BRYAN T. CLARK

Acknowledgments

The quote, *"Anything is possible when you have the right people there to support you,"* comes from Misty Copeland, the first African American Female Principal Dancer with the prestigious American Ballet Theatre.

And so, a special thank you to Dean, Program Director of HIV Services, at **The Source LGBT+ Center**, and Daniel G, for assisting me; answering my calls at all hours of the day, and returning the many emails and texts regarding living with HIV. Your assistance has been invaluable. To my fantastic team of Beta Readers, Alma C, Amy R, Brian R, Erin L, Israel S, Kelli C, Lana B, and Valerie G, it truly does take a village, and you are mine. And to Brian, my beautiful husband of thirty plus years, thank you for shepherding me and keeping me true to stories that I want to write, stories that have yet to be told.

He might be Mr. Right, but their timing is *all* kinds of wrong…
Gideon Miller is done letting his heart do the thinking for him. Been there, done that, still has the emotional scars to prove it. Besides, he's leaving Los Angeles soon. There'd be no point in starting up a new romance now. But when he meets the off-the-charts sexy, ex-military man next door, Gideon starts to question everything…

Isaiah Williams needs a fresh start. With his time in the Navy—and a painful, toxic relationship—behind him, he's ready to start a new life. Now all he has to do is figure out how to keep his matchmaking mother out of his business…and how to not fall for his sweet, nerdy, and entirely too attractive neighbor…

They're complete opposites with nothing but trust issues in common. Their timing? Terrible. And yet…none of that matters when they're together. Will love be enough to get Gideon and Isaiah to happily ever after? Or are they destined to remain star-crossed?

"*Gideon's Wish*, a standalone, steamy, lightly angsty, M/M contemporary romance, features a loveable, openly gay handyman and the not-so-openly gay alpha male of his dreams. HEA guaranteed. Download today and get ready to fall in love with your next favorite read."

Chapter 1

"Oh my God! I'm surprised Dad didn't throw them out!" Gideon howled into the receiver to his mother as he stretched across his bed.

"It was three a.m., and I was begging your father not to go out there." His mother laughed along with Gideon as she continued to tell him how noisy their latest guests who had checked out of the lodge this morning had been.

Gideon, his younger brother Andrew, and his parents had been running the Pacuare Rivers Ecolodge on the edge of the Pacuare River in Costa Rica since he could walk. The lodge was used by the local tour companies that ran whitewater rafting expeditions on the river.

It felt good to laugh on the phone with his mother. It wasn't that many months ago that his weekly calls had had a more ominous tone and had been nearly impossible for him to make. It had only been the last couple of months that he'd felt like his old self again and wasn't facing what he thought was his own imminent mortality. Now, although he wasn't missing the family business, he was missing his family, and in six weeks, he would be back home.

As he listened to his mother, Gideon stretched his naked body across the queen-size mattress and box spring that lay directly on the bedroom floor. Only after a body stretch that mimicked a bear coming out of hibernation did Gideon have enough energy to climb out of bed.

With the phone clutched to his ear, he walked down the hall toward the kitchen. "I bet Dad's exhausted and pissed off this morning." He ignored the demands of his woody screaming for attention. Certainly not while he was talking to his mother on the phone.

"We heard a couple of them screaming all night down by the river." His mother laughed.

Gideon snickered as he inserted a pod into his coffee maker, the

1

only appliance that he owned. He knew exactly what she meant: *Somebody was having sex last night down on the riverbank.* It's exactly where he'd lost his own virginity five years ago on his nineteenth birthday.

"Oh, I almost forgot, your brother's going to be working for Bluewater Rapids in a couple of weeks. He's hoping to get certified by the end of the season," his mother said.

"Mom, please don't tell me they're actually letting him take people down the rapids." Gideon tried to play it off that this was the first he was hearing about Andrew's new job.

Last month, when Andrew had texted Gideon that he was going for the job and not to tell Mom and Dad, the new job came as no surprise to him. He'd always known Andrew had no interest in sticking around to help run the family business. Although Andrew was the more masculine of them, Gideon prided himself as being more loyal to their parents. Now, with Andrew gone from the lodge, coupled with their dad's severe rheumatoid arthritis, they were definitely going to need him home if they were going to keep the doors open another season.

She laughed. "Your father's a little freaked out you're both going to be gone from the lodge." Her subtle way of reminding him he'd been in Los Angeles longer than they had agreed upon was loud and clear. The project of fixing up his deceased grandmother's house that they now used as a rental property was supposed to have been a couple of quick cosmetic fixes until he'd realized it needed more than repairs to the fence, a new oven, and new carpet. Now, eleven months later, he'd repaired the roof leaks, demolished and remodeled the kitchen, dining room, and living room. Last month, he couldn't stand to look at the yellow stucco, and the avocado green trim any longer, so the entire outside, as well as inside, received a fresh coat of paint. Two days ago, he finished the last of the new flooring he installed throughout the house. At twenty-four years old, he was proud of his carpentry skills—skills developed while working side by side with his father since he could walk.

"Why doesn't Dad just tell him to wait until I get back?" Gideon wasn't expecting an answer from her. He was really expressing that they expected more from him than from his brother. He was needed to return home while Andrew got to run off and do his own thing. Gideon eyed the stream of freshly brewed coffee pouring into his cup. It was only going to brew a half cup, but for five dollars at a garage sale, it worked well enough for him. If only for a few seconds, his five-dollar find stole his attention away from the fact that, like Andrew, he too had no desire to run the family business.

"You know your father. He'd just as soon not fight with your brother."

"But he can't do it by himself." On cue, the coffee machine shut off at half of the cup. He rested back on the counter as he eyed his plants in the window sill and took his first sip of coffee.

His mother huffed. "Anyway, you'll be back in what—"

"Six weeks." He finished her question for her. Now that he was mentally in a better place, they would never need to know that he'd been sick. He'd spoken with his doctor during his last visit to the health clinic about how to keep his treatment going when he returned to Costa Rica.

"Your dad and I are so proud of you and the work you've done on the house. I admit, I thought your dad was crazy to want to take the loan out to do this…But it really looks nice."

He knew she was referring to the latest pictures he'd sent her. Although he'd spent every bit of the twenty grand from the home equity loan they'd taken out for the project, they saved so much money in labor by him doing the work himself.

Gideon groaned into the receiver. He hated talking money with her. It was always 'we can't afford that.' "Well, I wanted to talk to you and Dad about the master bathroom. I was thinking we should redo the bathroom before we put it back up for rent. I can pay for it with the money I'm making, and…" The sound of a door closing caused Gideon to look over his shoulders, out the window, and into the carport that he and his neighbor, Daisy, shared.

Jesus! Gideon's lower jaw dropped as he stared at the young man coming out of Daisy's house holding a trash bag. Shirtless, his gorgeous brown chest muscles were like two rounded mountains.

As the guy walked across the carport, Gideon's eyes traced down his picture-perfect six-pack abs to a tapered waist and strong thighs. He had the classic military hair cut, trimmed short all the way around except for the top of his head.

"Hold on! Your father's walking in. Talk to him about that. I love you!"

"I love you, too," he tried to say before she was gone. As he waited for his dad to get on the phone, Gideon now remembered Daisy saying last week that her son, Isaiah, was coming home and would be staying with her until he got on his feet. *Was this who this gorgeous specimen of a man was?*

Gideon's gaze fell below the guy's waist. *Holy shit! What the hell is that swinging in his black nylon gym shorts?* Obviously, commando under the tight shorts, the sheer size of it sent blood flooding into Gideon's own groin.

The man's warm chestnut skin tone complimented his black hair and thin, neatly-trimmed mustache that dropped to his jaw line. If this was indeed Isaiah, he was way better-looking than his brothers and in great shape. He was all kinds of sexy.

After a second and what sounded like his dad dropping the phone, Gideon's father got on the line. "Hey, Gid."

"What's up, Old Man?" His dad's voice made him smile as he watched his neighbor toss the trash bag into the bin. The man then wheeled both Daisy's and Gideon's cans out to the curb. Gideon's breath caught as he watched the big, nearly naked man walk down the driveway. His biceps were incredible, but it was whatever the hell was flopping under his shorts that really got his attention.

"How are you?" His father's exuberant voice was a constant. "Have you run into Salma Hayek yet?"

His father's long-time crush on the beautiful Hollywood actress coaxed a grin from Gideon. "Um... no, not yet." Gideon released a pinned breath. "But as soon as I do, I'll be sure to let her know how much you love her." He laughed at his father's notion that famous actors and actresses were all around him, all the time. The truth was, Gideon hadn't seen one famous person since he'd been here. Gideon continued staring out the window, waiting for his neighbor to return.

"What's going on with the house?" his father asked. "I saw the pictures you sent mom of the new floors. I really like it."

"Thanks. I finished the backsplash in the kitchen. It turned out nice too." Gideon moved to the side of the window when he saw his neighbor walking back up the driveway. "I'll send pictures to Mom. I think I'm going to start the bathroom in the master bedroom next. It's a total gut-job." He couldn't see doing all the work he'd done to update the house and leaving that nineteen-sixties' bathroom. It was not only old but ugly too.

"Really? You think you have to tear it all out? What's going on in there?"

Gideon was about to answer when his neighbor looked right into Gideon's kitchen window. With a raised eyebrow and a smile, the guy nodded at him.

Busted! Gideon gave him the classic beauty queen wave before sinking back further behind his plants in the window. "Um... Dad..." It took him a second to collect his thoughts. "It's super outdated, and there's no shower. The tub, sink, and tile are all pink. The sink is the size of a cereal bowl."

"I'm starting to think you have no intentions of coming home," his dad laughed. "With all the work, we should be able to bump up the rent a couple hundred dollars a month more, don't you think? Your mom is really harping on me to get the house back up for rent. We need that money coming in to cover the loan payment. Let's do the bathroom and get it rented."

Gideon tuned out his dad's ranting and watched as his neighbor went back into his house. "Yeah... I know." His dad's comment was a reminder that the twelve hundred square-foot house was a profitable business for them before the loan, and he was only there to fix it up and get it rented again.

"I wish I was there to help you," his dad said.

"Yeah. Me, too. I miss you guys." This was the truth. He did miss being with his family, being outside all day in the open air. The camaraderie, the bantering, the teamwork... they were more like three brothers instead of father and sons. With his neighbor now gone, he settled back into his conversation with his father.

"Your mother's looking forward to you coming home—we all are."

As much as Gideon didn't want to return to the business, he was missing his mother's cooking. Some nights, he actually dreamed of her pineapple chicken and saffron rice pilaf.

His father asked, "You picking up any other jobs?"

"Yeah. This morning I'm tiling a bathroom at a church over in Glendale, and on Monday, there's a lady who needs some work done on a house she's putting up for sale. That might be a big job. I'll use that money for the bathroom."

"Where's the house you're going to on Monday?"

"North Hollywood." Gideon heard the envy in his dad's voice; Dad liked fixing and building stuff as much as he did.

"Hey, son, your brother's yelling for me. I have to go. Send pictures to your mom's phone. I lost mine the other day and haven't found it yet."

"Okay. I will. I love you."

"We love you, too," his father said before disconnecting.

After hanging up, Gideon poured himself a giant bowl of cereal and plopped onto the counter to eat his breakfast. As he ate, he combed over a stack of receipts and recorded expenditures in his log. Besides being a pretty damn good handyman, thanks to his dad, his mother had taught him everything she knew about accounting and bookkeeping. If he'd ever had a chance to go to college, he would have been an accountant for sure.

When he finished his bookkeeping, the clock on the microwave showed it was almost nine o'clock. If he didn't get a move on it this morning, he'd be late for his tiling job.

In the shower, he was a little surprised at the strong reaction that not only his mind had at the sight of Daisy's son, but how his body responded as well. He'd sworn off dating and had been doing well until now, but Isaiah's hotness and his reaction to it also brought up emotions he'd worked hard to not have: anger, revenge, disbelief, and, the worst, shame at what his ex had done to him.

Stop thinking about it! Don't go there. He rinsed the soap out of his hair. *You're healthy, you're alive.*

He attempted to switch his focus on his work for today. He had an appointment this afternoon about another job that also sounded promising and could lead to more work. Without the house's monthly rental income, his handyman jobs were only making up about half of the lost income and provided him the income to do all the remodeling after the loan money ran out.

After his shower, he rinsed out his cereal bowl as he peered out the kitchen window at the sporty midnight blue coupe that had been parked on his neighbor's side of the carport for the last couple of days. This had to have been Isaiah's car since Daisy didn't drive.

Daisy's house, which was the same floor plan as his family's, was well-maintained, in stark contrast to their rental that hadn't seen any TLC in about fifteen years.

When Gideon moved into the house, Daisy had been the first neighbor on the block to welcome him. A vibrant, talkative, and portly African-American woman, she'd been elated that he wasn't another renter moving into the house, but the owner—well, the grandson of the deceased owner. She'd been even more delighted to hear that he was here to fix up the old house.

She'd told him she'd been living next door back when his grandmother had still been alive and had lived here. She'd run down the list of all the renters who had lived in the house.

Daisy was a single mother of three grown boys. Gideon had met two of her adult sons, Josiah and Elijah. He hadn't met her youngest son, Isaiah, yet, who he presumed was the man in the lovely shorts earlier. Daisy had mentioned several times to him that her son Isaiah was in the Navy and was stationed in Hawaii.

Daisy often talked about Isaiah. Although she never came out and said it, she talked about him as if she was trying to set them up. It was kind of cute how she threw out little bits of information about him: how charming he was, that he was a police officer in the Navy, and—more than a few times—that he was single. Gideon shook his head. Daisy had forgotten to mention how fine he was.

He grabbed his keys off the counter and exited the house. He was two steps away from his van when Daisy's kitchen door opened, and Isaiah stepped out.

"Hey." Isaiah stopped next to his car, his smoky dark eyes locked onto Gideon. "Hope you don't mind that I took your bin out." A smile danced on his lips as he winked.

Gideon felt the force of Isaiah's penetrating stare. It was so strong that he wanted to look away. Instead, as if Isaiah had telepathically instructed him to do so, he smiled as he swallowed the lump down in his throat. "Um, no, not at all... Thanks... I always forget to put it out." He licked his lips as if they'd just been kissed.

"Yeah, it's been smelling the last couple of days. I wasn't sure if you were home or not." His voice was a low, sexy rumble.

"Sorry." Yeah, he tended to not put it out until it was really ripe. Looked like that had worked in his favor this time. He followed Isaiah's hand as the guy adjusted his gym shorts. *Good Lord...* It had been a long time since a guy had been able to jumpstart Gideon's libido as fast as Isaiah just did—a year almost. His sex life now was in the top drawer of his nightstand. Heat from his cheeks told him he was blushing.

"It's not a big deal. I had to take ours out."

"Um, okay... Thanks." Gideon fidgeted for a second before sticking his key into the door and unlocking it.

"By the way, I'm Isaiah. My mom is your neighbor." He pointed to his house.

"Um..." Flustered by Isaiah's consuming stare, he tried to snatch hold of his words and make sense of what he was trying to say, "Um... I'm Gideon." That was all he had—until his manners kicked in, taking him around to the front of his van to shake hands.

"Yeah, I know. My mom's mentioned you a few times." He took a strong hold of Gideon's hand and held his stare for a second before a warm smile broke across his face. There was a spark in his eye that went hand in hand with his smile.

"Nice to meet you." All the oxygen poured out of Gideon's lungs with his words, leaving him breathless. His gaze drifted from Isaiah's brown eyes to his lips, to his bright white teeth... back to his lips. This guy had to have been the sexiest man alive. A forced smile broke through Gideon's nervousness.

"Well, it was finally nice to meet you." Isaiah pressed his key fob and unlocked his doors. He nodded and smiled before jumping into his car.

The last sixty seconds of Gideon's life somehow had been wiped from his memory. He didn't even remember getting into his own car. His world was scrambled. *Did I say bye? Did I just walk away? Was he staring like I think he was?* Gideon drew a breath as he glanced over the seat and into Isaiah's car.

He placed his fingers over his mouth as if trying to hide his smile. *Why is my heart fluttering?* He took a breath to calm himself as he attempted to steal one last look at the man who just short-circuited him, but Isaiah had already backed out of the driveway.

That was crazy. The man was beautiful. Gideon scoffed, unsure what had just happened. It felt like something happened. Gideon replayed the last five minutes of his life.

Nothing happened. They simply met. However, the avalanche of tingles running down his spine said it was far from just a meeting.

Chapter 2

Exhausted, Isaiah pounded out another set of reps on the bench press machine in his new gym.

He looked up as the two blondes who'd been circling him for the last hour were walking right toward him. He returned a polite smile at the women before grabbing the handles and pumping out a fourth set. Earlier, he'd felt the heat from their stares from across the gym, as well as from a young guy that couldn't have been a day over twenty. And now, they were all circling him like vultures who'd spotted their next meal.

The idea of picking up random strangers in the gym—or anywhere else for that matter, was not his thing. He preferred it happen organically, from friends to lovers, learning the quirks of someone before moving them out of the friend zone.

He moved to the next weight machine and adjusted the weight to his liking. *Mom's neighbor seemed nice... Young... A little Femme... those eyes—Sky-Blue eyes against his olive complexion and dark hair—super sexy. His blue eyes were a surprise.* Most Latinos he'd known had brown eyes. In a passing thought, he imagined what it would be like to hold Gideon, his bare skin next to his. Surprised that he was actually attracted to Gideon, he snickered at the smile that crept across his face.

Twelve years in the military, he'd learned to be cautious on who he dated. He stayed away from two types of men; overtly flirtatious men and those who were visibly feminine. An association with either might lead others to question his own sexuality. He avoided this happening at any cost under the pretense of keeping his business private.

Gideon wasn't *that* feminine, he reasoned as he reminisced their exchange. Years of being in the closet in his personal life, as well as his professional life, coupled with his police training, he was a master

9

at people reading. Body language, eye movement, speech pattern, they all told a story. You just had to pay attention to what they were saying. As a gay man, he prided himself on having exceptional gaydar. Being able to quickly identify tiny traits and characteristics, some more pronounced than others, that over the years, he was rarely wrong. The warning bells sounded in his head. *Yes,* Gideon was more feminine than anyone he would—*could* date.

He dismissed his lingering thoughts of possibilities as whimsical. He wasn't looking to date anyone, especially someone who lived right next door to his mom. To shake Gideon from his thoughts, he added twenty more pounds to his weights and powered through two more sets.

With the strain felt in his arms and his heart racing, he paused a second to catch his breath. He glanced over and saw that the two women who'd been cruising him were now working out on the weight machine next to him. Unable to avoid eye contact, he civilly smiled, looked around at the crowded gym, and then resumed his workout.

It was great that this gym was twice the size of his gym back on the base. However, since it was packed with civilians in the middle of a Friday afternoon, he wasn't sure he would like working out here.

In one week, his life had completely changed. This time last week, he'd been on the island of Honolulu and had completed his last patrol on the naval base. Now, he was an unemployed civilian who lived with his mother. Ah, the glory of the service was already missed.

He'd moved from Honolulu, his home for the last four years, back to Los Angeles, to start the police academy this coming Monday.

The original plan was to get out of the Navy and take a month off before his training at the academy began. He'd hoped to find a place to live before starting, but when he'd received a call from someone at the academy advising him that they had one slot open in the next cycle that started in a week, he'd taken it.

So now, here he was again, living with his mother, sleeping in his childhood room that was now half his old room and half his mother's crafting room. With only a week between leaving the Navy and starting the academy, the new plan was to stay at her house until after he graduated and was working. Then he'd have time to look for his own place. It was only six months… How bad could it be living with his mother again?

He ignored everyone around him and concentrated on his workout until he was good and tired. Exhausted, he sped toward the water fountain at the back of the gym to quench his thirst before heading out. After several long swallows of the cold water, he felt the presence of someone standing behind him. Sure, he wanted another gulp or two, but he'd play nice and let this person have their turn. As he stepped aside and out of the way, he saw that the person behind him was the same guy who'd been eye-fucking him for the last two hours.

"Hey. How's it going?" the gym bunny asked with a leer that suggested he liked what he was looking at.

"Hey." Isaiah barely glanced at him before walking away. Yeah, this gym didn't work for him. There was no doubt he was the *new meat* in town, but he had no interest in fulfilling that role. All he wanted was a good, exhausting workout to keep in shape. Twelve years in the United States Navy and staying fit was part of a military lifestyle. Random hook-ups were not.

There was a lot that he was going to miss about being in the service. He had adjusted to the steady regimen that never changed much from day to day. Even as a Master-at-Arms, the Navy's equivalent to the Military Police, patrolling the base had been pretty routine. Most of the time, he'd sat in his patrol car under the tree at the entrance to the base, hoping to deter those who didn't want to obey the posted thirty-five mile-per-hour speed limit. There had been the calls to respond to a domestic dispute on rare instances and occasional calls from the Honolulu police to come to get a detained drunken soldier.

He skipped the showers and was back in his rental car, where he retrieved his phone from the glove-box. Surprised to see a text from Ronnie, Isaiah's heart skipped a beat as he read the text.

Hi Bro, hope you're settling into Cali. I'm about to board my flight to Amsterdam. Pearl Harbor won't be the same without us. The flight to Amsterdam is about fifteen hours, so I'll hit you up in a couple of days.

Isaiah held off sending a reply, not because he knew Ronnie wouldn't get the text on board the military's C-17, the Air Force's personnel transport plane, but because he didn't want to give in to the notion that he couldn't live without him.

11

As he pulled the vibrant, midnight blue Mustang into the driveway, he noticed his neighbor's VW bus was gone. *Wonder where he's at?* With the mere thought of Gideon, the corners of his lips quirked into a light smile. Not that it was any of his business, but he'd inherently learned to keep track of those around him—and especially those around his mother. Actually, he didn't trust anybody.

He hadn't gotten any negative vibes or red flags from his two-minute exchange with the guy. In fact, for some odd reason, the guy had kind of knocked him off his feet, so to speak. He was used to sizing people up quickly, but in that two-minute exchange, something in the universe told him, *Not so fast!* The world had slowed for a minute, standing in Gideon's presence.

Although his mother hadn't come out and said it, Isaiah had already gotten the feeling that her matchmaking skills were already in play. She'd mentioned the guy—Gideon—a half-dozen times before Isaiah had even made it back to California. He'd been home less than a week, and she'd asked him at least three times if he'd met him yet. Each time, she'd reminded him of how sweet Gideon was, that Gideon was single, or that Gideon owned his own business. Isaiah had seen right through her. He'd never actually hidden his sexuality from his family; it was something that just wasn't talked about. Over the years, he'd had many conversations where she hinted at knowing, but as long as she didn't ask, he wouldn't tell.

She played matchmaker with everyone and had about a dozen weddings under her belt so far. One of those weddings had been for his older brother Josiah and his wife, Tammy. Thank God they'd found each other because he was damn sure no one else would want either one of them with their *holier-than-thou-church-three-times-a-week* stupid-asses.

Isaiah grabbed the bag of groceries he'd picked up for tonight's dinner from the seat next to him. With Mom working all day at the bank, the least he could do was cook dinner for her. With his self-trained incredible culinary skills in the kitchen, people joked that he should have been a chef with the way he could whirl a knife, and it was less dangerous than being a cop on the streets of L.A.

He tossed what items needed to go into the refrigerator before jumping into the shower. Today's workout felt good. With the chaos of moving back to California, it'd been nice to expel some of the edginess this afternoon. Other than the constant cruising reminding him that he was the new meat in town, he'd felt like his old self again.

After his shower, Isaiah began prepping dinner. He'd picked up a couple of nice steaks and a medley of veggies to roast. He wasn't a carb eater and hoped his mother wouldn't miss them. The clock showed a little past six. Mom normally hit the door around six. He would hold off on cooking until she actually walked in. He spent some time combing through the kitchen drawers, getting reacquainted with his mother's kitchen. Once he was satisfied that he was organized and ready, he relaxed back in his bedroom. Since his room faced the street, he was able to see the same white Honda that had picked his mother up this morning pull up to the curb. He made his way down the hall to the kitchen as she came through the kitchen door.

"Hey, Mom." He stood at the counter as she emptied her used lunch containers into the sink. He'd noticed yesterday that there was a different faucet on the sink than what used to be there. "Who put the new faucet in?" He was sure she was going to say Josiah since he was handier with tools than Elijah.

"Gideon did it for me a couple of months ago. I told him what I wanted, and he went to the store and installed it in a couple of hours. He wouldn't even let me pay him for it. Said he owed me for all the times I've fed him." His mom looked at the raw steaks and veggies on the counter. "Whatcha got going on here?"

Isaiah gave her an incredulous look, amazed at how quickly she could work Gideon into any conversation. He wasn't sure how he felt about a stranger in his mother's house with no one there to protect her. "Thought I'd cook us some steaks to celebrate me returning to civilian life. You still eat meat, don't you?"

"Not as much as I used to." Mom retrieved a wine glass from the cupboard and poured herself a glass of the white wine she'd opened last night.

"Oh? I can fix you something else."

She waved her one free hand as she took a sip of wine. "No, no, no. I still love a good steak, especially if you're cookin' it. Just trying to watch my cholesterol and blood pressure." Daisy walked around to the other side of the kitchen island.

With his mother out of the way, Isaiah moved to the sink and washed his hands. "What's going on with your blood pressure?"

"The doctor said it was running a little high. He put me on a different blood pressure medication." Mom sat on a stool at the island. "We ain't goin' to talk about my health. How was your day?"

His mother had always been heavy. Maybe, since he was home, he could talk her into making some dietary changes, but he wasn't holding out any great hope. "It was good. This morning I drove over to the Ford dealership and checked out the new F150, then I went by the gym, worked out, and went to the grocery store to pick up some stuff."

"What's an F1-something?" she asked.

"It's a truck."

"Why do you need a truck?"

Isaiah shrugged. "I feel safer in something big."

"You should talk to Elijah. He's managing that Honda dealership in Thousand Oaks. He'd give you a good deal on something. I don't know if he's got any of those F1-somethings you're talking about." She eyed the tub of protein powder on the counter. "Are you used to being a civilian yet?"

"It's only been a week, so it feels like I'm on leave. It's weird." It was good to be back in L.A.—his home, with his family. Even if his family did drive him a little crazy, he still missed them. Isaiah poured a little olive oil over the assortment of veggies he'd already chopped up and seasoned with sea salt and pepper and his favorite mix of fresh thyme and fresh rosemary. He used his hands, digging down into the large bowl to stir the veggies, ensuring they were well-coated.

"I got a text from Josiah today. He said he and Tammy are wantin' to stop by this weekend with the baby. I told him that I thought it would be all right, but to text you to make sure." She reached for her phone that was lying next to her purse. "Did he text you?"

"Yeah, I got his text." By the way his mother was looking at him suggested that she was waiting for more, like the entire conversation between him and his brother. He broke eye contact with her. He could use a couple of more days before he had to look at Tammy and his brother. Josiah and Tammy had bought a house in Pasadena a year ago to be closer to their church. Every time Isaiah talked to his mother, it sounded as if they were constantly remodeling something in it. "I'll text him after dinner." He checked to see if the oven was hot enough before sliding the cookie sheet full of veggies into it.

While they waited for the veggies to cook, he asked his mom

about her work, the things that needed fixing around the house, and his brothers.

"I'm kind of…" Mom drew a visible breath as her eyes fastened on Isaiah.

Oh God—was she…? "What? What? Are you dating someone?" Her eyes said he'd guessed right. *She was.*

"Well… kind of. His name is Charles. He's a senior loan officer in the bank. We've worked together for years."

"Oh?" Isaiah nodded as he listened. He didn't care that his mother was dating. In fact, it made him happy. He hated that she'd lived alone ever since Elijah had moved out last year.

"He and his wife were separated about a year ago, but I told him I wasn't goin' to see him until his divorce was final. That happened recently…."

"What does this Charles look like?" Isaiah was intrigued. He'd never known his mother to date after his father had died fifteen years ago. She'd always seemed perfectly content being a widow.

"He's a handsome man. A little darker than your father."

"How old?"

"Fifty-two."

"Any kids?" Isaiah's eyes widened.

"Four. Three girls and a boy. His youngest, Joseph, is sixteen."

"Sixteen, Huh? Those are tough years for a boy. Are you ready to do that again?"

"I ain't doin' nothing. Them's his kids. I raised mine and ain't lookin' to raise nobody else's."

Isaiah checked the veggies, stirring them around before putting them back into the oven. "And the girls?"

"He has one daughter in college, Tiffany, and the two oldest are married." His mom took a sip of her wine. "What about you? You seein' anyone?"

Isaiah was caught off guard with her question. The answer was easy—*no*—but the straightforwardness and the discussion that could arise from it would be new ground for them. It was one thing for her to hint about the possibilities between him and her neighbor, but to discuss it would be different. He talked about his sexuality with few people, and his mother was not on that list.

He'd come out to only a select few at work, and he kept tight control on the conversation around dating and anything else involving his personal life that might take the conversation somewhere he didn't want it to go. Even those who knew about him didn't necessarily know who he was sleeping with. He handled his family in the same manner.

"Well?" His mother wasn't letting him off the hook.

"No... not really." He nodded, content that he'd answered her question truthfully.

"What does *not really* mean?" She took her seat back on her stool.

Her proximity made him uncomfortable... or was it the conversation? He jumped up to start their steaks. "No. I'm not." That was direct enough. He wasn't seeing anyone—*anymore*. He pulled out a large cast-iron skillet from under the counter and placed it on the stove.

"You know I ain't got a problem with it," Mom said.

"I know, Mom." His voice stalled, turning his words into little more than a whisper.

"My friend Gideon next door is nice. You should ask him out."

"Mom!" He cringed. He refused to have this conversation with her. Plus, the neighbor looked like he was sixteen years old. Too young for his liking.

His mom folded her arms under her breasts. "What? I'm just askin' a question."

He didn't want to talk about dating with her. "Yeah. Um, yeah, I got a lot going on. I'd like to get settled and get through this academy."

"You shouldn't be nervous, baby. You'll be fine. You got this."

Isaiah breathed a sigh that he'd successfully changed the topic.

"You could probably teach the classes. You've always been my smart boy. I ain't ever had to worry about you." She cocked her head. "But you should still get to know Gideon."

Isaiah rolled his eyes as he used a match to light the gas stove. "What you need to do is get this burner fixed. You got me lighting this stove like we're living in the fifties."

Mom poured herself a little more wine and then took a sip. "You know, Rose was his grandmother."

"Old lady Rose?" *The white lady? He hadn't thought about her in years.* "I thought he was from Costa Rica?"

"He is. He's here fixing up his grandma's place."

"They still own it?" He'd never given it much thought as to who the owners were since it had been a rental for so long.

"I thought maybe they were going to sell it since they were cleaning it up, but he says no. They're keeping it." She opened her phone case up and swiped at her screen.

He welcomed the silence that took over while she scrolled on her phone, and he could just focus on their steaks. He mulled over the fact that Gideon's grandmother was old lady Rose. He hadn't thought of her in years. *She was sweet.* He wouldn't have guessed in a million years that Gideon and old lady Rose were related. He glanced at his mother a few times while she was busy on her phone. *Good.* As long as she was playing with it, she wasn't up in his business.

With the steaks about ready, he tossed two slices of butter on top to melt into them. The sound of a car pulling into the carport caused him to look out the window. Gideon was parking his hippie-looking van on his side of the carport.

"Sounds like Gideon's home." Mom looked out the window.

Gideon exited from his side of the oxidized red van. The VW bus somehow totally fit him. His long wavy brown hair and sideburns screamed *Seventies* and his multi-colored Mexican Baja hoodie, tight jeans, and flip-flops shouted *hippie*. His tight jeans showed off the contour of his legs and a small round ass. *Damn, that's a fine ass.* Although younger and not as masculine as someone he would normally go out with, he had to admit, Gideon *was* nice looking.

"Hmm." She eyed Isaiah as he stared out the window.

"Don't hmm me." Isaiah turned from the window. "He's a puppy!" Stationed all over the world, he'd gone out with guys of every possible race, ethnicity, and size. He didn't think he had a certain type; however, the one common denominator they'd all shared was that they'd all been as discreet as he was. Knowing that Gideon's grandmother was Old Lady Rose, it now felt as if he somehow knew the guy.

In Hawaii, before meeting Ronnie, he'd gone out with a couple of surfers. He'd liked their laid-back, anything-goes, hippie attitude. The free-spirited attitude was probably because of all the weed they'd smoked, which had been problematic for Isaiah. Given the job he held in the military—a cop... the weed thing was definitely a problem.

With Gideon now in his house, Isaiah focused his attention back on the steaks. "Are you ready to eat?"

"Yes, I'm starving." Mom retrieved plates and silverware for them. She smirked at him; he wasn't fooling anyone. She'd caught him staring.

He tensed at his clever momma. *She obviously knows. She's trying to set me up with the guy. She wants to talk about it... but I don't.*

Isaiah pushed Gideon from his thoughts, switching his attention back to dinner as he removed the veggies from the oven. Usually, cooking put him in a chilled mood; the chopping and dicing vegetables, and the more burners he had going, the better. But, at the moment, it wasn't enough to stop his thoughts from drifting back to Gideon, nor his conversation with his mother. *Do Josiah and Elijah know as well? She's a match maker and a damn good one—Him and Gideon? No. No. No. My focus has to be on the academy. That's my focus. Damn. Why did I come back here?* He swallowed the sudden lump in his throat. *How am I going to keep all of this separated?*

Chapter 3

It was almost six o'clock on Friday when Isaiah pulled into the driveway. He'd completed his first week in the academy and was mentally exhausted. Although class was over by five every day, he'd stayed behind to help another young cadet named Aaron Lewis this afternoon.

Cadet Lewis was a twenty-two-year-old skinny kid who looked as if a mouse would scare him. Over the years, in the Navy, Isaiah had seen plenty of new recruits who'd looked like Lewis and turned into incredible soldiers. Earlier in the week, Lewis had failed the first written exam due to poor writing skills. He'd been permitted to retake it, and that time had passed—which was a good thing since failing twice meant immediate expulsion from the academy.

When Lewis had asked him for help with next week's exam at lunch today, he hadn't been able to refuse him. One cadet had already dropped out of their class of forty-five, and Isaiah didn't want to lose a second one so fast.

As he retrieved his duffel bag and lunch box from the trunk of his car, he glanced into Gideon's van. It was a cop thing, something he did without thinking.

There were no dead bodies on the seat, no bags of cocaine in plain sight. Nope, just a tool belt on the passenger seat and a bunch of milk crates filled with stuff in the rear. He shook his head at the naivety of people. He should probably say something to Gideon about leaving things in plain view. He couldn't count the number of car break-in calls he'd responded to on base. What riled him were the purses that were left on the seat of the car and reported stolen. He wanted to ask the women, *What the hell did you expect?* But his job was to assist, not judge or parent. The person was already having a bad day; he didn't need to shit on them even more… But he'd definitely thought it.

Isaiah entered the house through the kitchen door off the carport and put his duffle bag that contained his work gear and duty weapon away, then unpacked the small cooler that he used to carry his protein shakes for the day.

Isaiah released a sigh as he reflected on the week. His days started at three-thirty in the morning, with him getting out the door by four. Although the academy was only twenty-three minutes from his house, he gave himself a solid two hours in case of heavy L.A. traffic and to ensure he was seated in the classroom, ready to go, by six. Any extra time he had before class, he used to study.

The academics weren't hard, nor were the physical exercises; he could do a three-mile run in under twenty-four minutes and welcomed the paramilitary setting. The training was a gentle reminder of his not so old life.

Within minutes, his mom entered the kitchen. "Well, you did it. One week done, twenty-five more to go." She was still in her robe from this morning. It was her Friday off, her three-day weekend where she did nothing for the first day of it.

Twenty-five more weeks? Damn, that was a long time. Except for his Spanish course, the next twenty-five weeks was going to be like a long remedial reenactment of his basic training and Master-at-Arms training.

"Well, we need to celebrate tonight. Let's go out for dinner. Do you have any plans this evening?" She slid her butt up onto one of the kitchen stools.

"No. I'm pretty tired. I want to take a shower, put my sweats on, and do nothing until Monday morning." He rinsed out all of his containers and left them in the sink.

"Okay, that's all fine, but Momma's gotta eat, and I don't feel like cooking. I've been craving Mexican food."

Isaiah exhaled. "I feel you. Let me take a shower, and then we can go out."

"I'm so proud of you, honey, and it's so nice to have you home."

Home... The word swam around in his brain. With the occasional visits for Thanksgiving or Christmas, he'd been gone for so many years... and yet she still called it his home. It felt like *her* home now. Just a temporary stop for him was all it was.

Last year, when it came time to renew his enlistment contract, he questioned whether to get out or stay another eight years. Another eight would give him twenty, and he could retire with a military pension. As much as he loved serving his country, reenlisting felt like something he didn't want to do. With the military, he didn't just get a career. It was a way of life. He was sure that being a civilian police officer, protecting and serving the city of Los Angeles, was going to be just as rewarding, and hopefully, a little more freeing. It would be nice having a life outside of the military, where his friends and neighbors weren't his co-workers.

Isaiah stripped his uniform off and wrapped the towel hanging on the back of his bedroom door around his waist. Within thirty minutes, he was ready, and he and his mother were heading out the kitchen door.

In the carport, Gideon stood between his van and Isaiah's car. With the side of the van opened, Gideon's head was down as he fished through one of the milk crates inside. He raised his head as they neared.

"Sorry. I didn't see you guys." Gideon's brows narrowed above his blue eyes as he stood between the two vehicles holding a gray crate he'd removed. The crate slipped, but he quickly stopped it from hitting the ground.

"It's all right, man," Isaiah remained at the front of the cars, giving Gideon time to finish whatever it was he was doing. Next to his vintage VW bus, Gideon's small frame was accentuated next to the van. *Five-five? Five-six?* Isaiah again went with his earlier assessment of his height. Years of training, he couldn't stop being a cop. He assessed everybody, and everything, continuously. Attention to detail was important in his line of work.

Isaiah crossed his arms across his chest as he eyed the guy who kind of reminded him of the actor that played in his favorite movie, *Call Me By Your Name.*

Maybe a hundred and twenty pounds. Like many of the young recruits fresh out of boot camp, there was an innocence that spoke to Gideon's youth. *Twenty-one, twenty-two? Young... a kid.* He laughed at the notion that his mom said for him to get to know Gideon. She didn't know his type at all.

Gideon brushed back his dark brown wavy hair from his face. Strands of gold and tan highlights in the front matched his olive complexion. The back of his hair, darker, draped to his shoulders.

Gideon set the crate in the back of the van and stood for a second. "Oh, let me get out of your way." He slid his van door closed and moved out from between the cars.

"You're fine." Isaiah took a step back to allow for him to pass.

His mom pulled on his arm. "Gideon, have you met my son, Isaiah?"

Isaiah looked at her as if she'd lost her mind. "Um, yeah. We met last week. How are you doing?" He held out his hand to shake Gideon's as their eyes met. Face-to-face, Gideon was about six inches shorter than him.

Gideon shook his hand. "We sort of met last week." His majestic blue-and-turquoise-flecked eyes gleamed as he let go. "Are you guys heading out?" Gideon asked Mom.

"Isaiah finished his first week at the police academy. We're going out to celebrate. Want to join us?"

Oh, God, she did not just do that. Isaiah's eyes widened, and his muscles tensed.

"Oh, no, I couldn't. But thank you," Gideon answered.

He knew exactly what his mom was up to. Thank God Gideon said no. Jesus, the next six months couldn't pass fast enough.

"Come on, Gideon. I know you ain't got no plans. You haven't left your house on a Friday night in months. Come hang out with my Isaiah and me for an hour. It's an *hour*. What could happen in an hour?"

Isaiah glared at her. She wasn't as slick as she thought she was, and while Gideon wasn't hard on the eyes, he didn't need his mother setting him up on dates.

"Thanks, but I'm not dressed to go anywhere." Gideon tugged on his T-shirt.

"It's just Don Pablo's, around the corner. You're fine. It's Isaiah's treat."

Isaiah looked down at his mom. She had some nerve to invite someone to dinner on his dime. He jiggled his keys. "Um, it's fine. Come on. Join us. The more, the merrier, right?" By saying it that way, it made it clear to *everyone*, it wasn't a date.

Gideon winced. "Um, really, thanks, but I don't want to interrupt your night."

Mom put her hand on her hip; she wasn't going to let this go. *Gideon ought to just hop in the car to make this easier on everyone.*

"Listen, Gideon." His mother took a big breath—which meant she was on a roll. "Since you ain't gettin' it, let me put it this way. I see you up in the window looking at Isaiah when he's out here. I don't blame you, he's a good-looking man and so are you. Both of you need to stop pretending to be shy. I know how fast you gays work, so stop playin' me."

Isaiah snapped his eyes closed. He wouldn't mind crawling into a hole right about now. He could only imagine what Gideon was thinking.

"Oh my God!" Gideon covered his face with his hands.

"Now get in. I'm hungry," Daisy ordered.

"I can follow you guys in my van instead."

"No need, just jump in." Isaiah was tired of the whole song and dance as he unlocked the car. "I'll drive." He glared at his mom. She better not say another word.

Gideon insisted that Daisy take the front seat as he squeezed into the rear seat behind her. "Nice car," he told Isaiah.

"Thanks. It's a rental. I had a Jeep back on the island, but I sold it instead of having it shipped over."

"Oh?" Gideon fastened his seatbelt.

Isaiah looked over his shoulders as he backed the car out of the driveway. "Sold mostly everything but a few personal items." He cast a glance at Gideon.

"Damn, so it's like starting over, I guess?" Gideon asked.

"I think of it as a cleansing. Sounds better than starting over." Isaiah looked at Gideon through the rearview mirror.

Daisy did most of the talking for the six-block ride to the restaurant, way over-stepping any boundaries by sharing Isaiah's life story in under fifteen minutes.

He had a feeling it wasn't going to get any better during dinner.

Inside the busy restaurant, they sat along the window in a booth. He and his mother sat across from Gideon. Once they finished looking at the menus, they waited for the waiter to return to take their orders.

"So, Mom says you're from Costa Rica?" Isaiah asked, probing this stranger that his mother, the matchmaker, was all sweet on for him. He was in cop mode, asking the questions that would tell him the most about this person.

23

"Yeah."

He kept going with the easy questions. "I was surprised to hear that ol—" He caught himself before he called Gideon's grandmother by the nickname he and his brothers had given her without her knowing. "that Ms. Rose was your grandma."

"Yep. But I only met her a couple of times though, when she came to visit us."

"She was super nice." Isaiah remembered her as if it was yesterday that he last saw her.

"I loved your grandma." Daisy's voice was overly sweet.

Isaiah didn't remember her loving Ms. Rose *that* much to warrant her tender, sweet tone.

Gideon nodded as he smiled at Isaiah and his mom as they were interrupted by the waiter.

After taking their orders and collecting the menus, the waiter asked if he could get them something from the bar.

"I'll have a Long Island iced tea," Daisy said as she folded her cocktail menu and placed it back on the table.

Gideon looked at Daisy and then Isaiah. "I think I'll have one, too." He fidgeted in his seat as he released a noticeable breath.

"I'll take a diet cola." Isaiah saw the nervousness in Gideon's eyes and body language. *What is he nervous about?*

"Okay. I'll have your orders right out." The waiter excused himself.

Daisy turned to Isaiah. "Doesn't the house look nice?"

"Much nicer. You've done a good job." Isaiah addressed his response to Gideon instead of his mother. "Mom says you did all of it yourself?" As he continued with his investigation, he glared over at her, signaling to cut it out. Perhaps she was the source of the poor guy's nervousness. If she was anyone else, he would have kicked her under the table.

"Yeah. To save money. Plus, I like doing that kind of stuff."

"Isaiah, you should go over and see it tomorrow." His mom looked at him as if she was begging for a puppy.

Really mom? You're going to be that obvious. Okay, he was going to kill her when they got home. Isaiah gave Gideon a non-committal nod.

"I wish he was staying. I like someone as handy as Gideon next door." Daisy added.

"Oh?" Isaiah's breath hitched. "You're not staying?"

"No," Gideon answered.

"Where are you going?" Isaiah thought his question may have been too intrusive, but it just slipped out.

"Home. I just came out to fix the house."

"I see." Isaiah drew in a shallow breath. He felt the letdown but tried to ignore it. "Have you lived in Costa Rica all your life?" Isaiah asked as the waiter showed up with their drinks.

"No. I was born here." Gideon picked up his drink and took a sip. "Oh, that's strong." He winced as he put his drink down.

Daisy followed suit. "Mine's perfect." She announced after taking a sip. "To Isaiah, for finishing his first week. I'm so proud of you." She held her glass up in the air, signaling a toast.

Isaiah took a drink of soda. He thought he was going to sneak a peek at Gideon. However, when he did, Gideon met his stare. In an attempt to cover up that he'd been caught gawking, he fired away with another question. "When did you leave the United States?" Isaiah's gaze drifted from the smooth skin of Gideon's cheeks to his eyes.

Gideon looked away for a second. "Um, When I was a baby."

"And where do you guys live in Costa Rica?" Isaiah assessed the nervousness in Gideon's eyes.

"We live outside of Bajo Tigre, in the Rain forest. Do you know where that is?"

"No. I've never been." A jungle with vines dangling from trees came to mind. *Tarzan swinging from vine to vine.*

"It's the most beautiful place in the world. It's on the Caribbean side of the country and has a cool, laid-back vibe. Our hotel sits between the Pacuare River and the most gorgeous rainforest you've ever seen."

"Your hotel?" Isaiah arched an eyebrow. "What do you mean *your* hotel?"

"My family. We have a camping lodge that we run. We built it ourselves."

They built it themselves? Surely, he didn't mean they were the actual ones that built it. "What made your family get into the hotel business?" Isaiah's interest was piqued.

"It just kind of happened. My dad and my uncle used to be river guides. Years ago, they started making overnight trips to camp in the forest with the guests. The business caught on. They finally were able to save enough money to buy this land next to the river."

"And you guys built *a hotel* next to the river?" The massive hotels along the beach in Hawaii is what he pictured.

"Not at first. For years the guests just camped on the property. After spending the day fighting rapids, they get to camp in the rain forest overnight as part of their expedition package. My uncle and dad first built just a kitchen. Then the bathrooms. After that, they started building the yurts."

"What's a yurt?" Mom asked.

"It's like a circular tent, but way bigger and taller, and they have a floor. They're made out of a heavy canvas." Gideon rubbed the back of his neck and then fidgeted with his hands for a second. "We have twelve of them now." He looked at Isaiah and gave him a reserved smile.

Isaiah forced himself to draw his eyes from Gideon's beautiful lips that formed a smile that sent a flurry of butterflies to his stomach. Gideon's top lip made a perfect bow. "All the stuff you've done to the house. I'm blown away that you can do all of this stuff. I can't believe you guys built a hotel."

"Well, it's not what you are probably thinking. Ours is a massive two-story A-frame open-air building. It has a giant thatch roof. It's the coolest thing you've ever seen. The guests sleep in the yurts. They come up to the main building to eat, shower, use the bathroom, and hang out."

"It sounds cool." Isaiah nodded.

"For the most part. It's a lot of work. After my uncle died, my dad stopped taking groups down the river. Now we contract with other river guides to use our place for their overnight trips. We just focus on the hotel now."

"Who does all the cookin'?" Mom asked.

"My mom. She'll usually cook her jungle chicken with roasted vegetables and black beans and rice."

A young teenage male approached the table holding a water pitcher. *"Más agua señor?"* He held the pitcher out.

"Si. Gracias. Cómo estás?" Gideon slid his water glass closer to the kid so he could fill it.

"*Bueno, gracias.*" After topping off everyone's water, the kid gave Gideon a polite nod before stepping aside so the waiter could set down their food.

"Your Spanish is good," Isaiah told Gideon. He wished his Spanish was as good as Gideon's.

"Thank you." Gideon picked up his fork.

"I guess it would be, growing up in Costa Rica and all." In his head, Isaiah tried to picture Gideon's life in the rain forest, his parents, the hotel; it was all pretty intriguing.

Daisy waved her arms, her hand waving. "Gideon. Tell him about the monkeys." Her voice loud enough to apparently catch the couple's attention at the table next to them as they looked over at their table.

Isaiah's brows narrowed. "The monkeys?"

Gideon met his stare again. He wet his lips before taking a swallow, never taking his eyes from Isaiah. A slight smile creased his lips.

Drawn in by Gideon's smile, Isaiah smiled back as warmth spread across his chest. His brain fizzed at what they were even talking about.

"There are lots of monkeys in the forest. I love the mantled howler monkeys. The males make this loud howling sound at five-thirty in the morning. It sounds like someone being murdered," Gideon laughed. "But my favorite is the White-Faced Monkey. They're super smart. Lots of people have them as pets. You can train them to do almost anything. We had one when I was a kid."

"You had a monkey for a pet?" Isaiah couldn't help a smirk.

"Yeah. His name was Frankie. We think his mother must have died or something because he was young when he started to come around."

"What's your favorite thing about living there?" Isaiah leaned forward in his chair.

Gideon's forehead creased. "I think being outside, surrounded by nature all day."

Isaiah appreciated his answer. He loved to hike. When he went to steal another glance at Gideon, again, he was caught as their eyes met. Gideon's return stare caused Isaiah to squirm in his chair. Gideon had great eye contact, was polite, and, yeah, there was no denying that he was attractive. He caught his mother out of the corner of his eye. If she wasn't sitting at the table with them, this could almost feel like a blind date going exceptionally well. "How old are you again?" Isaiah flirted with the idea of dating him.

"Twenty-four... and a half."

Damn, that was young. Even if he considered dating him, he was his mom's neighbor. That's just too close. It was hard enough keeping her out of his business. *But...this guy is cute... smart...his lips are beautiful... his eyes, I can't stop looking at his eyes.*

Isaiah was in the depths of rationalizing why he couldn't date him with why he liked him when Gideon spoke.

"You're in the police academy? That's cool. Have you always wanted to be a cop?"

"Always."

"He wanted to be a fireman when he was little." Daisy offered.

Isaiah glanced over at his mom but ignored her. "I liked being a cop in the Navy."

"I didn't know they had cops in the Navy. That's cool. When I picture the Navy, I picture guys on a ship at sea." Gideon continued asking lots of questions about the military as they ate.

Halfway through dinner, when the waiter returned to check on them, Daisy and Gideon ordered a second Long-Island iced tea.

By the end of their meal, although Gideon continued to chatter, his words were now slurred. Yep, the guy was drunk. He should probably get him home. Isaiah looked around for their waiter.

"Can you guys excuse me for a minute?" Gideon stood up and braced himself on the table before heading to the restroom.

"Well, what do you think?" Daisy asked in a whisper even though Gideon was out of earshot.

Isaiah took a second before answering. He glanced back at Gideon, his eyes drawn to his adorable ass in his tight jeans as it swayed between the other tables in the restaurant. Yes, Gideon was a beautiful man. The long dark hair and striking blue eyes were hard not to appreciate. "I think he's drunk." Isaiah gave her the only safe answer he could. The last thing he wanted was for her to get excited that she'd matched another couple.

Daisy leaned in closer. "He's just nervous."

"Mom, I know what you're doing." He needed to shut this down.

There were so many reasons this was wrong, the main one being that she was sitting right here with them. The rest were equally important, however: he'd just gotten out of a relationship, he was trying to make the switch to civilian life, he needed to focus on the academy, Gideon was leaving, Gideon was too young, Gideon was.... was... Too damn hot for his sanity.

Damn it. As much as Isaiah wanted to deny it, he wanted Gideon.

"What am I doing? I'm merely having dinner with my son and my neighbor." She brushed off his allegation with a dismissive wave of her hand.

"Don't have me hook you up to a lie detector. You're matchmaking. I bet you timed the second we walked out the house so we would run into him." *Me and Gideon, with you involved... Hell No. It will never happen.*

"Now you're being ridiculous. I had no idea he was out there. Anyway, if anyone should be worried about taking a lie detector test, it's you."

"Mom?"

"What?"

"I'm thirty-years-old. I don't need my mother being my wingman." He'd always been close to his mother, especially after his father was killed, but this... This was a whole new level of closeness.

Gideon showed up out of nowhere and plopped down back into the booth.

"Are you all right, buddy?" Isaiah mentally noted that Gideon's pupils had constricted, and he'd lost a little color in his face.

Gideon didn't answer him but, instead, closed his eyes for a very long blink.

It was time to get the check and end this bizarre dinner—*date*—or whatever it was. He raised his hand, and caught the waiter's attention, then signaled for the check.

Gideon took a sip of his water. His eyelids were shutting down fast.

As soon as the waiter brought their check, Isaiah signaled to his mother to move out. He paid their tab on their way out and got everybody back to the car.

Gideon was quiet on the way back to the house. A couple of

times, Isaiah looked at him through the rearview mirror. His eyes were closed, his chin on his chest.

When they arrived back at the house, it was a little after eight. Gideon was the last to climb out of the car. He stood in the carport for a second before he doubled over and vomited onto the driveway, splattering his shoes.

Isaiah raced around to the passenger side. "Mom, you go on in the house. I'm going to make sure Gideon's okay." He put one hand on Gideon's back to soothe him.

"First, I'll take care of this, then meet you inside." Daisy frowned at the mess as she set her purse on the hood of the car and headed toward the garden hose.

"Okay, buddy, let's go." Isaiah stood Gideon up.

Gideon didn't say anything as he straightened up. His eyes were almost closed as he stumbled toward his house.

Getting the poor kid in the house was only the beginning. Isaiah needed to put him to bed. Since the floor plan was the same as his mother's house, he led Gideon to the master bedroom and sat him on the edge of the bed.

"I got it. Thank you." Gideon's eyes were closed as he yanked his T-shirt up over his head and off. He mumbled something inaudible.

Isaiah shook his head. "I know you've got this, but let me get your shoes off." Isaiah grabbed the first vomit-painted shoe and tore it off without untying it. He'd certainly dealt with enough disgusting things in the military, so a little puke was a piece of cake. With both shoes off, he then removed Gideon's socks.

Isaiah wouldn't say he was into feet, but Gideon had beautiful feet. Whiter than the skin on his face and arms, they were narrow, his toes, straight and thin. The nails were clipped and manicured.

Gravity and an alcohol-induced lack of balance pulled Gideon back onto the mattress, and Isaiah saw some vomit around the bottom of Gideon's jeans. He exhaled. He really couldn't put the guy to bed with vomit on him, so…He tugged the jeans off, thanking God Gideon wasn't one of those guys who went commando.

He would leave Gideon there like that. When he sobered up, he'd be able to get himself into bed.

When Isaiah reached down to take the soiled shoes and pants, Gideon sat up. "I gotta puke!" He tried to get up but staggered.

30

Isaiah helped him into the bathroom, realizing just how short Gideon was as he held on to him, barely getting Gideon to the toilet before the guy puked up his guts into the bowl.

Isaiah took a few steps back to give Gideon his space. The poor guy only had two drinks, and he was as messy as a sailor who'd been drinking all night. Isaiah grinned. It was kind of cute.

Despite Gideon moaning into the toilet, Isaiah found himself mesmerized by how adorable he was. Stripped down to a pair of tiny red underwear, Gideon's V-shaped back and little ass were beautiful. His tanned legs were lightly peppered with black hairs.

Shame on me for lusting after a man who was puking his guts out. And yet, he couldn't draw his eyes away from the beauty kneeling before him. Thank God his mother had raised him right, and he was way too much of a gentleman to take advantage of someone drunk.

Soon, Gideon got off the floor by himself. "I'm sorry." He didn't look at Isaiah as he walked past him and climbed into his bed. "If you want to come to bed with me, you can." Gideon slurred as he pulled his covers up over his head.

Isaiah stood in the doorway and stared at the mound laying still on the mattress. The room had fallen deathly quiet. He was sure he knew what Gideon was offering, *but...*

Chapter 4

Gideon's eyes opened to the sound of the birds chirping outside his bedroom window. He looked over at the shut blinds and saw a little light bleeding through. He reached for his phone on his nightstand, but it wasn't there. *Where's my phone?*

In the dimly lit room, it took a second for the pain in his forehead to communicate that he had a blistering headache. Gideon exhaled a breath, trying to wake up and shake the pain. Bits of last night came to him. He'd gone to dinner with Daisy and—Shit, this was a hangover. He'd gotten drunk last night.

His mind raced as he began recalling last night. He remembered sitting in the car coming home, and his head had been spinning with the movement of the car. He was pretty sure he vomited, and it wasn't because of the foul taste in his mouth at the moment. *I need water.*

Gideon got out of the bed and stood. His chest and legs exposed, he realized he wasn't in his usual sleeping sweats but had slept in his underwear.

In the kitchen, the clock on the microwave read six-twenty-three. He poured himself a glass of tap water. The first sip washed the harsh scent of puke from his mouth. By his third sip, his dry mouth had dissipated some. He twisted the wand on the blinds, letting the morning light filter in through the carport.

"Good morning."

"Jesus!" He wasn't used to another voice in the house. He spun around to see Isaiah stretching in the doorway.

"How are you feeling this morning?" Isaiah stepped into the kitchen.

Gideon answered with a gasp and an eye roll. Did he look as bad as he felt? His memory of last night was foggy, but details were, obviously, pretty important. Why was Isaiah here? His last conscious memory of last night was climbing out of the car when they got home.

Isaiah walked over and opened the cabinet to the right of the sink. He pulled a glass out and poured himself a glass of water from the tap.

The two stood in the kitchen for a minute in silence. *He's wearing clothes, but I'm in my underwear... What happened last night?* He was awake enough now to realize that he was standing in his kitchen, damn near naked, with someone he barely knew. He crossed his arms in front of his stomach as if that was enough to cover him. *Why is Isaiah here... in my house?*

"What are you doing here?" His dull headache seemed to be intensifying. Bed-head, dragon breath, a killer headache, and a lack of memory; this wasn't good.

"I stayed over. You don't remember?"

Gideon closed his eyes, searching for a memory of last night. *Did we sleep together?* He had zero recollection of anything happening between them. He drew a breath. "No. I don't." He shut his eyes again, this time more out of embarrassment than his hangover. *What had he done?*

Isaiah stared at him and ran his middle finger between Gideon's nipples. "I had a nice time last night."

"*OH DEAR GOD!* Please tell me we didn't!" Gideon's head pounded with the rush of blood to his brain. He put his hands against his temples to stop the aching.

Isaiah's smile widened before opening into a laugh. "No. I was a perfect gentleman."

A wave of relief washed over Gideon. It would have sucked to have had sex with this God of a man and not have remembered it. *Thank God we didn't have sex.* "Where'd you sleep?"

"In the chair, in the living room."

"Why?"

Isaiah shrugged. "Do you remember anything about last night?"

"Like what?" *Since drunken sex didn't happen, what happened?* Gideon's chest tightened. He took a breath and grimaced. He had to figure out how to breathe without breathing. He took a breath. *Ouch!*

"After I put you to bed?" Isaiah leaned back against the counter.

You put me to bed? "What happened after you put me to bed?"

Isaiah crossed his arms over his chest. "Nothing... You crawled into bed and fell asleep." Isaiah glanced over at him. A hint of a smile crept to one corner of his mouth.

33

Gideon tried to read the smile. Combined with a slight furrow between Isaiah's brows, it didn't feel like nothing. Silence fell between them as he thought about last night. He'd never been a big drinker, and he hadn't had a drink in nine months. Alcohol was discouraged with the medicine he was taking. He should have never ordered the second one.

As silence lingered, Gideon didn't know what to make of it. What was Isaiah thinking? What wasn't Isaiah telling him? As if drawing a breath jarred another memory, he remembered he'd been barfing in the bathroom at some point. "How bad was it?"

"You were fine." Isaiah took Gideon's glass from him and refilled it, and then handed it back to him. "Hydrate yourself."

"I'm sorry. I was freakin' nervous." Yesterday had been a rough day. He'd been especially missing his family, and yet the reality that he was heading home in six weeks caused more trepidation than comfort. When Daisy and Isaiah came out and invited him to dinner, the invite caught him by surprise. Isaiah was beautiful, and yesterday Isaiah's proximity caused him to melt into a puddle of hormones and liquid lust right there in the carport. The stress of having dinner with him, the alcohol helped to calm his nerves.

"Nervous?" Isaiah asked in little more than a whisper.

"Uh... yeah. Last night, I had, like, the hottest guy in Los Angeles staring at me from across the table." He stopped, realizing what he'd just said. Which explained the arch of a brow Isaiah was giving him, as well as the smile on his face. *Could this get any worse?* He needed to just shut up. "I'm sorry. I don't drink... I mean, I do drink, but not lately. I don't have a problem or anything like that—" *Shut up. You're rambling.*

"It's fine. You got it out of your system and then went to sleep." Isaiah stared at him.

He remembered that same stare last night. It was as if Isaiah was studying him. He'd never had anyone stare at him with such intensity. *Why?*

"Watching someone spew their guts out isn't fine. You didn't have to sleep over, though." Though him doing so spoke volumes about who he was.

Isaiah yawned. "I've had drunk sailors in the back seat of my patrol car aspirate. Just wanted to make sure you were all right."

Gideon wasn't sure if he should be offended by the association with drunk sailors. His head hurt too much to pick up that argument. "Well, I'm sorry."

"Maybe we can try the night again." A flicker of a smile passed Isaiah's lips. "Without my mother, of course."

Mesmerized by Isaiah's cinnamon brown eyes, Gideon nodded. When he was feeling better, he'd find a way to get out of it. As beautiful and as lovely of a person that Isaiah was, he'd made a promise to himself, no more dating. The promise had been relatively easy to keep the last nine months until now. The pressure between his eyes and the headache was all he could manage at the moment.

"I should be going." Isaiah pushed off the counter. "See you around?" He dawdled for a second. "You know where I am." And with a smile and just a few steps, Isaiah walked out of the house.

*****

When Gideon woke, the pressure in his head had subsided enough that he could actually get up and do something. He looked at the time on his phone. It was almost one o'clock in the afternoon. The luxury of staying in bed until the middle of the day was the exact opposite of what was likely going on at home right now. *Andrew and Dad were probably somewhere on the property, maybe cutting wood, sweeping down the paths, repairing whatever was the latest thing to break or stop working.* He forgot to ask the other day if the new generator had arrived. *Maybe they were working on it now. If they had guests coming in this evening, Mom was prepping dinner.*

The operation of the lodge was a lot of work, especially being a man down. As much as he loved his life back home, he didn't want to run their lodge, day in and day out, confined to its existence. He didn't know how many more years his dad had in him, keeping up with the physical demands of it, and it would all fall to him in a few years. But being here sucked too.

He had the same number of friends in California that he did in Costa Rica, a big fat *zero*. But, at least back home, he had an excuse for not having any friends: He lived in the freaking rain forest, worked sixteen-hour days keeping the lodge up, and his brother and dad were his best friends.

He wondered exactly when the loneliness had started. He wanted to blame one person for his loneliness, and that was his ex, Shawn. Yes, it was Shawn who begged him to come to California, but Gideon knew he owned what occurred afterward. He was an adult and had made the decision to have unsafe sex with Shawn that night.

Nine months ago, when he'd first tested positive for HIV, he'd been so scared, scared he was going to die alone, scared to ask his family for help, scared to trust another soul after Shawn cast him aside. Everyone at the clinic had been so nice, connecting him with a case manager and benefits counselor.

The thought of dating again, seeing Isaiah, all the feelings rushed back: the immediate thoughts of dying, the loneliness, the shame, and deep depression that he felt for months. If he refused Isaiah, he wouldn't have to tell him. It was that simple.

He used to resent every time he read that he shouldn't be ashamed of being HIV positive, that he could have a normal life. How on earth could his life ever be normal again? Sure, he knew he wasn't going to die, but *normal*?

After many conversations with his doctor and his caseworker at the beginning of his diagnosis, he realized that growing up as isolated as he was, he wasn't as knowledgeable on HIV as he should have been. The last several months had been an enormous learning curve for him, understanding the drug industry's remarkable strides over just the last ten years. They had changed the diagnosis from being a death sentence to a manageable disease. But what it hadn't been able to do was take away the shame and embarrassment he carried with the diagnosis.

Gideon rolled over in the bed and stared at the bathroom entry. He hadn't intended to start the bathroom remodel this weekend, but he had to get up and do something to shake off the loneliness. The job of demolishing the bathroom took no thought process. He could zone out and tear it out with his eyes closed. A small part of him regretted convincing his dad to let him do this because it was only prolonging his stay. He should have just torn off the bandage a month ago and gone home.

As he ripped out the toilet and then the sink and countertop, it did little to occupy his thoughts. He thought about calling Andrew and telling him everything: that he'd been sick, the truth about why he'd come to California—to be with Shawn, the man who'd broken his heart. Every time he talked to Andrew, he hedged on telling him everything. It just seemed like a massive lie he'd woven, and now he didn't even know where to begin to unravel it all. He was healthy now. His parents would never know he'd gotten sick or how stupid he'd been.

A couple hours in what was left of the bathroom, taking a sledgehammer to everything in there, had been therapeutic, at least in the form of releasing pent up energy. He felt a little better.

The time on his phone showed it was later than he'd thought. He'd been at it for almost five hours.

Gideon measured out the new floor plan. The room wasn't big enough for a tub and a shower, so he would do a combination shower-tub enclosure. Two sinks, side-by-side, would look nice opposite the enclosure.

He had two nice sinks in the shed that he'd ripped out of a bathroom two months ago when he'd installed a new counter in Mrs. Digger's bathroom. Like he did with a lot of stuff from jobs, he saved material if it was reusable.

When he finished what he could do in the bathroom for one day, the beginning of another headache drove him to bed. Back in bed, he watched a rerun of *Love It or List It* as he played on his phone. His mind drifted back and forth from Isaiah to the thought of being back home.

He couldn't believe Isaiah had actually asked him out. He wondered what Isaiah saw in him. He was nice-looking, but he was also short and entirely out of that guy's league. Isaiah was tall, muscular, smart, military, and several years older than he. Isaiah had stayed all night with him to make sure he was okay. If that wasn't sweet, what was?

Gideon hadn't actually said *yes* when Isaiah had asked him out, and he wondered if a nod actually counted as a *yes*. Surely, he could get out of it because he never wanted to date again. He couldn't.

Isaiah was the first guy since being sick that actually made his heart flutter. Was he actually thinking about rescinding his allegiance to his dildo for this alpha male? Johnson, the name he'd given his dildo, was a good partner; Johnson never lied or cheated and was always there when he needed him, no questions asked. He and Johnson had a good thing between them. Why would he ruin it?

The thought of Isaiah instead of Johnson caused him to shudder. The guy was absolutely gorgeous.

Gideon rehearsed in his head several versions of what to say to Isaiah, letting him know he couldn't go out with him. There was the truth, and then there were several versions of the half-truth. None of them seemed to work because the truth was, he wanted to go out with him.

The sound of his stomach groaning alerted him to the fact that he hadn't eaten. He'd been nursing his water all morning, but there was no mistaking that the grumbling in his stomach said he was ready for some food.

In the kitchen, he opened the refrigerator. A half-gallon of two-percent milk and an egg carton with one egg in it was on one shelf, and on the other shelf was a Styrofoam container of six-day-old Chinese food. Next to it was an unopened bottle of wine that had come with a basket of chocolates he'd won with a raffle ticket about four months ago. He opened the Chinese food container to see if it would pass the sniff test. He didn't even have to hold it to his nose to smell the shrimp had gone south. Ready to toss it into the trash under the sink, he changed his mind because he didn't want it smelling up his kitchen if it sat in there another couple of days.

He dumped the rancid Chinese food into the trash and hauled it out to the garbage bin under the carport. He'd make himself a peanut butter sandwich and a glass of milk when he returned inside.

As he tossed the trash bag into the bin and was about to step back inside, Isaiah exited his house out onto their side of the carport.

"Feeling better?" Isaiah walked towards him. He was wearing a pair of black nylon gym shorts and a blue T-shirt with NAVY in large yellow font across his chest.

"Um... better." Gideon's voice shook as a flush of adrenaline sent a tingling throughout his body. He stared, fixated on the bright lettering on Isaiah's chest as if in 3-D.

"You look a hundred percent better."

Awestruck at Isaiah's chest muscles, Gideon dismissed his compliment. "Um... On your way to the gym?" Like a straight eighteen-year-old virgin in a brothel full of women, Gideon's heart raced.

"Yep."

The copper color in Isaiah's eyes gleamed, causing Gideon to swallow and look down at the ground. To stare into Isaiah's eyes was like staring directly at the sun. You couldn't, even if you wanted to.

"Hey, you up for doing something this evening?" Isaiah's voice was low and husky.

For a second, the sexiness in Isaiah's voice took a backseat to the question itself. Gideon was powerless and looked up as if Isaiah had commanded him to do so.

As beautiful as Isaiah was, Gideon couldn't go out with him. He had to get out of this. "Um, about that. I'm sorry I said yes this morning. I shouldn't have."

"Oh?" Isaiah's voice dropped.

"It's not you." Gideon held out his hands. The sound of Isaiah's voice said he'd been wounded, but victory was just over the horizon. He felt it. "It's me. I've kind of sworn off men for a little while. I've been doing the whole celibacy thing." He tried to say it as if it was no big deal as if he was doing the latest fad diet or something. His thoughts scattered, elated that he could say no, yet he mentally berated himself for doing it.

"So how long is this celibacy thing lasting? Like until your wedding night kind of thing?"

Gideon wanted to tell him that there would never be a wedding night. "I don't know."

The two stood in silence for several breaths.

After a minute, Isaiah spoke. "All right, then let's just hang out. Maybe throw something on the grill or something. Two friends, who don't have shit to do on a Saturday night?"

No, no, no! Gideon's stomach tensed. *What would be the harm in just hanging out?* "I should just relax. Low-key is even probably more energy than I have right about now."

"I'll come over early. I'm a master on the grill. We'll have dinner, and then I'll roll out. I promise I won't keep you up past midnight."

A flare of adrenaline fired to the brain the moment Gideon knew he was going to say yes. "Well, since you put it that way, and I can be in bed before my carriage turns into a pumpkin, okay." He wasn't breaking his commitment to Johnson. He and Isaiah were just going to hang out. Friends. His gaze cut to Isaiah's nipples poking the fabric of his T-shirt. Yeah, *friends*.... Except he didn't just want to be *friends*, and he knew it.

"I'll come by later this evening." Isaiah gave him a thumbs-up, accompanied by a huge grin.

"What should I get?" A trip to the grocery store was needed since all he had in the house was a box of cereal and two boxes of rice pilaf in the pantry.

"Don't worry about it. Let me handle it." Isaiah insisted.

"Okay. Cool." Yeah, this sounded good. He could do this. It would be fun to hang out with someone, and he wouldn't have to have rice for dinner.

"Then I'll see you in a couple of hours." Isaiah pulled out his car keys. "Looking forward to it." With another flash of a grin, he jumped into his car and left.

Back in the house, Gideon had to do a little cleaning up in the kitchen if he was going to entertain this evening. A simple wipe-down turned into a deep scrubbing once he realized it had been too long since anything had been cleaned. He was once a neat freak, but apparently, he'd been slacking off lately and hadn't realized it.

With the master bathroom demolished, he used the hall bathroom to shower and get ready for his... he wasn't sure what to call tonight since he'd never entertained.

He picked out his outfit as if he was going on a date. *These jeans sag in the ass, these jeans are old, and these jeans...* Jesus Christ! Even his clothes were pathetic. He wanted to scream. *When did I turn into a hermit?* He again told himself this wasn't a date; they were just hanging out. *It's okay to have a friend,* he repeated in his head.

It was almost seven o'clock when he heard the Mustang roar into the driveway. He'd been listening for it for the last thirty minutes. He told himself to relax, and then he jumped up and ran to the kitchen window.

He peered out as Isaiah pulled a brown shopping bag from the rear seat of his car. *Damn!* Saliva pooled in Gideon's mouth.

Although sex was not even in the realm of possibilities for them, Gideon couldn't keep his titillating thoughts at bay. Isaiah was the stuff that would cause Eve to say *fuck it* and take a second bite from that damn apple before she offered it to Adam.

Chapter 5

Isaiah walked into his mother's kitchen from the carport. He could smell her perfume still in the air. He was at the sink mixing his post-gym protein shake when Daisy rushed in.

She was holding up her red dress against her chest. "Hey, baby, can you zip me up?" She spun around and lifted her hair up off the nape of her neck.

"Are you going out?" Isaiah located the tiny pull tab and lined up the zipper.

"Yes, Charles called. He scored two tickets to see the Temptations tonight. They're playing at the Kauffman Center. I've got to hurry."

"Oh, Okay." *I wouldn't mind seeing them either.*

Daisy looked at the shopping bag. "Whatcha get at the store?"

"Salmon. I was going to throw it on the grill for dinner. I talked to Gideon earlier, and I was planning on kicking it over there this evening." He zipped her up, dodging a couple of loose strands of hair.

"Really? You and Gideon?" Daisy spun around. "Again tonight?" Her eyes revealed her suspicion.

"Mom, we're just hanging out." Isaiah tucked her tag inside of the dress for her.

"I know what you kids call *hanging out.*"

Isaiah ignored her insinuation. Yes, he was actually feeling the guy more than he was willing to admit, but there were so many reasons they would only ever be friends.

"I also know you didn't come in until seven o'clock this morning."

Isaiah thought about their moment in the kitchen this morning when Gideon called him hot and confessed to being nervous around him. Gideon's body was nice, and his bed head was cute. "Nothing happened last night. I hung out there to make sure he was all right." *Although something could have if I'd acted on Gideon's invitation.*

"Uh-huh." Daisy looked him up and down.

"Don't uh-huh me. Nothing happened." *And if it did, I wouldn't tell you anyway.* This morning, Gideon had only verbally confirmed the vibe Isaiah had been feeling from him during dinner last night. The eye contact, the nervous smile that almost appeared forced... Isaiah was good at judging body language. Everything about Gideon said he was interested—including his drunken invitation to his bed— which didn't make sense if he'd had indeed sworn off men and wasn't dating. Whatever it was, it didn't change the fact that he wasn't looking to date either. In fact, none of this mattered. He couldn't date someone who lived right next door to her. *Can we talk about something else?* "Is the grill still working?"

"Yeah, but I think we're out of propane. The last time Josiah used it, he said it was almost empty."

"No worries. I'll check it." He released a pinned breath, knowing they'd moved on.

"Well, you kids have fun." She adjusted her dress around her hips as she headed back to her bedroom. She stopped at the doorway. "Don't wait up for me." With a wink, she disappeared around the corner.

"Don't wait up for me either!" he yelled back at her, throwing fuel on the fire.

Showered and dressed, Isaiah packed the last of the dinner preparations into two shopping bags. He was pretty sure he had everything. He wanted to believe that he was just going next door, that they were only hanging out. However, the vision of Gideon in those adorable red bikini briefs had been seared into his brain, and he wasn't trying to forget it.

In ten paces, he was at Gideon's kitchen door. He knocked and waited.

"C'mon in!" Gideon yelled.

Isaiah's brows wrinkled as he turned the unlocked door. "It's me!" He walked into an empty kitchen and put the bags on the counter.

Within a few seconds, Gideon emerged from around the corner. "Hey!"

Isaiah turned around to find a cleaned-up version of the Gideon from earlier. The color had returned to his face as well. The two stood fairly close to each other in the small kitchen, close enough that Isaiah saw the gentle essence in the hues of blue in Gideon's eyes. They drew him in closer, wanting more. He changed his mind about scolding him for leaving his door unlocked. The importance of it lost on the vision of Gideon.

The top of Gideon's head barely reached his shoulder. Isaiah's gaze dropped to Gideon's lower body, jeans that pooled around his bare feet. The sight of Gideon's feet—pale ivory, triggered the recollection of the night before, seeing Gideon in his skimpy red undies.

"Oh wow, you're able to rock a man-bun. I respect someone who can pull it off." Isaiah admired Gideon's narrow neck.

Gideon stood next to him. "What all did you bring over?"

A mix of peppermint and amber aroused his senses and caused his nose to tingle. *Soap? Shampoo? Hair product?* Those scents would forever belong to Gideon. "I was planning to throw a piece of salmon on the grill until my mom said we're out of propane. I can broil it, though."

"I like salmon. It's been a while since I've had it."

"I have it marinating in a little home-made teriyaki sauce and thyme. I also picked up some asparagus that I'll toss under the broiler as well. I'm not a carb eater, but I figured tonight I'd sacrifice for you and make us a spicy coconut risotto with lime shrimp."

"Damn, that sounds good. I love my carbs."

"Yeah, well, we all aren't gifted with a perfect hot body like yours. Some of us have to work at it." Gideon's long, thick eyelashes caught his attention. He'd never seen eyelashes so long, so beautiful, on a guy. Isaiah mentally shook his head. He needed to focus on dinner. Still… he took one more look at him, then licked his lips.

Gideon winced. "You're the one with the great body… Um, about last night, I'm sorry about that. I swear I'm not a drunk or anything."

"That's cool. We're all entitled to let go once in a while. It's all good." Isaiah looked around the kitchen. "Okay, show me the lay of the land, and I'll make the magic happen."

Gideon's right eyebrow shot up. "Nobody's ever made the magic happen in this kitchen."

"Well, that's too bad." Isaiah wondered if Gideon was talking literally *or* figuratively… Surely *somebody* had made the magic happen for him. Isaiah thought of Gideon's invitation to his bed last night. *Stop it. The guy was just drunk.* "Okay, so where are your pots?"

"I don't have much." Gideon did a quick one-minute tour pointing out where the pots, bowls, utensils, and dish towels could be found. "I have a bottle of wine if you want me to open it." Gideon walked to the refrigerator.

"Sweet." Isaiah laid out and organized everything he'd brought over.

"Um, I don't know. It's a Sauvignon Blanc." Gideon grabbed the wine.

Isaiah had meant sweet as in *yes, he'd take it,* but didn't correct him. He dug around in a lower cabinet in search of a cookie sheet. "I like to cook with a lot of spices. I love flavor. But let me know if you don't like something. Mom hates garlic."

Gideon poured a glass of wine for Isaiah and slid it toward him. "I'll eat anything except mushrooms. Oh, and I hate Thousand Island dressing." He twisted the top off his bottled carbonated raspberry water and took a sip.

Isaiah was clipping the ends from the asparagus but stopped to look up. "Who the hell still eats Thousand Island dressing?" *The stuff is nasty.*

"My mom loves it. It's hard to find it in Costa Rica."

"I'm that way with marshmallow spread. I can't stand it. I can't even believe people eat that." Isaiah snickered.

"C'mon now, don't be hating on marshmallows."

"It's all sugar." Isaiah glanced up. Gideon's long, curled eyelashes grabbed his attention again. It had been Gideon's soft, refined features that Isaiah had been noticing since last night's dinner. His brows, his lips, even his thin cheekbones, things that didn't usually stand out to him, caused him to pause and take them in with adoration.

Gideon laughed. "That's why I like them."

"Carbs and sugar? Dude, you're killing me." Isaiah grabbed his chest, pretending to have a heart attack. "You freakin' hippies... carbs, sugar, and pot, and you stay skinny and live forever."

"I'm not a hippie. Why do you say that?"

"Really? The hair. For God's sake, you drive a VW bus. I would have bet money you grew up on some compound out in the desert somewhere." *Okay, so I'm flirting a little, so sue me.*

Gideon laughed as he touched his bun. "You should meet my parents if you think I'm a hippie." He shook his head. "I don't think my dad's ever had a haircut."

"Besides your brother Andrew, do you have any more brothers or sisters?" Isaiah was intrigued by this guy. He wanted to know more about him.

"No, it's just me and Andrew. He just turned twenty-one last month."

"I have two brothers." Isaiah laid out his asparagus on a cookie sheet and tossed a mixture of spices and herbs over them.

"I know. Josiah and Elijah. I've met them and Tammy. Their baby is a doll."

Isaiah looked up at him. It was a little weird that Gideon knew so much about his family and had met the baby already when Isaiah hadn't yet.

"What's your mom up to this evening?" Gideon asked as he glanced over to the window toward their house.

"She's on a date."

"Good for her."

"Yeah. Some guy on her job."

"You don't sound that impressed."

"I'm happy for her, but he's newly divorced with kids, and I don't know how I feel about that."

"The divorce or the kids?"

"Divorce. I don't want some guy rebounding with my mom. She deserves better than that. I don't mind the kids."

"Do you want kids?"

"No, not really. They seem to be a lot of work. I don't know how people do it." *I like my freedom.* "How about you? Do you want kids?"

"I used to. I saw myself with a boy and a girl. I wanted the boy to be older so he could look after his sister." Gideon hopped onto the counter and watched Isaiah.

A boy and a girl? "What do you mean you used to?"

Gideon shrugged. "I don't know. I just don't see how it could ever happen for me."

Neither did Isaiah. The only gay men he knew with kids had them from a prior marriage they were in.

As Isaiah committed a full-on assault on Gideon's kitchen, he

45

steered the conversation toward much lighter topics: movies, tv shows, cars, and food, while he cooked.

After Isaiah plated their dinners, he looked around. "Where do you want to eat?"

"Um...." Gideon looked around. "I don't have a table. I usually eat here at the counter or in bed."

Isaiah raised a brow. "Okay, then, here it is. Not sure it would be kosher to eat our first meal together in your bed." Isaiah pushed Gideon's plate toward him.

Gideon jumped off the counter, retrieved a couple of forks and knives, and passed a set to Isaiah. He then hopped back onto the counter and put his plate on his lap.

Isaiah stood next to him as they ate and talked. "I'm still in shock that Ms. Rose was your grandmother. Was she your mom or dad's mom?"

"My mom's." Gideon took the first bite of his salmon. "Oh. This is good." He took another bite.

"Thank you." He loved seeing that look of surprise on someone's face that had never tried his cooking. "Is your dad from Costa Rica?" Isaiah glanced at Gideon's thick brown eyebrows and long lashes. That would explain his Latino features.

"No. He grew up here."

"Is he Latino?" Isaiah looked at the smooth olive tone that graced Gideon's cheeks. Without a doubt, Old Lady Rose was white, so maybe Gideon was mixed, maybe half Latino.

Gideon narrowed his brows. "No. He's white. Why?"

"I guess I thought you were Latino or something because of your olive complexion, but the blue eyes threw me. You have a tiny bit of a Latino intonation that I catch every now and again. That inflection made me think English wasn't your first language."

Gideon laughed. "I do?"

"Maybe it's from living in Costa Rica your whole life. I think it's cute." He was flirting again, but it was harmless flirting. He was just enjoying himself. This evening had been relaxing, easy, and fun. He thought for a minute as to the last time he'd spent an evening with a guy where it was this relaxed.

"My mom grew up in this house," Gideon said with a mouth full of food.

"I can't believe what you've done to it. It feels so different, more open." Although Isaiah grew up next door, Old Lady Rose was already living alone when his family moved in. He'd known she had a husband who'd passed some years prior and that she had adult kids. She was just the old lady who loved to dote on them and make them cookies.

"It's amazing what twenty grand will do." Gideon walked to the stove and scooped up more of the risotto and shrimp.

"Wow, you only spent twenty thousand?" Pleased to see Gideon going for more, Isaiah looked around the kitchen. "You've done a lot."

"I actually did more than just this. I'll show you when we're done. When I left Costa Rica, I was going to do only the repairs that it needed. But when I got here, I realized it should be a total gut job." Gideon climbed back onto the counter with his plate.

"Your grandmother lived here before we moved next door. Back then, the front yard was super pretty. She was into her flowers."

Gideon looked up from his plate. "My parents talked about selling it, but like the money it brings in as a rental."

"Before I joined the Navy, I used to cut the lawn for her, and she'd cook these peanut butter cookies for me in return. I'd cut her lawn just to get those cookies."

Gideon smiled. "I wish I'd known her better. She seemed nice. Tell me something else about her."

"Well, she used to make sun tea. Every Saturday morning, she would put this big jug on the front step and let it sit out there for hours. I swear to God, she put like four cups of sugar in it. It was damn near as good as those cookies. We lived here about eight years before she died. She actually died one year to the day that my dad was killed."

Isaiah stopped as he stared at nothing in particular for a second. "That morning, she was supposed to be going with us to the cemetery. Your grandfather is buried at the same cemetery, and she wanted to put flowers on his grave. I came over and knocked on the kitchen door to get her..." Isaiah stopped, realizing what he was about to tell Gideon. "I'm the one who found her."

Gideon's eyes widened. "Are you serious? All I knew was that she died in her sleep."

Isaiah nodded. "That's true." He paused again. Maybe he shouldn't continue talking about it. But Gideon was leaning in, so he continued. "She never locked the kitchen door—kind of like someone else I know. When I came in, I knew something was wrong. I called for her and didn't get an answer. All the lights were still off, and the TV in the living room was off. I could tell that she hadn't gotten up yet. It was almost noon. I walked down the hall and called her name. When I got to her bedroom, the door was open. She was still in bed with her back to the door. I called her name several times, and she never moved. I knew she was dead." Tears formed in Isaiah's eyes. "Yeah." He cleared his throat. "Um, yeah. She died in her sleep."

"Wow. It's kind of weird that our paths have crossed like we're connected somehow—like through my grandma. Can I ask, how did your dad die?"

"He was in Iraq, and his Humvee was hit by an IED."

"What's an IED?"

"Sorry. An Improvised Explosive Device. Basically, a homemade bomb or landmine. He was getting ready to come home. He only had three weeks left." Isaiah released a slow breath. Except for being gay, he was sure his dad would have been proud of him, his military career, joining the Los Angeles police department, being here, for Mom.

After dinner, they left the mess in the kitchen and went into the small living room. Isaiah stood at the entrance to the elongated but narrow room that faced the street as he looked around. The room was barely furnished with the mid-century armchair that he'd slept in, in the middle of the room, and a small sofa against the window. The only other piece of furniture was a tall ugly floor lamp.

"I can't believe you got rid of the dining room." Isaiah looked back into the kitchen. Now it made sense why the kitchen felt so much bigger than his mother's. Gideon had integrated the dining room into the kitchen and living room.

The fireplace had been sheet-rocked over and was now an entire wall. His mother should do the same thing since they never use their fireplace.

"Wow, I like how you've decorated the place. Do you have something against pictures on the wall?" Isaiah laughed as he eyed the stark white walls.

"Um, no, not really." He shrugged. "I didn't want to put holes in the walls. I kind of want it to be perfect for whoever moves in here. It's a cool feeling knowing that you're creating something nice for someone to have. Okay, don't laugh. I get excited seeing how happy people are when I fix something for them, like a new toilet, or that I fixed their garbage disposal. They're so grateful."

Isaiah raised a brow. "So… you like making *other* people happy?"

Gideon shrugged. "Yeah."

"Well, this should make someone very happy. You've done a nice job. It's like a new house." Isaiah kicked off his shoes and sat on the sofa. "Are you excited to get back home?"

Gideon sat in the chair and brought his feet up, under him. "I guess."

"Oh? That didn't sound convincing."

"I am. I miss my family like crazy." Gideon's mouth twitched to one side. "I love living in the forest, by the river…but my dad… he has terrible arthritis. Some days, he can barely work. They really need my help."

"How have they been managing while you've been out here?"

"My brother's there, but he got another job, so he's leaving."

Isaiah stared at Gideon. Yes, Gideon was a beautiful man, even with his brows furrowed. His gaze dipped to his slight frame, curled in the chair. *It's too bad that you're leaving, especially since it sounds like you don't want to.* He looked away before he was caught. He thought about what he would do if that was him. *I wouldn't do it.* But this wasn't his problem to solve. Gideon was a grown man… and hadn't asked for his help. The few beats of silence between them suddenly felt awkward. He searched for something to say, *anything, just say something.* "Mom says you can fix anything."

Gideon nodded. "Mostly."

"Business must be pretty good."

"Why do you say that?"

"Well, your van is gone most of the time. Sometimes you're gone all day."

Gideon shifted his ass in the chair before propping the small square pillow between him and the armrest. "Are you keeping track of me?"

"No. I'm keeping track of those around my momma."

"Oh. Well yeah. I like to stay busy." He again repositioned the pillow under his arm. "Damn... This chair isn't comfortable at all." He moved to the sofa.

"You're not telling me nothing I don't already know. Why'd you buy it?" Isaiah slid to the corner, ensuring Gideon had enough room to sit down.

"I didn't. I found it at the flea market."

"The flea market? Well, aren't you a thrifty motherfucker?"

"I come by it honestly, from my mom. She can stretch a dollar into two, but I've used all the money we had for repairs."

"Spent most of it on the kitchen, I bet."

"Pretty much, as well as the new roof and all the flooring. Now that I'm here, we've lost that income, so money is tight."

"Well, they need to charge your ass for living here."

"Oh, hell no. If anything, they should be paying me for all of this work."

Isaiah released a halfhearted snicker. He was less interested in the chair and Gideon's finances than he was about Gideon's offer last night. He floated the idea of them dating for a second. His breath caught, and he forced a series of short quiet breaths to bring it under control. "What happened that made you swear off men until you're... what did you say, a hundred?"

A one-sided smile crept to the right side of Gideon's mouth. "I didn't say a hundred. But maybe until I'm ninety-nine and a half." Gideon pressed his back to one side of the lumpy couch, placing his bare feet on the middle cushion between him and Isaiah.

Isaiah did the same, their feet now inches apart from one another. "What happened?" Gideon's toes' proximity to his, as if they actually were touching, caused a warmth to travel from Isaiah's feet, up his leg, and into his chest. When he looked at Gideon, their eyes met for a second before Gideon looked away. Isaiah seized the moment to stare. The look on Gideon's face reflected he was deep in thought.

Gideon took a deep breath. "Been hurt and lied to too many times. Not sure if I'm ready to do it again."

Isaiah gazed for a half-second at Gideon's beautiful lips as they moved. "Did they cheat on you?"

Gideon shrugged.

"I don't know what happened, but I can tell you that when someone cheats, it's about them, not you, no matter what they say." Years of being with Ronnie qualified him to speak about cheating.

Gideon nodded. "I hate all the drama. Why can't people be up front and honest about who they are?"

"The guy that hurt you—how'd you meet?" What he wanted to know was exactly how Gideon was hurt, but he'd start with an easier question.

"His name was Shawn. He was a guest at the lodge one weekend."

"And?" He wanted to know how, the why, the details. All of which fed him information on who Gideon, the person, was.

"That afternoon, when he and his group came down the river, Andrew and I met them and got them out of their rafts and wetsuits. It was like Shawn, and I spotted each other at the same time. He was freakin' gorgeous."

Isaiah tried not to react to Gideon's strong immediate attraction to Shawn.

"When Andrew took the group up to the lodge, Shawn had lingered, chit-chatting with me as I secured their rafts and sorted out their gear. His stare, his voice, the compliments, Shawn made it obvious he was interested in me. That night, at dinner, we both just started flirting a lot with each other."

Isaiah had questions, lots of questions: *What was attractive about Shawn? Did they have sex that night? What did the perpetrator... Shawn, do exactly to hurt him?* His years of training told him to just let Gideon talk. The story usually filled in all by itself.

"After dinner, I was working the bar, and the group was sitting around drinking. He came over, and we started talking. Everyone was getting pretty wasted, but Shawn wasn't drinking. He just hung out at the bar, and we talked. He's an airline pilot. He talked about his Mercedes, his motorcycle, his house in Los Angeles, and all the wealthy people he knew."

Isaiah nodded as he listened. *Was Gideon into this guy because he was gorgeous and they were both horny or was it the dream life he was flaunting?* "Did you guys hook up that night?"

"Yeah. After everyone went to bed. In his cabin."

Isaiah didn't need to hear those details. He was more interested in how Gideon ticked and how he was hurt. "Is that how you meet most guys, working at the lodge?"

"Yes and no. I'm on Studfinder, so sometimes, I would drive to San Jose for supplies, and I would use Studfinder to hook up while I was there."

"How far is San Jose?" Isaiah's foot slipped and touched Gideon's toes. It sent another wave of warmth to his chest. He waited to see if Gideon would pull away. What he got instead was a sad grin and lake blue eyes staring back at him.

"Two and a half to three hours. It's a big city, like L.A."

"How often did you go to San Jose?"

"Maybe two or three times a year. Not much. I didn't have my own car."

"That might be part of the problem, using this *Stud* finder site?" He put the word *stud* in quotations with his fingers as he said it. He didn't do random hook-ups, but it was common in the gay culture *and* in the Navy, especially while visiting other countries.

"Come on. Don't tell me you've never hooked up from a dating app?"

Isaiah sat up as he scowled. "Actually, no. I haven't." Maybe Gideon's offer last night wasn't just because he was drunk. Maybe Gideon wasn't the person he thought he was getting to know. He swallowed down the sour saliva that rose from his gut. He didn't want Gideon to be that person.

Gideon leaned forward. "Are you serious? Come on!"

"I'm not interested in hooking up. I'm a grown-ass man. That shit is for kids. I'm not sure that most people on those sites know the difference between love and lust."

Gideon's cheeks turned crimson. "So, how do you meet guys?"

"At the moment, I'm not looking to date either." He said it aloud to serve as a reminder to himself. "But when I am, I won't be shopping for them online, that's for sure." He could count the guys he'd dated, and it was under ten. His feelings for Gideon were all over the place. It was too bad Gideon was leaving in a couple of weeks—but he also lived next door to his mother.

"I see. You just take out the trash, and men fall out their doors for you." Gideon chuckled.

"I *wish*, but that doesn't happen." Isaiah brushed his toes against

Gideon's on purpose. He'd heard from people that he was intimidating, so he forced a smile to ensure Gideon was getting a clear signal as to how he was feeling. The two locked eyes. Isaiah wanted to kiss him.

"You're smooth." Gideon's voice was little more than a whisper.

"No, I know what I like." And it was too bad that what he was liking would be gone in a couple of weeks.

Gideon took a sip of his water. It was a slow drink followed by a slow swallow as he stared at Isaiah. "And… what do you like?" Gideon licked the moisture from his lips.

Damn, that was sexy. Blood rushed to Isaiah's groin as he took a second to refocus his thoughts. "Men, for starters. I don't play with boys. I want someone who's into me as much as I'm into him. I like a guy who's smart and can hold a conversation, but not so smart that he doesn't know how to laugh. What I like is a man who's willing to be vulnerable and show me his heart and what's in it." *Can you do any of that?* It was funny to hear himself say all of that because Ronnie hadn't been any of that.

"What was your last relationship like?" Gideon asked.

Isaiah didn't know how to answer that. *What exactly had Ronnie been? A boyfriend? A friend-with-benefits? A co-worker he slept with? His* definition of their relationship and Ronnie's definition of it had never matched up. It'd never been as clear as it should have been.

Isaiah looked at Gideon and then broke eye contact. He hadn't planned on getting this deep this evening, but here he was. It spoke volumes of how comfortable he was with someone he hardly knew because it wasn't in his nature to so easily and quickly trust someone he didn't know. Yet, with Gideon, he did. He tried to pin down why that was. What was it about Gideon that tilted so much of his world out of sync? "I was kind of seeing this brother named Ronnie. He was actually my commanding officer at one point. That's how we met."

"Aww, sleeping with the boss." Gideon wiggled his toes against Isaiah's toes.

Isaiah hated that term but couldn't deny it. It was what it was. "Yeah. I guess."

"How long were you guys together?"

"Well, we weren't exactly *together*. It was kind of like friends-with-benefits for a couple of years."

"O... kay." Gideon raised a brow.

"Well, not on my part. I was into Ronnie. Unfortunately, I didn't realize it at the time, but he was on the down-low. He'd had no interest in coming out or committing."

"So why didn't you end it?"

"Have you ever been with someone who was almost perfect for you, but then there was that one thing you always said would be a deal-breaker, but when you're actually faced with it, it might not be one anymore?"

A line etched across Gideon's brows. "What's a hard no for you?"

"In the beginning, with Ronnie, I didn't know what was going on. It was like, are we together, or aren't we? One day, after weeks of speculation, I asked him what the deal was. He hemmed and hawed, doing the whole *I don't like labels* shit. After about six months of that, I was ready to break it off with him. I told him I didn't want to do it anymore. He cried and begged, saying he would do better, and he did, for a while. But then, he slowly reverted back to doing his own thing, calling when his ass had an itch. Months turned into a couple of years, and I put up with it. I don't know how it is for you, but things are different in the military. You're always on guard, keeping your gayness a couple notches below who you are. They can know that you're gay, and for most people, that ain't an issue, but you're not putting your shit out there. Like, with guys I was seeing before Ronnie, I kind of kept things on the down-low. Most straight guys in the military don't want to see that shit. It's one thing to *know* someone's gay. It's another to see it. With Ronnie, we told ourselves that it was also because he was my commanding officer when, really, he just didn't want to commit."

"Who broke it off, you or him?"

"I'd say it was mutual. We were both up for reenlistment. I knew he wanted to make captain. I felt that if we didn't have the Navy, he'd be more comfortable committing, so I told him that I was getting out... and he said he was staying."

"Let me guess. You were hoping he'd say he was getting out, too."

Isaiah nodded, impressed that Gideon was so perceptive.

"Are you in love with him?"

"God, no." Isaiah winced. "Well, maybe at one time. But you know, once you're out of it, you can see how toxic it was."

Gideon's mouth twisted. "I think that's why it was so hard for me. I look back at it, and I still can't find those little clues that should have told me my ex was a scum bucket."

Isaiah shook his head. "I used to tell myself that cheating on me was a deal-breaker for me."

Gideon nodded. "Are you saying that you would actually take somebody back who cheated on you? Cheating is a *hard no* for me."

"No, that's not what I'm saying at all. I'm saying that you don't know what you'd do if it happened to you; you tell yourself that it's a hard no. I never caught Ronnie cheating on me. But I also wondered how many other friends-with-benefits did he have?"

"You never asked?"

"No."

"Why?"

Isaiah didn't answer right away. He thought about how much more he wanted to disclose of himself because the answer was painful. He took a deep breath. The risk of exposing something he shouldn't didn't seem so high with Gideon. "Afraid to rock the boat. That I'd lose what I had as if it was better than nothing. By his definition, we were only friends-with-benefits, so I took it as I didn't have the right to place limitations on him."

"Your feelings are your feelings. You have the right to set limits on how someone's going to treat you, even a friend."

"I agree, but when it's happening to you—the drama, the turmoil, the ups and downs, and wanting things to be better—you don't always see things as clear as you do once you're out. A part of me knew when I told him I was getting out what he would do. Deep down, I knew he would stay in, and that would be the end of us."

"But you guys are still friends?"

"He's in Amsterdam now. He took another enlistment overseas. I haven't talked to him since he left."

"Is this guy, Ronnie, the reason you're not ready to date?"

"Yeah and no. I think I need a little time to figure out exactly what I want. Ronnie's certainly not it. I don't know… with the move, the academy, living back at home with my mother… it doesn't feel like a good time to start anything."

"Was it hard to be gay in the military?"

"Yes and no. You have your core group of homies that you see and work with every day who are cool with it. Occasionally, you come across some dickhead from the backwoods who doesn't have a clue about life, and his only chance of getting out of the woods was joining the military. They usually think that every gay guy is checking out their ass, and they're threatened by it."

Gideon laughed, "Yeah, those are usually the same dudes who are whistling at women and hitting on anything with boobs."

Isaiah liked that Gideon was so inquisitive and wanted to know so much about who he was. Most dates—*if this was a date*—were usually filled with trying to impress the other person, not genuinely trying to get to know them. There was much he wanted to know about Gideon. "Growing up in the jungle and all, where'd you guys go to school?"

"My mom homeschooled us."

"Did you go to college?"

"No... Not yet."

Not yet? Yes, you're *young. What would you study? Who are you? Who will you be in five or ten years?* "What makes Gideon happy? What feeds your soul?"

"Besides my family, I think I'm most happy when I'm outside. I love being outside. Andrew and I hike in the jungle for hours. You'll see things you'll never see anywhere else all on one trail: Toucans, the red-throated ant-tanager, and loud-ass howler monkeys. The fresh air against my skin is like a drug. Sometimes I think I even crave it."

"You mean like the sun—"

"—no, day or night, rain or shine, I love air."

"Wow, I don't believe I've ever heard someone talk about air with such passion." It made Isaiah think about being out to sea on the ship. After being below deck for sometimes days, to make it to the deck, to have the wind in his face, when the ocean air filled his lungs... it was the best feeling in the world. Just thinking about it caused Isaiah to take a deep breath.

"The second-best thing is being barefoot. I freaking hate shoes, but socks are the worst. It's like my toes are wrapped up like a mummy."

With a snicker, Isaiah stared at Gideon's bare feet. "Shoes and socks?"

"Yeah. I hardly ever wore shoes as a kid. They were too binding for me."

Isaiah laughed internally at Gideon saying *as a kid* as if it was decades ago. "But you wear them now, right?" Isaiah smiled.

Gideon shrugged. "When I have to. Do you want to know what else makes me really happy?"

Isaiah leaned in.

"Being naked outside… and just hanging out and talking with you."

"You want to be naked outside with me?" Isaiah sat up.

"No. I didn't mean it that way. I meant being naked in general. Not… with you."

"You don't like being with me? Is that what you mean?" Isaiah saw Gideon's cheeks blush. He was easy to tease.

"No, I like being with you, just not naked."

Isaiah laughed inwardly at the panic on Gideon's face. This was fun. "You want to be with me, just not naked?"

"Come on, you know what I'm trying to say. Quit giving me a hard time." Gideon chuckled.

Isaiah couldn't hold back his smile, seeing that Gideon finally caught on to his teasing, but he wasn't quite ready to let him off the hook yet. "You don't like wearing shoes and socks…. or clothes… You really are Tarzan!"

"I'm not telling you anything else."

The vision of Gideon barefoot in the jungle as a kid made Isaiah smile. The image of Gideon, as an adult, in the jungle in a loincloth, well, that was flat out sexy. If Gideon wasn't leaving, if he didn't live next to his mom… *he entertained them dating:* kissing Gideon, making love to him, being with someone so out of the closet, and unapologetic for who they were. This guy was nothing like he'd ever dated. Mom loved him. She was playing match-maker with them. There was no need to keep Gideon a secret from her. S*he already knows…. But I don't want her in my business.* Isaiah drew in a frustrated breath.

*****

They had been talking for several hours, the evening filled with ideas of how dating Gideon could work. The only challenging obstacle was the fact that Gideon was leaving in six weeks. There was little Isaiah could do to change this.

It was a little after one a.m. when headlights illuminated Gideon's living room window.

"I think that's mom." Isaiah listened to the low idle of the car beneath the carport.

"Sure is taking her a long time to get out of the car." Gideon grinned.

"I know, right?"

When the car door opened, the living room was so quiet that Isaiah heard the chimes from inside the car. The chimes continued for another two minutes before the car door shut.

Gideon grinned at Isaiah. "I wonder how it went?" His grin widened.

"C'mon, man! I'd rather not go there!" The last thing he wanted to do was picture his mother having sex. The room went quiet again.

After a minute, Isaiah got to his feet. "I should get going." Isaiah slipped his shoes on and stood up and stretched. The last thing he wanted to do was overstay his welcome. He'd promised Gideon to keep it a short night. "See how her date went."

Gideon rose, too. "Tonight was nice. Thanks for cooking."

"We should have probably cleaned up the kitchen before coming in here to talk. Do you need some help?" Yep, he was stalling.

"Nah, don't worry about it. I'd much rather have talked."

They stood in Gideon's small living room a foot apart. There was a flash of awkwardness, like at the end of a good date when there should be a kiss, but it doesn't happen. To break the tension, Isaiah turned and walked to the kitchen. Gideon trailed behind him.

At the door, Isaiah stood there. "Um, okay. I guess I'll see you later." Their eyes met, and Gideon's eyes were doe-like and dreamy as he stared back at him. *I want to kiss him. Should I?* Isaiah took a step back from the door.

"Yeah, um… thank you for cooking." Gideon reached down and opened the door. "Good night."

"Yes, it has been." Everything Isaiah thought he knew about what he liked in a man had been shattered this evening. He liked Gideon more than he could ever imagine liking someone like him. He was different than anyone he'd ever dated… but he was also Mom's neighbor and leaving in six weeks. Their timing really sucked… or *maybe,* it was a blessing.

Chapter 6

This morning, Gideon had been painting Mrs. Garza's vaulted living room, covering the olive-green walls with a fresh winter white. He'd painted her bathroom, and she was so happy with him that she'd hired him to spruce up the living room as well. She was a dream client, not only because she paid in cash, but she fed him as well. Whatever she was cooking today had his stomach grumbling for the last hour.

As he rolled his paint roller on the wall, Gideon prioritized the many reasons he shouldn't fall for Isaiah. *One,* neither was looking to date. *Two,* he was leaving in five weeks. *Three*, he didn't want to get hurt again; and, *four*, he would have to admit to someone for the first time that he was positive.

In the last couple of weeks, he'd finally felt like his old self again. The HIV antiretroviral treatments were working. His viral loads were now at an undetectable level. He couldn't pass the virus on to another person. There simply wasn't enough of it in his blood to infect someone else. As his doctor put it, he was healthy; however, being deemed "healthy" didn't take away the feelings of being extremely self-conscious or ashamed.

Among the medical profession, HIV counselors, and his Living with HIV group, there was an ongoing debate as to when it was appropriate to tell someone they were dating that they were HIV positive. Although the answers varied, the one thing everyone agreed on was that it had to be before the relationship turned sexual.

The thought of telling Isaiah that he was HIV positive scared the shit out of him. This was one of the reasons he'd been avoiding dating.

It all felt like a tremendous responsibility to possibly hold someone else's life in your hands. It wasn't enough to simply practice safe sex; the other person had a right to make an informed decision if he wanted to be a part of it—something that asshole Shawn had never afforded him.

"What do you think about painting the hallway as well?" Mrs. Garza appeared out of nowhere, jerking him out of his head. She stood at the entryway with her arms folded across her breasts, looking at the walls.

"I can do that." Gideon crawled down the six-foot ladder and put his paint roller into the paint pan. "What color were you thinking?"

"Well, I love how new and fresh the white is. What do you think about the same color as the living room?"

Gideon was relieved to hear her choice of colors. The current coffee-brown walls made the hallway dark and appear narrow. "That would look nice, but I don't think I'll have enough paint. I'll run out and pick up some more at lunch, then start this afternoon."

A big smile emerged on Mrs. Garza's face. "Thank you."

"No problem. Let the paint dry in here for a couple of days before you put anything back up against the wall or hang your pictures." Gideon's phone pinged in his pocket. "Excuse me."

It was a text from Isaiah—*Finishing up lunch and was thinking about you. Had a good time Saturday night. Thks.*

Gideon smiled as he stuffed his phone back into his pocket. He'd text him back later when he was alone. He knew he was grinning from ear to ear, but he didn't care. Isaiah said he was thinking about him. He forced himself not to giggle as his grin widened.

"From the smile on your face, I suspect that text must have been from a girl," Mrs. Garza probed. "You're beaming."

Embarrassed, Gideon tried to dodge her questioning with a snicker instead of actual words. The simple text from Isaiah was a reminder of how much of a good time he'd had on Saturday, but Mrs. Garza didn't need to know this. Sure, he was excited over Isaiah's killer gladiator body, who wouldn't be, but something more profound than that was drawing him to Isaiah. It was as if there'd been an instant connection that morning through his kitchen window. Isaiah was easy to be around, and Gideon had never met anyone as direct and honest as Isaiah. But was all this for nothing? He was leaving in five weeks.

Anyway, what would happen once Isaiah knew he was positive? If things did get serious, Isaiah had a right to know. It was a stupid idea to think anything could happen between them. They'd spent two evenings together, and he was already trying to make it as if they were dating or something. He had to stop being silly.

"If you're hungry, I made enchiladas this morning. Mr. Garza can't eat them any more because of his acid reflux, so I thought I'd make some for you and me for lunch. Do you eat pork?"

"Oh, yeah!" His mouth watered at the thought of eating what he'd been smelling all morning. "I'll be done in about an hour. Is that good?"

Mrs. Garza smiled. "Perfect. Come join me in the kitchen when you're ready." She turned and disappeared down the hall.

Gideon went back to work. When he was done, he cleaned up his mess in the living room and then met Mrs. Garza in the kitchen.

She was at the stove with her back to him.

"I'm done." He said to her more to let her know he was there in the kitchen than to apprise her of the completion of the living room.

"Good." Mrs. Garza moved a plate of freshly made flour tortillas from beside the stove to the table. "Sit."

Gideon took a seat, and she spooned a large piece of her cheesy enchiladas onto his plate and then added two tortillas to it.

"Here you go, *mijo*."

Her calling him *mijo* made him smile. He knew she meant it as a term of endearment. She was sweet and easy to talk to. He'd learned the first time he was here that she used to be a schoolteacher and had retired last year. He'd only met Mr. Garza once, but he seemed like a nice man as well.

"Was that your girlfriend that got you smiling earlier?"

With a mouth full of possibly the best enchilada he'd ever eaten, he shook his head. "No, ma'am. Just a friend."

Mrs. Garza laughed. "You kids. You call everybody a friend. My grandson, Christian, called his wife a friend for three years before he announced they were engaged. My oldest, Emilio, growing up, had a new friend every two weeks. You guys aren't fooling this old lady." She spooned a small piece of enchilada on her plate.

Gideon laughed. She was right. "I hate dating." It slipped out of Gideon's mouth by accident.

"Why?"

He thought for a second of what he could tell her before the truth seemed easy enough. "I don't know... Because it's hard. You put in all this time and energy into someone and then find that the person isn't who they said they were."

"Hmm. When Mr. Garza and I met, I fell in love with him on our second date. On our first date, he invited me to a dance at his church. Back then, the girls stood on one side of the room, and the guys stood on the opposite side. Then the bravest walked to the middle to dance. I was sixteen and had never kissed a boy. My mother came with us and sat at a table and watched us all night. I didn't care; it was a magical night. On our second date, he took me to dinner at his folks' place. They were so kind to me that I knew I wanted to have a family and home like theirs. That night, when Eddie drove me home, he parked up the street from the house. We sat in the car and talked for an hour before he worked up the nerve to kiss me." Mrs. Garza slid her hand across her napkin on the table. "I knew I wanted to marry him that night." Her face lit up as if reliving that night all over again.

Gideon sighed. Times had changed, and her methods didn't work these days. He and Shawn had hit it off instantly, too. But other than him, Gideon's dating resume was short—in fact, Shawn was it. Prior to Shawn, his hookups with other guys had been about sex. He had a few that had asked to keep in touch for a while, but they never did. And now, he didn't see a future with Isaiah either, not just because he was leaving in five weeks, but because he also didn't see himself telling anyone he was positive. He couldn't imagine *how* to tell someone. "I think I might have met someone like that... but I don't think it's going to work out."

"Why not?"

"Um." There was no way he could share that he was positive with her. "I don't know. His name is Isaiah. He lives next door to me. Super sweet."

Gideon watched Mrs. Garza's face for a reaction, but she didn't seem to flinch hearing that he was into guys.

"But, I'm heading back to Costa Rica in five weeks." The excitement he'd had last week about going home had lessened since meeting Isaiah.

"For a visit?" she asked.

"No. My family and I live there. I'm out here fixing up our rental, then I'm heading home."

"Oh, I see. That's too bad." She frowned. "They say timing is everything, but I guess in your case, it couldn't have been worse for the two of you. But if you like him, then maybe just see what might happen. Who knows? Fate has a way of its own. Sometimes, to find true love, you have to take the risk. Tell me about this Isaiah."

Gideon's chest tightened as a sigh escaped his lips. "Besides being gorgeous as hell—I mean, *heck*—he's kind, sweet, and real. He just got out of the Navy and moved back home. His mother is my neighbor; that's how I met him. He's going to be a cop."

They talked for another ten minutes before Mrs. Garza looked at her watch. "I guess I should get this kitchen cleaned up."

Gideon knew he needed to get back to work too. "Thank you for lunch, Mrs. Garza. It was delicious."

"Sonia," she corrected him.

"Um, okay, *Sonia*... I have to get to the paint store. You're not paying me to sit here and eat your wonderful enchiladas. There's a hallway with my name on it." Gideon pushed back from the table. She'd given him a lot to think about.

Mrs. Garza walked over to her cabinets. "Please take some leftovers home with you when you leave this afternoon. Eddie can't eat them, and I shouldn't."

"Thank you." Gideon stood. "Okay. I'm leaving for the paint store, and I'll be back."

He hurried to his van, where he re-read Isaiah's text. *He says he's thinking about me. He had fun.*

Gideon thought about what Mrs. Garza had said, but she didn't have all the facts. Yes, their dinner the other night was fun. There was no denying he was attracted to Isaiah. He was sure Isaiah had been flirting with him while they were sitting on the couch. A tiny giggle escaped with the thought of the evening. But Isaiah *also* said he wasn't ready to date. *I told him I wasn't ready either... But... Damn, why do I have to go home?* Him taking a risk wasn't an option. His knee trembled as he weighed out several versions of a reply to text Isaiah that would end whatever this was that had started between them.

Thank you again for Saturday night. I had a good time, too. He hurried and sent the text before he could change it. His message didn't end anything. If anything, it opened the door wider.

He held his phone in his hand, staring at the screen. With each passing second, his heart pounded. He was flirting with danger, and it had his heart in his throat. After what seemed to be an eternity, Gideon started his van. He was about to back out of the driveway when his phone pinged.

Between classes. Only have a couple of minutes. Glad you had a good time too. Let's do it again!

Gideon's heart leaped into his throat as he read the text over again.

Do what again? Gideon texted back.

Gideon's phone pinged with another message from Isaiah.

I want to see you.

Gideon's breath hitched, the cause of his chest tightening. As much as he wanted to see Isaiah again, it wasn't that simple. He re-read the text. Isaiah had to be asking him out because this conversation didn't feel like it was two friends arranging to *hang out*.

Like hanging out? Gideon texted back.

Gideon's phone pinged at the oncoming message.

No. A date.

Gideon read the word *date* as he processed what it meant. Thinking about it gave him palpitations. *I thought you weren't ready to date?*

That was before I met you.

He read Isaiah's response at least three times as he stared at the words. He saw the words, but his brain was buzzing with static. This would never happen—it couldn't. Fear clenched like a tight fist around his throat. The lack of oxygen caused his breath to hitch as he sent Isaiah the text that would end all of this right here and now. *We need to talk.*

Chapter 7

About?

Gideon read Isaiah's response. Uh oh. He'd opened Pandora's box, and now he was going to have to deal with the fall-out.

With a sense of panic, he typed out his next text. *There's something you need to know about me.*

????

Gideon was having difficulty swallowing. Bile rumbled deep in his gut and pushed upward at the thought of telling Isaiah that he was positive, that he was careless and stupid, and now unworthy of any attention from him. The idea of just ignoring the message, going into hiding, running, all seemed like better options. His cheeks burned. *What have I done? How do I get out of this?*

He leaned back into his seat. If he pushed hard enough, he could melt into it and disappear. He looked at his phone. If he didn't respond, would Isaiah show up at his door? He couldn't face him and say it. That would be worse. Gideon shoved his phone into his jeans.

Sweat beaded across his forehead. Isaiah would be the first person other than medical personnel that he said it to. He couldn't even do it via text. He stared at himself in the rear-view mirror. He didn't look sick. He pondered the definition of sick. *What exactly is sick?* He wasn't sick. He felt fine. He was undetectable, and yet he was still classified as positive by the health care profession. This was now part of who he was. For the rest of his life, this would never change. *When do I start telling people?*

Gideon pulled his phone back out. His hand shook as he typed out his text. *You should probably know that I am HIV+ but currently undetectable.*

He waited a moment before he hit SEND. There. It was out there.

It was over.

His phone pinged.

He took a breath before looking at it.

So much was riding on Isaiah's answer...

Okay

Okay? Okay? That was it? Did that mean, *Okay, nice knowing you? Or Okay, I'm cool with it?* What the hell did okay mean?

Air slowly escaped from his lungs as he grimaced. He put all of who he was out there, and he got an okay back. *Okay, what?* About to overheat, he cranked his window down for air.

Gideon's phone pinged again.

I can handle it. I've dated positive guys before and would like to see you again.

Gideon exhaled. Was it going to be that easy? Was there no hesitation on Isaiah's part at all?

His phone pinged again.

So? Will you have dinner with me on Friday?

Gideon could hardly breathe as he typed his response. *Yes.*

As soon as he pushed SEND, he thought of something else to add. The adrenaline pumping throughout his body caused his fingers to shake as he typed out his message. *FYI, I'm not only +, but I'm also smart, can hold a conversation, and know how to laugh.*

I'm liking you, even more, Isaiah responded.

Although Isaiah's response made him smile, the bile in his gut and adrenaline hadn't begun to dissipate. *Was this happening?* Mrs. Garza said to take a risk, *to find love, sometimes you have to take a risk.* He inhaled a large breath. He exhaled through the large smile that was plastered to his face. He rubbed his face and then tapped out another text—*Can't wait to see you again.*

Me too.

He stared at Isaiah's response. The smile on his face cemented. *Dear God, what am I doing? I'm leaving in five weeks.* It didn't make any sense to start seeing someone now. His heart, however, didn't agree.

*****

The next morning, Gideon went back to work on Mrs. Garza's hallway walls, applying the paint's final coat. Last night, he'd listened for Isaiah's car until around midnight, but then he must have fallen asleep.

When he'd woken this morning, Isaiah's car was still not in the driveway. Had Isaiah not come home at all last night, or had he come and gone while he'd been asleep? If Isaiah *hadn't* come home, where could he have been? Gideon tried to push down the jealousy he was feeling. It was stupid; they hadn't even gone on a date yet. Isaiah had a right to do whatever he wanted, but it still bothered him, the thought that Isaiah may have slept at another guy's house.

Although... Isaiah *had* spent the night with him, and it'd been completely harmless. Besides, it was too soon to change his relationship status from single to married in his social media profile, but a guy could dream...

By late afternoon, Gideon was done with the Garza's hallway. He was putting things away in his van when Mrs. Garza came outside with cash in her hand.

She handed him several folded bills. "A Volkswagen bus? My dear, I remember some fun times in one of those." Mrs. Garza looked over Gideon's shoulders into the messy van.

"Did you have one?" He glanced at the money in his hand, seeing that it was all one-hundred-dollar bills, before slipping them into his pocket.

"No. In high school, I had a girlfriend whose parents had one. Every once in a while, she got to drive it to school..." Mrs. Garza glanced again at the van before turning her attention to Gideon. "I was talking to Eddie last night, and we'd like you to paint our bedroom and the kitchen before you leave. Can you? The white makes everything so bright and new."

"Yes, Ma'am. I can get it done." He could use all the money he could get. He had zero saved. The worry of money seemed to be a constant now for him. Prior to coming to California, he rarely gave it a real concern. Sure, he'd heard countless conversations between his parents about the lodge's finances and overdue bank loans. Mom was always pitching a fit about something Dad bought without telling her. The lodge's survival was utterly dependent on the rafting season, more so than it needed to be. He blamed this on his parents, though. They'd refused to listen to his suggestions of expanding and reaching out to other groups besides the rafters. It was nature's paradise:

Campers, hikers, a weekend retreat center, the possibilities on how to grow the business were limitless. He smiled at his one option that he really thought would be fun... a clothing-optional resort.

When he was done at the Garzas', he knocked out two small jobs and picked up a quick three hundred dollars before calling it a day.

After exiting his van, he balanced three bags of groceries he'd picked up on his way home. He'd tried to convince himself that it was ordinary grocery shopping, but it was about Isaiah. He didn't want to be caught with old Chinese food or no food at all if Isaiah happened to drop in one day this week. He walked through the unlocked kitchen door and thought of Isaiah. *Damn, I did it again.*

Thank God Isaiah wasn't with him to see that the door had been left unlocked all day. After his shower, tucked into his sweats, he reclined on his bed with what remained of the leftover enchiladas he'd brought home from the Garzas' yesterday. Stretched on his back, he had started out watching a show about a guy building a house underground but fell into multiple daydreams of Isaiah. Filled with nervous anticipation, his thoughts were scattered.

I can't believe I told him.

I'm going home.

I like him.

The thought of being with Isaiah, on a date, a real date, he constructed the evening at a restaurant, with white linen and staff dressed in black. Would they kiss? The thought of them kissing caused him to put down his dinner and adjust himself in his sweats.

From the moment he'd set eyes on Isaiah, he was taken by his neighbor. So tall, built, his eyes—flecks of gold and brown that matched the sandy shores at home. He could hear Isaiah's low husky voice as they talked on his couch.

Damn, his voice is sexy.

He tugged on his sweats, feeling his erection.

Maybe I should take care of this?

His fingers gently caressed his erection beneath the soft fabric of his sweats.

So much had happened since coming to California. Was it really true that he couldn't pass the virus to Isaiah if they had sex? His ass twitched at the thought of them having sex.

He smiled at the thought of snagging a man like Isaiah. It didn't seem possible. He thought about the men in his past. None of them remotely compared to Isaiah. *Well,* the Scandinavian dude came close, body-wise, but he knew nothing else about the guy. Isaiah was in the Navy—He's going to be a cop—He's freakin' funny. He giggled under his breath as a giant smile emerged.

In his fantasy, he already had them as a couple until the cold reality pushed its way into his dream. He was leaving. What if Isaiah came to Bajo Tigre? He pictured them sitting on the bank of the Pacuare River. What if he didn't have to return home?

It angered him that he was never asked if he wanted to run the lodge. It had always just been implied. The joke was that Andrew couldn't do it. *That would be a disaster.* He never told them no. He would never have a life if he ran the lodge. His parents had each other. It's not fair. But without him, there was no way they could do it with Dad's arthritis worsening.

How can I make it all work?

He pictured them together in his bedroom in the lodge. Could they run it together? Would Isaiah want to do something like that? He released a deep sigh at the thought of them making love.

Gideon's hand brushed against his erection. His ass twitched again. It took little imagination to actually feel Isaiah in there.

He loosened the drawstring on his sweats and was about to take matters into his own hands when his phone pinged. He expected that it was either his mom or Andrew as he grabbed his phone. He was surprised to see it was a text from Isaiah.

On my way home. You got a minute to talk?

Gideon's breath hitched. The first thing he thought was that Isaiah was canceling their date. He'd had a day to think about it, and now he was canceling. Gideon exhaled as he typed his response. *Sure.*

Within minutes, his phone rang.

"Hello." Gideon tried to sound as casual as he could.

"Hey. What are you up to?" Isaiah's voice was chipper, not the voice that was calling to cancel out on him.

"Just watching TV. How's it going?" Gideon braced himself for whatever Isaiah was calling for. *You got a minute to talk* sounded serious.

"It's been a long day. We had a surprise exam today. I aced it, but we lost another cadet this week. He couldn't qualify on the range. Poor guy had never shot a gun in his life." Isaiah cleared his throat. "I was thinking... I don't know if you were worried about telling me about being positive or not, but, really, I'm cool with it. I'm sorry if I came off the other day like it's no big deal. I know it is for you, and I'm sorry that I didn't acknowledge that. Thank you for telling me."

An apology from Isaiah was not what he was expecting. "You changed your mind about dating me? You do remember that I'm leaving in five weeks?"

"Yeah, I know, but...Why shouldn't we enjoy each other's company until then? Enjoy life, have fun."

Have fun? Gideon wasn't sure what he meant by have fun. *Fun in which way?*

"How are you?" Isaiah's voice was guttural.

"With being positive?" Gideon wondered aloud.

"Yeah."

"Okay." Not really, but blurting out that he was positive was a big enough burden to dump on someone; if he started piling all his fears on top of the diagnosis, the guy would run. God knows, he would if the situation were reversed. So he went with the non-committal "Okay" to avoid awkward silence. "I found out almost a year ago. We caught it early, and I was able to get on the meds almost right away. I found out a couple of months ago that I'm undetectable."

"Hey, that's great. You know the new saying is U equals U."

"U equals U?"

"Yeah. It means that if you're undetectable, then you're un-transmittable. *U* equals *U.*"

"Oh yeah, I did see that somewhere." He and his doctor had talked about what it meant to be undetectable.

"Anyway, thank you for trusting me enough to tell me. Because we travel so much in the Navy and some of the guys are so young, we do a lot of training on HIV and other STDs. These guys pull into port in some of these countries after being out to sea for thirty days, and, I swear, they run off the ship with boners." Isaiah cleared his throat. "I started taking PrEP about three years ago because, you know, dudes will straight-up lie to you these days."

Gideon knew the drug PrEP was for HIV-negative people to

reduce the possibility of contracting HIV. "You've dated a positive person before?"

"Yeah, but I just assume everyone is positive. I have to take care of myself, and I, for damn sure, didn't trust Ronnie."

"I haven't had a lot of experience talking with people about it. You're actually my first—the first person I've agreed to go out with since being diagnosed."

"Really? I'm flattered."

"You better be! I was hella nervous about telling you." Gideon's mood lightened. He was very proud of himself for doing it.

"I feel you, and thank you again. I can't wait to see you this Friday."

"I, um, have a bottle of wine if you, ya know, what to come over when you get home." God, he was really putting himself out there.

"Yeah, I'd like that... but I know myself. I have to study Spanish tonight. It's kind of kicking my ass. I know if I come over there, I won't want to leave."

Disappointed, Gideon said goodnight, feeling that Friday was a lifetime away.

Gideon fell back onto his bed and stared up at the ceiling. They were really doing this. They were talking. He was going on a date with Isaiah. An involuntary twitch cracked the edge of his mouth. He put his hand over his mouth to stifle his giggle, but it wasn't enough as a laugh broke from his chest.

"I'm going on a date with Isaiah!"

Chapter 8

By Friday, Gideon had envisioned his and Isaiah's date in every detail. With excitement that he could barely contain, he was somewhere between *Cinderella*—ready for an enchanted evening— and *Pretty Woman*—filled with self-doubt and hesitation. He knew the reality, and that was that no matter how well the evening went, he was still leaving in a month. He had zero control over this.

Out of the shower and dried, Gideon chose the jeans he'd worn last Saturday night along with a nice blue and white pin-striped button-down shirt. He walked several times from his bedroom to the kitchen window to see if Isaiah's car was there. It wasn't until he checked a little after eight that he spotted a car in Daisy's carport, but it wasn't Isaiah's.

An hour later, he heard Isaiah knocking on the kitchen door. Adrenaline fueled his steps as he hurried down the hall from his bedroom to the kitchen. He could see Isaiah through the small square window in the door.

Gideon tried to act casual as he opened the door. "Hey there." His gaze shot from Isaiah's smile to his chest. *Just fuck me now!* Gideon swallowed hard.

How could someone rock a plain white short-sleeve knit shirt like that? The top two buttons on Isaiah's shirt were unfastened. The next one under that looked as if it was struggling to hold the two sides together. Isaiah's biceps were testing the strength of the fabric around his arms. *Shit, I could work out forever and never have arms like that.*

"You ready?" Isaiah grinned as he took a step back on the single step.

"Yep." As soon as Isaiah turned his back to walk toward the car, Gideon took the opportunity to enjoy his butt in a pair of light blue slacks. The thin fabric and his trimmed waist accentuated one hell of a voluptuous ass. High and round, Isaiah's ass moved as if it was its own entity.

Isaiah spun around. "Lock your door."

Gideon narrowly avoided smacking into Isaiah as he stopped. "Yeah. Of course." *Protective and sexy, oh yeah, daddy.* The goosebumps rose on his arm as he returned to the door.

After locking the door, Gideon joined Isaiah in the car. "What happened to the Mustang?" Gideon asked as he opened the passenger's side of the four-door Honda Accord.

"That was a rental. Elijah works for a Honda dealership in Thousand Oaks. After class today, I drove over there and got it."

The new car smell was present as Gideon strapped in. "This is nice." He adjusted his ass in the leather seat.

"Thanks. I wanted something new. I wasn't sure what. I'd originally thought about a truck, but when Elijah called and told me about this car and that they were almost giving it away, I had him save it."

The sleek black Honda with blackout windows and alloy rims was quieter than any car Gideon had ever been in. "Where are we heading?" So far, Isaiah had kept him clueless about tonight's itinerary.

"The L.A. Zoo does this thing called Zoo Night once a month during the summer. It looks pretty cool, and I thought you might be missing the jungle animals a little. There are a bunch of food trucks there, a D.J., and it's all lit up. Tonight's theme is Motown. I thought since you were raised by monkeys in the jungle, we might run into some of your old friends."

Isaiah teasing him made Gideon smile. "Cool. Are the animals out?"

"It said that most of the animals are in their nighttime enclosures, but there are some that are still out. I can't remember which ones they said."

Gideon had never visited an American zoo. The flicker of a smile passed his lips. He couldn't wait to see the monkeys.

Within an hour, they were standing in line in front of the Lobster Roll food truck. It was a hard decision between the ten trucks on location, but the lobster po'boy sounded good to Gideon, and the shrimp tacos excited Isaiah, so the Lobster Roll truck was the winner.

They found a spot where they could hear the band banging out all of Motown's greatest hits, but be far enough away that they could talk. On the drive over, Gideon had asked a lot of questions about what it was like in the academy. Between bites from the greatest po'boy in the world, Gideon asked more about the life of a cop. He'd pieced together that it was an extensive process to get hired, one that he knew little about. He'd never gone out with a cop. The uniform, the badge, the gun... *the handcuffs.* His mind drifted to a fantasy that involved being shackled to the bedpost.

"What's the hardest thing about becoming a cop?" Gideon savored the meaty lobster in his sandwich. The fresh seafood was a little bit of home with each bite.

Isaiah hesitated. "I think it's learning Spanish. I know a little, but—shit. Some of it doesn't even make any sense."

Gideon looked up from his dinner. "I don't get why you have to know Spanish."

"Fifty percent of Los Angeles is Latino," Isaiah muttered through a mouth full of food.

"I can help you if you want." A warmth radiated in Gideon's chest, knowing he had something that he could offer, that he could be of some use.

"I'd love your help."

Pleased that Isaiah had accepted his offer, Gideon was also excited that it was an opportunity to be together. "I don't get why, if you were already a cop, you have to do all this training over again."

"Being a cop in the Navy versus on the streets is like apples and oranges. Stuff like criminal law, juvenile law, search, and seizures... it's all different from the military."

Gideon admired that Isaiah was so smart and could learn all of that stuff. To be in the military, and now to want to be a cop, took courage. That, in itself, Gideon found incredibly sexy. "You have to be in good shape too?"

"In the academy, you do. Right now, we're jogging anywhere between six and ten miles a week. Plus, circuit training on top of that. There's a mountain behind the academy that we run up. It's a bitch."

This explained why Isaiah was in such great shape. He envisioned Isaiah leading the pack up the mountain. "How long is the training?"

"Six long-ass months."

"Wow! How long before you get handcuffs?" Gideon smiled at the thought of his fantasy.

Isaiah grinned. "Okay, I got you. I see what you're interested in."

Embarrassed that he was so easily read, he broke eye contact. *I was only teasing. God, I hope he doesn't think I'm some kind of a freak.*

Isaiah was working on his third taco when Gideon finished the last of his sandwich. "Do you want this last one? The shit is delicious." Isaiah moved the paper bowl that contained his dinner to Gideon's side.

"You're not going to eat it?" Gideon wanted it but thought he should be polite.

"No. Go ahead. I'm stuffed."

Gideon grabbed the taco and went to work on it. It was better than his sandwich; he regretted not ordering these.

When they were done with dinner, they strolled around the event. Only about a third of the zoo was accessible. Everything else was roped off with signs. In case the sign wasn't enough of a deterrent, an employee was standing nearby to stop trespassers.

Gideon caught the sweet scent of eucalyptus every now and again as it mixed with the zoo's otherwise pungent odors. The various scents were another reminder of home.

"Your mom seems pretty cool with you being gay. I think she was actually trying to set us up." Gideon reflected on the many times Daisy brought Isaiah up before he came home. It now made a lot of sense.

"You think? My mother is the queen of matchmaking. She's got, like, twenty couples under her belt. I think she's going for her first gay couple."

"Has she always been cool with you being gay?" Gideon's heart thumped a little harder hearing Isaiah talk about his mother with such affection. Their relationship reminded him of his relationship with his mother. He liked that he and Isaiah shared this.

"I guess. I didn't come out until after I left for the Navy. It wasn't actually a coming out, as much as she figured it out, and we both just rolled with it. Josiah, I think, has an issue with it, but he's never said anything. It's not like I've ever dated anyone around them or brought someone home for them to meet. How about you? How'd your parents take it?"

The same held true for Gideon. He'd never had a coming-out experience with his parents either, other than the day his mother had made it clear she'd heard him and that guy on the rocks down by the river. "My parents are so laid back. I guess I've always shown signs that I might be gay. My mom said that she and my dad talked about it when I was only four. I'd liked playing with dolls, combing their hair, pretending they were my kids. I've never been like that big macho kind of guy."

"Trust me, I've met some of the most masculine gay men. The two are not mutually exclusive of each other. You don't still play with dolls, do you?"

"And if I did?" Gideon playfully punched Isaiah in his arm. It was like hitting a rock.

"My brothers would have kicked my ass if I'd tried to play with a doll. My dad played football in college. He was recruited by the *Jets* during his last year in college."

"Oh, wow." Gideon didn't know that much about football, but enough to know his dad must have been good to have been recruited.

"He played for them only for a half-season before blowing out his knee. My mom was pregnant with Josiah at the time."

"What's the age difference between you guys?"

"Elijah's fourteen months older than me, and Josiah is three years older."

"Damn, your dad was knocking them out. Did he ever play again?"

"My dad rehabbed his knee, but it wasn't enough for the NFL, so he joined the Navy when we were young. It was the only thing he could do that gave them medical benefits and paid a decent wage."

"We didn't have a lot of money growing up either." *Another thing in common.* "Did you and your brothers play football like your dad?"

"In high school, Josiah ran track, and Elijah and I both played football. What about you? Did you play any sports growing up?"

Gideon laughed. "Nope." *With who?* He loved his childhood, but being homeschooled in the forest didn't exactly come with any type of social life.

"Did you play any instruments?"

"The flute when I was little. I taught myself how to play the guitar."

"The flute? Isn't that a girl's instrument?"

"There's no such thing as a *girl's* instrument! You're a dick." Gideon chuckled at Isaiah's off-humor. "Thank God you don't have kids."

They stopped in front of a neon-lit ice cream truck. "Can I treat you to some ice cream?" Gideon was in the mood for a banana split.

"Sure." Isaiah stepped up next to Gideon.

Gideon ordered his banana split with three scoops of mint and chip, with extra hot fudge, and Isaiah ordered a single scoop of the bubble gum ice cream.

When the lady handed Gideon his bowl, Isaiah laughed.

"What's so funny now?" He had no idea why Isaiah was laughing now, but he had a good suspicion it was at him. *What did I do?* The grin that had been on his face for most of the evening returned.

"The bowl is as big as your head. There's no way you're going to eat all of that."

Gideon took his first bite. His eyes rolled to the back of his head. "Wanna bet?"

"I want to know where you're putting all of that." Isaiah pulled out his phone. "Hold it up."

Gideon held the bowl of ice cream up near his face and smiled. It was endearing that Isaiah wanted to take his picture. The thought alone caused his grin to widen.

After several photos, Isaiah put his phone back in his pocket. He held Gideon's waist and wiggled him. "What size waist do you have?" He grinned as his eyes gleamed down at Gideon.

I like how you look at me. "I'm not going to tell you because you're only going to make fun of me." Gideon playfully walked off with his banana split. He didn't let Isaiah see his cocky smirk. He could be just as silly.

Isaiah caught up to him. "No, I'm not. What size? Thirty, I bet."

Gideon wished it was a thirty. "Twenty-eight... most of the time."

"Damn! Where do you buy your clothes, Forever15?" Isaiah broke into hysterical laughter.

It's not that funny. "See? I knew you were going to say something smart." He bit his lower lip, trying not to laugh.

"Okay, okay, sorry. Come here, my little 4T." Isaiah began laughing again.

"You suck!" Gideon couldn't hold his own laughter back any longer as a half chuckle-half splutter came out.

It took a moment for Gideon to regain his composure. Isaiah was as funny as Daisy. She often made him laugh. "I remember the week I moved into the house. Your mother came over with this cake. She said that she made it for me as a welcome to the neighborhood present."

"Was it her hummingbird cake?"

"Yeah, that was it."

"Oh, that's a cake she only makes for weddings or when she's really trying to impress someone."

A burst of giggles stirred in Gideon's belly and mingled with a thousand butterflies that she wanted to impress him. *Why?* "Oh my God, that cake was so good."

"Damn, she started working on you right away. It's like her signature cake. People show up at the reception for that cake and then go home."

"Really?" Cinnamon, vanilla, pineapple, bananas, pecans… he'd never tasted anything like it. He remembered how creamy the three-layer cake covered in cream cheese frosting had been. "I can see why. Okay, but the funny part is, for two days, your mom showed up at the house, and we ate that cake, piece by piece, in two days. Damn, I wish I could have that cake again."

"Yeah. She was playing you. Did she ask you a ton of questions?" Isaiah rubbed his chin.

Gideon thought for a second. *As a matter of fact, she did. She wanted to know everything about me.* "She grilled me."

"Did I come up?" Isaiah arched a questioning eyebrow in his direction.

Gideon's eyes widened as it all started making sense. "Oh yeah. But she never said you were gay. I thought she was bragging on you. It was cute."

Isaiah made a tsk-ing noise with his mouth. "There's nothing cute about it. I'm going to get her when I get home." Isaiah shook his head. "She had this whole thing planned out."

She did? She did… An impish smile made his mouth twitch. *She thought I was perfect for you. I love her.*

They continued walking as if they were the only ones amid the thousand people that had turned out for the event. The music was faint as they strolled the zoo and arrived at a circular moat. There was just enough light to see that on the other side of the moat was a small island that contained the hippopotamuses. It sounded as if one was sloshing around in the water below them.

They paused to see if they could count how many were in the enclosure. Gideon counted three massive figures as he finished up the last of his ice cream.

"Yeah, I think there's only three." Isaiah swiped his index finger across Gideon's chin. "You got a little something there." He then licked it off his finger. "That's good."

There was a moment when Gideon thought Isaiah might kiss him. He was prepared for it, but it didn't happen.

"If you weren't working with your parents, what would you be doing?" Isaiah's gaze lingered over him.

Gideon had to reorganize his thoughts from being kissed and those warm brown eyes staring attentively at him to talking about himself. "I don't know. I used to think it would be fun to work in a nature park as a naturalist guide. Being outside with the animals all day, taking people into the wilderness, hiking and camping would be fun. But I also love working with numbers. If I could go to school, I wouldn't mind being an accountant. I'm actually kind of an egghead." Out of the corner of his eye, he saw a group of girls walking toward them.

The girls stopped next to them, asking what was in there. After a brief chat with the strangers, Gideon sensed a change in Isaiah's demeanor as they took a couple of steps away from the girls. The warmth in Isaiah's eyes was gone, his playful mood suddenly absent as they stood there in silence, looking over at Hippo island.

Gideon caught that Isaiah had glanced over at the girls at least twice. Did they make Isaiah nervous? *Why?*

When Gideon looked over at the girls, they didn't seem to be paying them any attention as they laughed and carried on.

"Shall we walk?" Isaiah asked. He didn't wait for an answer before walking.

Gideon fell into step behind his date, taking four steps before catching him. He looked back at the girls. *What was it about them that made Isaiah nervous? They were just girls.*

On a narrow path, just the two of them, the low lighting provided a sense of seclusion as they meandered through the wooded park. Gideon eyed the dense vegetation of bamboo and ivy that lined their path. It was a reminder of his nighttime hikes up behind the lodge.

"This is nice." Gideon finally spoke, ending their silence.

"You having a good time?" Isaiah's voice was low, the inflection caring a genuine concern.

"I am."

"When did you know you were gay?" Isaiah asked through his own laughter.

"What's so funny?" Gideon snickered at Isaiah, teasing him.

"I can picture you as this sweet little kid playing with his dolls and wanting to play the flute, and your parents saying to each other, 'Shit, we've got to tell him that he's a homo.'"

"Playing the flute and playing with dolls doesn't make you gay. Man, you're such a sexist." Gideon playfully pushed Isaiah away from him. "I'll have you know, my parents are super cool. When I was thirteen, I hung this poster up in my room of a shirtless Zac Efron. I was in love with him. One day, my mom saw it. I remember thinking, 'Uh-oh!' She looked at me, and then back at the poster and then said, 'I love his eyes.'"

Isaiah nodded. "You even had good taste back then. It's so cool that she did that."

Gideon nodded in agreement. He sensed the old Isaiah slowly returning. He exhaled, letting go of whatever that was that occurred back there with the girls.

This evening so far had been incredible. A smile parted his lips as they strolled. It just might have been the most magical evening of his life. Until this trip, Gideon had never spent more than one night of his life without his family. They were a tight family, which made his failed attempt with Shawn that much harder because he'd traded his family for something that had failed miserably. Him staying away while he'd been sick wasn't just because he didn't want them to know he'd been sick. He was embarrassed that he'd done something so stupid.

Side by side, they chatted as they walked. He held onto every word Isaiah was saying; Isaiah's dry sense of humor, his confidence in speaking his mind, his intelligence… Isaiah checked all the boxes for him. In the occasional silence, Gideon savored the moments just to take the evening in. Being here, so much of it spoke to his heart: the breeze carrying various odors from neighboring animals, the earthy decomposing leaves. It was the most he'd felt like being home since he left. But this evening was even better because Isaiah was by his side.

Isaiah's hand lightly brushed against his. The simple touch sent a tingle up Gideon's arm to his heart.

Gideon wanted to feel it again. As they approached a couple walking in their direction, Gideon went to clasp his fingers with Isaiah's, but Isaiah pulled away. Gideon let his hand drop to his side as well.

Does he not hold hands? Maybe I shouldn't have done that. What just happened? Gideon retraced the last ninety seconds.

At the end of a path, Isaiah stopped Gideon in front of a large steel cage. They were completely out of view from anyone, tucked in a corner of the zoo.

A black panther paced back and forth in its small cage, only stopping long enough to hiss. Alone, just them and the angry panther, the beast in the cage, was the least of Gideon's concerns. Why did Isaiah not hold his hand? Was this evening not going as well as he thought it was? This felt important to get right, to understand what was happening here. It was different than with other guys, even stressful in some way. He knew exactly where he stood with other guys. The end game was sex. It was pretty straightforward, happening within hours of meeting. Even with Shawn, the only real relationship he'd had, no matter how short it was, there was a degree of certainty—that was until it all fell apart with one phone call.

Isaiah turned towards him, his proximity just inches from Gideon. He waited for whatever Isaiah was going to say, but instead of talking, Isaiah leaned in and kissed him.

Gideon's breath hitched at the unexpected kiss. In an instant, any concern he was having about the evening dissipated as Isaiah's warm lips touched his. His eyes closed as he tasted Isaiah.

One light kiss, followed by a long lingering kiss, the kiss deepened as Isaiah's tongue slipped into Gideon's mouth. Isaiah pulled Gideon against him, his hand sliding up Gideon's back to the back of his head. Blood rushed to Gideon's head as Isaiah's mouth took control of him.

Gideon took a step, positioning his body in between Isaiah's legs. He attempted to use Isaiah's biceps for leverage, to hold on to, but they were too big to grip. Blood pumping in Gideon's veins, the crotch in his jeans tightened as his erection grew.

Isaiah's mouth, his hands, his body pressed against Gideon, it was more than a kiss. It felt as if Isaiah was making love to him, fully-clothed, in the middle of the zoo. Gideon let go of everything around him and surrendered his body to him. Passionately, they kissed. The onslaught of raw physical desire that Gideon was feeling made time and place irrelevant.

When Isaiah pulled back, breathless, Gideon released the pent-up breath lodged in his gut, followed with a moan. He licked his lips, savoring Isaiah's sweetness. His heart pounded, his breaths coming rapid and shallow.

The zoo was abnormally quiet. One minute he was questioning the date, and now… this. As he looked into Isaiah's piercing stare, it took a second to realize that the background music had stopped.

He was hungry for another kiss. God, his lips looked so good. I should kiss him again. He didn't want to stop, but anything more could get them arrested. "Damn, you can kiss." He rubbed his swollen lips as he stared into Isaiah's eyes.

Isaiah rubbed Gideon's shoulders before his hand slid down his arm. "I like you," Isaiah whispered.

Gideon released another pent-up breath. "I like you, too." *I'm going home in four weeks. What are we doing? What am I doing?* He tried pushing away the thought of them having sex. He would never let it get that far. They were just having fun.

"I think we should head back." Isaiah released his hand from Gideon's arm.

Within a couple of steps, a zoo employee met them on the path. "Hey, guys. Zoo Night is over. I need you to make your way to the exit, please."

Gideon replayed the evening in his head in a fog of emotions and feelings on the walk to the car and began toying with ideas on how the rest of the evening would play out.

On the way home, a sultry song echoed from the speakers in the dark cabin of the car. They'd both been quiet for the last ten minutes as Gideon's thoughts mixed with the lyrics that filled the car.

"Who's this?" Gideon asked.

"Annie Lennox." Isaiah tapped the audio screen in the middle of the dashboard, where information showed what was currently playing.

Artist: Annie Lennox
Title: The Nearness of You
Album: Nostalgia

Gideon committed the information to memory. It was the most beautiful love song he'd ever heard. He would download this song first thing in the morning. He had to have it. He liked Isaiah, and, with Annie Lennox singing about someone falling in love, this evening felt like so much more than them just having fun.

Was Isaiah as deep in his head as Gideon was in his own? Was the night as magical for Isaiah as it was for him? What was going to happen when they got back to the house? *Should I invite him in, or not?* He had condoms, he had lube, and he had clean sheets on the bed. In a mix of emotions, the thought of having sex freaked him out a little. Was it too soon? This *was* their first date—

Actually, *technically*, it was their third if he counted dinner with Daisy and last Saturday's dinner. He'd had plenty of sex within hours of hooking up with someone, but this felt different. He wasn't craving sex. He desired intimacy with this one person, Isaiah Williams. He glanced at Isaiah. Why couldn't he have met him instead of Shawn?

Isaiah took Gideon's hand and lay their entwined hands on the console.

He does hold hands! Gideon tried to suppress a quiet sigh.

Isaiah's hands were not just large, but they were also warm and soft. Gideon realized that no guy had ever held his hand.

When they pulled into the driveway, it was a little past midnight. Gideon wouldn't have minded if the drive home had been another hour just to avoid this moment. He wasn't ready to say good night and, yet, he was uncertain if he could have sex with him. He wasn't sure if he was prepared to cross that bridge yet. The darn bridge hadn't just collapsed on him the last time he'd been involved with someone. The damn thing had blown up and could have cost him his life. "I had a nice time tonight." He unfastened his seatbelt, ready to bolt, but his butt remained firmly in his seat.

"Me, too." Isaiah unstrapped his seatbelt but didn't move either.

"Do you want to come in?" Gideon questioned his offer as soon as he said it. *Come inside to do what?* He didn't want this evening to end, but from this point forward, the rest of the night was a dark abyss, and he had no idea where it could go. He lowered his head, staring down into his lap.

"If it's not too late, sure."

In the dark cabin, neither of them moved. "Are you okay?" Isaiah's voice was soft, a little more than a whisper.

"Truth?" Gideon's voice shook.

"Nothing but." Isaiah's fingers massaged Gideon's hand.

"I had a really nice time tonight. I like you... I think a lot." Gideon's admission caused him to draw a breath. But it was what he was about to admit that felt like a full exposure. "I'm kind of freaking out."

"Why?" Isaiah's fingers stopped.

"Sex... I haven't had sex with anyone since finding out that I'm positive." Heat rose in Gideon's cheeks.

"Really? Oh...We can wait. When you're ready. No pressure." There was an earnestness in Isaiah's voice.

"Okay." Gideon nodded. He felt his shoulders and chest deflate.

Isaiah leaned over and kissed Gideon on the lips. He pulled back and stared into Gideon's eyes. "You're the boss. We'll do it your way." He gently kissed him again.

A nervous smile rose along the edges of Gideon's lips. He'd never met anyone like Isaiah. He didn't even know people could rise to such a level. Yep, he was falling fast.

"Thank you." Gideon stared at Isaiah in his eyes, searching for who this man was. "Well, good night." Gideon moved as if he was about to get out but stopped. "You know... I'll probably go inside and start looking for venues for an outdoor wedding." He cringed at what he just said. *Why the hell are you talking about a wedding? Shut up!*

"Really?" Without cracking a smile, Isaiah nodded as if thinking. "Well, I'll probably go inside and make a couple of phone calls."

"Oh yeah, to who?" Gideon was relieved to hear how fast Isaiah had changed the conversation. He would run with it. "It's a little late for a booty call, isn't it?"

"That's exactly what a booty call is. A late-night call for booty. But that ain't me. However, you're right; it's probably too late to call my buddy and have him run a background check on you. I'll maybe surf the internet and read up on living in the Amazon, maybe watch *Tarzan* or the *Jungle Book*."

"God, you're funny!" Gideon leaned over and gave Isaiah another kiss. "I wasn't raised by monkeys." He kissed him again. "Good night... And thank you." In a state of bliss, Gideon exited the car and floated into his house. He stood in the dark kitchen against the door as he released a large, slow exhale. He replayed the evening in his mind. Endorphins sprung into every part of his body, causing him to quiver against the door. He closed his eyes. He could feel Isaiah's warm lips touching his. *Oh my god... What a night—*

"Lock your door!" Isaiah's voice echoed through the carport and into Gideon's kitchen.

Chapter 9

Gideon had woken up several times in the night, and, each time, his thoughts had been of Isaiah. The date was wonderful. He'd never met anyone like Isaiah, so comfortable to be around, who made him laugh as much as Isaiah had done last night. He hadn't had that much fun since…. He couldn't come up with anything that matched last night. *And God, is he sexy.*

When the sun began to creep through the blinds in his bedroom, he figured he needed to stop obsessing over Isaiah and get up. In the end, it really didn't matter anyway. He was heading home in a few weeks. Inwardly, he winced as his throat tightened. He'd never hated his life on the river or the lodge, but this morning he resented it.

He headed to the kitchen for coffee. After that, he went to work on his bathroom, installing the new sheetrock. However, even the power of a nail gun did little to stop him from thinking about Isaiah.

It was noon when his stomach started to grumble. He fixed himself a bowl of cereal out in the kitchen and retreated to his room to watch TV.

After two bowls of cereal, Gideon hopped in the shower with the plan to head out to do one of his favorite things: walk the aisles of a gigantic hardware store.

Although everything he'd actually put in the house so far was inexpensive and considered standard in any new tract home, he'd fantasized of building a lavish bathroom, with a spa tub and a shower for two, with massive dual shower heads and lots of jets. He dreamed of what he would do to it in his fantasies if it was a bathroom he and Isaiah would share.

Once dressed, he sat in his van while it warmed up and saw Isaiah heading to his new car.

"Hey!" Isaiah waved. "Heading out?" He walked around to the driver's side of Gideon's van.

Gideon hand-cranked the window down. "Yeah. Redoing the bathroom and going to pick up a few things." He saw Daisy coming out onto the carport.

"Good morning, Gideon!" Daisy waved to him as she approached the passenger side of Isaiah's car.

He waved to her before shifting his attention back to Isaiah, who had walked around to his window, and now leaning into the car.

Without asking, Isaiah kissed him.

Wow! Okay... I liked that. Gideon licked his lips.

"I know I'm supposed to wait a few days, observing the man code and all, but I can't. Can I see you again tonight?" Isaiah stared intently at Gideon as he leaned up against the door.

Mesmerized, Gideon couldn't look away, nor could he find his voice as he stared back. Isaiah's eyes were as potent as a drug. Isaiah looked at him like no man had ever looked at him. He wondered what it was that Isaiah was looking at as if Isaiah had unearthed something that Gideon didn't even know was there. He wanted to know what that was. He sucked in a breath. "Does that mean I passed a background check?"

"Yeah, you checked out okay." Isaiah's dimples emerged as he smiled.

Dimples... You're funny and gorgeous. "You're not concerned with the arrest? In my defense, I didn't know all that cocaine was in the suitcase."

"What?" Isaiah reared back.

Not being able to pull it off, Gideon laughed. "I'm joking."

"That shit's not funny!" Isaiah's grin widened.

"Of course, I would love to go out with you again. I had a good time last night. What time?"

"Mom and I are heading out to Pasadena to see the baby. I'll come by around eight. We'll get dinner."

"Okay." That was hours away, and Gideon didn't want to wait that long to see him again.

Isaiah kissed him. A simple peck that drove heat down Gideon's spine and throughout the rest of his body. A little giddy, a little self-conscious, he glanced over to see if Daisy had seen the kiss. She was already in Isaiah's car, but he couldn't see her through the tinted windows. He could bet she was watching and hadn't missed the kiss.

Bryan T. Clark

*****

That evening, under the steamy hot water, Gideon carefully trimmed back the hair around his pubic region, paying close attention to his balls. It had been a while since he'd given his body a good trim, and it was long overdue. He'd gotten used to the caveman look, but now it all had to go—just in case they did have sex tonight, he needed to be ready.

Every thought involved Isaiah in some way. He couldn't remember the last time he was this excited about a date, this excited about someone—this excited about anything in life.

Although Gideon hadn't had a lot of men in his life, there was something different about Isaiah. His straightforward candid voice in which he spoke his mind was filled with insight and wisdom. Gideon had never met anyone like him. When Isaiah stared at him, those cinnamon-brown eyes of his were like kryptonite. He couldn't be responsible for what he might do when they were staring at him.

Would having sex with Isaiah move them out of the just-having-fun zone? Being HIV positive and having casual sex—safe or not—didn't feel like something he should be doing.

Over the last couple of months, as he'd begun to feel better, the fear of rejection because he was positive, the fear that something could go wrong during sex, was one of the reasons he'd sworn off men. Would sex even be the same?

Isaiah excited him in many ways, enough so that he wrestled with his own courage to push forward with this, whatever this was. Sex or not, tonight he couldn't do the caveman look any longer.

He was now semi-erect from holding himself as he shaved. He loved the way his balls felt freshly shaved, and it had been way too long. Slick and wet, he fondled his balls in search of any hairs that he'd missed. If he wasn't going out tonight with the hottest guy in Los Angeles, he would definitely do something about the woody that continued to grow under the caress of his hands.

He then moved to his butt, ridding his ass of the fine fuzz that covered his cheeks. When that was done, he again ran his hands over his slick wet ass, feeling for any rogue hairs. He imagined it was Isaiah's hands on him. Slick to the touch, a rush of blood pumped into his cock, imagining that Isaiah liked what he was feeling. *You better stop touching yourself.*

88

That evening, at exactly eight o'clock, Gideon heard Isaiah knock on the kitchen door. He tried to calm his breathing as he hurried down the hall and into the kitchen.

"Hey." Gideon swung the door open.

"Is my little Puppy ready?" Isaiah looked Gideon up and down, and then a slight smile emerged.

Gideon had changed a half dozen times and had done his hair three different ways before settling on pulling it back into a nice man-bun. Gideon looked down at Isaiah's fancy brown dress shoes, then back up his navy-blue slacks, past his tapered waist, to his massive upper body covered in a lavender-and-white fitted dress shirt.

He felt under-dressed and out of Isaiah's league. He didn't have a lot of clothes, and what he did have, didn't make him look like that. Back home, the entire outfit of the day mainly consisted of a pair of board-shorts and T-shirts. In a moment of insecurity, he regretted committing to this evening. He pushed past his discomfort and smiled as he stepped out of the house and locked his door.

In the restaurant, he was relieved to see it wasn't an over-the-top restaurant with a maître d' in formal wear, but a young girl in jeans and a sweater. She didn't ask if they had reservations, but simply the size of their party.

They were escorted to a booth in the far back corner of the restaurant. They both slid in and scooted to the back of the booth, sitting side by side.

Gideon scanned the menu, pleased that he had so many great choices to pick from. They stared at their menus until a woman approached their table.

"Good evening, guys, I'm Tyla, and I'll be taking care of you tonight." She pulled out a pad of paper and her pen. "Are you guys together?"

Gideon looked at Isaiah, who was wide-eyed as if he'd seen a ghost. He looked back at Tyla and then again at Isaiah.

Tyla spoke, "Separate checks or is this all on one—"

"Just one!" Isaiah blurted before she even finished. He slid over a little, putting a bit more room between him and Gideon.

"Okay... Can I start you off with a cocktail—" Her eyes glanced over at Gideon, "—or something to drink?"

Gideon hesitated, still assessing Isaiah's sudden change in

demeanor. *What was this about? Is Isaiah actually nervous?* In his hesitation, he also realized that Isaiah was waiting for him to order first. "I'll have an iced tea, please." He wanted to order a glass of wine to prove he was actually an adult, or maybe something even a little stronger to settle his nerves. It was a flashback of how the night had ended the last time he drank in Isaiah's presence that stopped him.

"Me too." Isaiah closed up his menu.

"Have you settled on dinner yet, or do you need more time?" Tyla went through her entire spiel, taking their orders and side orders then left them alone.

Just the two of them... Gideon felt the clumsy silence between them. "Are you okay?"

Isaiah gave a bitter laugh. "She kind of freaked me out for a second when she asked about the check. I thought she was asking if we were together-together, like a couple."

Gideon laughed under his breath. "Were you freaked out that she thought you were gay, or that she thought you were with me?" So, it was nervousness that he'd seen in Isaiah's eyes a minute ago. *Wow!*

Isaiah's brows drew together. "I don't know. That she knew we were on a date, maybe." A hushed tone wedged itself between his words.

"Why do you care?" Surprised that Isaiah even cared what she thought, it hurt a little that Isaiah may have been embarrassed to be with him. This was a different side to the man he thought he was getting to know.

Isaiah's shoulders dropped with a sigh. "Years of being in the military, we're just not that *out*."

Not out? "So then, are you glad to be out of the Navy?" Isaiah's admission that he wasn't out was a little surprising. He'd never been with someone who wasn't out, and Isaiah just seemed so sure about who he was. Confident and assertive didn't go with not being out.

"For the most part. I joined right out of high school. It's been good to me." Isaiah paused long enough for the waitress to drop off their iced teas. "I miss going to work and my patrol car. I can't wait to get through the academy and actually start working again."

"Besides not being out, was there anything you didn't like about being in the Navy?" Gideon took a sip of his tea.

"Not really. It wasn't like I was totally in the closet. I just had to be careful. No matter who I was with, or how good of a friend someone was, I still was always cautious, never letting down my guard."

"Are there a lot of gay people in the military?" Gideon began to understand Isaiah's reaction to the waitress a little better. It also added a reason why Isaiah appeared nervous last night at the zoo when the group of girls came over to them. When he pulled his hand away when he tried to hold it. Now it made sense.

"Not out, but they say it's like six percent overall, but the Navy is more like around nine percent.

The Navy didn't sound like a place he'd do well in. He'd never been one to hide his gayness. In fact, his gayness had always worked in his favor. It eliminated the whole *is he or isn't he*, and afforded several occasions between him and a few of their resort guests who'd been looking for a nightcap. "Are there any females who are gay?"

"Way more than men. It seems to be a little more accepted with lesbians. What about you? Living out there in the jungle, did you have many gay people around you?"

Gideon wondered what life in the military was like for Isaiah, having to suppress his sexual identity. "No, not really. We spent our days running the lodge. There was always something to do whether we had guests or not. There is Perlita, a little town about ten miles from us that had one older gay man. Most gay people live in the capital, San Jose. There's also a lot of gay people in Manuel Antonio."

"How far are they from where you were?"

"San Jose is about three hours. Manuel Antonia is farther, like five hours."

"Who was your first?" Isaiah asked. "Please don't say the old man."

"Nooo! It was a big ass six-foot blond rugby player from Scandinavia, who was on a rafting trip with his buddies."

"How old were you?"

"It was on my birthday. I'd turned nineteen."

"What happened?"

"It was late. Everybody had gone to bed except three of the guys and me. They were sitting down by the river, drinking by the fire. I was up at the lodge cleaning up. I saw two of the guys come up from the river, but there was this one guy… He'd been watching me all night. You know that look. Anyway, I asked them if he was still down there, and they said yes. As soon as they were gone, I went down there under the guise of getting him something."

"You little hussy!"

"I'd never done anything like that before. Never even kissed another guy, but I was ready. I'd only thought about it my whole life."

"So you knew you were gay?"

"Oh yeah."

"What happened down on the riverbank?"

"He said he was fine and asked me to stay. We hung out and talked for about an hour or so, and then he said he had to go pee and would be back. When he came back, he had two beers."

"How old was this guy?"

"I don't know. Early twenties maybe." They both sat back when the waitress appeared with their dinners.

After several bites, they traded little pieces of their meal for the other to taste.

Isaiah swallowed and washed his salmon down with his tea. "Okay, you're not going to leave me hanging. Finish your story."

"What? You want details?"

"Yes!"

He'd never told the story to anyone. "We were drinking the beers, and then he leaned over and kissed me. It got pretty hot, pretty fast. Then he stopped. He told me to wait there. He was gone like forever. When he came back, he undid his pants and dropped them below his knees."

"Wait a minute. Were you, like, freaked out?" Isaiah leaned forward in his chair.

"Hell no, I was totally ready." Gideon laughed. "He stripped my shorts off, and then he suited up. He lubed me up and fucked me over the rocks. It took all of five minutes."

"It was your first time, and the dude just stuck it in? That must have hurt."

Gideon cocked his head. "It might have been my first time with a guy, but it certainly wasn't the first time anything was in there. And trust me, I'd had way more in there than what he had."

Isaiah covered his eyes with his hands. "Oh my God! Welcome to the *First Time, and It Sucked* Club."

Gideon shrugged. "I guess. I didn't know any better. I didn't think it sucked, other than my mom hearing us—*me*. Since there were no girls in the group, it wasn't that hard to figure it out that two dudes were having sex."

"But how'd she know it was you?"

"My damn brother. Andrew."

"He told your mom? How'd she react?"

"After the guests left that morning, she gave me a big ol' lecture about being professional around the guests and that it was a business. She said that it was Andrew who told her it was me that was making all the noise last night."

"Did she say anything about you actually having sex?"

Gideon shook his head. She didn't have to. He knew exactly what she was talking about.

"Why didn't Andrew come here with you?" Isaiah asked.

Gideon laid his fork down. "Truth?"

Isaiah raised a brow. "Nothing but."

Gideon thought about his story. "For one, my brother can be a sloth sometimes. If there's nothing in it for him, he's not doing it. Secondly... coming out here was kind of the plan I'd made up. I convinced my parents to let me fix up the house so we can rent it. But the truth was that the guy I had told you about, Shawn, who I hooked up with at the lodge, lives here, in L.A. After he left, we stayed in contact, FaceTiming and chatting a couple of times a week. We'd been talking for a couple of months."

"The jungle has internet?" Isaiah smirked.

Gideon snickered. "He kept begging for me to come out to visit him. All the stuff we could do, and how much fun it would be. When the opportunity came up, with the house and all, it was perfect timing. Then I got sick and started treatment. I couldn't go home. I didn't want my parents to know I was sick. I told them how bad the house was and that I wanted to stay out here longer and do a total remodel on the kitchen and bathrooms."

"They don't know that you're positive?"

Gideon shook his head no. "When I was initially diagnosed, I couldn't tell them because I was still processing that it had actually happened to me. How could I tell them I could be dying? It would've devastated them. Then I started treatment and couldn't leave because I saw my doctor at the clinic every two weeks. After a couple of months, when my levels had reached an undetectable level, it was simply out of embarrassment that I never said anything to them. I still can't believe how stupid I was for having unprotected sex."

"I think we've all made mistakes in our lives. I couldn't imagine going through something like that alone." The sparkle in Isaiah's eyes spelled sincerity.

"It was pretty depressing. This last year has to be the worst year of my life." Gideon picked up his fork and resumed eating.

"And now?"

Gideon winked as a smile crept to one side of his mouth. "It's getting better. I wish I wasn't leaving in a month."

"Oh yeah? Why is that?" Isaiah raised his chin as he eyed Gideon.

Gideon held off putting a fork of food into his mouth. "I don't know. It would be nice to..." *See what would happen with us.* Yeah, Isaiah said they were only hanging out—having fun, but... "It would be nice if I didn't have to go back."

"So why do you have to go home?" Isaiah stared at him.

Gideon looked down at his plate. *Why do I have to go home? Because I'm the responsible one. Andrew's not going to be there. My parents need me.* Up until two weeks ago, there hadn't been any reason to stay. The house was almost done, and his parents wanted it back on the market. His life was in Costa Rica. "It's where I live."

Isaiah nodded. "Okay..."

Gideon sensed that Isaiah wasn't accepting his answer. "My dad's arthritis is pretty bad. It's in his fingers, arms, back, and legs. The inflammation in his joints causes a lot of swelling and stiffness. Sometimes, he can barely pick up a hammer. The lodge is a lot of work. Without me and Andrew, there would be no way they could run it by themselves. Plus, we've talked about me taking over the business someday."

Isaiah straightened as he grimaced. "But you don't really want to run the lodge—do you?"

"Not really." Up until two weeks ago, him running the lodge was neither here nor there. It was the plan. It made sense. It was what he was going to do. Sure, if he had his way, he would go to college. Move to the city where he could have a life.... A boyfriend... His own life.

Isaiah tilted his head. "Then why do it. Let your brother run it."

Gideon snickered as he shook his head and rolled his eyes. "My brother can't even run a blender."

"So, then it falls to you? Could they sell it?"

"Nah, they'd never sell it. It's like my dad's and his brother's dream."

"But not yours?" Isaiah raised his chin and stared at Gideon.

"Not really." Gideon lowered his head, cutting off eye contact.

"And they couldn't just hire someone?" Isaiah's voice was laced with skepticism.

"No." Why that wouldn't work was too difficult to try to explain. The job was twenty-four hours a day. He and his dad worked well together. Sure, they could probably hire someone to replace Andrew, but there was no way they could afford to hire two people and have them work the hours he did. His dad really wanted him to run the business, keep it going. It was his dad's dream to be able to hand it down to him. His dad was so proud that he had this to give to his sons, and Andrew clearly didn't want it. How could he tell his dad he didn't want it either? It would break his dad's heart, and he couldn't do that.

Isaiah stared at Gideon before drawing a breath. "I like you. I wish you weren't leaving."

"Me, too. Our timing sucks." Gideon's gut tightened at their reality. He forced a breath down into his lungs. *If things could be different.*

"I'm glad you're healthy now and feeling good enough to go home."

"I used to worry about being sick all day, every day. I don't do it as much anymore. Other than taking my meds every morning, I can get through the day now without thinking about it. Every once in a while, something will happen, and it's a cold dose of reality hitting me in the face."

"Like what?"

"Seeing my own blood for one thing. In the beginning, it was like looking at this deadly poison."

"I get that. Before the Navy, I didn't know that much about HIV other than how not to get it. The military was good about training us on blood exposure and how to stay safe. You learn to treat all blood exposures the same because you never know." Isaiah took a bite of his dinner. "They've come a long way with the medications these days. I remember this guy, a couple of years ago, he had like seven different drugs he had to take."

"Yeah, I take only one."

"Any side effects?"

Gideon released a slow, long exhale. "No, not really." He looked up at Isaiah.

The warmth cast from the brown hues in Isaiah's eyes spread across Gideon's chest, warming his entire body. It was as if they had melted him, turning him into a puddle of liquid lust. He was unable to look away.

"Do you know how handsome you are?" Isaiah's gaze held their focus.

Gideon had never been described as handsome. He was generally described as cute, at least to the guys who hit him up on Studfinder. That was the word they all used: *cute*. He actually hated the word. What he heard when they called him cute was that he looked young. Cute was a baby or child. He was neither. Isaiah used the word handsome. *I want to kiss you.* Gideon drew in a long deep breath before speaking. "Thank you."

Gideon rested his hands on the table. He was surprised when Isaiah placed his own hand next to his. Their fingers barely touching, and yet it was enough to send a dose of adrenaline up his arm and into his chest.

"Okay, so what scares the shit out of you?"

He thought about Isaiah's question for a minute. Nothing really scared the shit out of him. He was as adventurous as they came. No, there wasn't much he was afraid of. His gaze cruised their hands. Isaiah had big beautiful hands. "I don't know, maybe... dying?" He wasn't even sure that held true anymore. He just stared at death earlier this year, or at least what felt like death. "Okay, maybe leeches. They gross me out."

"What do you require from a boyfriend?" There was a twinkle in Isaiah's eyes as he stared at Gideon.

What do I require? Gideon looked down at Isaiah's hand next to his as he thought about it for a second or two, unsure if he even understood what Isaiah was asking. *Fidelity? Honesty? Tall? Someone attentive to him?* The one thing for sure was that he certainly didn't want to get hurt again, especially to the depths to which Shawn had done. Since Shawn was the closest thing he'd had to a boyfriend, he didn't know how to answer the question. "Dude, where did you come from? Why weren't you around a year ago?"

"Because our connection is bigger than Studfinder. I mean it, Gideon. When you were at your kitchen window, I felt something from the first day I met you. I remember this feeling of warmth inside of me. It was like electricity was jumping through my body. I walked into the house asking myself what the heck was going on?"

"You couldn't even see me. All you saw was my head."

"It's not about what you look like. It was like, wow, *I want to know this person.* I can't explain it because it's never happened to me before. In the two weeks that we've been seeing each other, I feel like I've known you forever. I know that you love your family, that they're important to you, and you're close to them. That you're sensitive to other people's needs, that you invest in people and relationships, and you don't take them lightly. I love that you can match my sense of humor and can be just as serious as me, too."

Gideon heard every compliment Isaiah gave him. While he wasn't going to dispute any of them, he had to be honest. "I have to admit, that morning I saw you come out of the house, I was like *Holy shit! Who's this?* You definitely had my attention." Gideon felt a little shallow that his initial reaction was more physical than Isaiah's had been. But, shit, Isaiah was undeniably gorgeous. He'd been wearing his infamous gym shorts that left little to the imagination that morning. Just thinking about that day made Gideon's mouth water as he glanced down into Isaiah's lap.

Isaiah rubbed Gideon's fingers, then pulled back. With a mischievous smirk, Isaiah held his stare. "Oh, Mr. Miller, you are so easy to read." Isaiah's grin widened.

A little self-conscious that he'd been caught, Gideon tried to play it off. "What?"

"You just checked out my junk."

Gideon was mortified. "No, I didn't!"

Isaiah laughed. "Yes, you did."

"Okay... So maybe I did." Gideon matched Isaiah's grin with one of his own. "But it was like... just there. How could I not?"

"Hey, you don't have to apologize to me. I'm glad you're interested."

Gideon's eyes dropped back down to Isaiah's lap. "Maybe a little."

When the waitress came to check on them, Isaiah slid his hand away from Gideon's and then leaned back.

"Are you all through?" she asked.

After clearing the table and being unsuccessful at tempting them with dessert, the waitress returned with the bill.

Gideon attempted to pick up the tab, but Isaiah snatched the black bill folder before he could get it. "No, I got it."

"You've paid for the last two dinners plus the zoo. I can get this one."

"Listen, Gideon, I'm only going to say this once." Isaiah had a stern look. "Whenever you honor me with your presence, the least I can do is pay. Don't take that away from me."

Gideon's breath stalled for a second as his gaze lingered over Isaiah's beautiful face, narrowing in on his lips. *I want to kiss you so bad.* "What do you say we get out of here and go back to my place?" Gideon tried to maintain eye contact, but he couldn't stop glancing at Isaiah's lips. The thought of them against his sent a surge of blood to his groin.

Isaiah rubbed his chin as if he was actually mulling it over.

Gideon couldn't help but laugh. Isaiah's teasing and sense of humor awakened something within Gideon. He was well aware of the flutter in his chest that Isaiah caused. He'd never been around someone who constantly made him laugh like Isaiah did. Yes, in the beginning, the first day he lay eyes on Isaiah, it was purely physical; he was unbelievably sexy. But now, his attraction to Isaiah expanded well beyond his looks.

"Come on. Let's get out of here." Well aware of his semi-erection, Gideon slid out of the booth and stood. He was not ashamed to let Isaiah know how he felt, should he see it.

*****

Back at the house, Gideon's heart raced as he fumbled with the lock. He could feel Isaiah's energy behind him. He wanted to turn around and kiss him right there. *No, unlock the door and get in the house.* He could hardly concentrate on what he was doing.

Once they were in, Gideon turned on the kitchen lights. With a slight separation, Gideon lost his nerve to kiss him. *But I want to.* "Do you want a glass of wine?"

"No, I'm cool."

"Water?" Gideon walked over to the cabinet. *Separation is good.*

"Yeah, I'll take some water."

Gideon retrieved two glasses and filled them with tap water from the faucet. He caught up with Isaiah, standing in the living room, and handed him the glass. Then he walked down the hall. "I don't really hang out in there."

They climbed onto Gideon's bed. Nervous, Gideon fidgeted before deciding to put his back against the headboard.

Isaiah stretched out alongside him. His massive frame took up so much of the bed.

He's so big. Gideon searched for something to say. *Say something.*

"You know, I don't have fond memories of this room." Isaiah adjusted his weight on the bed, scooting up closer to the headboard.

Oh, right. The last time you were in here, I was puking my guts out in the bathroom. Not my finest moment. "Don't be hating on my room. It was the bathroom where the evil shit happened."

"True. I can't ever go in there again." Isaiah shook his head as he frowned.

"You don't have to worry about it. I couldn't either, so I ripped it out."

Isaiah sat up. "You did what?"

"Check it out." Gideon was proud of what he'd done in there so far.

Isaiah walked to the bathroom and turned on the light. "Holy shit!"

"I did the drywall today," Gideon said. "I'm going to use the same tile as the kitchen since I have so much of it left over. I found a tub and vanity that are coming next week."

Isaiah walked back into the bedroom and took his place on the bed. "I can't believe you can do all of that. That is crazy talented." He lightly ran the tips of his fingers up the side of Gideon's jeans.

Gideon watched Isaiah's fingers as they moved up his thigh. "Bathrooms are easy. If I had more time and money, I would redo the one in the hall." Gideon's pulse quickened as Isaiah's hand came to rest on his thigh. As the sexual energy rose between them, heat coursed through Gideon's veins. He fought not to look at Isaiah, afraid Isaiah would see he was nervous. He tried to distract himself by looking at his bare feet as he wiggled his toes. "I love doing stuff like that."

Isaiah scooted a little closer, closing the gap between them. "I think my talents are reserved for under the hood."

Is he going to kiss me? Although their bodies weren't touching, the heat from Isaiah's body made it nearly impossible to think of anything else. "I bet you're pretty good under the hood, too," Gideon mumbled, hoping Isaiah caught the double meaning.

Isaiah repositioned onto his stomach before sliding his hand over onto Gideon's upper thigh. "Mr. Miller, I do like checking out what's under the hood."

"Well, no one said I'm lifting my hood... or my trunk, but feel free to check out the rest of it." Their playful banter caused Gideon's heart to skip a beat or two.

"Indeed, I will..." Isaiah lifted up and moved in, stopping just shy of touching, and then, softly, their lips touched.

Fireworks! Explosions! Intense heat! A wave of ecstasy surged up through Gideon. Their kiss deepened as Isaiah's large hands moved him from up against the headboard, allowing him to lay down.

Gideon released a low moan that originated from the back of his throat. He'd been waiting, wanting this, for so long, and now... *Oh God... that feels...*he squirmed even closer to Isaiah. Side to side, he pressed his body against Isaiah's.

They continued kissing as Isaiah gripped Gideon's ass. With a firm grip, Isaiah's strong hands slid up under Gideon's shirt, resting on the small of his back.

They caressed each other, mapping each curve as if time was going to run out on them, and this would only be a memory. Isaiah's hardness pressed against him. He imagined what it must look like. The most lascivious thoughts caused him to push harder against it. He wanted more than to feel Isaiah's cock through his pants.

And with that thought, the chatter began. *Dude! What are you doing? We should stop... You're P.o.s.i.t.i.v.e.*

Stop! Gideon tried to control the chatter that was beginning to dominate him. *You're HIV positive, and he's not.* He opened his eyes but quickly shut them, hoping to shut out the chatter.

What am I doing?

When do I stop?

Are we going to have sex?

Is a condom really enough? Panic knocked all other thoughts aside.

I'm not ready; I can't. Gideon pulled back, his lips already beginning to swell. "We should stop," he murmured. Their eyes met. *We're only kissing.* His heart seized control from his brain as he plunged his mouth back against Isaiah's lips.

Gideon wasn't sure how long they'd been kissing. It felt like an eternity when Isaiah pulled back this time. The two panted, their breathing ragged as they stared at one another.

"You're shaking." Isaiah brushed Gideon's hair back.

"I'm fine." Gideon drew in a shallow breath as he leaned back farther. He was anything but fine. Waves of nausea disrupted his thought. His shallow breaths threatened to suffocate him. *What am I doing? I can't do this.* He wanted to flee.

Isaiah gently kissed him, his lips lingering for a second or two. "It's okay. We're doing this at your pace. You're still shaking."

Gideon rolled off Isaiah. His erection had completely subsided. He didn't know what to say to Isaiah. He wanted to have sex with Isaiah, and yet he was panicking over something he'd done with people that he knew far less about than Isaiah. *What are you afraid of?*

Finally, able to catch his breath, he knew he owed Isaiah some sort of an explanation of what just happened, but he wasn't even sure himself. *I'm undetectable. At least, I was two months ago at my last check-up. I'm fine. Everybody said sex was safe as long as we're careful.* The word careful rang in his head.

Careful... because I don't want to get hurt... again. This was about more than keeping Isaiah safe. It was about his own fears, about being hurt again. Gideon inhaled a large breath and exhaled slowly. "I'm sorry."

"For what?" Isaiah sat up.

"For leading you on. For doing this and then stopping."

"You don't owe me an apology for stopping. Us kissing doesn't come with a hall pass for anything else. If that's all that you want, you have a right to say so." Isaiah squeezed Gideon's thigh. "Look at me."

Gideon looked into Isaiah's eyes.

"This is your body." He squeezed Gideon's thigh again. "It's *your* body."

"Yeah, I understand that. I also feel like it's poisonous, and I have to ensure that I don't infect anyone."

"You can't infect anyone. You're not poisonous, damaged, or ruined. You're beautiful, loving, kind, and safe. Do you remember that second text you sent me after you agreed to go out?"

"What text was that?" Gideon racked his brain, trying to remember what he could have said.

"You said you were not just positive, but also smart, could hold a conversation, and knew how to laugh. You defined yourself as more than positive. You revealed all of you that day to me. You were so honest about who you were, even though it scared the shit out of you to say it to me. It could have gone wrong after that, and yet you still stayed true to who you are. I have a lot of respect for who you are." Isaiah kissed Gideon's forehead.

Yes, he was more than a person living with HIV, but it often didn't feel like it. He knew what Isaiah was saying was true, but he only knew half of it. Isaiah didn't know how scared he was about getting hurt again. Nausea filled Gideon's gut. He wanted Isaiah to know the whole truth, more of who he was. He drew several breaths to collect his nerves. "Do you feel like talking?"

"Of course." Isaiah rolled onto his side, facing Gideon.

"The night I think it happened... I was with Shawn. I'd been here about a month. I was staying at his place every night. Except when he was at work, we were with each other twenty-four-seven. We'd been using a condom until that night. That night, we were at a Christmas party, at a friend's house. I was drunk and went to the bathroom to pee. Shawn followed me in. He was wasted, too, and all over me while I was trying to pee. He was begging for it. I told him no that we didn't have any lube. He grabbed the bottle of lotion that was on the counter. I told him he didn't have a condom. He kept begging and begging, saying he was negative, that we'd been together all month, that he hadn't been with anybody since I got there…. He kept begging." Gideon paused as he heard Shawn's voice in his head begging, *Come on! Come on! It'll be all right.*

Gideon felt the swell in his chest. He didn't want to cry in front of Isaiah. He had no right to cry—after all, he was the one who'd said okay.

Isaiah's hand glided softly up Gideon's pants leg. "I get it. I've been there."

Gideon wiped back a tear. He wondered if Isaiah really got it. If he'd ever been there. He couldn't imagine Isaiah doing something that stupid. It was a night he relived over and over, a night that seemed to have changed his life forever.

Gideon laid his head on Isaiah's chest. He was embarrassed that he was tearing up. "You're welcome to stay… if you want." He hoped his invitation wasn't another mixed message, but he wasn't ready for Isaiah to go. *What I want is to be held by you and in your arms, against your body.* That seemed a little needy to say, though. "We can hang out and talk if that's okay."

Isaiah brushed Gideon's hair back and tucked it behind his ear. "I'd like that." He wrapped his arm around Gideon and brought him in close.

It took a moment before Gideon released an exhale, fully appreciating the comfort from Isaiah's warm body. "You know, earlier, when we were talking about triggers? What reminds me that I'm positive is not just seeing my blood… It's liking you."

"What do you mean?" Isaiah stroked Gideon's hair.

"Before meeting you, I hadn't dated in months. Then I met you, and it was like, ah shit, I'm HIV positive, this won't work. Being positive changes everything. I think about the virus every day, wishing it wasn't so, wishing things were different. It's like you don't want to like anyone because then you have to face the truth, or worse, that they'll reject you once they know. You don't feel like you're equal to other people anymore; you're less than them because you're positive. And the last thing I would ever want to do is infect you. Just by sleeping with you, I could kill you."

"But you know that's not true, right?"

"What's not true?"

"That you're less than someone negative and that you could kill me. Today, you are as healthy as I am. Mr. Gideon Miller, I think you're worth dating, worth getting to know, worth trying to impress. Your HIV status isn't a factor, and I'm not going to reject you because of it, whether you're positive, negative, detectable or undetectable, ever." Isaiah adjusted his body and arms around Gideon. "You're sweet, smart, honest, freakin' hot, and a ten in my book. Me judging you on your status is like me saying I wouldn't date someone who had cancer."

"But I can't give you cancer. It's not the same." Isaiah's words didn't sound like someone who would hurt him.

"It *is* the same. You're healthy. You can't give me HIV either." Isaiah thumped Gideon on his forehead. "You're special, Gideon Miller. Please don't deny me the chance to get to know someone as dynamic as you, the very person who may only come along once in a lifetime."

Warmth pooled around Gideon's heart. Isaiah was right. He *was* healthy. He had to stop looking at himself as this walking zombie. For the first time since being diagnosed, Gideon had a thirst for more information about living with HIV. Embarrassingly, his knowledge of HIV extended little beyond what his doctor had told him during his appointments. He'd gone to two group counseling sessions right after being diagnosed but hadn't clicked with the group. It'd seemed as if they were all best friends, and he was an outsider. He'd tried a couple of times to explore some stuff on the internet, but that only depressed him even more than he'd already been. It was time to take his head out of the sand and really understand how to live again.

He listened as Isaiah told a story about a bully in fifth grade who had reigned terror on everyone except him. Even in fifth grade, Isaiah seemed to possess the ability to reason and deescalate even a bully. The conversation continued into their childhoods, sharing trivial yet memorable details of their past. Isaiah was a breath of fresh air, someone who inspired him to be more. Gideon felt as if his heart was a flower, blooming for the first time. With certainty, he'd never felt this with Shawn.

It was crazy that he already thought this was something more than it was. They were both clear in the beginning that this would only be about hanging out, having fun.

This is what Isaiah wants. Gideon closed his eyes and summoned a deep breath. As he exhaled slowly, he opened his eyes and looked up at Isaiah. He took in every detail of his face.

Isaiah smiled at him as he continued to talk. His voice came low as he talked about a day Elijah accidentally hit him with a baseball bat when they were kids, which led to a hospital trip, eighteen stitches, a spanking for Elijah, and a permanent scar between his eyes. Isaiah rubbed a finger between his eyes.

Although listening, Gideon thought about his situation. *What are we doing? What am I doing? I don't want to get hurt again.* His stomach tightened as a wave of uncertainty washed over him. *You're leaving, you're going home. You're falling for this guy. What if you stayed?*

Dad would be pissed.

Gideon contemplated his options, none of which seemed plausible. The one thing he knew was that he really liked this guy.

Chapter 10

After church this morning, Isaiah drove his mother out to Pasadena to visit Josiah and Tammy and their new baby.

Isaiah cooed over baby Simone as she lay in her crib. He attempted to tune out Josiah and his mom's conversation about her pastor's sermon on *Psalm 55* this morning. He found it hypocritical of his brother to be speaking of not being afraid of betrayal by your enemies who you thought were your friends. It's what Josiah would do to him if Isaiah was honest with him about being gay. He knew his brother's beliefs on homosexuality and the judgmental, narrow-mindedness that came with it. Although they'd never talked about his sexuality, he was sure Tammy and Josiah knew he was gay. He'd never made any attempt to hide it, but then again, he'd never owned it either. His entire childhood, he'd kept his thoughts and fantasies of the same sex to himself. He took girls to high school dances, pretended as if he were interested without ever fully committing. He'd listened to his brothers throw around the words *fag* and *queer*. As much as he loved his family, there were many times he didn't like them.

It was hard enough being a Black man in a White world; it was even harder to be a Black gay man in a Black family whose members weren't allies.

The thought of such a harsh judgment was also the very reason he didn't let other people get close to him either. The pain of rejection, not being accepted by people who love you was too great of a pain to bear, and the ultimate betrayal.

"She's looking more and more like her daddy every day," Tammy whispered to Isaiah.

"God, don't say that about her," Isaiah replied, only half-joking.

"Ah ah ah, watch your words," Josiah said in mid-sentence with

106

his conversation with their mother. "We don't take the Lord's name in vain in this house."

Isaiah rolled his eyes at his brother's holier-than-thou correction.

"Are you glad to be home?" Tammy asked.

Isaiah picked up Simone. "I am."

"Now that you're home, maybe we can introduce you to some ladies at church." Tammy watched as Simone rested her head against his chest.

Although Isaiah didn't flinch, he'd heard exactly what she'd said. *Let's all pretend that you're not gay, that maybe some female could interest you.*

"A lady at church as in... to date?" He stared at her. He hated this bullshit game of talking in code with his own family. *I can't do this anymore.* He forced a smile as his mouth went dry. He hesitated, giving himself a moment to back out of coming out to her.

"Of course to date." Tammy slid a small towel between Simone and Isaiah's shirt. "She just ate. Be careful."

Isaiah lightly patted Simone on her back as he mentally weighed whether it was worth having this conversation with her at this particular time. He knew the day would come when he would have to put it out there but didn't imagine it would be today. "Tammy, do you really want to have this conversation?" he mumbled as he felt Simone burp. He resonated with her burp. He, too, had something that he needed to burp up: the truth. Acid swirled in his stomach. He was not scared easily, but this threatened to knock his legs right out from under him.

Tammy's mouth fell open as if she'd been slapped. "Isaiah, you know it's a sin."

He tried to moisten his mouth. He grappled for the courage to do what he needed to do. She wanted to have the conversation. "What's a sin?"

Tammy slammed her hands onto her hips. "Isaiah, you know. Leviticus 18:6 says you shall not lie with a male as one lies with a female."

Isaiah gasped as he rocked his head, not believing what was happening. He took a breath, not wanting to pass any of the negative energy to the baby. "Look, Tammy. I'm trying to respect you and Josiah. I'm trying to have a relationship with you guys. But I'm not going to do it in the closet anymore. If you can't accept the fact that

I'm gay—" air stalled in his lungs, "that the God I know has no judgment on my sexuality, then let's not have the conversation."

"But, Leviticus says—"

"If you want to recite Leviticus, then let's talk about what it actually says. It also prohibits tattoos..." He looked to the tattoo on her wrist before continuing. "And working on the Sabbath, and wearing clothes of mixed fabric, and eating pork and shellfish—and we all know you like your bacon and shrimp, as well as your polyester-cotton blends. That old-ass shit was written three thousand years ago, but you go on and live by it if you think it still applies. Just make sure you live by *all* of it, not just the comfortable parts."

"Whoa, bro!" Josiah spoke up. "You want respect? You're the one who's come here taking the Lord's name in vain like you don't know any better. Talking to my wife like you ain't got no sense. Leviticus 20:13 says—"

"Hey! Hey! Boys!" Daisy jumped in. "What do you say we sit down for lunch?"

"Do the collard greens have pork in them?" Isaiah glared at Tammy.

Everyone ignored Isaiah's question, which was actually a statement. Tammy took the baby from Isaiah and followed her husband and mother-in-law into the kitchen.

Isaiah shook his head. He'd rather fight and arrest drunk sailors on a Saturday night than listen to Josiah and Tammy's bullshit interpretation of the bible and their judgment.

Isaiah's phone pinged. He pulled it out.

Had a great time last night. Specially sleeping in your arms. xoxoxoxo

The boiling blood racing through Isaiah's veins cooled a little as he read the text. He had a strong desire to be with Gideon instead of where he was right now. *Maybe I'll go see him when I leave here.*

Torn, Isaiah knew the academy was his priority, and hanging out with Gideon, later on wasn't possible. He had a ton of studying this evening; at least a couple of hours of Constitutional Law, and, of course, Spanish.

He thought about how nice it was this morning, waking up with Gideon in his arms. As much fun as the date had been last night, what he'd truly enjoyed yesterday was laying in the bed talking with

Gideon. At first, he'd been caught off guard when Gideon had expressed how he viewed himself and that he was still struggling with his HIV status. In just a couple of weeks, his and Gideon's conversations were far more profound than the years of conversations he'd had with Ronnie. His ex had liked to keep it light, none of that *feelings* stuff. In fact, the only time it'd ever come up was when Ronnie had begged him not to leave. Gideon was one of the sweetest guys Isaiah had ever met. Gideon seemed to put everyone's needs first, in front of his own... a people pleaser.

Anger simmered again in his chest. Forced not to talk about who he was his entire life, and now to sit here with his people—who supposedly cared for him—well, it didn't feel like love. It felt like censorship. Like control, rejection, and judgment—everything he'd fought his entire life not to feel.

Being an African American gay man, judgment seemed to come from all fronts. It had been the standard in which he'd lived. People being surprised that he was a cop, or intelligent, or gay... he got it from everybody: classmates, fellow soldiers, even other gay men who were out and proud.

But still, even being free from the Navy's judgment, he was trying not to be *too* gay, *too* black, *too* tough... He was having a harder time than he thought adjusting to civilian life, where nobody knew him from Adam. Last night, when the waitress had asked about the check, it'd freaked him out, the thought that she saw they were on a date. Even though he'd realized that wasn't what she'd been asking, the panic had been real.

Because he and Ronnie were both black, he assumed people naturally saw them as just two guys having dinner when they went out to dinner. He'd been asked that question from a waitress a million times, and it had never freaked him out because he'd never thought about it any other way than it'd been intended. But, last night, he'd heard it as a judgment, as if she'd been asking if they were queer. He realized that, other than Ronnie, most of his dates hadn't been in such a public setting where it could be construed as something intimate.

Now, to just sit here and be judged by his family was brutal. Was there such an existence where he wasn't playing a version of himself that he thought people expected, a version of him that didn't sacrifice who he truly was?

Being out of the military wasn't as freeing as he'd anticipated. He was envious of Gideon's unapologetic way of life. Isaiah had spent his entire life attempting to keep his own gayness out of his conscious awareness, disassociating it from who he was most times, yet Gideon had no such qualms.

His and Ronnie's relationship had worked at some level regarding the discretion they'd desired. And while they'd both wanted concealment, Isaiah no longer wanted it from Ronnie. He wanted more from him, and Ronnie didn't give it to him. On some level, he and Ronnie were more alike than he wanted to admit.

He'd never been around anyone like Gideon—so open and free about his sexuality. But yet, for everything Gideon was, he was afraid as well. He'd been hurt by that Shawn dude. Some of the things Gideon had admitted last night about being afraid to date again had broken Isaiah's heart. The wall Gideon had built around himself to protect his heart was obvious. Isaiah understood all too well the need for a wall to protect oneself.

He re-read Gideon's text. *Had a great time last night. Especially sleeping in your arms. xoxoxoxo*

He typed his response. *Me too. FYI, you snore.*

Isaiah stopped short of sending it. He smirked as he looked up and around the empty room. He heard his mother and Tammy laughing in the kitchen. He released a sigh and hit SEND.

I do not!

Reading Gideon's response gave him a chuckle. *Yeah, you do.*

K, maybe a little.

xoxoxox back at you. Isaiah hit SEND and put his phone away.

His grin grew wider as he envisioned Gideon last night. He wanted to be with him again this evening, but he told himself to slow down. This thing, whatever it was, was burning hot, but his focus *had* to be on the academy and getting through these next six months. And yet, since that night when the two of them had sat in Gideon's living room talking into the late hours of the night, he did nothing but envision his future with Gideon in it. His mother was absolutely right about Gideon; he *was* a great guy.

Given Josiah's issues with him being gay, his brother was going to have an issue with Gideon being White as well. He used to tell himself that it never mattered that his brother or his wife didn't fully embrace his gayness, but to not fully embrace Gideon because of his skin color was reprehensible. *Christians, my ass...*

His personal life and his family life had always been separated by thousands of miles. But now, his two lives were living next door to each other. His natural impulse was to continue to keep them separated to minimize any shame over something he wasn't shameful about... *or was he?*

In silence, Isaiah stared at the crucifix on the wall. Over on the bookcase, there were several tchotchkes with religious overtones. Josiah would never say anything to Isaiah's face, but being raised in a conservative Christian Black community, he knew many believed that not only was being gay a sin, you did *not* date outside of your race. In a world that beat him up every day, the one place he should be safe was in his own home. But he wasn't.

In the military, although the culture was certainly changing for the better for gays and lesbians, homophobic ideology was still there. Yes, you could be gay, but you couldn't be queer. Femininity was viewed as weakness in the military for both men and women, but especially men.

Isaiah liked to think of himself as a strong individual. It was a little disheartening to admit to himself that he wasn't as strong and put together as he portrayed. If he was, he would have never hung in there with Ronnie as long as he had. Even the way he'd ended it with Ronnie had been a lie. Yes, he'd walked away from Ronnie—but with the hopes that, if he'd turned around, Ronnie would have come with him. Instead, Ronnie had walked the other way... all the way to Amsterdam.

If he was totally honest, he'd been guilty of judging Gideon when he'd first seen him. Although they were only six years apart, Gideon looked like he was fifteen.

Initially, his age had been an issue, mainly because Isaiah had—incorrectly—assumed Gideon was immature and had no depth.

Isaiah could have never envisioned dating someone like Gideon in a million years. He wasn't even sure how it had even happened. It'd been unexpected and fast. He hadn't been looking to date, but as soon as he'd met Gideon, he'd been drawn to him.

Gideon and Ronnie couldn't be more different. Gideon was funny, laid-back, and intriguing.

On the other hand, Ronnie was a serious, obstinate person who revealed little about himself, even to those supposedly close to him. Isaiah remembered one day when he asked Ronnie why he was attracted to him. Ronnie mentioned that he only dated light-skinned dudes, that he was only attracted to *dulce de leche* brothers. Isaiah remembered feeling as if his worth had been tied to his skin color even by someone who was Black.

Isaiah joined his family in the kitchen to fix his plate, but he wasn't hungry anymore. He'd rather wait outside in the car than sit in this house. He watched his mother take her plate into the living room. They weren't leaving anytime soon, so he had to play nice.

In the past, during short visits when he was on leave, they all played nice because it had been only for a couple of days. Now he had to do it because Mom said so. Not wanting to offend his brother or Tammy any further, Isaiah made himself a plate.

Back in the living room, he balanced his plate on his lap as he thought about having a conversation with Tammy about how she justified the pork in her greens. *Play nice,* he told himself, but it was hard to sit there as they wallowed in their own ignorance and bigotry. *What if I just came out to them? Right here, right now. What would happen?* He ran down the possibilities of what could happen. He wouldn't lose his livelihood, a career... just his brother. Gideon made it look so easy. How is one able to be so free. How does it not matter what people think of you? He'd been clenching his jaw so tight that the muscles in his face hurt.

"How do you like your car?" Josiah asked.

Isaiah knew he was only trying to make conversation. "I like it."

"Did Elijah get you a good deal?" Tammy asked.

"Yeah." If Josiah wanted to know how much he paid for it, then he'll make him ask.

"I need to get a hold of him and see what he could do for Tammy. With the baby and all, I'd feel safer if she was in something a little bigger, like a minivan or something," Josiah said.

"Well, as long as she lets Jesus take the wheel, she should be all right." Isaiah popped a piece of cornbread into his mouth in an attempt not to laugh in her face.

His mother glared at him, the look that said, *Knock this shit off!* "Tammy, is Simone sleeping all night now?" Mom asked as she continued to glare at Isaiah. Back when they were kids, she would have already thrown her shoe at him.

For the next ten minutes, Mom and Tammy chatted about Simone's sleeping pattern as if it was the most important thing in the world.

"How's the academy?" Josiah asked him.

"It's fine," Isaiah answered.

"Man, not sure if Mom told you, but we're so backed up, we have jobs scheduled six months out. I keep trying to hire more guys. They work a couple days, then never show up again. Construction is the one job machines ain't taking from people, and I can't even hire a brother to do it. The only ones who are willing to work are the illegal aliens."

Isaiah rolled his eyes. "Aliens? What planet are they coming in from?" *Be nice. He's an idiot.*

Josiah must have not caught that Isaiah was calling him out, as he kept talking about the cost of lumber and how it was the government's fault.

Isaiah was barely listening as he rambled on—until something Josiah said went off in his ear like a bomb.

"What was that?" Isaiah turned his full attention to his brother.

"I said that I have this new sister in my office helping with the bookkeeping. Single, you know. We should all go bowling this Friday."

"Who is *we all*?" The muscles in Isaiah's jaws tightened.

"Me, you, Tammy, and Denise. Man, she's badass looking," Josiah whispered as he glanced over at Tammy and then back to Isaiah.

Isaiah's pulse quickened as muscles in his jaw tightened. He wasn't going to sit here a minute longer pretending to be someone who he wasn't. *Gideon wouldn't pretend.* Adrenaline tore through him, causing his back, chest, and neck muscles to stiffen. His throat went dry, likely the body's attempt to stop him from doing what he was about to do.

No, he was going to do this. He was coming out to his brother. He cleared his throat. "Nah, I can't. I'm already seeing someone… Mom's neighbor, actually. The guy next door." Isaiah's heart pounded. He'd been less apprehensive or intimidated breaking up barroom brawls or pulling someone from a burning car fire than he was sitting here ready to take the judgment that was about to come from his own brother.

"Oh..." Josiah looked as if someone had smashed a pie in his face. The room was quiet. Tammy and Mom had stopped talking.

"The White guy?" Josiah's face was stoic.

"You're correct. He's White, and he's a guy."

The room again fell silent. Isaiah looked over at his mom, whose face showed disappointment that he couldn't sit there and behave. But he couldn't. Not even for her. Not for a second longer.

Josiah rose to his feet. "Look, bro, I can't understand how you could date someone who's not Black. It's wrong."

Isaiah couldn't hold back. Josiah was an idiot. "You know, for a Christian, you got some fucked-up shit going on in your head."

Their mom stood and stomped her foot. "Boys!" Her tone said *No more*!

She was right. No more. He wasn't going to give his brother—or any family member—a free pass to be a self-serving judgmental hypocrite ever again. If it meant losing his brother, he would rather lose Josiah than give up another ounce of what was left of who he was.

Chapter 11

With buds in his ears, Gideon whistled and rocked out to Adam Lambert as he laid down the Russell's laminate flooring in their small dining room. The young couple had hired him to lay the flooring in the dining room, living room, and bathroom in their recently purchased home. As newlyweds, the Russell's had just moved into the small sixty-year-old Craftsman, and lucky for Gideon, they hadn't yet filled the rooms with wall-to-wall furniture.

Gideon planned for the project to take him a week to complete. With both the homeowners at work, they had a neighbor come over and house-sit while he worked. The young woman looked to be maybe a little younger than Gideon. For most of the morning, she'd spent her time in one of the back bedrooms, and he'd spent it in his head thinking of Isaiah. On occasion, he would see her walking about with one eye on him, and one ear pressed to her phone as she walked and talked.

By early afternoon, he was in a groove with almost half of the living room done. He wouldn't be able to finish that room today, but he would be at least three-quarters done. Down on all fours, there was a moment when Gideon envisioned Isaiah behind him, taking him like that, right here. Deep in fantasy, Gideon was surprised when Mr. Russell walked through the open front door.

"Oh wow, this looks good." Mr. Russell stood at the door.

"Thank you." Gideon straightened and turned off his music, embarrassed as if Mr. Russell had actually caught him being fucked on his newly laid floor.

"When Linda picked this floor, I wasn't that crazy about it, but now I like it." Mr. Russell walked around the edge of the room Gideon hadn't covered yet.

"I like it, too." Gideon's eyes followed the man around to the other side of the room. Mr. Russell looked to be a couple years older than him, but the gray suit and drab tie he was wearing made him look older. Clean-shaven, his blond hair, and blue eyes now showed the stresses from the day. Gideon wasn't sure what he did for a living. Other than the suit, he resembled Shawn.

Mr. Russell continued to walk around the room as he studied Gideon's work. "I like it." Eventually, he excused himself and retreated into the kitchen.

Gideon returned to work, Mr. Russell's likeness to Shawn now in his thoughts. He thought about what he would say or do if he ever saw Shawn again. He'd like to think that he would confront him, that maybe Shawn would admit that what he did and how he acted was wrong. This still pissed him off; that Shawn had never taken any responsibility for what happened. Gideon accepted his own actions in what happened that he should have been more responsible for himself... but still, an apology would be nice. He'd come to terms with having the virus but still had so much anger with how Shawn had treated him.

He measured the next plank to go down and marked where to cut. *Stop thinking about Shawn... I wonder if he's infected anyone else? How can someone be so cruel?* He could never forgive himself if Isaiah were infected by him. His stomach heaved with the thought of it.

Before meeting Isaiah, Gideon wondered when and if he would ever date again. He'd read that some people who were positive only dated other people who were also positive. That made sense and would certainly be a lot easier to deal with emotionally for both partners.

He was shocked that Isaiah was as okay with it as he was. In the beginning, he hadn't been totally convinced Isaiah could be, but hearing Isaiah say that he was worth dating, worth trying to impress, was the most beautiful thing anyone had ever said to him. An impish smile made Gideon's mouth twitch as he carried several planks outside that he needed to cut.

His smile slipped away at the reality of the situation. He certainly couldn't infect Isaiah if they weren't having sex. The other night, had he not gotten in his head, he would have had sex with him. He *wanted* to have sex with him. Who wouldn't? The guy was

116

absolutely the definition of tall, dark, and handsome. His smoky brown eyes were impossible not to stare into. *Damn,* the way Isaiah looked at him as if they were seeing something that nobody else sees, the seriousness on his face that said he wasn't afraid of anything, that he controlled the situations in his life, whatever they were, it was such a turn on. Was that a cop thing or the military?

Isaiah was certainly more of a man than Shawn in more ways than just their stature. Gideon thought of his parents' love. His dad would follow his mother to the ends of the earth and would do anything for her. His dad never batted an eyelash at what Mom said. Gideon smiled, hearing his dad's voice saying, "Because your mother said so." It was his standard answer for everything. Gideon wanted to be with someone who loved him as much as Dad loved Mom.

Back in the house, Gideon stood in the middle of the living room and assessed how much was left before dropping to his knees with the freshly cut planks. Isaiah was right. He was healthy—healthy enough to have sex with him if that's what he wanted. And it *was* what he wanted. He loved having sex, being fucked... It was gratifying. In the past, sex had been the goal, with the possibility of a relationship coming second. With Isaiah, it was different. Yes, he wanted to have intercourse, but that wasn't the driving force. With Isaiah, he wanted more than sex; he craved intimacy. He wanted an intimacy like he witnessed between his parents. Their ability to read each other's mind, to speak the same language on matters of the heart... he wanted that deep and loving friendship with the person he called his best friend—with the added bonus of great sex. He thought about Isaiah all the time, and it was time to start living again. Living with HIV.

They would be careful. He was undetectable, Isaiah was taking PrEP. If Isaiah could deal with it, then he certainly could too. He hadn't known Isaiah for two weeks, and yet he liked everything about him. Isaiah excited him, made him thirsty for life. He wondered what Isaiah was doing at this very moment. Was he in the classroom, dressed in his black suit, or in his gym shorts, running up the side of some mountain with his unit? *Isaiah in those shorts....* The thought of what was under those shorts caused Gideon's cock to pulse. He took out his phone and checked the time. It was almost the end of Isaiah's day at the academy.

He text him. *Missed you the last couple days.*

I missed you too. What R U doing this evening?

Gideon smiled at Isaiah's response as a warmness filled his chest. *No plans.*

Can I cook you dinner? I have something I have to tell you.

It'd been two days since they'd seen each other, and yet it felt like a week. What did Isaiah have to tell him? It sounded important. Gideon typed as he walked. *Sure.*

Heading to the gym now. I should be home by seven. What time do you want to eat?

Eight or nine??? Whatever works. Is everything okay? What was it that Isaiah wanted to tell him?

I'll be there by eight.

See you then.

Gideon stuffed his phone down into his pocket. This gave him plenty of time to get home and clean up. He especially wanted to ensure his body was clean, specifically where it really counted. A naughty snicker escaped him as he tucked his phone into his jeans.

He worked for another half hour before Mrs. Russell showed up. Dressed in pink nursing scrubs, her name tag said Linda Russell, RN, Providence Saint Joseph Medical Center. Her excitement over the room was even more than her husband's as she walked across the new flooring, shrieking, "Thank you!" over and over.

With both homeowners home, it was time to call it a day. He was at a good stopping point. After he and Mrs. Russell agreed on what time he could come back tomorrow, he packed up his equipment and got out of their way.

*****

When Gideon pulled into the carport, Isaiah's car wasn't there. Good. Now he had time to take a shower and pick up the house before his date arrived this evening. He wondered what Isaiah was going to cook tonight. The thought of another home-cooked meal caused his stomach to grumble. What was it that Isaiah had to tell him? He could run with several great possibilities if he let his mind wander.

In the shower, the lengthening of his cock under the warm water was all Isaiah's doing as Gideon thought about their evening to come.

After his shower, while in the kitchen, he saw Isaiah's car pull into the carport. Gideon peeped through the window and watched Isaiah bolt from the car into the house. *Jesus!* There was no denying the ass on that man was a gift.

Within a half-hour, Isaiah was knocking on the kitchen door. As Gideon entered the kitchen to let him in, Isaiah smiled at him through the door window and then let himself in. "I'm assuming the door is unlocked because you knew I was coming?"

"Exactly." Gideon lied. "How are you?" He shut the door behind him and locked it.

"Great." Isaiah kissed Gideon before laying his shopping bag on the counter.

The scent of amber and lavender wafted under Gideon's nose. "Mmm, you smell good."

"Thank you. How was your day?" Isaiah started unpacking his bags.

"Good. I was in Santa Monica today." *What the hell did you want to tell me?* Gideon drew a breath at the sight of Isaiah standing in his kitchen and the possibilities of the evening. His flesh tingled at the thought of making love to him, of seeing him naked, having him on top, touching his smooth skin, feeling his weight. His cock came to life with this thought.

"What were you doing in Santa Monica?" Isaiah looked around the kitchen as if looking for something.

"I have new clients. I'm putting new flooring in their house." Gideon leaned against the counter, hoping to conceal his semi-erection.

"Damn, is there anything you don't do?" Isaiah opened several cabinets and looked in them. He pulled out and held up a ten-inch fry pan. "We need to get you some better pans."

"What's wrong with my pans? They're new."

"I like heavier stuff. No worries, these will work… for tonight. Does a person have to be licensed to do all of the stuff you do?"

"Not really. There are a lot of contractors and people who are licensed, but nobody ever asks." *Did he forget that he wanted to tell me something? Maybe he changed his mind. Maybe it wasn't as important as I thought it could have been.*

Isaiah looked up. "I need to hire you when I buy my house." Isaiah turned the oven on and set the temperature to three-fifty.

"You want to buy a house?"

"Yeah. I've been saving for years. Measuring cup?" Isaiah asked.

Gideon grabbed it from one of the bottom cabinets and handed it to him. "Will you buy something around here or closer to work?"

"I like this neighborhood, and it would be nice to live close to Mom." Isaiah removed a baking dish from his bag of tricks.

Gideon couldn't take it anymore. "What did you want to tell me?"

Isaiah's brows furrowed for a second before his eyes widened. "Oh! That's right. You'll never guess what I did on Sunday." He grabbed a white onion and began chopping.

Gideon knew he was visiting Josiah and Tammy, but he had no idea what the big news could be.

"At their house, we were about to eat lunch, and Tammy started in on wanting me to date this woman at their church. Then Josiah started in talking about double dating and shit." He tossed the onions and celery in the frying pan along with a half stick of butter.

Gideon didn't like hearing that they were attempting to set him up. He didn't like the idea of Isaiah seeing anyone. "What'd you tell them?"

"At first, I was really nervous. I knew I was going to come out to them. I wasn't ready, but I couldn't sit there and pretend like I wasn't gay or something. It just felt wrong." Isaiah shook his head. "Not only did I come out, but I told them that you and I were seeing each other."

"Really?" He was surprised that Isaiah told his brother that they were seeing each other... *like really seeing each other, not just hanging out?* As much as he wanted to comment on this, he didn't want to interrupt Isaiah and his story.

"Yeah. I kept thinking about you. How secure you are about being gay, being who you are. Just not giving a shit about what people are thinking about you."

Me... strong? Prior to contracting HIV, Isaiah would have been right about who he was. He honestly never gave it any thought to what people thought of him. He liked who he was and assumed everyone else did too. He'd never been ashamed of being gay. His parents and Andrew just accepted it. Other than this last year, which felt like five years, life had been relatively easy, living and working in the rain forest. His only reservation in life was talking to his parents about not wanting to run the lodge. It was a conversation that he never had because it was a moot point. Now, it felt as if Isaiah was talking about someone else when he called him strong. If anything, he was envious of Isaiah. He was the strong one to stand up to Josiah.

Gideon caught a whiff of the onions that were frying in the pan. "What are you making?" He snapped several pictures on his phone of Isaiah working his magic in his kitchen. He wanted more than a memory of this moment.

"Chicken Tetrazzini. I thought I'd keep it simple tonight and sauté some string beans to go with it. I like to sauté them in white wine, but I can do something else if you don't want the alcohol."

Gideon waved it off. He didn't know what Chicken Tetrazzini was, but it didn't sound simple. "Wine's fine. How was training today?" he asked as he watched everything Isaiah was doing.

"It's going good."

"I'm glad I texted you." Gideon climbed up onto the counter.

"Oh yeah… Why?"

"I'm getting a free dinner out of it." *and maybe more.* The thought of *more* put a grin on Gideon's face.

"Yes, you are."

Gideon's cock stiffened a little more. He had to stop thinking nasty thoughts, or Isaiah was bound to see his erection. "Is the training hard?" He envisioned Isaiah running up the side of a mountain.

"Not really. I think it might be a little easier for me because I've had experience. I'm used to following orders and the training that we're doing."

"Are you excited?"

"Yeah, I am. I miss not working. The Wednesday morning exam always makes me a little nervous, though." Isaiah lifted the frying pan and tossed the contents up into the air several times.

"What happens if you don't pass your test?" Gideon watched, amazed that everything didn't fly out the pan.

"We get one chance to retake it on Thursday. If we don't pass the retake, then we're out." Isaiah went to work on his string beans as he continued to talk.

Isaiah made cooking look easy. It was like watching the pros on the cooking shows where everything was done at lightning speed. In no time at all, Isaiah had assembled his casserole. When the oven beeped, Isaiah slid the casserole into it and set the timer for one hour.

"What do you like most about being a cop?"

Isaiah looked as if he was thinking about it. He walked over to where Gideon was sitting on the counter and moved between Gideon's legs. "Well, I think it's going to be a lot different from the Navy. Dealing with the public instead of soldiers and their families, I imagine, will come with its own set of challenges. But, with that said, there's truly nothing like the feeling that you've done something to make someone else's life a little better. It's never routine like sitting at a desk, crunching numbers for eight hours."

Gideon was eye level with him. "Man, you're tall. How tall are you?" He always had a thing for tall men.

"Six-one." Isaiah leaned in and kissed him.

Gideon sighed as endorphins swirled to his head. Their heads inches apart, Gideon wanted another kiss. Isaiah's kisses were addictive. He couldn't just have one. This time, it was Gideon who leaned in, Isaiah meeting him halfway. The kiss was another light kiss followed by one that lingered a little longer and left him lightheaded. He squirmed, trying to shift his semi-erection in his pants.

Isaiah brushed his thumb across Gideon's lips. "You're a pretty good kisser, Mr. Miller."

Gideon licked his lips. "So are you." He glanced at Isaiah's lips, glistening. He wanted to kiss him again. It was getting warm in the kitchen, and it had nothing to do with the oven. He had to cool his jets, or he just might cream his pants right here on the counter. "Um... so, where did you learn to cook?"

Isaiah ran his fingers up Gideon's thighs. "My mom mostly. My dad was the master behind the grill. I remember watching him BBQ as a kid." His stare lingered around Gideon's mouth.

Gideon's pulse quickened with the thought of Isaiah kissing him again. Lost in Isaiah's stare, there was a softness in which Isaiah looked at him, and yet, there was a hunger as well that said *I want you.* Gideon licked his lips. He tasted Isaiah. He thought about leaning in and just taking another kiss. He wanted another kiss. His erection pressed in his pants. *No... you have to cool it.* He squirmed, trying to adjust his cock without Isaiah noticing. "I wish I could cook."

"Can you cook anything?" Isaiah softly kissed him.

"Maybe a peanut butter and jelly sandwich."

Isaiah laughed. "Um, you don't exactly cook them."

"Okay, whatever, make them." He leaned in, and they kissed again.

"Don't worry, I'll take one of your peanut butter and jelly sandwiches over some of the stuff in the Navy?" Isaiah's hand moved up Gideon's thigh before they kissed again. "They can't even make them right."

"How can they mess up a PB&J?" Gideon looked down at Isaiah's hand, which was inches away from touching his growing erection. *Does he see what he's doing to me?* Like a dry sponge soaked in water, his erection struggled to find room to expand in his pants.

"I love a good PB&J on soft white bread. The peanut butter spread thicker than the jelly." He ran his hands up and down Gideon's thighs again. "I like my peanut butter nice and creamy." He squeezed Gideon's thighs.

Isaiah's grip felt as if they were transferring currents of electricity, setting Gideon's skin on fire. "What's your favorite jelly?" Gideon was so over talking about food. He wanted Isaiah more than ever. He needed to take matters into his own hands and speed this up before he exploded right here in his kitchen.

Isaiah's hands moved to Gideon's waist. "Strawberry."

"What brand?" *His hands are so big.* Fully hard, Gideon's cock pulsated in his pants.

"Are you interrogating me?" Isaiah leaned in for another kiss.

Gideon held his hand up in between their faces. "Answer the question, sir," *I swear, don't kiss me again, or I'm going to cum right here.*

Isaiah grinned. "I see... Okay... Smuckers, sir. Now can I have a kiss?"

Gideon shook his head. "It's against policy. Not until you're cleared."

Isaiah leaned in, his mouth inches from Gideon's. "Then I want a lawyer," he whispered.

"No." Gideon took in Isaiah's breath. His lungs expanded, wanting it all.

Isaiah chuckled as he stepped back.

"What's so funny?"

Isaiah continued laughing. "You can't deny someone if they ask for a lawyer."

"Yes, I can."

Isaiah's laughter increased. "No, you can't!"

"I can do anything I want. It's my kitchen." Gideon grabbed Isaiah's shirt and pulled him back. "Now you've got me thinking about dessert." He wanted this man in bed, naked, right now.

"I brought brownies and ice cream for you," Isaiah mumbled. His eyes were at half-mast as he stared at Gideon.

"Yeah… Not what I'm craving at the moment." Gideon pulled Isaiah in, and the two began kissing… Deliciously wet, fiery, and hard.

After kissing for several minutes, Isaiah stopped them. "Damn, that's nice." He planted a single kiss on Gideon's bottom wet lip. "What exactly is my Puppy wanting?" Isaiah kissed up and down Gideon's neck.

Gideon moaned as Isaiah's breath pressed upon him. "You."

"Now?" Isaiah's voice was low and husky.

"Are you going to make me wait?" The fire within Gideon smoldered just a little. With a simple fan of air, it would kick up and surely burn the house down.

"Are you sure?" Isaiah nibbled on Gideon's ear and then dragged his tongue down his neck.

Gideon gasped at Isaiah's warm tongue against his skin. "I'm not quite ready for the full tune-up, but maybe I'll let you check my oil. Study my dipstick. You can show me some of your mechanic skills that you were bragging about." Gideon tried to meet Isaiah's lips, but Isaiah teased him and drew back out of his reach.

Isaiah looked at the clock on the oven. "We have a little bit of time."

"Okay." Gideon's voice trembled.

Isaiah wrapped his arms around Gideon and cupped his ass, then he scooped him into his arms.

Gideon wrapped his legs around him. "Are you sure?" He would give Isaiah one last chance to back out.

Isaiah winked at him. "I've never been more sure of anything."

Chapter 12

Isaiah laid back on the unmade queen-sized bed in the bedroom and brought Gideon down on top of him. The only light in the room came from the hall.

This is happening. Gideon moaned as he rested on top of Isaiah. A gasp of air left Gideon's lungs.

With Isaiah under him, their kiss deepened as Gideon's body moved against Isaiah's. He could hardly contain himself as Isaiah's hands worked their way around his body before gripping his ass. In a fiery kiss, their mouths pressed hard against each other. Gideon squirmed on top of Isaiah, fighting to hold back and yet wanting more. *Oh my God, you feel so good.*

His hand slipped under Isaiah's shirt and across his stomach to find his nipples. Isaiah's skin was warm to the touch. He rubbed a finger over the nipple, feeling its hardness. He palmed Isaiah's chest muscle, feeling the sheer size.

Their bodies firmly together, chest to chest, Gideon thrust against him, but their clothes prevented the friction he craved.

Isaiah moaned, shifting his body on top of Gideon. He bore his weight on his elbows, his body barely touching Gideon's.

He grabbed the side of Isaiah's shirt and brought the full weight of Isaiah down on him. "Oh my God! Yes!" Gideon moaned as Isaiah's body buried him between the bed and his lover.

Isaiah kissed his way up Gideon's neck, then up to his ear. The sensation of his warm lips touching his ear, his breath; Gideon gasped again, the air draining from his lungs as if it was his last breath. He felt Isaiah's cock against him through his clothes. He wanted their clothes gone.

He pushed as hard as he could, attempting to communicate that he wanted up.

Isaiah rolled to one side. "Are you okay?"

Gideon nodded as he sat up and pulled his hoodie over his head. "Get undressed." Gideon unzipped his own pants as he stared at Isaiah. *I want you.*

They frantically peeled off their clothes, finishing almost at the same time. He knew Isaiah's body would be nice-looking, but never in a million years did he expect the very definition of perfection. His chest, muscled abdomen, his skin a glistening brown… and his cock—holy shit!—it stretched all the way to his belly button. Gideon had never seen anything like it, and yes, fucking him with that would definitely have to wait for another night. *That thing is going to hurt!* He licked his lips as he peeled his eyes away from it and back up Isaiah's chest.

His breath labored as he looked at Isaiah's dark brown nipples before crawling on top of Isaiah. The sensation of Isaiah's burning skin touching his sent a quiver up Gideon's spine.

Gideon's cock pulsated. *Shit!* Was he about to cum that freaking fast? It had been way too long, and he was way too excited. He froze, trying to stop the onslaught of what he knew was to come if he ground even a little. Clearly, Johnson hadn't been exciting him to this degree.

Isaiah continued kissing him. Like in the kitchen, their kiss was slow and tender now. Isaiah glided over his body, exploring and feeling each crevice, each line, with his hands.

Gideon was glad Isaiah had changed the tempo and slowed things down. He could think now, without fear of ejaculating too soon. He appreciated all of the sensations Isaiah stirred in him: the warmth of his hands, that sent a tingle everywhere they touched; his breath, like the sun warming his back on a hot summer day.

They lay as they kissed, every couple of minutes trading who was on top. Cautiously, Gideon measured his hunger, not wanting to get too excited again, losing control, and cum too early. He moaned in ecstasy as he took in the tenderness of Isaiah's kisses.

Dear God. This man feels so good. Gideon's hunger increased with every passing second, every touch, every moan from his mouth. It was as if it had been years since he'd been touched like this. He'd forgotten how good it felt. He ran his hands over Isaiah's arms, his biceps so prominent, and over his shoulders, and then down his back.

Isaiah's back muscle filled his hands. There seemed to be no end to them. Every inch of him appeared to be muscle.

Isaiah slid his hands over Gideon's ass, squeezing it. This caused a spontaneous guttural response from Gideon.

Then... one of Isaiah's fingers slipped between the cheeks of his ass and pressed against his opening.

Gideon clenched his butt as his eyes opened. *Whoa... Stop... Not that... Don't put your bare finger in there. It's not safe...*

As if Isaiah heard his thoughts, he moved his hand, caressing his cheeks again for a second, and then moved up the small of his back.

That was close. Okay... okay, get out of your head! Get out of your head! He *wanted* this. He *wanted* to make love to Isaiah; he *wanted* the guy's hands all over his body.

With Isaiah's touch, his panic dissipated. He closed his eyes again.

Their naked bodies ground against one another, the physical friction of their cocks as they rubbed together amplifying the sexual tension that was building. In a deep kiss, the room, as well as any fear Gideon may have had completely evaporated. Deep in nirvana, he squirmed and mewed as Isaiah made love to him.

Gideon's cock pulsed, signaling his brain that he was close. The sensation was too strong to stop. "I'm close!" Gideon barely got the words out before he was engulfed in ecstasy. His vision went gray as he spilled between them. The sensation powerful enough to cause a long throaty moan as his body jerked.

With the newly deposited lubricant between them, Isaiah's thrust was like satin brushing against Gideon's skin. Each thrust sent another wave of euphoria as he tried to hold on to Isaiah. The only thing Gideon was able to absorb in that moment was that the deep grunts from the back of Isaiah's throat sounded as if he was getting close. Moments later, Isaiah released a moan and a cry as his body jerked and quivered before stiffening.

Chest to chest, Isaiah lay still, his breathing ragged as he whimpered and moaned. Gideon was quiet as he lay there recapturing what just occurred. *Damn, that was good.*

When it sounded as if Isaiah might have caught his breath, Gideon slid closer to him. He needed to touch Isaiah, to be closer if that was possible. They had made love. The virus hadn't taken this from him forever.

Isaiah pulled him in even closer and wrapped one arm around him. As if he'd been caged for years, Gideon took a breath and exhaled as he lay his face against the side of Isaiah's chest. *I'm going to stay right here, forever.*

They lay side by side, motionless, the only sound in the room for several minutes was their breathing. Savoring what happened, heat radiated from Gideon's body. It hadn't been full-on intercourse, but he'd gotten something way more than sex. He'd gotten a little bit of his self-worth back.

Isaiah was the first to move as he sat up. The touch of Isaiah's hand as he softly slid it against Gideon's face caused him to open his eyes. *Did I fall asleep?* He tried to account for time.

Isaiah was staring at him. His smokey eyes held the same tenderness in them as if making love to him all over again.

"That was nice," Isaiah murmured as the tips of his fingers gently brushed the long strands of hair from Gideon's face out of the way. His fingers then moved across Gideon's chest and into the gooey mess that coated his abdomen. He swirled his finger in it as if writing something.

Gideon wasn't quite ready to talk. The sensation of Isaiah's fingers caused neurons to refire. He closed his eyes and moaned. It was all he had. He was relishing in what had happened when the oven timer buzzed.

"I'll get it." Isaiah rolled out of bed.

Wow! I can't believe that was forty minutes. Yes, he'd for sure lost time somewhere. Gideon watched as Isaiah leaped from the bed. His back, a beautiful light brown, was wide and massive and tapered down to his waist. His perfectly symmetrical ass was like two luscious melons at the peak of ripeness.

Within seconds, Isaiah was gone, and the room was quiet.

Gideon drew a breath and exhaled as he stretched his arms out across the bed. In a strange dreamlike state, he tried to grasp that this was real. That gorgeous naked man who'd just left his room had made love to him. He released another sigh as he took it in. His body felt like mush and, yet, as light as a feather. When he closed his eyes, he felt the drumming of his heart.

When he opened his eyes, his gaze drifted to the bare walls around him. He heard Isaiah whistling out in the kitchen, the oven door slam, and cabinets closing. He sure did know his way around the kitchen. *That's another plus.*

He looked at the four-by-four window on the far wall. *That window needs to be bigger. If I lived here, I would also extend this room out about another ten feet and turn this room into a master suite. I'd build Isaiah a barbecue grill out back. I'd use Clinker bricks... six burners, a built-in refrigerator... and bar seating. Isaiah would like that.* He pictured himself and Daisy on a hot summer day, sitting there, watching Isaiah do his magic on the grill. A giggle broke from his chest as the corners of his lips moved into a grin. *Man! I love this man!*

No sooner did he think it, his smile wilted. *You don't love him, you like him... a lot. It's just a saying. You can't possibly love him. You've only known him for what—two weeks?*

He lay there waiting for Isaiah to return. He regretted how panicky he got when Isaiah's finger touched his ass. *That was stupid. It was a finger. Nobody's going to catch anything through a finger. No. that's not true. If they had cuts on their finger, maybe. He released a sigh. Okay, knock it off, you're being stupid. You're undetectable. You can't transmit anything. Get out of your head.* He contemplated if he should get up and wash off the physical remnants of what had occurred, but that required more energy than he had. He shut his eyes and exhaled as he thought about them making love and just how much he liked... *his new friend?* What were they?

Isaiah reappeared. "Are you thirsty?" He held out a glass of water for Gideon.

Still on his back, Gideon looked up. Isaiah stood over him, his flaccid cock dangling inches from Gideon's face. The length and girth of the damn thing made it impossible not to hunger for it. His sphincter twitched at the thought of it inside him.

He took the glass. "Thank you." His gaze never leaving Isaiah's body as he drank almost all of the cool tap water.

Isaiah crawled back onto the bed and used a towel that he'd brought back with him to clean Gideon's abdomen. He then tossed the towel onto the floor and nestled up against Gideon. Isaiah wrapped one arm around him and kissed him.

"So you cuddle and kiss afterward?" Gideon teased.

"Not normally. My go-to is to tell them the money is on the dresser and turn the light off on their way out." Isaiah chuckled.

"You better not!" He gave him a kiss. *You are so funny... I like that.*

"Was that a whimper?" Isaiah asked.

"No... That's what satisfied sounds like." Gideon burrowed beneath Isaiah's arms, attempting to quell the emotions he was feeling. The thought of going home, leaving this.... it wasn't fair. Why... why him? Why did it have to be him taking over the lodge? *I never asked for it.*

For the next half hour, they dozed with Gideon's ass spooned inside the curve of Isaiah's body.

When Isaiah shifted, Gideon opened his eyes.

"Hey Puppy, you awake?" Isaiah whispered in his ear.

"Yeah." Gideon stretched out of the spoon onto his stomach. *Puppy...* He liked his nickname. "I fell asleep." He turned his head and gave Isaiah a kiss.

"Mmm, I like those lips. Are you hungry?"

Gideon nodded. What he really wanted was to stay right where he was, forever.

Isaiah patted Gideon's bare ass. "I have to cook the string beans." His hand rested on Gideon's butt. "Your skin is soft." His massive hand stretched across both of Gideon's ass cheeks and squeezed them. "I love this ass." He jiggled Gideon's butt.

Warmth spread through Gideon as Isaiah's touch caused him to squirm and smile.

*****

Back in the kitchen, Gideon sat on the counter in his white undies and watched Isaiah plate his food. Isaiah wore only his jeans, hung low around his waist. This man had beautifully made love to him and took him to a place that he hadn't been in a long time. He'd been nothing but honest with Isaiah, and Isaiah was still here in his kitchen, cooking him dinner. "Are you that perfect?" Gideon couldn't believe this could be true. *No one is perfect.*

"What was that?" Isaiah brought him a plate and handed it to him.

"Nothing." Gideon took his plate and leaned back against the cabinet.

"What'd you say?" Isaiah asked again.

"Truth?" Gideon used the playful dialog they'd invented for themselves. He wanted to ask if they were still just having fun? Okay, so they'd had sex; it didn't mean he had to put a ring on it.

"Nothing but." Isaiah set his plate on the counter next to Gideon's body.

"I'm used to guys who appear perfect, and then I find out they're not actually who they portrayed themselves to be," Gideon muttered.

"Are we talking about your guys on Stud Man?"

"StudFinder... but yeah, and no. I'm talking about guys in general." Gideon took a bite of his casserole. "Mmm, this is good. They say they're this or that or have this or that, and then I find out it's all a lie." He was talking about all guys. However, Shawn was the face that came to mind.

Isaiah smiled. "I know exactly what you're talking about. But if you're hooking up for sex, does it really matter? It's not like you're sticking around long enough for the truth to come out anyway. For some guys, dating is just the means to have sex."

Although Gideon never lied about why he was meeting someone, he'd been guilty of hooking up just for the sex. But he was usually genuinely interested in the person as well. Gideon attacked his dinner as he mulled over his past with guys. They were all liars.

"I call that shit selfish greed. Some people think they're so much smarter than everyone else. Like their shit ain't going to get caught." Isaiah took a bite of food.

"I don't follow?" Gideon asked with a mouth full of food.

Isaiah signaled to give him a minute to swallow his food. "What I mean is, they lie to you with the guiltless idea of impressing you. Subconsciously, the lie doesn't matter because the truth will never be revealed. The greed part is that the relationship continues long enough that they have to start managing the lies. Instead of confessing the truth, they want you and the lie to stay intact."

"That's such bullshit. Why do that to someone?"

"Because it's about them."

Gideon thought about what Isaiah had said as he debated asking his question. It felt safe to ask. "Besides being gay, is there anything about you that you're afraid for someone to know?"

Isaiah leaned against the counter. He was silent for a minute.

"Not really afraid, but…" His mouth twisted. "I'm probably not as secure with myself as you might think I am."

"Really? You seem confident to me. What do you worry about?"

"Being black… being gay… No matter how hard your parents try to raise you to be secure, the world is constantly reminding you that you're different. Sometimes, I worry about being perfect and not being whatever negative stereotype someone has about black people or someone who's gay. Some people are clueless about their own ignorance. Like I have to constantly prove myself. I heard the jokes about gay people from people who didn't know about me in the military. That we don't belong, or that they would never shower with a gay dude."

"I totally get what you're saying. When I was first diagnosed, I was so afraid of what people would say or how they would react if they knew I was positive. You hear these stories of people not wanting to drink out of a glass you used, or if I touched them, I could give it to them. Would they even let me in their house to fix something? You feel like an outsider, that, if they knew the truth, it would be this horrible reaction."

"Growing up in Costa Rica, did you feel like an outsider?"

Gideon thought about it. "Most of the time, I was the only white kid. I knew I was different, but the difference didn't seem to matter to anyone. Everyone treated us normal. Shit, when I was little, we were as poor as the rest of our neighbors."

"Makes me think of when I was stationed in the Philippines, I couldn't believe how nice and accommodating everyone was."

"Costa Rica is that way too. The Ticos are super nice. But most of the time, at the lodge, our guests were from another country, and mostly White. To them, we were just employees."

"That's one thing I have to say about being in the military— you're with people of every ethnicity and race. And, as a Master-at-Arms, I got a certain amount of respect, especially if I was in my patrol car."

"Master-at-Arms? What's that?"

"It's what the Navy calls their police like the Army and Marines have the Military Police."

"Oh." Gideon wondered why they didn't just call themselves police as he hopped off the counter and walked over to the casserole.

There was so much he didn't understand about the military. Isaiah seemed so much older than him, so mature. Was that because of the military? Compared to Isaiah, his life had been so simple. "What's this called again? It's hella good." Gideon carved out another big piece to suppress his negativity.

"Chicken Tetrazzini. It's my mom's recipe, but I've changed a couple of things to put my own twist on it." Isaiah walked behind Gideon. "I left the mushrooms out for you."

Focused on getting the loose spaghetti noodles onto his plate, Gideon jumped when Isaiah reached around and tugged him back against him. It was like being pressed against a wall—a brick wall. "Mmm." Gideon rolled his head to the side as he enjoyed the kisses landing on his neck. Isaiah's warm lips touching his skin sent heat coiling down his spine. He closed his eyes as Isaiah's kisses moved down his neck to his shoulders and back.

"I love kissing you," Isaiah murmured through his kisses.

"Mmm. *I love...*" The word caught in Gideon's throat for a second. "*I love* kissing you, too." The word love dangled in his thoughts as Isaiah's kisses began to stoke the smoldering fire from earlier. Each kiss elicited a low incoherent whimper from Gideon.

When Isaiah stopped, Gideon was light-headed. "Mmm, *I'm in love* with those lips." He was in a daze.

Isaiah cupped Gideon's erection. "I see that." He softly kissed the back of Gideon's neck once more, then he squeezed Gideon's cock.

"Aw, come on—how's a guy *not* supposed to respond to that? It's like crack." He spun around to face Isaiah. He lifted onto his toes for a kiss. "Let's just say I'm ready for a second round after dinner."

Isaiah's brows rose as he took Gideon by the hand. "I think I can handle that."

Chapter 13

This morning was anything but a typical morning for Gideon. For starters, he had a warm and naked man back in his bedroom sleeping like a baby; two, he was attempting to cook breakfast, and three, it was three o'clock in the morning.

As hard as it was to leave Isaiah's side, he'd snuck out of bed for a crazy idea that he would fix him breakfast before he left for training.

Gideon checked his pan, ensuring it was hot enough for his first try at pancakes. How hard could it really be? He'd seen his mother do it a thousand times. The back of the pancake mix that he slipped out to buy said to mix it with water. That seemed easy enough.

He carefully spooned his lumpy batter into the pan, making five cakes the size of a half-dollar. They looked smaller than his mom's, but maybe they grew as they cooked.

While those cooked, he climbed onto the counter and waited. He was still basking in the pleasures of last night. It was phenomenal. Isaiah's body and that cock of his was nice, but how he kissed and made love... *Now that's what I'm talking about.* He questioned if he really could be in love that fast? It was crazy that he already thought this was something that it wasn't. He'd been a fool eleven months ago to think that he would have traded his entire life for Shawn. Now, it didn't seem as foolish when he thought of doing it again with Isaiah. Had he learned nothing from Shawn? Anyways, they were both clear at the beginning of this that this would only be about hanging out and having fun. He was sure he'd moved past having fun a while back.

He caught a whiff of his pancakes. Why did they smell like they were burning? He jumped off the counter to check them. The tops of his cakes weren't cooked and resembled the moon, riddled with craters.

He grabbed his spatula and lifted the side of a cake. *"Shit!"* The damn thing was black. He flipped it over and checked another one, and then another. They were all burnt.

He'd just flipped the last one over when Isaiah entered.

"What are you doing in here?" In two giant steps, a naked Isaiah was at the stove.

"I was trying to make you breakfast."

"Puppy." Isaiah grabbed the spatula from him and checked one of the cakes. "That's sweet of you... but I think these can't be saved."

"The box said to cook them for four minutes."

"Four minutes?" Isaiah's brows furrowed as he looked around before grabbing the box and reading the back. "Four minutes total. Two minutes on each side." He took the pan off the stove and dumped the cakes in the sink. "Let's try this again. Have you ever made pancakes?"

"No."

"First of all, your fire's too high." Isaiah reduced the flame by half before looking down at his lumpy batter. "This won't work."

"But you're supposed to be sleeping. Let me try it again." Gideon eyed Isaiah's beautiful ass.

"I can't sleep if the house is on fire." In a matter of minutes, Isaiah whipped up another bowl of batter and had four cakes cooking in the pan. "Don't let them burn! I'm going to get my underwear."

Deflated, he succumbed to his defeat as he watched Isaiah run out of the kitchen and then return in less than a minute.

"Damn, I liked you better naked."

"I bet you do." Isaiah kissed him before checking his cakes.

"Do you want me to make you coffee?"

"Yes, please." Isaiah flipped over his cakes.

Gideon brewed the first cup of coffee and set it on the counter next to where Isaiah was cooking. "Thanks." Isaiah plated the four cooked cakes and poured more batter into the pan.

Gideon watched for a second before making coffee for himself. "By the way, this is way too freakin' early to be up every day."

"You get used to it." Isaiah nodded to the four cakes that were already cooked. "Go ahead. Start before they get cold. These will be ready in a sec... Syrup?"

Gideon's eyes widened. "Syrup? Shit. I don't have any."

"Really. You got stuff for pancakes but no syrup?"

Gideon shrugged. "I didn't think about it."

Isaiah checked the underside of his cakes. "That's fine. We can eat them without syrup."

"But I love syrup!" *Who eats pancakes without syrup?* He retrieved the plate of cakes. *This sucks.*

Isaiah removed his four cakes and joined Gideon at the counter. "What's a typical day for you when you're at the lodge?"

"It starts early. But not this early. We're up by six, trying to get things ready before the guests start waking up. Every night, it rains at least a couple of times. Since the lodge is all open in the morning, Andrew and I have to wipe down everything and make sure the chairs and tables are dry for breakfast. Sweep down the walkways and paths, so it looks like they'd left it the night before. My mom is in the kitchen getting breakfast together for the guests." He took a bite of his pancake. *They really suck without syrup.*

"What's a standard Costa Rican breakfast?" Isaiah took a bite of his breakfast.

"For us, or for them?"

"Both."

"We have coffee in the morning until after the guests leave."

"What does your mom cook them?"

Gideon's mouth twisted. "Always a fruit mix, like pineapple, papaya, mango, bananas, and melons. She usually makes banana pancakes with home-made coconut syrup, bacon, sausage, and eggs. After the guests are gone, we'll eat whatever is left. Mom always cooks way too much, ensuring there is plenty for them. By ten o'clock, the river guides like to have the group back on their rafts for their second day on the river. Once the guests are gone, we clean the rooms, change the sheets, and get everything ready for the next group that will show up by four o'clock." Gideon paused to take a bite of his breakfast. "If we don't have a group coming in, then we do maintenance, cut back brush, and repair anything that's broken or worn. There's also a constant need for dry firewood that we have to keep up with."

"Jesus. And you want to go back to that?"

Gideon nodded as he chewed.

"What do you miss about being in Costa Rica?"

136

"Being on the river. Hearing the rush of it all day and night. Rainstorms out of nowhere. Oh man, can it rain. Sometimes we can fill up a five-gallon bucket in one storm."

"I think that's why they call it the Rain Forest."

Gideon ignored Isaiah's sarcasm. "I love seeing a bird or a frog or a snake that I've never seen before. Camping on the beach. The beaches on the Caribbean side have beautiful coral reefs, and the water is so warm."

"You like camping?"

"Oh yeah. I love to camp. For Christmas, we go camping every year."

"Camping for Christmas in the winter?"

"Yeah. December to April is our dry season. Things slow down a little for us. The lodge closes for the week of Christmas. It's the only time we can get enough time off to go."

"What's the temperature like in December?"

"We have nice weather. It's around seventy-five during the day. The nights might drop to the low seventies. But we get some rain. On Christmas day, my mom makes the best-ever paella over the campfire." Gideon licked his lips, sorry that he traded in last year's camping trip for his trip to California.

"You said you hike a lot?" Isaiah finished the last of his pancakes.

"I love to hike. Anytime we don't have a group and are caught up around the lodge, Andrew and I take off hiking."

Isaiah began brewing a second cup of coffee. "Have you had a chance to get up to Griffith Park?"

"Is that where the big Hollywood sign is?" Gideon finished the last of his crappy breakfast.

"Yeah."

"That's on my bucket list."

Isaiah grabbed his coffee from the brewer. "Okay, I got to go, or I'm going to be late. The views from up there are exceptional. How about tomorrow, after I get out of training, we hike up there?"

Gideon was surprised that he offered to take him. "Are you sure?"

"Yeah, I think it might be fun to take my Spanish flashcards with us. If you're still offering, you can help me go through them." Isaiah signaled for him to follow him.

Although Griffith Park was on Gideon's bucket list, it took a backseat to spending the day with Isaiah. It didn't matter where they were. "Okay, it's a date."

Back in the bedroom, Isaiah gathered his clothes and got dressed. "We can pack dinner to take with us."

The excitement in Isaiah's voice coaxed a grin from Gideon. A picnic on top of a mountain sounded fun and romantic. Tomorrow couldn't come fast enough.

"Okay. I'll pack some sandwiches." Gideon thought about what he needed to get for sandwiches.

"We're not taking sandwiches. I'll take care of the food." Isaiah buttoned his shirt and slipped on his shoes.

"What's wrong with sandwiches? I can make PB&J, or ham and cheese, or turkey."

Isaiah laughed. "My point exactly. You don't have to worry your pretty little head over it. I got this." Isaiah hurried over to him and kissed him. "I got to go."

With Isaiah gone, the house suddenly felt very empty. It had been just him in it for months, and it hadn't ever felt empty, but now, yes, it very much felt empty. He yawned as he crawled back into his bed. Even the bed was cold.

This morning was fun. He liked that Isaiah took over and made them breakfast. How the hell did he forget to buy syrup? Isaiah didn't seem to care that they didn't have syrup. He wondered if Isaiah ever got mad at anything. He tried to picture him mad. Isaiah was too sweet. He couldn't picture it. Was this what it felt like being married to someone?

This could be his life, waking up with Isaiah, watching him go to work… The thought of Isaiah naked in the shower sent blood to his groin.

It really sucked that he was leaving.

Chapter 14

Isaiah stopped along Brush Canyon trail, the three-mile footpath up to the iconic Hollywood sign. After tying his shoe, he shifted the heavy backpack, regretting stuffing so much into it. Before resuming his hike, Isaiah read the sign adjacent to the trail.

Caution

Rattlesnakes

Shit. Are you kidding me? There better not be. Isaiah quickly refocused his attention on Gideon's ass as he hiked up the trail ahead of him. His butt looked really cute in those jeans. He pictured Gideon naked... yes, it was a very cute ass and soft.

"Wait up!" Isaiah yelled as he snapped a picture of Gideon's backside as Gideon practically ran up the dirt trail.

He wished he had the same energy as Gideon, but his academy class had done a five-mile run this morning, then they'd spent the afternoon on the firing range. The temperature outside was peaking at almost ninety degrees now. With the L.A. sun on him, it felt as if it was well over a hundred degrees. He used the front of his tee-shirt to wipe the sweat from his brow.

"Come on, old man!" Gideon shouted as he waved for him to catch up.

"What is this, a race?" He sprinted in a full run until he caught up to Gideon, then he grabbed Gideon by the waist and lifted him off the ground, spinning him in a circle. "I got your *old man* for you!"

Gideon squealed, his voice echoing down the canyon as he squirmed. "I meant it as a compliment, I swear! I'm into old dudes!" Gideon squirmed to break free.

"*Old dude*! You're a little shit, you know that?" To prove his point, he threw Gideon's body over onto his shoulder and playfully patted him on that cute behind as he carried him up the mountain.

"Okay! Okay! Okay! I'm kidding!" Gideon shrieked.

He whirled Gideon off his shoulders. "Now, walk like you have some sense. This ain't no Goddamn race!" Isaiah's heart was pounding from the exertion, but he would never confess that to Gideon. He tried to bring his heavy breathing under control by taking several large breaths.

Out of breath as well, Gideon pulled his jeans up and adjusted himself.

"And I don't know how you can run in those tight jeans anyways." Isaiah smacked him on his ass.

"They're not tight."

"Yeah, they are."

"They're not." Gideon pulled on the waist to show that he had room in them.

Isaiah went to grab him again, but Gideon was too quick as he jumped back.

"I love it up here," Gideon said, as they both looked down the canyon through a haze of smog that filtered the views of the city below them.

"That's Santa Monica, right?" Gideon pulled his tee-shirt up and over his head.

Isaiah's gaze fell to Gideon's small dark nipples. He wanted to kiss them, touch them, devour them. "Yeah, on a clear day, you can actually see the ocean from up here."

"That'd be cool." Gideon's fingers brushed his hand.

For a second, Isaiah thought Gideon was going to try to hold his hand again. Public displays of affection with another man were ingrained in his head as something he didn't do. Years in the military, he'd overheard enough gay-bashing to know people didn't like to see it. Then he remembered his conversation with Josiah the other day. *I'm not doing it anymore.* It was a little empowering to come out to Josiah and to be able to say, I don't give a shit. He looked around to see if anyone was around. They were alone. He took Gideon's hand and clasped his fingers with his. He took a breath just as Gideon looked up at him and smiled.

Isaiah took another breath. *This is my life now. Really. What would happen if someone did see us?*

There weren't any consequences. He wouldn't lose his job or face harassment from co-workers.

This is my life now. He repeated it, trying to believe it. His only reservation was the new job. It, too, was a testosterone-filled environment. But one of the reasons he'd chosen the L.A.P.D. was their zero tolerance towards harassment against one's sexual orientation. They even had an L.G.B.T.Q. police association that did recruiting and participated in Pride events. More than anything, he wanted to be as free and comfortable about being gay as Gideon was.

In some way, it seemed as if Gideon gave him the strength to come out. Isaiah couldn't stay away from him. He didn't care what Mom thought or his brother. He lived right next door, less than twenty-five feet away from the guy, and that was too far away. He wanted to be in Gideon's presence every second that they could find to be together.

Lying next to Gideon the last two nights, he'd felt something for Gideon that he'd never felt with Ronnie. Although he and Gideon hadn't talked about their feelings for one another yet, Isaiah knew he was falling for him. Outside of Ronnie, the only other serious relationships he'd had was six months with Eric and a year with Steven. Everything else had never made it out of the exploratory phase.

They walked up the gradual incline that continued to steal their breath away with the views of the city below them. He'd been in his head thinking about his relationship with Ronnie when Gideon spoke.

"You got quiet. What are you thinking about?" Gideon's forehead creased with worry.

Isaiah was embarrassed to admit the truth. Here he was on a date and thinking of someone else. That seemed wrong. But it wasn't like that. "Ronnie, my ex."

"Do you miss him?" Gideon's brows pulled together in harmony with his question.

Isaiah debated how to best answer without freaking Gideon out. "When you've been with someone for that long, there's a lot of history there. We had some memorable moments." He had to clean that up a bit. "But it's not like I want to get back together with him. I'm glad that's over, but still, it's like losing a friend. You think about what went wrong and whose fault it was."

"I got the feeling that you were still friends."

On the surface, yeah, of course, they were friends, but were they *really friends*? "That's a hard one. Friends in the sense that we're not enemies. But would I want to spend time around him? Probably not."

"Why's that?"

"It wasn't a healthy relationship for me. I wanted something he wasn't willing or capable of giving me. And yet, I hung in there, believing that one day he would be the person I wanted him to be. He knew what I wanted—which was not what he wanted—and yet, he kept dangling that carrot in front of me like it could happen."

"I don't see you with that type of person."

Isaiah laughed. "Me neither. Never again." He coordinated his step with a kiss. "Why do you ask?"

Gideon shrugged. "Just wondering how you feel about him."

"If you're wondering would I get back with him if I could, the answer is no. I've learned a lot about myself because of that relationship." Isaiah felt Gideon's grasp tighten on his fingers.

They were both silent for several steps before Gideon spoke. "When I had sex with Shawn that night, I knew better. I used to ask myself every day why in the hell I'd done it. I still don't know why. It was the stupidest thing I've ever done, and now I'm paying for it for the rest of my life. I got sick about a month after we'd had sex at that party."

"Got sick? How?" Isaiah was sorry that he interrupted him.

"One morning, I woke up with a sore throat and feeling like I was coming down with something. When it didn't go away after a couple of days, I went to Urgent Care. I told the doctor that I thought it was the flu. When the doctor saw me, she suggested they run an HIV test. I had forgotten about us having unprotected sex until she brought up the test. I kind of panicked right there in the office while waiting for the results. When she came in to tell me I was positive, I was in shock. I called Shawn that night. I wasn't blaming him; I was telling him he needed to get tested, too. That he might be positive. He got weird, saying that I must have gotten it from someone else. That he wasn't positive. When I told him that he was the only one that I'd been with in a while, he told me that it wasn't a big deal, just get the meds."

"Really? What an ass."

"I know. I was so scared."

"Just curious, had you had unprotected sex with anyone else?"

"Well yeah, about a year before that, but I never got sick."

To hear someone say this always surprised Isaiah. He just couldn't understand why someone would have unprotected sex these days, and yet, it seemed to be so common, especially among younger gay men. "Had you been tested between that guy and Shawn?"

"No. I'd never been sick. That's why I know it was Shawn."

"Had you *ever* been tested?"

"No."

Isaiah couldn't believe what he was hearing. How was it possible that Gideon hadn't been tested until then? It seemed a little reckless. Was this Gideon's youth, a lack of maturity? Though he was in no way promiscuous, Isaiah made sure he was tested every six months regardless of how much or what kind of sex he'd had. "You know, the virus can live in you for a while before you get sick. Maybe it was a coincidence that you got sick after having unprotected sex with Shawn because you'd already contracted the virus."

Gideon let go of Isaiah's hand. "But there was something about how he reacted," Gideon muttered. "He flat-out denied that it was from him." Gideon shrugged. "I guess you could be right..."

There was so much Isaiah wanted to say to Gideon about unprotected sex, the virus, being tested regularly, about life, but what he had to offer felt so preachy, too, *Father-Knows-Best*. The last thing he wanted was to come off as someone who knew everything. Isaiah changed the direction of the conversation. "Are the antiviral drugs expensive?"

"Yeah, they are. But luckily, I was able to get into a program that covers them. I have a co-pay." As Gideon shared information about his doctors and the medication, they reached the end of the trail.

"Ah, man! There's a fence around it!" Gideon whined. "I wanted a picture with it."

Isaiah stared at the tall chain-link fence that kept hikers off the forty-four-foot-tall white letters. "I wonder when they put the fence up?"

"Do you want to climb it?"

"No. Wouldn't be a good idea for me to get arrested while I'm in the police academy."

"Good point." Gideon tried several angles for a selfie with the sign. "That sucks! I wanted a picture on it."

With sweeping panoramic views of the eastern ridges and peaks of the Santa Monica Mountains and the city below, Isaiah pulled out his own phone. "Stay there!" he ordered, as he snapped several pictures of Gideon with the sign behind him and then directed him to stand with the city below as the backdrop.

After their impromptu photoshoot, Isaiah found a spot they could eat the picnic he'd packed for them.

Gideon kicked his shoes off and then tore off his socks. He looked at the sun and released a breath. Perspiration glistened on his shoulders and chest from the intense sun, his beautiful blue eyes matching the pale blue sky.

Isaiah wasn't into feet, but Gideon's feet and wiggling toes were adorable for some reason. "I wish you could see the ocean better." He hated that he brought Gideon all the way up here, and the smog was so bad that they couldn't see the ocean.

"I know. I have to say, the ocean and the beach are like some of my favorite places to be." Gideon stared at the haze of white clouds in the far distance.

"Me, too." Isaiah glanced out over the ridge. "What do you want to do first, flashcards or eat?"

"Um… Let's do flashcards first."

Nervous about looking stupid in front of Gideon, Isaiah dug in his bag until he found the deck of cards. He handed the deck to Gideon. He was starting to regret this idea.

"Which side do you want to read?" On one side of the cards was a Spanish word, and the flip side had the word in English.

"Show me the Spanish side. I'll say it in Spanish and then tell you what it means." Isaiah took a breath as he mentally prepared himself.

Gideon held the first card up.

"Volar… Fly." *Okay, that was an easy one.*

Gideon held up the next card.

"Noche…. Night." *Easy.*

Nombre… Name." *Easy.* Isaiah took a breath as he settled into the lesson. The next fifteen cards, Isaiah knew the word immediately.

"You're good." Gideon held up the next card.

"Encima…" Isaiah studied the word. He wasn't sure. "Enter?"

Gideon shook his head. "Encima."

Isaiah listened to Gideon's pronunciation. His intonation as he said the word back was incredible.

"Vi flamas encima Roma," Gideon said slowly.

He thought about what Gideon said in Spanish. He pieced together the words he knew. *I. saw. flames? Rome. What's the word?* "Encima…"

Then he got it. "Over! You said I saw flames over Rome." He laughed at Gideon's sentence and that he was able to get the word from the sentence. "Damn, your Spanish is good."

"Gracias." Gideon smiled as he held up the next card.

Over the next half hour, they completed the entire deck of cards. It wasn't near as embarrassing as Isaiah thought it would be. In fact, it was fun. Gideon was a great teacher and way more appealing on the eyes than his instructor at the academy.

"Let's eat." Isaiah took the flashcards back and put them in his bag. He then handed Gideon a small container as he kissed him. "Here you go."

"What is it?" Gideon cracked the lid and peeked in the container.

"It's a strawberry quinoa salad." Isaiah removed the lid from his container.

"Did you make it?"

"Oh yeah. In between classes, the gun range, and running five miles today, I whipped up a little salad for us." He chuckled. "I got it at this little deli down the street from the academy."

Gideon dug into his salad. "Mmm, this is good. Is it rice?"

"Kinda sort of. You've never had quinoa?" It was nearly impossible for Isaiah to stay focused every time he looked at Gideon, who was too damn sexy, sitting there with no shirt. He could make love to him right here.

"No." Gideon nibbled some of the grain.

"It's kind of like rice, but it's a seed. It has way fewer calories and carbs than rice and is a good source of protein." He watched to see if Gideon liked it. He was so cute, just to watch. "Okay, you asked me about Ronnie, and I only know what you told me about Shawn. I don't mean it disrespectfully, but have you ever had a *real* boyfriend?"

"Where the hell am I going to get a boyfriend in the freakin' rain forest?"

"I'm just asking."

"Has your mom said anything about us?" Gideon asked.

Isaiah shrugged. "Not really. A couple of times, she's asked how you were, trying to be nosy without asking. I haven't seen much of her this week. I feel a little bad." Isaiah remembered what she had said on Sunday on their drive home from Josiah's. "The other day, she was talking about some wedding and asked me if I ever wanted to get married."

"What'd you tell her?" Gideon's left brow arched.

"At first, I was caught off guard. But yeah, I told her that sure, I'd love to… One day." Isaiah looked at Gideon. "How about you?"

Gideon put his salad down and took a drink from his bottled water. "Of course. I haven't thought about it a lot, but yeah, I'd like to. Why do you think she asked you that?"

"You know she calls herself a professional matchmaker. She loves getting people together. I swear to God, she'll meet someone in line and, before the end of the conversation, she's setting them up with someone. She's got at least a dozen weddings under her belt."

"Really?" Gideon laughed.

"It's not funny. I tell you, she's got her sights set on a gay wedding."

Gideon squinted. "Like you and me?"

Isaiah nodded as he frowned.

Gideon pouted. "Why do you make that face? I'd make a good husband!" He skewered Isaiah with an unflinching look.

"You're a little young to be thinking about marriage."

"I'm not that young."

"Okay, who was the president before Obama?" Isaiah attempted to prove his point.

Gideon's forehead wrinkled. "Um… I don't know. I was, like, fourteen back then."

"Exactly." A nervousness crept into Isaiah's gut. His question did prove a point: Gideon was young, maybe *too* young for him. At thirty years old, Isaiah had already had had an entire career and was now starting a second. He was ready to buy a house, settle down, even get married. Gideon was still learning about protected sex and the responsibilities of getting tested and knowing your sex partners. The military had a way of maturing people well beyond their age. Maybe he was too old for Gideon.

146

"My parents were married when my mom was eighteen," Gideon said. "You should see them together. He still holds her hand and kisses her all the time. They've been married forever, and they still do Date Night. They never leave the property but will have dinner down by the river or in the pavilion by themselves." Gideon's grin widened.

"I think that's cute. My parents were high school sweethearts. They got married pretty young, too. I think my mom was twenty."

"Twenty? Then why do you say I'm too young?" Gideon folded his arms across his chest.

"Good point. But, back then, people got married earlier than now. How old were your parents when they had you?"

"Mom was seventeen."

Isaiah's brows rose. "Oh, I'm smelling a scandal."

"My mom said that when Grandma found out she was pregnant, she made them break up. She tried to keep them apart when my mom was pregnant. My mom had me two months before she turned eighteen, and, on her eighteenth birthday, she and my dad got married."

Out of the corner of his eye, Isaiah saw something moving about five feet in front of them. It took a second for his brain to process that it was a snake. He jumped to his feet, screaming. "Snake! A snake!" He pointed toward the small twelve-inch, brownish-gray creature as it slithered away from them.

Gideon took two steps toward the snake. "It's a baby gopher snake." He snatched it up with his right hand, grabbing it behind the head.

"Oh, dear God! Don't come near me with that thing!" Isaiah shrieked. "It could be a baby rattlesnake. The sign said Rattlesnakes, not Gopher snakes."

"It's not a rattlesnake. This guy is harmless. They don't bite." Gideon held it up as he laughed.

"That's not funny. Put that thing down. How do you know it's not a baby rattler?" Isaiah pointed away from them. "Over there! Put it over there!"

"Because I know what a rattlesnake looks like." Gideon carried it about ten feet away, then dropped it down into the bushes. "So you don't like snakes?"

"Let me guess. You had those for pets, too?"

Gideon wiped his hands on his pants as he walked back to Isaiah. "In Costa Rica, we have huge boa constrictors that live in trees. You'll be walking along and look up into a tree, and there would be twenty of them just hanging out."

"That's nasty! Can we talk about something else?" Isaiah cut his gaze to the brush as if expecting the snake to come out again.

Gideon's phone chimed in his pocket. He pulled it out and barely glanced at his screen before stuffing the phone back into his pocket.

"Who was that?" Isaiah was being nosy and probably wouldn't have asked if Gideon's facial expression hadn't changed like it did.

"My brother. I'll text him back later. So... I was thinking.... Tonight, you want to do something a little different?" Gideon's cheeks flushed.

"What?" Isaiah was intrigued.

Gideon swung a leg over Isaiah's and an arm around his neck. The gleam in his eyes said whatever he was thinking was naughty. Gideon kissed him. Initially a light kiss, but followed it up with a second, longer kiss that involved a little tongue and a gentle tug on his lip.

Isaiah put down his salad. "I'm listening," he murmured through their kiss as he glided the tips of his fingers over one of Gideon's soft nipples.

"Well... I was thinking..." Gideon moved up completely on his lap and kissed him again. "Tonight, maybe... What do you say you check out my trunk? See if there's enough room in there for that luggage of yours?"

"Are you sure?" Blood rushed to Isaiah's groin at the thought of it. He'd forgotten how aggressive a young gay man was.

Gideon kissed him again, this time putting his hand over Isaiah's growing erection. "I'm sure... but that thing does scare me a little."

Isaiah released a sinister laugh. "Don't be scared. Just think of it as a boa constrictor." He loved that Gideon was this weird mixed bag of innocence and yet had this assertive side as well.

"Trust me, I'm scared." Gideon snickered.

The two gathered up their things and descended down the mountain at lightning speed.

Chapter 15

On the way home, he continued his seduction of Isaiah. With his hand on Isaiah's groin, he softly massaged Isaiah through his pants. He could feel that his light touch had Isaiah very excited. He managed to get Isaiah's pants undone and open with little resistance, feeling the beloved cock that he'd asked for on the mountain top. He couldn't keep his hands off of it, keeping Isaiah in an aroused state for most of the drive home. Yes, he was leaving in three weeks, but they were both adults. It was just sex. They could handle keeping it casual like they'd both agreed.

Oh, God! Isaiah squirmed. "You've got to stop." He lightly guided Gideon's mouth off of him. "You're getting me way too excited."

When they pulled into the driveway, Daisy was out front watering the potted plants on her side of the carport.

"Ah shit. My mom." Isaiah navigated the car into the carport and, at the same time, tried to stuff himself back into his pants.

"That thing ain't going back in there. Not like that." Gideon laughed.

"It's not funny." Isaiah slowed the car to a crawl, stalling for time. "I hate those damn plants!" With one hand on the steering wheel, Isaiah continued to tuck himself into his pants.

Gideon snickered. "I figured out a long time ago that she only waters them when she's being nosy. Do you know how many times she's caught me coming and going using those damn plants?"

Daisy moved onto the step and waved.

"Don't open that door!" Isaiah shrieked. "Not yet!" He finally got himself back into his pants and fastened up. "Okay."

The two exited the car. "Hey, Mom. What are you doing home? I thought you had bingo tonight?"

"I wasn't feeling well. Called Cathy and told her not to pick me up. Been dizzy all day. Thought I'd give these guys a little water before I lie down for a while."

Gideon moved to his side of the carport as Isaiah moved to his side. "Anything I can do? Did you call your doctor?"

"No. It's just my blood pressure, I'm sure. Been eating too much of the good stuff lately."

Isaiah moved closer to his mother. "Do you want me to fix you a salad for later?"

"No, I don't want no salad."

Gideon stopped on his step as he listened to Isaiah and Daisy. If Daisy wasn't feeling well, he and Isaiah might have to postpone their little escapade for another time.

"How about some soup?" Isaiah glanced back at Gideon and then back at his mother.

"I got a corn dog that I didn't eat for lunch. I'll eat that later. How's y'alls hike?" Daisy directed her question to Gideon.

"It was fun. I've never been up there." Gideon looked at Isaiah. "That sign is sooo big." He couldn't stop smiling, seeing Isaiah give him the stink-eye. He watched Isaiah to see if he was heading into the house with his mother. "Hey, I'm going inside to clean up. Thanks, Isaiah, for the hike. I had a lot of fun."

Isaiah's face sobered. "Um, okay. Me, too. I'll come over later." Isaiah looked at his mother.

"Yeah, come on over." With a half-wave, Gideon said goodbye, with hopes that Isaiah wouldn't be long.

Inside, he turned on the hot water in the hall bathroom shower and, as it heated up, he went to his room, undressed, and tossed his dirty clothes into the corner of the room. Naked, he made his way back down the hall to the only working bathroom. If he didn't pick up any jobs for Saturday, he'd like to get the master bathroom done this weekend.

The warm water cascaded down his body, stripping the sweat and dust from the hike. Today had been fun. It'd been nice being outside in nature again. Sitting up there on that mountain, talking like they did, had fed his soul. The views from the top of the mountain had been spectacular. He snickered, thinking about Isaiah squealing at the snake. That had surprised him. *Why is Isaiah afraid of snakes?* He snickered again as he played out the scene of Isaiah jumping up and down and screaming.

After shampooing his hair, Gideon squeezed out a heap of his rosemary and mint conditioner into the palm of his hand. As the aromatic rosemary reached his nose, he gently massaged the cream in, ensuring every strand of hair was coated. While the conditioner sat in his hair, he scrubbed his body with his soapy loofah. A noise caused him to pause. He listened for a second before continuing his routine.

With his eyes closed, he rinsed the conditioner out of his hair and away from his face. When he opened his eyes, he was no longer alone.

Isaiah stood in the shower, grinning. *Naked.*

"Jesus! You scared the crap out of me."

Isaiah smirked as he looked behind Gideon. "I hope not."

Gideon cleared water from his face. "That's not funny. You could have killed me."

"How's that? I'm not Norman Bates."

"Who the hell is Norman Bates?" Gideon asked as he turned around and positioned his head under the water to finish rinsing the remaining silky conditioner out of his hair.

"From *Psycho*? Anthony Perkins? Alfred Hitchcock? Really? You've never seen the movie?"

"Nope." Copious amounts of conditioner slicked around their feet as Gideon turned back around. He cast a look at Isaiah's glistening cock. His hand followed and lifted Isaiah's flaccid cock as if he was weighing it. *I want this.* "Did you put Mommy to bed?" He grinned as he gripped Isaiah's cock and tugged lightly.

Isaiah took a step closer and kissed him. "Yes, Mommy's sleeping, so we can play." He grasped Gideon's wet hips and pulled their bodies together. He softly kissed Gideon as he stroked his hair. "Don't think I didn't catch that shit about how the sign was soooo big. You're so naughty. I can't believe you didn't hear me come in."

"Me neither." Gideon moved closer, his hardening cock pressed against Isaiah. "You're like a ninja." The warm water acted as a lubricant between their skin.

Isaiah brought him up into his chest. "Not a ninja." He gently kissed Gideon. "I walked through the kitchen door—"he kissed him again—"the door you didn't lock." He delivered two more tender kisses.

I love your kisses. Gideon released a pent-up breath through a moan as Isaiah drew back. Gently, Gideon licked his own lips, savoring the taste of Isaiah. "Well, I guess you're going to have to arrest me to teach me a lesson." He stared into Isaiah's eyes. *God, you're beautiful.* His heels rose off the floor of the tub for another kiss—*one more.*

As they kissed, Isaiah's hands slid around to Gideon's slick ass. Isaiah's massive hands cupped his butt, and then he pulled him up closer. Gideon's cock firmly against Isaiah, he began thrusting up and down.

The sound of the water raining down on them echoed as if music set to the sexual tension that was building between them.

He continued to rub against Isaiah's slippery skin as he lightly kissed his nipple. The water cascading over Gideon's mouth made the nipple the perfect temperature, like a warm hors d'oeuvre. His desire surged. He sucked harder, wanting more of the nipple, as much as he could devour. Isaiah's chest muscle flexed in his mouth. Gideon wanted more. He moved in between Isaiah's legs, needing to be even closer, twisting his mouth over Isaiah's chest. They'd been having sex all week and were *very* familiar with each other's bodies. He knew how much Isaiah liked what he was doing, and he loved feeling his massive chest as he kissed it. It was a win-win for both of them.

Isaiah pulled him off his chest. He smoothed the hair from Gideon's face and tucked it behind his ears.

Gideon was light-headed as he gazed into Isaiah's eyes. His heart pounded with the anticipation of Isaiah fucking him. A low groan escaped him. He ran his hand across Isaiah's chest. "Mmm, I'll never get tired of this big chest and those kisses."

Isaiah sighed as he released Gideon. "I've got plenty of those for you. But first, I better get clean before we run out of hot water." Isaiah took ahold of Gideon's erection. "I can't wait to get you in that bed." He released Gideon and grabbed the soap.

"Hurry." Gideon stood under the cascade of warm water as he watched Isaiah cover his body with lather. *God, you're sexy.*

Isaiah playfully teased Gideon's hunger as he slid his soapy hands over parts of his own body. He couldn't decide what was sexier: Isaiah's shiny skin coated with foamy soap or the way the water made his skin glisten as he rinsed off. Isaiah's unbelievably gorgeous six-foot frame and broad shoulders took up most of the shower enclosure. In more ways than one, he was easily the largest man that he'd ever been with. The thought of letting Isaiah fuck him right here, right now, in the shower excited him.

When Isaiah was done rinsing off, he shook the water from his ears. "What do you say we get out of here and you let me make love to you?" He pulled back the shower curtain and waited for Gideon to step out first.

After drying off, naked, the two raced to the master bedroom. Isaiah lay him down on the bed.

Gideon took a deep breath and exhaled as he watched Isaiah climb on the bed. He knew what was to come, and he wanted it more than anything.

Isaiah stretched out on his side against him and kissed him. His hands, as gentle as a feather, traced the length of Gideon's side and then across his abdomen.

As the tips of his fingers scrolled over Gideon's bellybutton, Gideon gasped, sucking air into his lungs as his abdominal muscles tightened.

Isaiah landed a kiss, and then another, before moving on top of him.

"Mmm… You feel so good." Gideon squirmed under the weight of Isaiah as they kissed. The friction of their bodies rubbing against each other caused Gideon to moan louder.

Isaiah stopped kissing him, his lips inches from Gideon's. "You okay?" he asked. He stared into Gideon's eyes.

Unable to speak, it was as if he had no voice. Gideon nodded. *Kiss me.*

"You have the most beautiful blue eyes I've ever seen." Isaiah's voice was low and husky. "It's like looking at a sapphire as light shines through it, specks of blue that flicker in different shades. Sometimes… I can't stop looking at them."

"I can't stop looking at you." Gideon found his voice but didn't want to talk. He wanted Isaiah's lips back on him. He hungered for them. Heat radiated from Isaiah's erection as it lay against Gideon's thigh.

Isaiah kissed him again. The tips of his fingers skimmed up Gideon's side and then across his chest to trace over his nipple. He kissed Gideon's shoulder, then traveled over his chest with soft kisses, and then moved up his neck.

"Yes... That's it—" Gideon rolled his neck, the sensation of Isaiah's kisses, his warm lips, it was maddening. Gideon released a series of low incoherent mews as he once again absorbed the weight of his lover.

After a few minutes, Isaiah eased up and looked into Gideon's eyes.

What? Gideon stared into Isaiah's smoky eyes that were at half-mast. He saw the hunger in them. He knew what Isaiah was asking. "I want you." His voice shook as he maneuvered out from under Isaiah a little, enough to reach across the bed and into his nightstand. He pulled out his lube and then a box of condoms.

Isaiah sat on his heels on the bed between Gideon's legs. With the lube, he slowly and gently prepared Gideon.

On his back, Gideon trembled with a mix of anticipation and concern as he stared at Isaiah's erection. It was twice the size of Johnson. He tried to focus on the tantalizing sensation of Isaiah's warm fingers as they caressed and stretched the ring of muscles in his ass.

When Gideon was ready, Isaiah rolled a condom on and moved in closer between Gideon's legs. Skin to skin, he bore down a little, but even that was too much. The stretch burned as pain shot up Gideon's spine and his abdominal muscles clenched.

It might not be possible to take him. This was disappointing... Another wave of pain hit him. *No. it was definitely not happening!* "Stop." Gideon eased his ass away from Isaiah. He forced air down into his lungs, trying to recover from the intense pain in his gut.

"Are you okay? I'm sorry." Isaiah sat back on his heels.

"Yes." Gideon could barely breathe. *Fuck, that hurt.*

Isaiah stared at him.

"Give me a moment." Gideon was nowhere close to accepting defeat. He wanted it. After a minute, the pain began to subside in his ass and gut. He took a deep breath.

Isaiah stared at him. As still as a sleeping sloth, he looked like a kid about to be scolded by his mother.

Within a few breaths, Gideon was ready to try again. "Okay. Let's try this again. Come on." He scooted his ass closer to Isaiah.

Isaiah pressed the tip of his cock against his ass. Gideon inhaled as Isaiah barely eased a little inside of him. With an exhale, he felt Isaiah move a bit more into him. *Come on. Give me that fucker.*

Never breaking eye contact with each other, Isaiah sunk deep into him.

Gideon's eyes slammed shut as the fullness devoured every conscious thought for a second. The reach of Isaiah's member felt beyond the muscles in Gideon's ass. The warm flesh boring into him, the sensation, it was overpowering. Through several large breaths, Gideon pumped air down into his lungs.

Isaiah's breathing matched his thrusts as he moved inside of Gideon. He felt the moment his body adjusted to the mass of Isaiah, and the pain turning to flames of desire spreading like wildfire within him. The intensity of each of Isaiah's thrust, gradually increasing over time, moved Gideon closer and closer to the edge of ecstasy.

Gideon cried out in the darkness of the room, "Oh my God!" as endorphins flew and Isaiah took him over the edge. His moans echoed off the walls of the small room that contained them. He was in a full onslaught of an orgasm when Isaiah's grunts began to match that of a raging bull. Consumed in his own rapture, Gideon heard the cry of release from Isaiah as his body stiffened.

When it was over, their damp bodies lay still, crossways in the bed, pillows, and sheets on the floor. The sound of an occasional car passing, the low hum of white noise emanating from something— somewhere in the house was the only thing Gideon focused on.

Bodies barely touching, Isaiah entwined his fingers with Gideon's.

They lay on their backs as Gideon listened to Isaiah's breath returned to normal. Gideon was completely satisfied, that was until Isaiah rolled over and wrapped an arm around him. Yes... *now* he was completely satisfied.

"That was nice," Isaiah said as he pulled Gideon closer.

"That was way better than nice." Gideon wiggled his toes, still trying to expel some of his energy. Isaiah had made love to Gideon like no one ever had. Slowly and tenderly, he'd taken Gideon on a voyage to heights Gideon hadn't known existed until each moment arrived. He'd known Isaiah all of three weeks, and yet, it felt like a lifetime. He barely remembered life before Isaiah. Everything he thought about involved Isaiah; their dates, the meals they shared, their hikes, just talking for hours about nothing. Their sex had been amazing, some of the best sex he'd had, but this, what just happened, went way beyond sex. They made love this evening.

We made love. He released a slow, quiet sigh. His heart pinged. He wasn't just having fun with Isaiah. He was in love with him.

It's too soon... No, it's not. He didn't want to argue with himself. He could be in love if he wanted to be. His heart even backed up his claim. He'd never felt this way about anyone, not even Shawn. There was nothing he didn't love about Isaiah. He thought about it; *nope, not a single thing.*

Chapter 16

Gideon stood at the kitchen sink, drinking his coffee. In his underwear, he stared out the window, past the dark carport, at Daisy's house as he thought about how her son had made love to him last night. Every so often, the muscles in his butt twitched. His ass was raw, and he loved the visceral reminder of last night. Isaiah had pounded his ass so hard; he wasn't sure what he wanted more, round two or an apology. The thought of it stole his breath, as well as his heart.

It was surreal how the universe worked. Meeting Shawn, traveling to California, physically moving into this house because he and Shawn had broken up, becoming friends with Daisy, meeting her son Isaiah... and now he was in love, only to end up moving away. His spirits fell with the thought of leaving.

How could he make this work? He could go home and simply tell his parents he wanted to move to California. His stomach knotted at the thought of disappointing his father. He could just not go home. That would be easier, but how could he just abandon his parents like that? His life really was in Costa Rica. The only thing here was this house... *and now,* the love of his life. Isaiah could move to Costa Rica. *Would he?* This caused an immediate adrenaline rush, but it was short-lived. Isaiah's home was here. He took a deep breath and exhaled.

"Good morning." Isaiah slogged into the kitchen in his underwear. He walked up behind Gideon and kissed him on the back of his neck. "How are you doing?"

"I slept like a baby." Gideon savored the kiss from his sleepy lover.

"Coffee ready?" Isaiah asked before kissing him again.

"I'll make you a cup." He bent his head, giving Isaiah more to work with.

"Thanks." Isaiah landed several more kisses before patting Gideon on the ass.

"Ugh! Still a little sore." Gideon tucked his ass under him as he set up his little brewer to brew Isaiah's coffee.

"Are you okay?"

"Oh yeah. Just been awhile." A tiny laugh escaped Gideon. "Last night, when I watched you put on that condom, I was like, there is no way that's going to fit in my ass." Gideon hesitated with what he was about to say, unsure if it would sound wrong. "I hate that I'll never be able to feel you without a condom, though." *I'm leaving, and we'll never be a real couple.*

"You mean because you're positive?"

"Yeah." He would go with that. It was easier than the truth for some reason. He pushed BREW to start Isaiah's coffee.

"Puppy, not wanting to contract HIV is not the only reason someone should suit up. There are other STDs as well, you know."

"I know." Gideon cringed inwardly, embarrassed that he'd stepped into a conversation that he hadn't intended on having. He wasn't stupid; he knew there were other STDs. Of course, condoms protected people from more than just HIV.

"Just curious, why do you not like using condoms?" Isaiah's brows drew together as he held his stare.

Gideon's thoughts were scrambled for a second as he stared into Isaiah's beautiful eyes. "I don't like the way they feel. It feels so much nicer bareback." The few times he had had sex without a condom, he'd consciously known he was taking the risk of contracting HIV, and yet, at the time, he rarely gave any of the other STDs any thought, as if those didn't apply to him. He wondered why in the hell that was, how that thinking came about.

"I've never had sex without a condom." Isaiah leaned back against the counter.

"Really?" Gideon suppressed a laugh; it really wasn't funny— nor were some of his other choices in life. The news that Isaiah had never had sex without a condom made him feel suddenly stupid. It was time to grow up and make better, more responsible choices. He wanted to be the man he thought Isaiah was seeing in him. In a moment of enlightenment, he remembered what his mother had once said to him: that once you've been awakened to something, it can't be undone. He relished the moment of growth that just occurred within him.

Isaiah wrapped an arm around Gideon's waist and pulled him back up into his body. "Last night was amazing, condom or not, it was simply one of the best nights of my life." He nuzzled Gideon's shoulder.

Gideon moaned.

"I might have to get you a gag. I'm sure my mother heard you, as well as the rest of the neighbors."

"I wasn't that loud." He broke from Isaiah's arms to retrieve Isaiah's mug out from the brewer and handed him a half cup of coffee.

"Thanks." Isaiah looked down into the cup. "Yes, you were." He took a sip. "I'm surprised the cops didn't come by to do a welfare check."

"Well, you won't have to worry about it in three weeks. I'll be gone." Gideon shocked himself with what he'd just said. He didn't mean it in a mean way. How *did* he mean it? He didn't know. The frown on Isaiah's face said he needed to clean it up somehow. "I mean… it's just that I'll be gone in a few weeks."

"And you don't think I remember that? It's all I thought about this last week." Isaiah sat his mug on the counter. He pulled Gideon by the waistband of his underwear closer to him. "You really think I wouldn't miss this?" He slid his hands down into the back of Gideon's underwear and held his tender ass in his hands.

"Mmm." Isaiah's hands on his butt felt so nice, even if it was still a little sensitive. His body responded immediately to the touch. "Oh? You're just going to miss my ass?" Gideon laughed as he playfully, but not really, attempted to wiggle out from Isaiah's grip.

"How about if I come by after training, cook dinner, and I can show you again just how much I'm going to miss you?" Isaiah held on to him, not letting him escape.

"Don't you have to study or something like that?" Gideon wiggled a little more.

Isaiah hung on to him. "Yeah." He planted a kiss on Gideon. "But I'm sure I'll be done before you get home." He finally released him. With their faces inches apart, Isaiah rubbed under Gideon's eye. "You have an eyelash." He held it out on the tip of his finger. "Make a wish."

"Make a wish?" Gideon didn't believe in wishes. Life wasn't a freakin' fairy tale with magical wishes. "Don't be silly."

"Come on! You've never done this? Make a wish!"

Gideon looked down at the eyelash. "No. Never heard of it."

"Geez, my sweet jungle boy has lived a sheltered life. My grandmother used to say it's like wishing on a star."

Gideon closed his eyes and blew the eyelash off Isaiah's finger.

"Nooo! You're not supposed to blow it!" Isaiah stared at where the eyelash had been but was now gone. "You were supposed to make a wish, and then I was supposed to throw it over my shoulder. If it leaves my hand, then your wish would have come true."

"Well, it's gone, so I should get my wish."

"That's not the way it works. You can't change an eighteenth-century Irish ritual."

Gideon shrugged. "We'll see about that. Do you want to know what I wished for?"

"No. You have to keep it a secret until it comes true."

"I'll tell you." *I want you to fall in love with me. Tell me you love me.* As if telling Isaiah would help to ensure this would happen.

"Puppy, let the magic work." Isaiah softly kissed him. "What time do you think you'll be home this evening?"

But I want to tell you. He thought of his wish. He had little faith that an eighteenth-century Irish ritual of wishing on a dumb eyelash could make it happen. What he could have was another kiss. "Maybe around seven?" He took what he thought would be another quick kiss, but Isaiah pulled him into his arms as his tongue sunk into his mouth. The kiss deepened immediately as Gideon leaned in and enjoyed the impromptu make-out session. It was a couple of minutes when they finally came up for air.

"You better be glad I have training." Isaiah licked his lips.

I wish you didn't. "Go home. You've got to shower, or you'll be late," he ordered, as he shielded his erection by turning around towards the coffee pot.

Isaiah was right behind him. "I'm coming back for this." He reached down into the front of Gideon's underwear and took ahold of him.

So, he did see it.

*****

From the bedroom, Gideon heard Isaiah's car leave about twenty minutes later. *Wow, not only was Isaiah fast, but these walls were really thin.* Embarrassed, he wondered if Daisy or the other neighbors had heard them. If they could, he wasn't to blame; it was Isaiah's fault.

A couple of hours into his morning, Gideon was ready to head out for his first job of the day when he heard his phone buzz. He grabbed the phone off his nightstand and saw that it was his brother. "What's up?"

"Hey, Dick Breath!" Andrew said. "How come you didn't text me back yesterday? Mom wanted me to find out what day you're coming in."

"I told her the end of the month." He'd forgotten to text his brother his flight plans. "Hold on. Let me find my flight plan, and I'll send it to you." Irritated that his brother's call was a reminder that he was actually leaving, he went through his phone looking for the information. He'd bought the ticket a week prior to meeting Isaiah. His breathing slowed at the heaviness of what he was doing. Yes, he was leaving.

"What's going on there?" Andrew broke their silence.

"Nothing." Gideon brushed off the question as he located his confirmation. "I'm coming in on the nineteenth. It's a Thursday, at six-forty-three." His stomach churned—that was only two-and-a-half weeks from now.

"Okay. I'm picking you up. Damn, I wish we could hang out in San Jose, but I have to work at Blue Fin on Friday, so we'll have to head straight back."

"That's cool. I'll probably be too tired to want to do anything anyway."

"I kind of wanted to introduce you to someone. Samantha."

"Who's Samantha?"

"She's a girl I met two months ago. She came down the river. She and her co-workers stayed here."

You have a girlfriend? And you wanted me to meet her? This made Gideon smile that he wanted his big brother's approval.

"She's super cool. She's a secretary. Lives in San Jose." Andrew cleared his throat. "Man, I think I'm in love with her."

"Good for you." Gideon had never heard Andrew say he was in love with any girl. In fact, Andrew was as secretive about his hook-ups as Gideon was.

"Mom and Dad don't know. I was kind of wanting to introduce you first. That's why I wanted you to meet her when I picked you up."

"Why can't I meet her after you pick me up? The three of us can do dinner before we head home."

"I guess we can do that." Andrew exhaled. "I'll see what time she gets off. Maybe she could meet us somewhere. So, what's going on with you? You hooking up with anyone?"

Gideon hadn't had any plans on telling his brother about Isaiah; there was no reason to. They were just hanging out. What he really wanted to share with him was that he, too, was in love. Andrew had never had any judgment on Gideon's sexuality; in fact, he'd often teased Gideon when he'd caught him checking out the guests. He'd been with Isaiah for less time than Andrew and Samantha had been, and Andrew sounded confident that he loved her. He and Isaiah had only known each other for a month, but, for the last fourteen days, they'd practically lived together. "I've sort of met someone, too. My neighbor. Actually, his mother's my neighbor. He's been in the military for the last few years and moved back home last month."

"What's his name?"

Gideon shook his head. He hadn't mentioned Isaiah's name—that whole secretive, gender-neutral way of talking about yourself. "Isaiah."

"Cool."

"I think I might be in love, too." His breath hitched as he waited for Andrew's reaction to confirm it was too soon to be in love.

"If you're in love with this guy, why in the hell are you coming back here?"

"Because I live there. And… I don't know how he feels about me." That was a partial lie—he just didn't know if Isaiah loved him. Isaiah had been clear in the beginning that he hadn't been looking for a relationship. They were "just having fun," as he'd put it.

"But you have actually met him, right? He knows you exist?" Andrew laughed.

"Yes, we've met, and, yes, he's into me, too. We've been dating for the last month."

"If you guys are all hot and heavy, puffing on the other's cigar, I don't get why you're coming home?"

"Because Dad can't do it by himself... And if you're leaving to go work for Blue Fin, what are my options?"

"Bro, they need to figure that out for themselves. Dad's not your kid. They're not your responsibility, and, at some point, you got to let go of Mom's tit."

Gideon's jaw tightened. Not because it was messed up to say, but because it was true. As the oldest, Gideon was also the responsible one, the one who did everything according to Mom and Dad. Andrew did the opposite and got away with everything.

"Gid. I know you ran away chasing some dude. Stay there if that's what makes you happy."

I didn't run away... "I didn't come out here for some dude." *How the hell does he know about Shawn?* "I came here to fix the house."

"Okay. Whatever."

Gideon heard the sarcasm in Andrew's voice. But saying any more just added to the lie he'd created. He let out a harsh breath. *Jesus. I don't want to run the fucking lodge. I'm in love, and I want to stay here. I want to be with Isaiah.*

This whole conversation was just too much. Gideon's brain fizzled, scrambling his thoughts. *Did I run away? Did I come out here to be with Shawn... or to get away?*

No, that's not true. I liked Shawn.

Was Andrew, right? He was so eager to believe everything Shawn had pitched to him, maybe because he needed it to be true, as the excuse for him leaving. He wasn't sure what was the lie and what was the truth anymore. His skin prickled as he stared at the wall. It felt as if the walls had shifted closer.

Nothing was making sense. Maybe he *was* running away. He didn't want to run the lodge. That was clear. Did *I use Shawn, the virus, the house, all as an excuse to get out of running the lodge? Damn. Am I using Isaiah as well? Noooo. I love him.*

"Where would I live if I stayed?"

"I don't know—in your car? With him? Figure it out."

"Is that why you took the job at Blue Fin and moving to San Jose, to be with her?" He couldn't believe he hadn't figured it out until now. San Jose was where Blue Fin picked up the groups that were going rafting. Andrew was moving to San Jose to be with his girl, not the job. How could he do the same? "I don't think I make enough to do it by myself."

"Then get a job." Andrew guffawed.

"I have a job." Sometimes Andrew irritated the shit out of him.

"Get a better job. Dude, you're making excuses. What's the issue?"

It made him mad that Andrew got the girl, the job, and out from under the lodge. "I don't want to run the lodge!"

"Oh… Do Mom and Dad know that?"

"No! And don't tell them." He regretted telling Andrew. He should have never said anything about Isaiah or the lodge. Why stay if all he and Isaiah were doing was having fun? Why should he stick around if that's all they're doing? Was he running from the lodge, or was he really in love with Isaiah? This conversation with his brother wasn't solving anything. He needed to have this conversation with Isaiah.

"I'll be there on the nineteenth. Just pick me up."

Chapter 17

It was almost three o'clock in the afternoon on Saturday when Isaiah and Gideon got the last fixtures in the master bathroom installed. They had been working all morning on the bathroom, and the only thing left was to grout the tile and caulk the sink and tub. Gideon could do that on his own sometime in the next couple of days. Right now, the plan was to shower and get out the door and start their beach date in Santa Monica.

While working this morning, there'd been so many times Gideon had wanted to blurt out, *I love you.* He was sure he was in love. Before meeting Isaiah, if someone would have asked him six months ago if he loved Shawn, he would have answered yes. But that was because he'd had no idea what true intimate love for another man actually felt like until now. He was never in love with Shawn. He was in love with the fantasy of being in love. His love for Isaiah was something completely different. He'd given it much thought over the last several days. This wasn't about the lodge or running away from it.

He finished getting dressed and walked to the kitchen, where he could see when Isaiah came out of his house. He was surprised that he'd showered and was ready before Isaiah. Within minutes, Isaiah walked out of his house wearing grey fitted pants and a dark blue polo.

Damn, he's fine. Gideon watched for a second before he started towards the kitchen door. The butterflies in his stomach made it painfully obvious that this had moved way beyond just having fun. He needed to talk to Isaiah about what he was feeling, tell him that he loved him. What was the worst that could happen?

I don't love you, Gideon. I thought we were just friends.

Yeah, that would be bad. Gideon tried to erase the thought from his brain as he met Isaiah in the carport.

"You ready?" Isaiah walked to the driver's side of his car.

"Yep. You look nice." Gideon forced a smile.

"Thank you. So do you." Isaiah smiled at him before getting in the car.

His conversation with Andrew yesterday plagued him—almost to the point of making him nauseous. *There's no way that I am using Isaiah as just another excuse to not go home? I love him.*

After leaving the house, Isaiah first drove him to the academy to show him around. They then drove to the Santa Monica boardwalk and the old yacht harbor. They strolled along a mile or so down Venice beach to the iconic Muscle Beach. There, they sat on the empty metal bleachers that faced the small fenced-in outdoor gym where three guys worked out together. Two looked to be in their mid-twenties and were massive, and the third was an older gentleman who looked a lot like Clint Eastwood. The old guy was tall and thin but looked to be in super shape. Though each of the bodybuilders made at least two of him, the old guy kept up with his counterparts. They were lifting such heavy weights, grunting, and making animalistic noises every time they completed a set. It was kind of fun to watch.

"Do you make all those funny sounds at the gym too?" Gideon asked as he admired the younger guys spotting the older guy as he bench pressed what looked to be more than Gideon weighed soaking wet. It wasn't the question he really wanted to ask, but he hadn't worked up the nerve yet to tell Isaiah how he was feeling, that he loved him.

Isaiah watched the bodybuilders. "No. I don't. These guys get a thrill at people watching them. They're showing off, being dramatic."

"Was Ronnie into the gym?" Although Gideon had no idea what Ronnie looked like, he pictured Isaiah in the gym working out with someone like the guys they were watching. He didn't think he was jealous of someone who wasn't in the picture anymore. More like curious as to what it was about Ronnie that Isaiah had been in love with.

"Yeah. We'd work out together a lot."

Gideon looked at the guys working out, envisioning they were Isaiah and Ronnie. "Can you believe I've never been to a gym?"

"Really?" A tiny bit of a grin crept to one side of Isaiah's face as he kept an eye on the bodybuilders. "I guess there's probably not a gym in the middle of the jungle." Isaiah leaned slightly, so his shoulder was touching Gideon's. "You don't need the gym anyway. I love your body."

The word *love* reverberated in Gideon's head. "Are you kidding? When I look in the mirror, I see someone who's kind of nice-looking, but I hate looking at my body. I have no shape and no ass." Gideon nodded to the bodybuilders. "I mean, look at their asses. They're huge!"

Isaiah arched an eyebrow. "I love your ass."

Heat rose to Gideon's cheeks. "I know you do. But I want a butt like yours, one that goes boom!"

"Well, you can lift weights until you're blue in the face, but you're not going to get an ass like mine. It's genetics. I get it from my momma." Isaiah stood and pulled his phone from his pocket.

"And exactly how is that fair?" Gideon looked at Isaiah's bulging crotch. As he envisioned what was behind that fabric, saliva pooled in his mouth.

"I know. Life sucks for the White male." Isaiah laughed as he moved his head closer to Gideon's. "Let me get a picture of us."

Gideon leaned in until their heads were almost touching.

Isaiah snapped a photo, then reviewed the picture before turning his full attention to Gideon. "When I first saw you—" His grin turned into a snort and then a laugh. "—I thought you were, like, twelve."

"Bullshit! I don't look twelve!" Although he couldn't deny that next to Isaiah, he felt like a scrawny kid.

"Okay, seriously, how tall are you?"

Gideon knew he wasn't going to win this one. "Five-six."

"How tall is your dad?"

"We're the same height, five-six."

"How about your mom?"

"My mom's the tallest." Gideon shrugged. "Maybe around five-seven. She might be a little taller." *We're all short.* Gideon studied the muscle mass of one of the bodybuilders. "My mom would love you." *...I love you.* "She always teases my dad when she sees someone who's tall and cute. I can't believe you thought I was Latino when we first met."

"It's your dark thick hair and your slim facial features. You just look Latino to me."

"Um, blue eyes?" Gideon raised his brows for Isaiah to look at his eyes.

"I know some Latinos who have blue eyes. Their skin is lighter than yours. Okay, and plus, your name... It's so biblical. I know a lot of Latinos who give their kids names from the bible."

"It is?" This was the first time Gideon heard that his name was biblical. His family didn't go to church.

"You've never heard of Gideon, the Great Warrior?"

"No. My dad's a huge Abraham Lincoln nerd. He named me after Gideon Welles."

"Who is Gideon Welles?" Isaiah's face scrunched.

"Come on. You, of all people, should know who he is. He was Abraham Lincoln's Secretary of the Navy." Gideon went on to tell Isaiah how Welles expanded the Navy almost tenfold and how he was praised as the person responsible for winning the Civil War.

"Man, you really are a geek, aren't you? I guess because my dad gave us all biblical names on purpose and thinking you were Latino... I just assumed that's who you were named after. If your dad's a history buff, how did your brother Andrew end up with such a modern name?"

"It's not that modern. He was named after President Andrew Johnson, Lincoln's vice president."

"I know who Andrew Johnson was, but thank you for that clarification." Isaiah laughed before leaning in.

Gideon was sure Isaiah was about to kiss him, so he was surprised when he stopped.

Isaiah looked at the guys working out and then back at Gideon. "Can I kiss you?"

The kiss was light, a little more than a peck, and yet it still took Gideon's breath away. He didn't believe he would ever get tired of Isaiah's kisses. "You know, that's the first time you've ever kissed me in public." *I love you...* The words lodged in his throat.

"No, it's not. I kissed you at the zoo and on our hike that day."

"But you've never kissed me in front of anybody."

"Well, that's because I've never dated anyone quite like you. I don't know how to explain it, but it's different. You make me want to be this more true-to-myself person."

"And I've never dated anyone like you either." Gideon hoped for another kiss from the gentlest, nicest man he'd ever dated.

"You mean Black?" Isaiah asked.

168

"Um, no… That's not what I was going to say…" Although he hadn't ever dated someone who was Black. "I thought we couldn't use the word Black anymore?" The conversation about race caused Gideon to straighten up.

"I don't mind it. It's a tricky one because, technically, I'm brown, but it's not offensive to me. I know some people who hate the word. You know what I do hate? When someone uses it as a descriptive when it's not relevant to what they're saying."

"What do you mean?"

"Like saying *the Black guy*, or *the Mexican woman*. If it's not relevant, why use it? I call you White, and you're not exactly White either, but I would never use the word to describe you unless it was important to the conversation."

Gideon wondered if he was guilty of that. If he'd done it, he certainly hadn't been trying to be offensive to anyone. Being White, living in Costa Rica where his skin tone clearly made him the minority… he was always aware that he was different, the outsider. He wondered if Isaiah felt like an outsider in his own country. That would suck. "What I was going to say was someone as hot as you, but still down to earth… it's like I got to meet the real you the minute we met."

"I'm not sure you did. I'm not sure I even know the real me."

"What do you mean?" This was a surprise to Gideon. Isaiah was as real as it got.

"Just that you're so comfortable about being gay. It's who you are, and you make no apologies for it… nor should you have to. I'm not as comfortable about it as you are, but I'm working on it."

Gideon didn't know how to be anything different. He'd never really struggled with his sexuality. If anything made him uncomfortable before being HIV positive, it was his small size. He always wanted to be taller.

Isaiah stood up. "It sucks that you're leaving."

"I know." *It sucks big time.* Gideon thought about what Andrew had said about him staying here. As much as he wanted to believe his little brother, Andrew was never right about anything. With Andrew gone, too, there was no way his dad could do it all. "My dad needs me to come back."

"I understand about his arthritis and needing help, but can't they hire someone to replace you?"

"No... Sure, when we have guests, we can bring someone in to replace Andrew. But I'm the one taking over the business."

"The business... that you don't want?"

Exactly. One day, when his dad couldn't work anymore, there would be nobody there to run it if he left. It was a family business. His uncle and parents worked hard to get it to what it was today. "We all can't leave. I'm the only one."

Isaiah nodded. He didn't say anything, but his stare told Gideon that he wasn't buying what Gideon was trying to sell.

"Are you ready for dinner?" Isaiah softly asked.

For dinner, they dined on the rooftop of Fiorello's on the Santa Monica Pier. In the low-lit dining room, overlooking the ocean, the full moon illuminated the white caps as they rolled toward shore.

Even in conversation, Gideon couldn't stop gazing into Isaiah's beautiful brown eyes as the light from the candle flickered in them. There was something about how Isaiah looked at him from the first day they'd met. It reminded him of how his parents looked at each other.

It was during dessert, as they shared a serving of rich and creamy tiramisu, that Gideon realized that he'd never been treated the way Isaiah spoiled him. Isaiah was in a league by himself. Yes, he was definitely in love with this man. *I love you* was now at the tip of his tongue. He was scared to death to say it first—or be the only one feeling it.

After dinner, the walk to the car was quiet. *Just say it. Tell him that you love him.* Gideon was deep in his head. He was in love. He didn't want to run the lodge. He didn't want to leave. It seemed as if he didn't get a say-so in any of it. How was any of this fair?

"You're awfully quiet. What's on your mind?" Isaiah asked just as they reached the car.

"Stuff." He was stuck. Isaiah knowing that he loved him, wouldn't change anything. He was still leaving. Then why tell him?

"Stuff? Do you want to talk about it?"

Gideon released a heavy sigh. "Not just yet."

In the car, Isaiah kissed him before starting the car and exiting the parking lot. At the light, Gideon sat quietly in the cabin as he stared at the man holding his hand. *I'm just going to say it... I love you... I don't care about anything else.*

When the light turned green, with the word about to come out of his mouth, out of the corner of his eye, he saw something moving as fast as a fireball roll toward the car. "I lo—"

The crashing of metal and glass was horrific, and the world spun uncontrollably for a second before the world went black.

*****

"Gideon... Gideon... Gideon," a voice whispered.

As Gideon opened his eyes, something sizzled like a kettle about to boil, and nothing looked familiar.

"Gideon... can you move?" Isaiah moaned. "We've got to get out of here."

Gideon had no idea where he was. Nothing was familiar. The windshield was shattered, with a large piece of it missing. He heard voices outside the car but couldn't see anyone. The car was on its side... They'd been in an accident. He was alive, and so was Isaiah.

"Gideon, we have to get out of here. Hold on, I'm going to undo your belt."

Gideon felt Isaiah pushing against him. Freed from his seatbelt, Isaiah was now pushing him up through the window frame.

As they made it to the sidewalk, sirens blared in the distance and, within seconds, police, fire, and medical were all on scene.

Little by little, life came back into focus for Gideon. Isaiah was holding something against Gideon's forehead. Was he injured? He felt a sharp pain, forcing his eyes shut.

"Sir... Sir! Let me take a look at you."

Through barely-opened eyes, Gideon saw someone move Isaiah out of the way as an unfamiliar pair of legs stood in front of him.

"What's your name?" the person asked him.

Gideon opened his eyes a little more, seeing that the young Hispanic man in front of him was wearing a blue uniform. He couldn't remember his own name for a second. "Gideon." It hurt to talk.

"Okay, Gideon, I'm Pete. You know what happened to you?"

"I think we were in an accident." Gideon looked at the street. Isaiah's new car was on its side in the middle of the intersection. There was a bright red pickup truck with its front end mangled and hood up. Yes, it was an accident. He tried to look up at Isaiah, but Pete held his head in place as his female partner handed him something out of their orange EMT case.

"Gideon, can you tell me what today is?" Pete asked.

Gideon thought for a second as the man dabbed something against his forehead. "I don't know." The man's hand in his face prevented him from seeing anything.

"That's fine." Pete continued working on him.

Gideon again tried to pull away from Pete to look for Isaiah. He didn't want anyone touching him. He wanted Isaiah. The female EMT rested her hand on Gideon's shoulder, preventing him from moving.

Gideon saw the latex gloves on the EMT's hands and then the blood on them. He was bleeding. "Please don't touch me!" Gideon tried again to pull away. "Please... Don't touch—"

Pete held onto Gideon's head. "Sir, are you under any medication, or do you have any medical condition I should know about?"

Gideon squirmed again. The EMT was making the pain unbearable. Worse, he was touching his blood.

"Gideon. Gideon, let him work on you. Hold still."

Gideon realized Isaiah was standing right there. *Medication? Why is he asking me about my medication?* If the EMT's knew the medication he was taking, it would reveal something so personal about him. Who was this person that he needed to bear his soul to, right here on the street, in front of a crowd of strangers standing around? He'd never shared his HIV status with anyone but his doctors... and Isaiah.

"We'd like to transport you to the hospital. Do you have a preference?" the female EMT asked.

This was all too much. It was happening too fast. He couldn't think. He didn't want to talk to these people. They were strangers; nor go to the hospital where his HIV status would have to be revealed. People he didn't know would be in contact with his blood. "No. I don't need to go!"

"Gideon, you have to go. You're going to need stitches on that. You have a head injury. They have to check you out." Isaiah squatted in front of him.

"I'm okay. Really." Just seeing Isaiah calmed him. He didn't need to go to the hospital.

Isaiah took Gideon's hand. "You've got a laceration that's going to need stitches to close it up."

Gideon again saw the blood on Pete's gloves. He had to be honest with the EMT. He had a right to know, so he quietly told him.

"Is that it?" Pete responded as if Gideon had told him aspirin.

Gideon nodded. "Yeah." He wondered about his blood on the glove. He'd been undetectable the last time he'd seen his doctor almost three months ago. There could be a chance the medication had stopped working since then. That's why they wanted to see him every three months for the first year.

Even with gloves, Gideon didn't like this guy touching his blood. He didn't want anyone touching any part of him.

After a cervical spine collar was placed around his neck, he was loaded in the back of the ambulance. The male EMT entered the back with him, as the female EMT shut the door and jumped into the driver's seat. He could hear her calling in that they were en route to U.C.L.A. Medical Center.

Though it hurt to talk, Gideon didn't want to go to the hospital. It was just a cut on his head. "It's really okay. You don't have to do this."

"Do what, sir? Transport you to the hospital?" Pete sat next to him.

"It just makes me nervous. My blood and all."

"How's your meds working?"

Pete's question sounded more genuine than gathering data. "Good. I'm undetectable."

"Congratulations." Pete continued working on the laceration.

"Thank you." Gideon wondered if the guy was gay too. Was that really why the guy knew what he was talking about? He told someone that he was HIV positive and the world didn't end. He was proud that he was healthy and could share that as well. He released a low sigh, realizing that he was less embarrassed and proud of his undetectable status.

"You're going to be just fine." The EMT placed his hand across Gideon's chest.

I'm going to be fine. And then, in a breath, he remembered. In all of the chaos of the accident, he'd forgotten what it was that he was about to tell Isaiah. It killed him that Isaiah wasn't here. That he couldn't tell him that he loved him. They'd left him back there. How on earth did that happen? Everything in him told him to get up. He had to get out of this van. He had to tell Isaiah that he loved him.

Chapter 18

They hadn't left the hospital until almost two this morning. Isaiah had told the doctors he was a cop and knew the signs to look out for in case Gideon had a concussion. Somehow, Isaiah managed to walk away from the accident with little more than a cut across his knuckles, which had been a relief when he'd called his mother to tell her what had happened and where they were. By the time he'd gotten Gideon settled in bed, it'd been after three a.m.

He lay next to Gideon, thinking about how frightened Gideon had been sitting on the curb.

He gently brushed his hand over Gideon's hair. He wanted him to sleep as long as he could. The bandage over Gideon's right eye didn't cover the entire massive lump on his forehead. The poor guy looked like someone had inserted an egg under his skin, and yet, he still looked like an angel sleeping.

Even if Gideon were to stay, was now a good time to be thinking about trying to have another relationship with someone? With all that he had on his plate right now, the academy being his number one priority, that should be his sole focus. It wasn't, Gideon was, and he was leaving.

He thought about going with him to Costa Rica. What if he offered to go with him, help them with the lodge? He would be Andrew's replacement. That would be an easy fix. Isaiah pondered this possibility, wavering back and forth on how ridiculous the plan was. He loved being a cop and really wanted the future he'd worked so hard at building. It was crazy to abandon everything he worked for, for a guy you've only known for a month. He liked Gideon a lot, so much so that he was lying here contemplating giving up everything. This was crazy.

God, how did I get into this situation? Would I really give it all up for love? Could I?

He never again wanted to love someone who didn't love him just as much. Although neither he nor Gideon had declared their undying love for the other, Gideon did excite him. When he was with Gideon, he was reminded of that thirst for life.

He and Gideon had a lot in common: they both wanted a committed relationship at some point, they were both adventurous and spontaneous, and they loved their families. Gideon was also smart, spoke Spanish fluently, a nature buff who knew his wildlife, creative and industrious, and from what Isaiah could tell, able to build anything he set his mind to… and above all else, Gideon was as cute as a freaking puppy.

It didn't seem so important that he didn't know that Bush had been president before Obama, or that he didn't know anything about quinoa, or that he was naïve about many things—things that could have cost him his life. Gideon was the kind of person who would figure it out, adjust and adapt, capable of correcting a wrong. *Could you really give up everything for him*? It seemed ridiculous, and yet he wasn't ready to dismiss the possibility.

Gideon stirred, stretched, and then opened his eyes.

"Ugh." Gideon ran a hand over his bandage. "Is it as big as it feels?"

"Worse, Puppy. You don't want to know." Isaiah brushed the strands of hair from in front of Gideon's face. "Do you want a painkiller? They sent a couple home with you."

Gideon closed his eyes for a second. "Not yet. How are you feeling?"

"I'm a little stiff, but okay. Are you hungry?" Relieved that Gideon was awake and not in much discomfort, Isaiah brushed his hand across Gideon's cheeks.

"For what?"

Gideon frowned at him. He knew precisely what Gideon was thinking. "No, not for sex." He removed his hand from Gideon's face. "Pancakes, you fool. Mom texted and said she'll make us breakfast when we get up since we're not going to church." Isaiah couldn't resist touching him, this time stroking his hair. It was still amazing how soft his hair was. And it always smelled like mint and rosemary.

"Oh good. I was hoping you were talking about food. I'm starving. But, first, I need coffee and a shower."

"I'll get you some coffee." Isaiah got out of bed. "Let me pee first?"

Gideon crawled out of bed. "Don't pee on my new floor in there."

"I'm a guy. That's what we do." Isaiah walked into the bathroom.

"I can get my own coffee."

Isaiah's neck was stiff, and his lower body felt as if he'd been hit by a truck… oh yeah, he *had* been hit by a truck.

*****

By the time they got to his mother's, she had a plate of pancakes on the table and was frying sausage patties and potatoes. She stopped what she was doing to tend to Gideon, ensuring he could sit okay, as she fussed over him as if he'd just returned from war.

"You want some eggs?" she asked Gideon in the same tender voice one would use as if talking to an infant.

Isaiah answered first. "Yeah."

She held the spatula as if it was a weapon. He knew the look she was giving him. He probably should have let Gideon answer her first.

"Yes, please." Gideon inhaled the aroma of the frying potatoes.

"Can you scramble them? Four for me." Isaiah asked, knowing if he didn't, she would fry them.

"Honey, how would you like your eggs?" she asked Gideon, as she rolled her eyes at Isaiah.

"What? What the hell did I do?" Isaiah tried to think of why she was mad at him.

"You know what you did! What did I tell you about those tinted windows on that car? You can't see nothing. Did you even see that truck?" Daisy slammed a hand on her hip.

Are you kidding me? "Mom, the truck ran the damn light. It wasn't my fault," *Are you really blaming me for this?*

Daisy retrieved the carafe. "Coffee?"

"Yes." They both answered at the same time.

She poured coffee into a mug and handed it to Gideon. "Cream or sugar, Sweetheart?"

"No, thank you. I like it black." Gideon arched an eyebrow as he looked at Isaiah.

I know you do. Not wanting his mother to catch Gideon's double

176

meaning, Isaiah sheepishly grinned at Gideon, whose cheeks were blushing. *You're being naughty... and I like it.* He was sure they were reading each other's minds. Damn, was he cute, even with that big ass knot on his head.

Daisy looked at the stitches and the knot on Gideon's forehead and shook her head. "Go on and start before it gets cold. Potatoes are almost ready."

Isaiah grabbed two pancakes first, and Gideon took four. Gideon coated his pancakes with butter and then flooded them with syrup.

"I see you like a lot of butter on your cakes." Again, Isaiah grinned at his naughty connotation. It was surreal that he was sitting in the house he was raised in, at the breakfast table, with his boyfriend... *Boyfriend?*

Isaiah couldn't get the word out of his head. *He's not my boyfriend. You need to have the boyfriend talk first before you can declare someone as your boyfriend.* They hadn't had that talk. He realized just how crazy his notion of moving to Costa Rica really was. *He's not even your boyfriend.* He looked at Gideon. *I can't believe you're leaving. I don't want you to leave.*

As they ate through the stack of pancakes, Daisy brought over the sausage, putting the plate in the middle of the circular table. After that came their eggs and the fried potatoes with onions. Once everything was on the table, Daisy sat down with them.

Isaiah told her the details of their accident and emergency room visit. At times, he was surprised at the parts Gideon said he didn't remember. He was so glad he was there to get Gideon out of the car and there with him when the EMT's were there. It felt as if the hours they spent in the E.R. was a bonding experience. The doctors and the nurses treated them as a couple and were great at their jobs. They had their first crisis together, and as bad as it was, he wouldn't undo it. He glanced at his mother and then at Gideon. Even though the knot on Gideon's forehead was covered by a bandage, Isaiah's breath took a hiatus as reality smacked him in the face.

He was in love with this guy, and he could have lost him last night.

"I'm so glad you two are all right." Daisy's gaze lingered on both of them.

Isaiah wondered what she was smiling about. It was suspicious.

"I used to worry about you, Isaiah. All them diseases and things out there. The minute I met you, Gideon, I knew you two would be perfect for each other."

"Mom!" Isaiah's heart leaped in his chest. *Did you really just say that in front of Gideon?* He looked at Gideon, who had the deer in the headlight look. He tried to imagine what Gideon was thinking. Isaiah looked back at his mother. *All those diseases? Really?*

Oblivious, his mom took a sip of her coffee.

I can't believe you said that. He thought of something to say, to erase the awkwardness at the table. "In a half-hour, Elijah's coming over to take me to the rental car place. I need to take care of that today because I won't have time in the morning before training. Do you mind keeping an eye on Gideon while I'm gone?" *I'm not sure that's even a good idea after what you just said.* He regretted asking.

"Sure," his mom answered.

"I don't need anyone to take care of me. I'm fine," Gideon chimed in. "In fact, I'm going back now to rest." Gideon scooted back from the table.

"You need help?" Isaiah tried to get a read on Gideon to see if he'd been hurt by his mom's words.

"No. I'm good." Gideon's downward smile said differently.

"Call me Honey, if you need anything." She sipped at her coffee.

Gideon walked out the kitchen door. Silence fell between Isaiah and his mother as they sat at the table. Isaiah debated with saying something to his mother about Gideon or staying quiet. He couldn't be angry at her. How was she supposed to know? But still, why would someone say that? Gideon's story wasn't his to tell, and he didn't have Gideon's permission, but he didn't want Gideon to be hurt by what his family might say because of their own ignorance. The fear he'd seen in Gideon's eyes yesterday after the accident, he never wanted Gideon to feel that way again. He wanted to protect him from anything that might be coming his way, and that included his family, especially Josiah and his racist views. He was in love with Gideon.

"What's on your mind, son?"

"What do you mean?" he asked.

"I can see it on your forehead. It's all frowned up. You're stressing about something. Is it him?"

"Mom, this thing with Gideon and me… It's serious. I'm really liking him." Isaiah drew a breath. He would have to ask Gideon for forgiveness instead of permission. By telling Gideon's story, she would know not to say that kind of shit anymore. He was protecting Gideon. "What I'm about to tell you is not for you to repeat, not even to Eli or Jo. Gideon is positive."

"Positive? Positive about what?"

Isaiah blew out an exasperated sigh. Of course, it wasn't going to be that easy. "He's HIV positive."

"Oh, Lord! Did you give it to him? Are you sick?" His mom made the sign of the cross over her chest. Her eyes were as wide as they could go.

"No, Mom. He's been positive for about a year."

"How'd he get it?" Her gaze swept over the plate and coffee cup Gideon had left at the table.

"That's not for me to say. One day, if he feels like it, he can share his story. I'm telling you, so you don't say something stupid again."

"What did I say?"

"Your comment about catching a disease."

"How was I supposed to know?"

"That's it. You *didn't* know."

"Well, I was kind of only joking." She rubbed her palm across the table.

"Yeah, and it was also kind of insensitive and not funny."

"Well, y'all ain't having sex… are you?"

Isaiah's brows rose. "That's actually none of your business, but I get why you're asking. As my mother, you're worried. Yes, we're having sex, and, yes, we're using condoms." He couldn't believe he was sitting at the breakfast table with his mother, talking about having sex with a guy and safe sex practices.

"Isaiah! Even condoms break! Ain't nothing truly safe anymore but abstinence. I know you kids think ain't nothing goin' to kill you, but this AIDS thing, it's killed a lot of people." His mom put a hand over her mouth as she sniffed. "I know I ain't ever said anything to you, but your father's brother—Uncle Paul—he died of this AIDS thing."

"He did?" Isaiah asked with a tilt of his head.

She pressed a hand to her throat. "Yes… He was gay too."

Isaiah's eyes popped wide. "Uncle Paul was gay?" He'd never met his uncle because he died years before Isaiah was born.

"He ain't ever said it. He lived in San Francisco when your father and I met. I only met him a couple of times. They weren't close. One day, before Paul died, I asked your father if he thought Paul was gay. Talk about a conversation stopper. Your father had a real problem with the gays. After you were born, I suspected that you might be gay when you were around eight or nine. I knew I had to do something with your father just in case you were. We had many fights over this gay thing."

This was the first Isaiah was hearing about any of this. It came as no shock that his father might have been homophobic, but hearing that his mom went to battle for him…. well, that was no shock either. "So how do you know Uncle Paul was gay? Just because he lived in San Francisco doesn't make him gay."

She stared at him, her face sour. "Boy, a woman knows these things. I ain't never said anything to your father, but when me and your Aunt Colette went to clean out Paul's apartment after he died, we found a whole lot of medication. I looked up some of them, and they were drugs for the AIDS."

It's not 'The AIDS,' but okay. "That doesn't make him gay." Isaiah could concede that his uncle might have died of AIDS based on the medication, but there were other ways of contracting the virus. Isaiah had never really given it much thought, but now it made sense since no one had ever talked about how Uncle Paul had died. Car accident, cancer, murder.

"Them stacks of nasty magazines and movies we found in the apartment was all the proof I needed to see. Even without them magazines, the pictures on the wall, the stuff we found under the bed… they left no doubt that a gay man lived in that apartment. To this day, I still don't know what some of that stuff was for." Mom shook her head. "He died alone. We knew Paul had been sick for years, but he kept his business private. It came as a shock to all of us when the news came that he'd passed that morning. Before your Uncle Paul died, I didn't know anything about AIDS except it was something that gay men caught and were dying from. But since I didn't know any gay men, I really didn't pay that much attention to it.

That was, until after your uncle died. I remember sitting in the doctor's office one morning. There was a magazine with several African American women on the cover. The headline read something like Black women were the second-highest group of people that the virus was killing. At first, I almost didn't pick up the magazine because I assumed the story was about lesbians. I don't know what made me pick it up; it was like those women on the cover were calling my name to read their stories. I recalled being shocked as I read the article that they were all straight, and there was this big percentage of them that had contracted the virus from their men. When I saw the number of how many people had died of AIDS and then read how little our government did to fight it in the beginning, all I could think about was your uncle dying without his family and how so many others probably died that same way."

Isaiah was shocked that the virus had hit so close to home, and he'd had no idea of it. "Mom, I get why you're worried." He understood her concern now, but things were so different than thirty years ago. "Mom..." Isaiah realized he was once again telling someone else's story, and maybe he shouldn't be. "He doesn't have AIDS. He tested positive for HIV, and it's not a death sentence anymore. People manage it with medication the same as you do with your high blood pressure and cholesterol. Studies show that I can't catch it from him because his levels are so low."

"Dear child, what does all that mean? Speak English. I ain't no doctor."

"It means that there is not enough of the virus in his blood—in his body—for him to transmit it to me. But even with that, we're still using precautions. So, if a condom breaks—" Isaiah tried to push past the visual of him inside of Gideon. "—there's not enough of the virus in him to give it to me." He exhaled a large breath. "Plus, I'm taking a drug called *PrEP*."

"Are you sick, too?" Worry shot across her face again.

"I'm not sick, and neither is Gideon. He's freaking healthier than you. *PrEP* is a pill, kind of like birth control. It's to prevent HIV like birth control does for pregnancy."

His mom stood in front of the table. "I'm not good with this AIDS thing. None of it. I don't see why you have to take medication for something you don't have."

He thought of ways to end this conversation and was relieved when he saw his brother's BMW pull into the carport. "Eli's here." Isaiah raised a brow. "Don't. Say. A. Word!" He stared at her ensuring she knew he meant it.

Isaiah stood. "In two weeks, you won't have to worry about it."

Two weeks. Isaiah realized the reality of his words. He'd never actually forgotten it; he'd just refused to think about it. By saying it out loud to his mother made it a reality that he could no longer ignore.

"In two weeks, Mom." He swallowed hard, pushing down the lump that had formed in his throat. "I'll be losing the love of my life, not by disease or to a car accident, but to life circumstances. That's what I'm thinking about… not about all this other stuff."

*****

When Isaiah returned from picking up his rental car, he first went to check in on Gideon. He'd been thinking of his earlier conversation with his mom, as well as about how Gideon had reacted to the EMT touching him and having to go to the hospital. He couldn't believe he told her he was in love with Gideon. He needed to tell Gideon as well. There was a lot that they needed to talk about if he was seriously considering moving to Costa Rica. He needed to know how Gideon felt about him as well.

He felt horrible about sharing Gideon's status with her without Gideon's consent. So first, he needed to tell Gideon what he'd done, tell him that someone else now knew he was positive.

He wanted to understand specifically Gideon's fear with the EMT and going to the hospital. Gideon was so comfortable about being out, it didn't make sense. Was it going to the hospital? That at least made sense. Lots of people hate hospitals.

He found Gideon in the bedroom. "Hey. How are you feeling?" Isaiah sat on the edge of the mattress.

Gideon scooted closer and set his head in Isaiah's lap. "Just tired."

"Do you feel like talking for a second?"

Gideon raised his head. "I don't like the sound of that. About what?"

Isaiah brushed Gideon's hair from the side of his face and tucked it behind his ear. "You seemed a little nervous with the EMT yesterday. I'd like to know what happened? But first, I have to tell you what I did." Isaiah wished he could stand, but he didn't want Gideon to have to move.

The muscles in Gideon's face went rigid.

"Earlier, after you left the house, I told my mom you're positive."

Gideon's head nodded, but he never looked up. "…Okay."

"I didn't like that comment she'd made about catching diseases and stuff. I saw your reaction when she said it. At first, I was pissed that she'd said it, but then I realized that it wasn't what she'd actually *said* but how it affected you. It killed me seeing you hurt like that. I wanted to protect you. I didn't want anyone hurting you, especially one of my family members."

Gideon tilted his head slightly. "But, really, I didn't take it personally. I know your mom. She wouldn't have said it if she knew."

"Exactly. I didn't want her to ever do it again, so I said something to her about it."

"And? How'd she take it?"

Isaiah thought for a second about what and how much to say. "She had questions. She's not that knowledgeable on HIV and all of that. We talked, and I told her about the medication and how well it was working."

"Was she afraid I'd give it to you?" Gideon said into Isaiah's lap.

"Sort of. At first. Apparently, my uncle…" Isaiah realized what he was about to say. He cleared his throat and continued. "I'm sure she'll have more questions for me, but she's good." At least he hoped she was. "What about you? Why were you so nervous with the EMT yesterday?"

Gideon sat up and brushed the hair out of his face. "I was embarrassed. Being HIV positive and stuff. I know he was doing his job when he asked me about my medicine. He had a right to know, but…" Gideon lay his head back into Isaiah's lap. "It's like I think they think of it like leprosy or something. That it's going to jump off of me and get them. Like I'm contaminated. But when I told him, he'd barely reacted. We talked about it in the ambulance. He actually congratulated me on being undetectable. He was nice."

Isaiah didn't expect that the EMTs wouldn't have been kind and professional. He knew Gideon wasn't that comfortable about sharing his status with people, but hearing that Gideon was terrified of people knowing, was surprising. Now it made sense—that feeling of being exposed. "I get it. I think it's like my fear of not wanting any of my homophobic superior officers—or my family, finding out that I'm gay."

Gideon looked down and then back up at Isaiah. "But that was your job, so I understand why you didn't want them to know about you."

"To some extent, but I also think that as gay men, we're experts at guarding our secrets, compartmentalizing different aspects of our life, letting the world believe the narrative we put forth." It was a protective mechanism that took on a life of its own at some point.

Gideon looked up at him. His blue eyes staring up at him like a puppy.

Isaiah tried to think back, as far as he could, for the moment that he realized he had to hide who he was. "Growing up, I'd heard the jokes from people who didn't know I was gay."

Gideon nodded. "I never heard any gay jokes or anything growing up. I knew I was different—gay, but it was never really a bad thing. But when I was diagnosed, for me, that was huge. Not only did I think I was going to die, but I thought that people wouldn't want me around because I could give it to them."

The image of his mom looking at Gideon's plate and coffee mug came to mind. He knew exactly what she was thinking when she was looking at it.

"I guess avoidance is an easier option than the truth. I especially couldn't tell my mom and dad that I was sick. They would think I was stupid for getting it."

You're not stupid. "I did the same thing. Every time weighing if I should say something. I guarded my secret growing up and all through my military career, only letting a few in, and always on my terms."

Gideon rubbed his hand up and down Isaiah's leg. "It's hard to want to educate someone if there's a chance they're going to reject you."

"If it were that easy, we wouldn't have to hide in the closet."

Now that he understood Gideon's fear a little more, it felt like a good time to discuss Josiah. "Truth?"

"Nothing but." Gideon looked up at him.

Isaiah smiled back at their little game. "Josiah and Tammy both have a real problem with the whole Gay thing. You and I are both going to Hell. And my brother," Isaiah shook his head, "is going to have a big issue with you being White."

"Really?" Gideon's face scrunched. "I never got that from him."

"That's because he didn't know we were kicking it. Trust me. He'll have a problem with it."

"What does *kicking it* mean?" Gideon's face sobered as he sat up on the bed.

A tiny laugh gave way under Isaiah's breath. "You've never heard of *kicking it*? It's like we're together, having sex."

Even with the giant knot on Gideon's forehead, Isaiah saw the frown across Gideon's forehead as he crawled out of bed.

"I have to pee." Gideon walked away.

The sudden change in Gideon's demeanor was strange. He wasn't quite sure exactly what it was that caused it. Was it because of what he said about Josiah or them going to Hell? Maybe he shouldn't have said anything. Or maybe Gideon was just tired. It had been a long day for the both of them. Isaiah thought he would just leave that conversation alone. He had so much more to tell him, starting with I love you.

Chapter 19

Gideon stood in the doorway between the bedroom and the bathroom as he stared at Isaiah. The love of his life, the person who seemed to have complicated his life, even more, was bent over drying his feet after his shower. Isaiah's strong back and muscles fanned out, accentuating his tapered waist and beautiful ass.

You're so beautiful... are we really only kicking it? I'm not. I'm in love with you. It hurt that they were, as Isaiah put it, kicking it. He'd been stewing over Isaiah's comment all evening to the point that he'd made himself sick.

Before the accident, he'd been about to tell Isaiah that he loved him. Either one of them could have died in that accident, and the words would have never been said. He was in love with this gorgeous naked man in front of him. He loved everything about him, every inch of his soul.

Gideon thought about what Andrew had said to him about not coming home, staying here if they were in love. Why shouldn't he go home if all Isaiah was doing was kicking it. To stick around only to be hurt again... He couldn't do it. The pain had taken too long to get over the last time; he didn't want to do that ever again.

The world was closing in on him *again*. His thoughts drifted back to the day he'd met Isaiah. The guy had taken his breath away. He could have never envisioned things would have worked out like they had, and so fast. From a simple meal they'd shared to this, to being in love with the guy. But why tell him that he was in love with him if all they were doing was kicking it? It seemed needy. Truth of the matter, it didn't matter. He was leaving. He resented the lodge with every passing day. No matter what he did, either he was going to hurt his parents or be the one who was miserable.

He stared at Isaiah's naked backside. He was as beautiful on the inside as he was on the outside. He'd never met a more caring and compassionate man. Yesterday, while sitting on the curb, he'd never been so shaken up in his life. Isaiah was his knight in shining armor, especially at the hospital. Just knowing Isaiah was with him, there by his side, he'd known he'd be all right.

He pushed out a large breath as he gathered the courage to speak. "What are we doing?" Gideon muttered almost to himself.

"What?" Isaiah turned around. "What's wrong, Puppy?" He raised a brow as he straightened, the towel dangling in front of him.

Gideon pushed off the doorway and walked into the bathroom. The look of concern on Isaiah's face said he'd read his mood; he saw it in Isaiah's eyes. He was never good at hiding his emotions, but now, he was good at reading Isaiah's.

I love you. He avoided Isaiah's stare to not give this away, looking, instead, around the bathroom he'd created. The only two people to ever step foot in it were he and Isaiah; it was *their* bathroom. He walked to the vanity and leaned against the gun-powder grey tiled countertop.

Gideon drew in a quiet breath. "When we met, we said we were just having fun… It doesn't feel like we're just having fun anymore." His pounding heart stopped him. *I love you.*

Isaiah hung the damp towel on the hook behind the door. He picked Gideon up, sat him on top of the counter, and then moved his naked body between Gideon's legs. He rested one hand on Gideon's thigh and brushed his hair out of his face with the other hand. "You need a damn haircut."

He stared into Isaiah's big brown eyes. The flecks of gold in them glittered in the light. *I love your eyes… I love you.* He fought off the tears. "Isaiah, what are we doing?" He was barely able to speak. His throat was closing up on him.

Isaiah's face went blank. "If you're asking what I think you're asking… I… I don't know, Puppy." The back of Isaiah's hand softly rubbed Gideon's cheek. "I've been asking myself the same question these past weeks. I don't want you to go. But I get it. Maybe I could come to visit you?"

Gideon cleared his throat, trying to force the words out. "I love you," Gideon blurted before he could stop himself. He wanted to turn from Isaiah but couldn't. He stared deeply into Isaiah's eyes as if they were a crystal ball about to reveal his future.

Isaiah's eyes softened, and his lips parted. "I love you, too." Isaiah never blinked as he stared at Gideon.

"You do?" Gideon's mouth fell open, and his breath hitched. *You just said you love me.* It took a second or two for it to sink in. He stared at Isaiah as it did. It was what he wanted, and now, it was as if he'd been completely blindsided by it. A tear swelled in his eye. *Don't cry.* His emotions were overpowering him. *Say something, so you don't cry.* "I thought for sure you were going to tell me that you didn't love me. That it was over."

"No." A faint snicker came from Isaiah. "I don't want it to be over. I want to be with you." He looked at Gideon's forehead before lightly touching around his wound. "I've been thinking… How would you feel if I wanted to move to Costa Rica?"

He was still processing that Isaiah had said he loved him. *Did you just say you want to move to Costa Rica?* He couldn't have heard that right. "Really?" *Hell yeah!* A second wave of adrenaline hit him. "You would really move there?" This was not the conversation he thought he would be having, not at all—an explosion of emotions and ideas of how this would look flooded his brain.

"I could work at the lodge and take Andrew's place. Then after your dad retires, we could run it together. Do all the things you want to make it your own, your dream."

You said make it my dream? The lodge had never been his dream. With or without Isaiah, that didn't change. Gideon pushed the thought aside. *Could this really work?* "But… but what about your training? Your mom? I thought you really wanted to be a cop?"

Isaiah moving to Costa Rica wasn't the answer. He didn't want to be tied down to the lodge. Day in, and day out, every single day. That would be his life, a life he didn't want. He wanted more. He couldn't ask Isaiah to leave his life for him, for something he didn't even want himself. "I can't ask you to do that." He felt nauseous again.

"You're not asking. I'm offering."

It didn't matter how great Isaiah's idea was. It wasn't the right answer. So much excitement and hope were gone just as quickly as it emerged. "Don't you want to be a cop?"

"I do. But I also don't want to lose you."

Isaiah's answer confirmed what he already knew. "You can't give up your dream… for me."

"Then we'll figure something else out." Isaiah leaned in and wrapped his arms around him. The sound of the clock on the wall ticked off the seconds as Gideon thought of returning home.

"Me leaving... why does it feel like the end of us?" Gideon asked.

"No. No. No. It's not the end, my Puppy. No, not even close," Isaiah said as he raised Gideon's chin. "I'm not letting you go that easy."

"This would be actually easier if we were just kicking it or having fun. But I fell in love with you."

"And I fell in love with you too. But I'm also having the time of my life with you. I might have fallen in love with you the day I met you. I admit I wasn't looking for love. In the beginning, yeah, neither of us was looking for this, but it happened anyway. Right?"

Gideon's mind raced. "So then, what are we going to do? I wish I could stay..."

"Baby, you're making that choice. If you don't want to run the lodge, then don't. Tell them it's not what you want. From everything you've told me about your parents, I don't see them resenting you for doing what you want. I don't see it."

Gideon lowered his chin again, avoiding Isaiah's stare. Hah. As if he *had* a choice. He didn't; he had to go home. There was no one to help his dad with Andrew leaving. Sure, if they had to, or wanted to like Isaiah had suggested, they could hire someone to help out, but that didn't solve the bigger issue of what would happen when his dad couldn't work anymore?

Gideon finally looked up at Isaiah. They gazed into each other's eyes. "Could you visit?"

"Of course, I can. As soon as I can get some time off, I'll be there. And if you have time off, I can fly you back here, even if it's only two or three days."

Gideon scoffed at how hard they worked, day in and day out. Even when guests weren't on the property, some things needed to be done. "We'll see." He didn't like the notion of a long-distance relationship either. How many times had he heard "*Let's stay in touch*"? That had never worked out, and, up until now, he'd been okay with past hook-ups dissolving naturally over time because of the distance.

"Gideon, look at me." Isaiah tilted Gideon's chin up. "We don't have to figure this whole thing out tonight. It will be all right." Isaiah smiled at him; the sadness in his eyes matched how Gideon was feeling.

A visit didn't seem like the answer. Gideon forced a smile back. "How long do you think it'll be before you can come?"

"I don't know. I imagine I won't get a vacation until after my first year. I'll still be on probation."

"A year?" Gideon hadn't expected that. He couldn't go a year without seeing him.

"But maybe I could get a couple days off at some point. Even if it's just my days off and one extra day, I'll come. What about Thanksgiving? The academy's closed that Thursday and Friday. I'll fly out Wednesday night. It's only four days—well, not even four days because I have to fly out on Sunday—but it's something. In two months, I'll be there. Would that work for you?" Isaiah's voice sounded as if he was pleading.

"I guess. It seems like it's the only option I have." Gideon thought about it. They rarely had guests Thanksgiving night, but the rest of the weekend was business as usual. He didn't know if it would work, but it would have to. It was only one visit, but it gave him something to cling to.

"Puppy, you can't please the world. You're a damn good handyman, but it's not your job to make everyone happy and fix everything that's broken in the world. You've got to learn to start telling people no if it's really important to you. If you don't, it will destroy you."

Everything Isaiah was saying was right. He needed to do better at saying no. He'd never thought that being nice was a bad thing. He tried to think of the last time he told someone no. "I just told you no—not to move to Costa Rica."

"But that's because you were trying to make me happy. You didn't want me to give up my dream of being a cop... Did you?"

Isaiah was right, yet again. Gideon didn't want to think anymore. He was worn-out and needed to sleep on everything they'd talked about.

Isaiah kissed him. "Don't be sad. Tonight, dream of how much I love you." Isaiah wrapped his arms around Gideon's butt. He nudged Gideon forward. "Let's go to bed."

Gideon eased his body off the counter. He trailed behind Isaiah as they walked into the bedroom and walked to their own sides of the bed.

Isaiah set his alarm on his phone. "I wish I didn't have training in the morning."

Gideon pulled the covers back. He wished that as well.

Wish...

"Oh my God." Gideon crawled into the bed. "I just remembered my eyelash wish. I wished that you would fall in love with me." He couldn't believe that it had worked. "I guess it worked."

The two met in the middle of the bed.

Isaiah pulled the covers over him. "Of course it did."

They kissed and then lay on their backs, looking up at the ceiling.

Gideon placed his hands behind his head. "*Buenas noches, mi amor.*"

"*Buenas noches,*" Isaiah replied.

As Gideon snuggled up against Isaiah, he smiled at how good Isaiah's Spanish was getting. He loved doing the flashcards with him. He closed his eyes and thought of his eyelash wish. Isaiah had confessed his love for him. His wish had come true, and yet it wasn't playing out like he envisioned. He was still leaving. Although he didn't have an eyelash, Gideon made another wish.

Chapter 20

With plans for a morning hike in the Angeles National Forest, Gideon was up early and getting their coffee going in the kitchen. He'd left Isaiah snoozing like a baby in the bed.

Gideon leaned against the kitchen counter and stared out the window as the coffee brewed. His gray baggy sweat pants hung low around his waist and pooled around his ankles and bare feet. He rubbed his bare chest, fighting off the urge to scratch at his stitches. Yesterday his stitches started itching really bad, reminding him of when he had Chickenpox when he was eight and had been told not to scratch. With most of the swelling down, the knot on his forehead was barely noticeable.

This was their last Saturday together, the last weekend, the last week they would have together. It was hard enough that the academy took so much time away from them, but then, with the car accident last week, Gideon felt as if time had been stolen from them.

With his flight on Thursday, he'd had planned to clear the house of all his belongings over these next few days. He had to downsize the last eleven months into one suitcase.

The sparse furnishings in the house was the easy part. He was donating all of it. But all his tools and left-over scraps from projects jammed into the shed in the backyard were a different story. He was happy that Isaiah wanted all of his tools, even offering to pay for them, but Gideon had refused to take a dime for any of them. He was glad to give them to Isaiah because it was good stuff; he hadn't been able to imagine junking tools. Now he wouldn't have to. But it was what was in his heart that he couldn't imagine parting with.

Conflicted by so many emotions, he tried to sort through them. He'd fallen in love, and he wasn't even sure when it happened. Being in love was supposed to feel good, but it hurt. He was sad because he was leaving and mad that he felt he had to. He felt guilty for resenting his dad and his illness and jealous and angry at Andrew, who was able to walk away from the lodge with no responsibility. Gideon had never been a person to carry anger, but Shawn changed that. He was still mad that Shawn had treated him like a piece of shit and discarded him the way he did. The thought of Shawn brought up its own set of emotions of shame that he'd contracted HIV and embarrassment that he used Shawn to run from the lodge.

The sound of his little coffee brewer signaling that it brewed its half cup pulled him out of his thoughts. He pressed brew again to get the second half of the cup. He had to stop thinking about all the shit in his head and more about everything he had to complete this final week. He'd put it off as long as he could. The *Out of the Closet* thrift store in West Hollywood was picking up on Tuesday, and the rental agency was coming to pick up the house keys from him on Wednesday. There was so much to do in the days he had left here.

"Good morning, Puppy." Isaiah walked into the kitchen in his underwear and leaned against Gideon. He wrapped his arms around Gideon's waist.

Isaiah kissed his neck, his morning stubble scraping along Gideon's skin. "Ahh, I love those kisses." All of the emotions he'd been sorting through evaporated, and he was left with just one—Desire. He pushed his butt against Isaiah until he found what he was looking for. "Mmm." He rolled his neck, giving Isaiah more access to kiss it. Sandwiched between the counter and Isaiah, he gyrated his ass on Isaiah's stiffening cock. "I'm going to miss this."

Isaiah lowered Gideon's sweat bottoms until they fell around his ankles. He leaned back up against Gideon as he kissed his neck. "I want you to miss it."

Suddenly naked, Gideon moaned as he raised himself up on his toes, his bare ass touching Isaiah's warm skin. His hardness took Gideon's breath away.

He released a low, long groan as he reached behind him and freed Isaiah's erection from his underwear. He pressed back up against him.

Finally! Skin to skin. Gideon knew they were going beyond playing. He wanted to be taken right there and now. "Get the lube."

In less than a minute, Isaiah was back with the lube and a condom. He prepared Gideon first and then suited up.

Braced against the counter in front of the window, Gideon inhaled as Isaiah sank deep within him. He gasped at the fullness that threatened to split him in two. His breathing was instantly labored. He pushed through the sting until he could breathe and then closed his eyes and dropped his head as Isaiah made love to him over the sink.

The sound of a door slamming jarred Gideon's eyes open. It was Daisy stepping down off her steps into the carport. Dressed in her pastel pink housecoat and matching slippers, she held a white trash bag as she moved around Isaiah's car over toward their trash cans.

Before Gideon could alert Isaiah, Daisy looked up and right into the window. "Good morning, Sweetie. How are you doing this morning?"

"Um... Fine." He came down off his toes, forcing Isaiah to slip out of him. He knew she couldn't see up and into the window, but still, that was Isaiah's mother!

Isaiah looked over Gideon's shoulders and out the window. "Um... good morning, Mom!" He rubbed his erection along Gideon's lower back.

"What are y'all up so early for?" Daisy asked as she tossed the white trash bag into the garbage and slammed the lid close.

"Going hiking!" Isaiah yelled over Gideon's shoulders.

"Y'all have fun. Tell Yogi Bear I said hi." She turned back toward her house.

"Ooooh, right," Isaiah answered as he found Gideon's ass and pushed back inside.

"Aaaahh!" Gideon gasped as everything in front of him went gray and his eyes closed, making Daisy and all of his problems disappear, even if it was only temporarily.

*****

Gideon and Isaiah arrived in the Day-Use parking lot across from the Buckhorn Campground. The sun had been up about an hour. However, the morning chill still hung in the air.

Out of the car, Gideon jumped up and down in place as he tried to keep from freezing. "Damn, I should've brought a jacket."

"I tried to tell you it might be cool." Isaiah shook his head before he dragged his own hoodie over his head and pulled it down over his body to keep warm.

Across the empty parking lot on the other side of the road were campgrounds. Through a collage of firs, ponderosa pines, and oaks, Gideon saw a mix of campers, RVs, and tents through the trees. Some campsites had puffs of gray smoke billowing up. He heard children screaming and playing.

Isaiah slung a backpack over his shoulder. "You ready?" he asked as he clicked his key fob to lock the car.

Gideon tore his eyes away from the campground. Camping had to be at least one of his top three favorite things to do next to hiking and tearing things apart, and rebuilding them.

They walked over to the trailhead and stopped to read the sign that described the route of each trail. "Which one are we doing?" A light twitch of Gideon's sphincter reminded him of this morning. *Damn*, Isaiah had fed him good this morning. He was for sure going to feel his man on this hike.

Isaiah stood behind Gideon and dropped his chin onto Gideon's shoulders as they looked at the large wooden sign.

"Well, how much are you up for?" Isaiah asked.

They all looked pretty easy to Gideon, but Cooper Canyon Falls caught his attention. He pointed at Burkhart Trail. "This looks interesting." He traced the trail that meandered along a creek down the mountain. "It looks like Cooper Canyon Falls is down there. I'd like to see that."

"Oh, I ain't been there since I was a kid. Okay, let's do it." Isaiah lightly rubbed Gideon's back.

Side by side, they left the trailhead onto their hike. The mountain terrain was lightly peppered with more firs, pines, and oaks, as well as lots of large boulders and manzanita.

"This is pretty." Gideon drank it in as he took in everything all around him.

"Does this make you miss home?" Isaiah asked as he clasped Gideon's fingers.

He loved Isaiah's large soft hands entwined with his. "Yes and no. I miss this a lot. Hiking, just being outside. But it's nice to experience it with you."

Isaiah lightly squeezed his hand. "I feel the same."

The babbling creek alongside them served as music in the absence of conversation. He never realized how soothing the sound was. He'd grown up his entire life hearing babbling creeks and never thought of it as anything but noise. It was a beautiful sound.

About a mile in, Gideon stopped and pointed. "There's a woodpecker," he whispered as he pointed to the bird. "Oh! And there's a warbler." Exhilaration filled his lungs as he inhaled a large breath of the fragrant smell of pine.

Isaiah laughed as he took ahold of Gideon's hand. "I love you, Puppy."

Gideon squeezed Isaiah's hand, and they resumed their hike. "I love you, too." He loved that they had said it to each other every day since he'd first said it last Saturday night.

"You promise not to replace me with some dude on Creepy-Stranger.com?" Isaiah joked as he frowned.

"It's Studfinder, and, no, I'm not going on it again. I already found my stud. But you better promise that you're not going to find some tramp to *kick it* with."

Isaiah laughed. "Not even if we're just having fun?"

"That's not funny!" Gideon yanked on Isaiah's hand. "Promise?"

"I promise," Isaiah laughed. "But you might see me sooner than you think. I might be floating down the river on a log, shouting your name." He raised Gideon's hand and kissed it. "You'll have to come out and save me."

"I swear, my parents are going to love you. You're so much like my dad it's not funny."

"Do you enjoy sleeping with Daddy?"

"That's gross!" Gideon playfully socked Isaiah on his arm. Every inch of Gideon craved this man as a warmth spread throughout his chest. He looked at Isaiah. "What? What is it?" He sensed an ominous look in his eyes.

Isaiah drew a noticeable breath, causing Gideon to be even more concerned. "What is it?"

"You know how I said that I get tested every six months regardless of my sexual activity?" Isaiah's steps slowed.

"Yeah." A nervousness swelled in Gideon's chest.

"Well, since we're joking about other guys, I think you know, but I feel like I have to say it out loud. I am in no way looking to have sex with anyone but you. You and I are a lot alike in so many ways.

A monogamous relationship is the only thing that really works for us. With all of my heart, I am one hundred percent committed to you." Isaiah stopped and turned towards Gideon. "I'm due for my next test next month. I'm not worried about it at all, but I've been thinking… When we see each other again, if you're agreeable and everything is fine with you, we could start having sex without a condom."

"You're really not worried?" Gideon stared into Isaiah's eyes, bewildered at how much this guy made him feel special. He'd always just assumed that because of the simple fact that he was positive, no guy would ever want to go without a condom with him.

"No, I'm not worried. You're my boyfriend. I love you. As long as your meds are working and your viral loads are undetectable, there's nothing to transmit. Why would I be worried? There's no reason to be… I love you more than I've ever loved anyone."

"I would like that." Gideon's voice shook. Other than his parents, no one had ever said they loved him more than anything. He loved this man more than anything as well. The day he'd met Isaiah, Gideon hadn't been ready to date; he'd wanted no part of it. It wasn't that he didn't trust men; Gideon didn't trust his own ability to spot friend or foe—someone who would hurt him again, who was lying about who they were. He hadn't trusted himself.

But Isaiah had the ability to quiet some of the chaos in Gideon's head. And while Isaiah had been doing this, he'd managed to steal Gideon's heart long before Gideon even knew he'd been offering it to him. He should be scared of someone as clever as Isaiah, but, from the first day they'd talked—the moment Isaiah had looked at him through that window—it'd been as if those big beautiful brown eyes of his had put a spell on him, causing Gideon to drop his sword—because Isaiah was safe. He was a friend, not foe.

"There's so much love for you inside of me that I feel like I could just explode and splatter love everywhere."

"I like when you explode." A full-face grin emerged across Isaiah's face.

"You know what I mean. And for the record, I could explode right now." What Gideon was feeling now was something that dwelled deep inside of every bone in his body. At times, the feeling was so strong that it caused him to quiver. Gideon took a long deep breath, filling his lungs to capacity with the morning's crisp air. He slowly exhaled before looking up at Isaiah. "I love you so much." He rose off of his heels and kissed Isaiah.

"I love you more." Isaiah kissed him again, and then they continued on their hike.

When the trail narrowed to a tapered path, Isaiah took the lead. Gideon, who was still reeling in Isaiah's declaration of commitment a few minutes ago, peered down a couple hundred feet of a steep drop. *Man, it'd really suck to fall to my death now.*

They stopped at the turn-off that led down to Cooper Canyon Falls. Isaiah handed Gideon the bottled water he'd been nursing. "You want to go first, or shall I?"

Gideon stopped drinking. "I'll go." He screwed the cap back on and handed it back to Isaiah.

Gideon carefully placed his feet firmly down with each step as he descended, not wanting to slip and fall. If he stumbled, he could slide several feet before stopping. That would hurt like hell.

Long before Gideon saw the waterfall, he heard the roar of the water as it cascaded down the mountain. A rope tied to a tree near the bottom helped hikers lower themselves the final ten feet.

When they arrived at the base of Cooper Canyon Falls, Gideon took a moment to take in the forty-foot waterfall. The water cascaded off of the mountain and down into a large pond. Large boulders around the pool that were likely completely covered in snow in the winter and underwater at the height of the snow-runoff in spring now served as warming beds to stretch out on.

"I'm so glad no one's here." Isaiah stood next to Gideon.

"It's beautiful here! I love it." Gideon dropped to one knee and unlaced his shoes.

Isaiah followed. They took off their shoes and stuffed their socks into them.

Gideon was the first to roll his pant legs up and head down to the pool. When the cold water touched his feet, it stole his breath. He stopped for a second before realizing that it wasn't as cold as his brain initially warned him. "Be careful. The rocks are slippery!" he shouted back to Isaiah as he saw small trout swimming in the calm, knee-deep water.

With the water rising near his rolled-up pants, he walked over the tiny multicolored pebbles below the surface of the crystal-clear water, staring down at it. He carefully navigated along the shallow parts, not wanting to go any deeper.

"Is it cold?" Isaiah asked as he scurried down to the edge of the water.

Gideon stepped over a larger rock and then slipped, sending him butt-first into the foot-deep water. "Jesus!" He popped up. "It's freezing!" He jumped up and down as he hugged himself, trying to shake off the chill. He finally unsnapped his soaked jeans and tore them off as well as his underwear to free himself from the clinging cold fabric. He tossed them up on the bank. Then he pulled off his shirt and tossed it, too. Before he could change his mind, he dove head-first into the deepest part of the pool. It was the quickest way to acclimate his body to chilly water. Within seconds, he came back up. The cool water soothed his itchy stitches.

"Are you crazy?" Isaiah stopped at the spot where Gideon had slipped.

"Come on! It's not that cold once you're in!" Gideon waved to him to come in.

"Oh, hell no!" Isaiah took a step back as if something was going to grab him and pull him in.

"Come on!" Gideon yelled again. This time he didn't wait for Isaiah to answer as he dove back under the water and disappeared. He resurfaced behind the falls. Through the cascading water, he could barely make out Isaiah, who was still standing in the same spot.

Gideon used both hands as he scooted his butt up out of the water, attempting to climb up onto a rock covered in moss. The rock was too slippery, as he lost his balance and slipped back down into the water. He tried it again, this time being successful.

Up out of the water, he worked to catch his breath. He brought his knees to his pounding chest and wrapped his arms around his legs, trying to warm his body. He looked for Isaiah through the falls but couldn't see him. Had he gone back up to the large boulders?

Then Isaiah popped up at Gideon's feet, gasping for air, his eyes bulging as he shrieked and puffed for air. He groaned as if he'd been drowning.

Gideon laughed at his theatrical performance. "Come on. Get up here." Gideon extended a hand out to help Isaiah climb out of the water. Isaiah grabbed his hand, and, before Gideon could do anything about it, his ass slipped off the rock, and he plunged into the water on top of Isaiah. He was laughing so hard that he took in water, spitting it out as he resurfaced. He climbed into Isaiah's arms and wrapped his legs around Isaiah's waist. "Get lower, so your shoulders are covered. It's warmer that way."

Isaiah did as instructed, sending both their bodies under the water. He felt the goosebumps along Isaiah's arms and felt bad. He rubbed Isaiah's back, trying to warm him.

"It's cold!" Isaiah shivered.

Their face's inches apart; Gideon knew exactly how to warm up his sailor. He pressed his wet lips against Isaiah's, and they sank into a deep full-on kiss. Isaiah's mouth was cold, his breath as crisp as the fresh waterfall that shielded them from the world.

Feverishly, they kissed, turning Gideon's penis shrinkage to a partial erection. He was lost in the kiss when Isaiah pulled back.

"It's not working! I'm freezing!" Isaiah flung him off of him as he bobbed in the water.

Gideon was about to climb back on him when Isaiah dove under the fall. Gideon was laughing so hard he had to wait for a second to stop so he wouldn't drown going back under.

Still laughing at Isaiah, he climbed out of the pool of water and walked over to where Isaiah was shivering on top of a rock. Isaiah's entire body shivered. Cold and wet, he was as innocent as a little boy standing up there, which made Gideon start laughing all over again.

"It's not funny! I could've succumbed to hypothermia in there!" Isaiah barked from the rock.

He reached for Isaiah and wrapped his arms around him to help warm him.

"Ugh! You're freezing!" Isaiah complained but didn't release him.

Gideon rubbed Isaiah's arm, trying to make the goosebumps go away. "I'm sorry." He tried to say it without laughing but was unsuccessful. Naked, they huddled together on top of the large boulder, attempting to warm their bodies back up.

"That water is like two degrees!" Isaiah's teeth chattered.

"Come here." Gideon moved out from under the wet spot on the rock they were standing on onto a dry part that was warm from the sun.

"It's warmer over here." Gideon's gaze dropped to the fullness of Isaiah's cock. He wasn't hard but full. "You're not *that cold,* I see."

Isaiah moved next to him and laid flat on his back over the rock.

Gideon lay next to him, so their bodies were touching. With the roar of the fall, Gideon slowly caught his breath. Under the sun, their bodies dried in a matter of minutes.

"Are you warm yet?" Gideon tilted his head to look at Isaiah.

"Yeah, better." Isaiah lay motionless with his eyes closed.

Gideon tried desperately to hold a laugh in, but a snicker escaped, then a louder chuckle.

"I can hear you laughing at me," Isaiah mumbled.

He was incapable of speaking without a full-on laugh bursting out first. When it felt safe to do so, he rolled into Isaiah and attempted to climb up on him.

Isaiah pushed him off. "Uh-uh! Nah! You're not going to laugh at me and then think you're going to get some of this. You keep your *Tiny-Mighty-Mo-Little-Ass* over there."

Gideon was laughing uncontrollably as he admitted to himself that it probably wasn't the best idea to climb up on him in public. But damn, he wanted to. His erection was proof enough. Naked on this rock in the middle of nowhere, he closed his eyes and listened to the water cascading down the fall.

The continuous chirping of a bird close by took him home. In his head, he dreamed of when Isaiah would come for his visit. There was so much he wanted Isaiah to see: the river, the lodge, the neat hiking trail that led deep into the rain forest where the moist soil smelled of sweet, decomposed earth. He wanted to share with him the plants, the insects, the birds. It wasn't possible to see everything Gideon wanted to show Isaiah in three days. Three days wouldn't be enough to share his entire world with the man he was in love with. When would their next visit be? Would that be their relationship then—a series of visits? Unsettled, he opened his eyes. The first thing he saw was a butterfly dancing over them. He watched the butterfly flutter down to the water's edge, then over a cluster of wild ferns before flying away. Fascinated by the insect, he waited to see if she would return. After a couple of minutes, it was apparent she wasn't coming back.

Would Isaiah disappear as well over time? He didn't like the long-distance relationship idea.

Being out here, so relaxed, he'd been seduced by Nature, but She'd shown her cards when the butterfly had vanished. So pretty, and it was just gone like that. The reality was that he was leaving this Thursday, and he wouldn't see Isaiah for months. They'd known each other for such a short time, and yet he couldn't understand how he'd lived without him. He certainly couldn't imagine living without him now.

Six weeks ago, tomorrow had been a lifetime away; it'd only been a date on the calendar. Now, it was the day his world would change as he knew it, with only uncertainty beyond that. He closed his eyes again, not wanting to think about it, to enjoy the moment, but how could he?

Maybe I should take Isaiah up on his offer to move to Costa Rica. Was the offer even still on the table? Isaiah didn't like snakes. *There're snakes everywhere there.* And that wouldn't fix his other problem... he didn't want to run the lodge.

The life in the jungle that had once held so much joy for him now seemed crippling, and there was nothing he could do short of simply telling his parents he wasn't coming back.

But if he didn't go, what would he do here? The easiest thing would be to continue doing what he'd been doing the last eleven months. He was good at it, and he enjoyed it. But could he make a living on it? He would have to pick up a lot more jobs to pay rent and everything else. He wasn't even sure what those expenses would be.

The thought of going to college appealed to him. He imagined himself walking through a campus. Now that was his dream.

Could I live in the house? Twenty-two hundred dollars a month was a shit load of money for rent. That would take a lot more jobs.

Are you really contemplating this? Dad would be hurt, and Mom would be pissed.

They were a family. What right did he have to just bail on them? There was no one else they could count on. The internal agony stole any peace that the falls had offered.

Chapter 21

Gideon had been awake ever since Isaiah climbed out of bed to get ready for training. It was the first and only time he'd ever spent the night in Isaiah's room. Last night, he'd had little choice since all of his furniture had been picked up by the donation company.

He rolled onto his side and pressed his face against Isaiah's pillow. He could smell Isaiah's scent. With a slow exhale, he had the crazy notion of taking the pillowcase home with him tomorrow. He hugged it and inhaled once more. In the dark room, Gideon imagined the pillow was Isaiah.

In no way did it feel as if he'd only met Isaiah six weeks ago. Now, in twenty-four hours, he was boarding a plane and heading home. It seemed a lifetime ago that he'd been so broken, so depressed, that love had been the furthest thing from his mind. He hadn't realized that he'd been in survival mode when he'd met Isaiah. He'd allowed his devastating diagnosis to continue to define him, even after he'd become undetectable. Isaiah had helped him see that he was more than his diagnosis. In fact, Isaiah had helped him learn a lot about himself, things he knew but never had quite put all the pieces in the right place, things he needed to change and work on.

He squeezed the pillow as he listened to the faint sounds of Isaiah across the hall in the bathroom. The reality that he was leaving this man penetrated his chest like a knife. The pain felt like a wound that he might die from.

"Hey, Puppy, I've got to go," Isaiah whispered into Gideon's ear, making him open his eyes.

He was surprised that he hadn't heard Isaiah come back into the bedroom. Gideon released a long, drawn-out moan. It was a moan that cried *Don't go*. He uncovered his arms and draped them around

Isaiah's neck, pulling him down onto the bed. Isaiah collapsed onto the bed alongside Gideon.

"I love you, Puppy. I'll be thinking about you all day." Isaiah kissed his forehead.

There were no words that Gideon could speak that accurately conveyed his grief and the separation anxiety bubbling within him. If he let go of Isaiah, the clock would continue chipping away at their time left.

"Puppy, I have to go." Isaiah pulled away slightly.

"Okay," Gideon murmured as he released him.

Isaiah rose from the bed, leaving a hollowness in Gideon's chest that threatened to stop his heart. To breathe, he rolled onto his side and propped his head up. "Good luck on your test today." He offered Isaiah a fake smile that was mostly downward. It was all he had.

"Thank you. I'll text you when I know something." Isaiah leaned over and kissed him.

"You'll pass." Gideon savored the tiny kiss as if it was their last. "Just visualize the flashcards. It will come to you."

"Okay, I will. I'll see you tonight. I love you."

"I love you, too," Gideon murmured. This evening couldn't come fast enough. They'd booked a room at the Marriott next to the airport for their last night. They wanted one last romantic evening without having to worry about Daisy hearing them. Since the hotel was next to the airport and close to the academy, they would have that much more time in the morning to say goodbye.

With the sound of the bedroom door softly closing, he laid back down and closed his eyes. It had to be close to four in the morning. He could sleep for another five hours before he had to get up and meet the agent in charge of renting out the house. He had to ensure the house was clean enough for her, as well as hand off the keys.

*****

When Gideon opened his eyes again, his phone showed he'd missed a call from the agent five minutes ago. He looked at the time; *Shit! It's nine-thirty!*

Half asleep, Gideon got out of the bed and stumbled over to the window that looked out onto the street. There was a red minivan with a woman sitting in the passenger seat on her phone.

Shit! Shit! Shit! He rushed back over to the bed where his sweats were lying on the floor, and he pulled them on. Within a couple of minutes, he'd hurried through his bathroom routine, brushing his teeth and combing his hair as he'd dressed, then was out the kitchen door and down the driveway.

She looked up as he approached the car then got out. "Hi! I'm Carla, from Hometown Realty. I just left you another message. Your mom told me nine."

"Sorry." *I can't believe I overslept. Mom would have killed me if I missed her.* He extended his hand. "Good morning. I'm Gideon."

Carla shoved a large plastic For Rent sign under her arm, then dug around in her purse. She handed him a business card. "The place looks great. I've driven by a couple of times, checking on it. You've done a great job. I don't know if your mother told you, but my office handled the house for the last couple of years. Shall we go inside to see what you've done?" She headed toward the front door.

Gideon dropped in behind her. As they walked through the front door, it seemed weird. He never used the front door.

"Oh my. You've done some work in here." She glanced at the flooring that had replaced the light blue carpet and then headed to the kitchen. "Oh, this is nice." She spun around with a look of surprise. "Your mom said you were doing all the work. You did all of this?"

Gideon combined a yawn with a nod. He drove one hand down into his pockets, still trying to wake up.

Carla put her purse and the sign on the counter. "New countertops, flooring, and appliances… Are the cabinets new?"

"No. I just painted them and added the trim molding." Even with sleepy eyes, Gideon saw himself sitting on the counter as Isaiah cooked so many meals at that stove. This place felt like his home, and she was here to take it from him. He released a sigh, moving his gaze to blink up at the ceiling for a few seconds, long enough to control the onslaught of emotions that were causing his eyes to water.

She smiled at him. "You're good."

The gleam in her eye jolted him a little more awake. He recognized that flirtatious smile. "Thank you." He broke off their eye contact. He was proud of the work he'd done to his house. In the beginning, fixing up the house had been an excuse to come to California, and then, after being diagnosed, demolishing something—

anything—had been a great way to expel energy. The last couple of months before meeting Isaiah, this house had been his solitude from the world that he'd hidden from.

She flicked on the hall bath light. "New paint? That looks nice."

"Thank you," he muttered as he remembered he and Isaiah naked behind that shower curtain as they'd showered and played together. The desire to be back in the tub with Isaiah burned a hot spot in the pit of his belly until her babbling doused it.

"Your mother said the master bathroom was redone?" She turned off the light and continued past the second bedroom to the master.

Gideon missed what she'd said as he trailed after her down the hall. Had she noticed the new baseboards or light fixtures in the hall? Did she think the white paint made the house appear bigger, the hall wider? Was she not saying anything because she didn't like it? He studied her, trying to get a read on her. Was this just another house to her? Did she even care who lived here? He'd poured his heart and soul into this house the last eleven months, and now seeing it completely empty left him feeling empty as well.

She walked into the empty master bedroom. There was nothing in there for her to see other than the four white walls and new flooring, but Gideon saw Isaiah making love to him in this room, where he woke the day after their car accident, and Isaiah held him that morning. This was his and Isaiah's room. His heart pounded. Was this what a heart attack felt like? He mumbled yes to something she asked him. What it was, he wasn't even sure.

He glanced out the window into the back yard. There were more dirt patches than grass back there. He'd done nothing to fix it up. He'd had dreams of what he would have done.... *If it was his house.*

He trailed two steps behind her as she walked into the bathroom. She turned the lights on over the large vanity. "This is beautiful. I don't think I would have gone with such a dark gray tile on the counters in such a small space, but it's certainly better than before."

He didn't see the gun-powder gray tile she was talking about; he saw the counter that he'd been sitting on when Isaiah had first said he loved him. *Lady, if you don't like it, get out.*

He followed her back out to the kitchen, where she grabbed the sign before walking into the living room.

"Do you live close?" she asked.

"I was staying here while I was doing the work. I leave tomorrow. Heading home." He'd been gritting his teeth so hard that his jaw ached.

"Costa Rica?"

"Yeah."

"Lucky you."

Yeah, lucky me.

"Thank you so much for cleaning the place, too. That will save us time getting people in to see it. It's going to go fast."

Yay... He ought to be happy for his parents, but the truth was, he was going to be sorry to leave this place. He was leaving part of himself here.

"You're good at what you do. The house really does look nice."

"Thank you." Initially he welcomed her compliment, that she did, in fact, like what he'd done—that he was good... *Good.*

I'm good.

His chest tightened as the word reverberated in his head. He'd always been *good*, his whole life. Being good was important to him.

"Okay, I think I'm out of here. I'll let your mom know that we met." Carla walked back into the kitchen and retrieved her purse.

He trailed behind her. Isaiah was right. He was a people pleaser. Being good was how he pleased people. The word *no* was not something he used often, nor did it make people happy to hear. His relationship with Shawn was the perfect example of where not being able to tell people no got him. He should have insisted that they not had sex that night without a condom. He said yes, and look what happened. *Wow.* He pondered this new revelation about himself.

"The keys?" she asked.

"Oh yeah, that's right." Gideon dug into his pocket and retrieved a key chain with a VW emblem and four keys. "They're all the same... except the small one. It's for the storage shed out back."

"Thank you. She opened the door and waited for him to exit first.

He walked out, and as he turned, *she* was locking *his* front door. This whole morning—the tour he'd given her—seemed to be moving in slow motion as he said good-bye to each room.

"Have a safe flight home." Her smile was warmer than earlier, more authentic.

207

Gideon looked at the door. He'd been locked out of his own house. A sadness tore at his chest. Yes, this was a nightmare.

He watched as she made her way back to her car. He waited for her to drive off before taking his phone out and checking the time, for no other reason than to keep himself from crying. A little after ten. He stared at it, not trusting what he was even looking at. In seven hours, he was going to meet Isaiah at the hotel. This was the end.

*****

Gideon stepped out of the elevator onto the seventeenth floor of the Marriott hotel as his phone pinged. With everything he owned stuffed into one carry-on, he slung the shoulder bag over his shoulder before pulling out his phone and seeing the text from Isaiah.

I'm on my way. Should be there in a few.

Inside, the room was warm, with a faint cigarette odor that tickled his nose as he stepped farther into the large suite. He tossed his bag onto the bed and typed a reply. *Room seventeen-twenty-one.*

He pulled the heavy curtains and sheers back, revealing the L.A. skyline off in the distance. The beauty of the expansive skyline—he was going to miss this city.

He slid the large glass door open that led onto the balcony and took a breath, filling his lungs with fresh air before walking back into the room and turning on the shower.

After a long hot shower, Gideon stood in the bathroom drying his body when he heard a knock on the door. He tucked the towel around his waist and hurried to the door.

"Do you always answer the door in a towel?" Isaiah was weighted down with his equipment duffle bag slung over his right shoulder and an overnight bag in one hand and his backpack and a bottle of wine in the other. A playful grin slowly emerged as he looked down at Gideon's towel.

"Not always." He released the towel from his waist with the flip of his thumb and let it fall to the floor.

Isaiah raised both brows. "Goddamn!" he shrieked as he pushed past Gideon and into the room. "Are you insane? Damn, that was hot!"

The look of panic on Isaiah's face made Gideon laugh. He shut the door and then bent over and picked up his towel. He wrapped it back around his waist as he headed toward Isaiah.

"Damn, Puppy!" Isaiah grabbed him by his narrow waistline. "You are beyond freaking sexy." His gleam conveyed his hunger.

Gideon's cock sprung to life under the towel as they kissed.

What Gideon thought was going to be a simple, affectionate kiss deepened within seconds beyond how they usually greeted one another as Isaiah pulled Gideon closer into his chest. Gideon closed his eyes as he savored Isaiah's taste.

Deep in the kiss, Isaiah's hand slipped under the bottom of the towel and cupped Gideon's ass.

Gideon moaned as Isaiah's massive hands rubbed and squeezed his butt. He pushed his pelvis against Isaiah's thigh, feeling the pressure against his cock.

Isaiah broke free, releasing Gideon to drop back down off his toes. "I have to take a shower first. I have to get clean." With his tongue, Isaiah wiped saliva from his own lips.

"That's so not fair!" Gideon patted Isaiah on his chest. "What did I tell you about kissing me like that and then stopping?" Isaiah's raised brows and doe-like eyes made him question his decision to not at least try to get what he wanted. He dropped the towel around his waist and exposed his full-blown erection. "Are you sure?"

Isaiah gripped Gideon's erection. "Now you're the one playing dirty. I'm going to take a quick shower, and then I'm going to take care of this for you."

Gideon exhaled at his defeat. Disappointed, he shook out of Isaiah's hand and walked back into the bathroom for his underwear. "How'd you do on the Spanish exam today?"

"I failed. Barely." Isaiah shouted from the other room.

It took a second to process what Isaiah said, to go from wanting to make love a second ago to hearing after all their work, he failed his test. "Are you kidding me?" Gideon stepped into his underwear, then returned to the room. "What happened?"

Isaiah's face was marred in sadness. *How had he not seen this before?*

"Dunno. I got a seventy-four percent." Isaiah's eyes fell to Gideon's bare, flat abdomen, and yet the sadness remained.

"Isn't a seventy-four good?" Gideon gave him a hug.

"Passing's seventy-five."

"So now what?" Gideon pulled away and raked his fingers through his hair, feeling how damp it still was.

"I'll take the test again tomorrow." Isaiah sounded as if it was no big deal.

"And pass?" Gideon dug around in his bag, pulled out a black tee-shirt, and slipped it over his head. He then moved closer to Isaiah and nuzzled against his chest again. Gideon's stomach churned— Passing the test tomorrow was a big deal.

"Yeah." Isaiah broke from his hug and looked at their bags on the bed. "Where's all your stuff?"

"What stuff?"

"All your clothes?"

"That's it." Gideon glanced at his bag.

Isaiah touched Gideon's bag. "This is all you're taking?"

"It's all I have. Most of my clothes were work stuff." The duffle bag was the same bag he'd had when he'd arrived eleven months ago. He was basically leaving with what he'd brought. "You know what they say: travel small, stand tall."

Still, behind Gideon, Isaiah palmed one of Gideon's butt cheeks and lightly squeezed as he kissed him on the back of his neck. "You're five-six; you're not tall."

Gideon moaned at Isaiah's playful touch.

"How was your day?" Isaiah asked as he brushed Gideon's hair to one side.

"It was okay." A moan escaped Gideon as he closed his eyes for a second to enjoy Isaiah's touch. "I met with the lady from the company that will rent out the house for us. I had to give her the keys. I wanted to say goodbye to your mom, but I overslept and, by the time I got up, she was already gone. I sent her a text."

Isaiah's hand glided up from the small of Gideon's back, up along his arm to his bare shoulders. "I missed you so much today. I was originally thinking about calling in sick tomorrow. Now, I can't because I have to retake that stupid test."

"Estarás bien." In Spanish, Gideon reassured him that he would be okay.

Isaiah took a second before he answered. "Um… you said, 'You'll be fine.'" His nostrils flared as he took in a large breath and exhaled. "Yeah. I know. I'll be fine." There was uncertainty in his voice.

"How would you say that in Spanish?" Gideon wasn't sure if the uncertainty was that he would pass tomorrow or that he guessed at what he'd said.

Again, Isaiah hesitated, this time a little longer. *"Sí. Lo sé. Estaré bien?"* Isaiah said slowly.

"That's right."

Isaiah grinned as he squeezed Gideon's ass cheek harder before smacking it. "Yeah, baby! Call me *Señor Papi!"*

Gideon laughed at Isaiah's excitement and sudden cockiness. "How about we stay in instead of going out for dinner? Order room service and work on your Spanish, *Señor.* I know you know it. You just have to stop second-guessing yourself." Isaiah's smack on his ass had sent a flow of blood to his cock again.

"Ah, no. It's our last night. I want to take you out. Someplace special."

"I don't need special. Let's stay in, order room service, and hang out. It's what I want to do." He was semi-erect as he closed the gap between them, hoping at another shot at what he wanted... no, needed. He needed that closeness that came after making love to soothe his melancholy mood.

"If that's what you want, we can do that." Isaiah stepped away from Gideon and unbuttoned the academy-required white dress shirt.

"I'm learning to say no." Gideon watched as he unbuttoned his shirt.

Isaiah smiled. "Okay... Good for you. I have to get in the shower to get this sweat off me because all I can smell is myself." He slipped out of his shirt. "There's a restaurant downstairs. If you don't want to order from there, I'm sure there're places around here that will deliver." Isaiah pulled his tee-shirt up over his head.

This was torture having to stare at Isaiah's bare chest. "What I want is not on any menu." He could no longer resist, reaching out and laying a hand on Isaiah's chest. He gently rolled his finger over the areola as his desire surged even more.

"Damn, Honey, you act like I've been gone a week. How are you going to make it for two months?"

"I don't know." *I'll have to take matters into my own hands.* If it was up to Gideon, he could have sex twice a day, every day of the week. Since throwing his plan of celibacy overboard six weeks ago, his sex drive had been in overdrive, as if he was trying to make up for lost time. He hadn't been so sexually aroused since he'd first hit puberty. It was like going through puberty all over again, only, this time, instead of jacking off in the woods every chance he had, he was attacking Isaiah. Sometimes even in the middle of the night, waking his poor sailor up. This overwhelming sensation to have Isaiah fuck him was too strong to deny.

Gideon wasn't ashamed of it. He loved Isaiah and couldn't get enough of the drug-like endorphins that exploded within his body during and after sex.

As Isaiah unfastened his belt, Gideon stretched out across the bed to watch.

"I see you." Isaiah grinned as he slid his belt off and folded it in half before snapping it, sending a loud *pop* throughout the room.

"Oh, Daddy… Are you going to spank me?" Gideon playfully squirmed on top of the bed. They hadn't done the whole fantasy-with-the-handcuffs yet, and he wasn't into the whole spanking thing, but it was fun teasing Isaiah.

"I should." Isaiah smirked as he toe-kicked off his black dress shoes and then removed his black dress pants.

Gideon watched as Isaiah neatly hung his pants, shirt, and coat on a hanger from the closet. In his boxers, he went into the bathroom and turned on the hot water. "Hey Puppy!" he yelled from the bathroom.

Out in the other room, Gideon squirmed on top of the bed as he ran his hand up under his Tee-shirt and across his abdomen before sliding his hand down toward his underwear. He resisted the urge to touch himself. "Yeah?" He envisioned Isaiah's cock, slamming into him as his own cock once again hardened.

"I wish you were going to be here this weekend. Mom's planning a BBQ at the house on Saturday. Josiah, Tammy, and Elijah are all coming over. We're going to meet her boyfriend, Charles, from the bank."

"Are you and Josiah going to rake the poor guy over the coals?" Gideon couldn't resist touching himself, caressing himself over his underwear. His stomach muscles tightened as he released a tiny moan.

"Probably."

Gideon heard the shower turn off, and then the glass shower door creak. Here he was, thinking about getting pummeled by that cock of Isaiah's, and Isaiah was in there thinking about the weekend.

He chuckled, knowing, eventually, he'd get what he wanted. Isaiah gave him everything and spoiled him in every way. Filled with desire, he took a large breath and exhaled it slowly. Was this the kind of love that his parents had? He'd watched their love his entire life: holding hands, kissing, doting over each other. It used to make him and Andrew sick watching them, and now, he was sure he'd found a love just like theirs.

Although Isaiah was without question handsome, and his physique was what had caught Gideon's initial attention, it was his attentiveness—like his parents'—to those around them—that was far more attractive to Gideon.

His yearning to be close to Isaiah—it was a craving so powerful that it felt as if he could explode. This wasn't entirely physically impossible either, as he slipped his underwear down and tossed them to the side of the bed. This evening—dinner, studying, talking, everything—would have to wait until after they made love.

Chapter 22

When the alarm went off at four a.m., Isaiah was jolted out of a deep sleep. It took a second for his brain to register that it was time to get up.

He silenced the alarm on his phone, then groaned as he dropped his head back onto the pillow. He dozed for a minute before a noise in the room made him open his eyes. His gaze zeroed in on a naked body standing in front of the wet bar.

"What are you doing?" Isaiah scratched his head as he took in Gideon's beautiful naked ass.

"Getting your coffee going." Gideon looked back, over his shoulder at him.

"Thank you," Isaiah muttered. Two hours of sleep just wasn't enough. After making love last night, they'd laid in the king-size bed, both facing the large picture window as they'd talked for hours. With the lights of the city of Los Angeles outside their balcony, it'd been after midnight when they'd gone from *not hungry yet* to, *I'm starving*. Since the hotel restaurant had already been closed, they ordered crispy chicken strips, French fries, and mozzarella sticks from a neighboring twenty-four-hour diner up the street.

"Here you go." Gideon put one knee on the mattress as he leaned over with a hot cup of freshly brewed coffee.

Isaiah grunted as he opened his eyes and sat up. The warm aromatic, freshly brewed coffee was heaven sent. "Thank you."

Gideon nestled his naked body back down beside him, laying his head across Isaiah's lap.

Isaiah took a sip of the hot coffee as his brain processed what today was.

Today... he was driving Gideon to the airport for his flight.

Today, Gideon was leaving him.

Today, he was taking his remedial Spanish exam, and if he failed it, he was out of the academy.

He stroked Gideon's hair; today was a shitty day, and it hadn't even started. But he was a soldier, and soldiers pushed past adversity. This morning, he didn't want to be tough. He didn't want to deny that Gideon's leaving hurt. He drew in a frustrated breath, feeling the hurt in his chest.

Gideon laid in his lap until Isaiah finished drinking his coffee. He grunted at what needed to be done. "Come on, Puppy. We have to get going." He stroked Gideon's hair.

Gideon nodded, but instead of getting up, he tightly hugged Isaiah's thighs.

"Come on, Puppy." He leaned over, put his coffee cup on the nightstand, and then leaned over and kissed Gideon on his temple. "Do you want to get in the shower with me?"

Gideon stirred and then sat up. He brushed the hair from his face and stared at Isaiah.

"I know, Puppy... I love you." Even in the dimly lit room, the grief in Gideon's eyes was irrefutable.

Gideon lay his head against Isaiah's chest and hugged him.

A lump formed in Isaiah's throat. He wasn't a crier by any means, but knowing Gideon would be gone in an hour hurt. He leaned back against the headboard and rubbed Gideon's back. He couldn't deny his puppy the affection he was clinging to so desperately this morning.

As he stroked Gideon's hair, Isaiah thought of a different outcome than what was happening. He could just say screw it, not show up for training and board the plane with Gideon. His heart was telling him that being with Gideon was more important than anything else. By this evening, if he followed his heart, he would be in a different country, with an entirely different life. He'd made the offer to go to Costa Rica, but Gideon refused him. As hard as it was to admit, he was glad Gideon said no. He really wanted to be a police officer—not just any police officer, but for the city of Los Angeles. The Navy had allowed him to live all over the world, but there really wasn't any place like L.A. It was home. When it came down to it, they'd both chosen their family over the other.

The mood was still somber forty minutes later as they gathered their bags and headed toward the door. Isaiah held it open for Gideon.

Gideon was about to pass through but stopped. He raised up on his tiptoes and kissed Isaiah. With their lips still almost touching, Gideon murmured, "I love you." Tears shimmered in his eyes.

"I love you, too." It pained him to see such sadness in Gideon's eyes. It was the same hangdog eyes that the old hound gave to potential adoptive parents as they walked past him at the shelter looking for the perfect new family companion. There was nothing Isaiah could do to make it go away. This was something he couldn't fix.

*****

Freeway traffic was light for early morning as they approached the airport. They'd barely said two words to each other on the drive. Isaiah had been in his head, trying to work on his Spanish, but his mind kept drifting back to Gideon. This whole thing with Gideon was a complete surprise. Gideon wasn't a person he would have ever gone out with if he had been still in the military for fear of being guilty by association. How stupid was that? Look at what he would have missed out on.

Deep in thought, Isaiah almost missed his exit to the airport and had to quickly maneuver the rental car across two lanes to not miss it. Thank god for his High-Speed pursuit training. *That was pretty damn good.* He looked in his rearview mirror, hoping not to see an accident behind him.

"Will you call me when you land?" As they crept along in bumper-to-bumper traffic, Isaiah saw Gideon's departure terminal ahead and began looking for a spot to pull along the curb.

"You want me to call or text?" Gideon asked.

"Call. I want to hear your voice." A car pulled away from the curb, and Isaiah pulled in behind it. Airport police were everywhere, blowing their whistles, attempting to keep the traffic moving. He and Gideon would have little time to say good-bye before he was shooed away by the hall monitors with badges. He should have more respect for his comrades, but he wasn't feeling them at all this morning. He wanted to kiss Gideon goodbye, but the rush of people around them stalled him from doing it. So many people would see him kissing another man. *Fuck them!* None of these people mattered as much as Gideon did.

He leaned over into Gideon's seat and kissed him. "I love you so much," he said through their kiss and then kissed him again.

"I love you, too." Gideon drew back slightly. "I can't wait for Thanksgiving."

"I'll be there that morning, I promise." Isaiah pictured landing in a strange airport. Although he had no idea what the airport looked like in San Jose, Costa Rica, in his mind, it was the most important place in the world and the only place in the world he wanted to be.

Gideon reached into the backseat to grab his bag and then grabbed the door handle but stopped. "I love you." He leaned over and gave Isaiah another kiss.

Isaiah resisted the urge to grab him, hold him, and stop him from getting out of the car. But this was something he couldn't stop, and he knew it. Gideon was leaving. Never in his dreams—and certainly *not* six weeks ago—could he have imagined that he would be hurting as much as he was right now. Never could he have imagined that he would fall so deeply in love with someone so fast. It didn't seem like it had only been six weeks. It felt as if they'd already spent a lifetime together. Isaiah was a person who always had a plan, and, in this moment, he had no idea how he was going to get through this separation. It seemed an impossible task.

Chapter 23

Inside the terminal, Gideon fell in line with the drone of travelers as they moved through the massive airport. He held onto the mental picture of Isaiah in the car as he stood on the curb and shut the car door. The sadness in Isaiah's eyes equaled the emptiness that now filled Gideon's soul. The metallic tasting saliva that swirled in his mouth said that he was at risk of spewing vomit all over the polished white tile floor. He tried to swallow down the saliva, but it wasn't going down. How was he going to make it for two months when loneliness already hurt this much?

I'm going home... I made the choice... Why'd I make that choice? His stomach muscles tightened around the bile that was trying to come up.

Because you're a people pleaser. You don't want to hurt Mom and Dad... But I don't want to hurt either. He heaved and quickly put his hand over his mouth.

Maybe I shouldn't fly today. The last thing I want to do is throw up on the plane. Isaiah wouldn't be with him this time to ensure he made it back to bed, *or in this case,* his seat. Shit, if he threw up in his seat, that would be really bad.

I can't fly... not today. He stopped at the back of the long line that zig-zagged towards the TSA checkpoint. He focused on his stomach, gauging how sick he was. Sick or not, he didn't want to go.

You're making yourself sick trying to please Mom and Dad. How could this be the right choice if it was making him so sick? Isaiah said he was a people pleaser, and it would destroy him. *No... If I got on that plane, that would destroy me.*

"Excuse me." A man pushed past him and stepped to what was now the back of the line.

Gideon looked at the man and then saw that the line had moved up about ten feet. He took three steps and rejoined the line. Two months was a long time before he saw Isaiah again... too long.

I can't do this. He tapped his passport in his hand as he took a step in the line every few seconds.

There's got to be a hundred people in this line. He anxiously looked at the crowd of people he'd been sandwiched in with. *Just get out of line.*

What do you want? The voice in his head was so strong, it was as if someone else was asking.

I want to stay here. I want to be with Isaiah... I want my own life. I don't want to run the lodge, not now, not ever.

Then pick one, the most important. What's the one thing you really want?

He thought for a second. *I don't want to hurt Mom and Dad.*

That was not the right answer, and he knew it... *No... what do I want?*

He knew exactly what he wanted, and yet he resisted saying it. *I'm not getting on that plane... I can't... I won't.*

He stepped up and handed his passport to the agent. *You can't do this.* He swallowed the massive lump in his throat.

"No... I changed my mind." Gideon snatched his passport from the agent. "Sorry."

He didn't give the agent another look as he stepped out of line and walked over to a pillar. He braced himself against it, unsure if his wobbly legs would hold him up. He reached for his phone in his pocket. *You have to call Mom.*

He gripped his phone but didn't remove it from his pocket. He was having difficulty swallowing.

You have to call them. Tell them you're not coming. It wasn't just Isaiah; he needed a life of his own. He didn't want to follow his parents. That was their dream, not his. He needed to tell them this. He clenched his phone harder as he removed it from his pocket and called his mom's phone. Right when he thought her voice mail would pick up, she answered the phone.

"Hey, Mom."

"Hi, Hon. I wasn't expecting your call. I was cleaning up in the kitchen." Her breathing was ragged. "Your dad had my phone last, and I had to find it."

"How's Dad doing?"

"He's had better days, but we're managing. I can't wait for you to get here. Are you at the airport now?"

"Yeah, that's why I'm calling. I wanted to talk to you and dad."

"Oh... Okay... Is something wrong?"

Gideon took a deep breath. "No... not really... I guess... I mean yes."

"Well, Dad and Andrew just took the guests down to the rafts. Is it something you can tell me, or do I need to get him?"

"No, I can talk to you about it."

Gideon pushed the lump down in his throat. "Um... I... I don't wanna run the lodge." His breath hitched, stopping him from saying anything else.

"What do you mean?"

"I mean... I know you and Dad wanted me to take over the lodge—I don't want to. I want to stay here."

"Really? Why?"

I'm in love... "Running the lodge isn't something that I want to do." He wished he could see her face to gauge how she was taking this. "It's not my dream. I want to do other things."

"Other things? Like what?" His mother asked.

"I'd like to take some classes at the college, maybe get my degree. I like what I'm doing now. I can make enough money to live on while I'm going to school."

"What brought all this on?"

Gideon gazed at the flow of people walking past him as he thought about what to say. "I like it here. I've never wanted to run the lodge. Don't get me wrong. I love the lodge; I just don't want it to be my life." Maybe it was better that he wasn't there to see her reaction.

"I can't say that I'm that surprised. I know your father will be, though."

"What will you guys do without Andrew and me?"

"Well... I don't know. I guess we'll have to hire someone."

"And when Dad can't work anymore?"

"Honey, that's not your problem. We're grown adults," Mom said. "You make it sound as if your father has six months to live."

"I know, I know. I just worry about you guys."

"Well, stop." His mother laughed. "We can take care of ourselves. I do have a question for you, though."

"Yeah. What's that?"

"Does any of this also have anything to do with the *someone* you met there, the one who lives next door?"

Gideon closed his eyes. *Goddamn Andrew!* His brother had a big mouth. He took a deep breath as he collected his thoughts. "Yeah."

He was sure she didn't care that his "someone" was a man. They'd never talked about his sexuality, but he always got the sense that they knew. They talked about Andrew having a wife one day, about tending to their grandchildren that they hoped to have someday from Andrew. Neither of his parents had ever attempted to pin any of their visions of a wife or kids on him.

"Andrew said you're in love with him."

Her use of the male pronoun confirmed what he already knew. He waited to see what else she knew.

"Are you still there?" she asked.

A glassy layer of tears glazed Gideon's vision. "Yeah. Yeah, I'm here. His name is Isaiah."

"How long have you been seeing him?" she asked.

"About a month and a half… and yeah, Mom, I do love him."

"You know… the day I met your father, I was a junior in high school. Your father ran track. I remember I was with my best friend, Cori. She was dating another guy on the team. She introduced your father and me. He asked for my number, and I gave it to him."

Gideon had heard this story at least a hundred times by both his mother and his father. He took a deep sigh, knowing not to interrupt her.

"That night, when he called, your grandmother was furious that a boy was calling the house."

Gideon automatically filled in the blanks in his head: '*Grandma was furious because you were only sixteen, and she said that you couldn't start dating until you were seventeen. Grandma wouldn't let you see Dad, so you guys sneaked around and dated anyway. It was love at first sight, then you got pregnant—*

Gideon's breath hitched as soon as he made the connection. Her acceptance and understanding of him was what she never got from her own parents.

"Does he look at you the way your father looks at me?" she asked.

Gideon smiled as he remembered the day they'd met. He hadn't realized it until the moment she said it. "Yes, he does. Definitely." He smiled as he released a big sigh.

"Then love him as much as I love your father. I'm happy for you."

"Really, Mom?" A tear floated at the base of his eye.

"We would love to meet him someday."

"Yeah, you guys will love him."

"Maybe you two can come for a visit."

"That would be good."

"I suspected that you might have met someone before your brother told me. Now it all makes sense why you weren't in a hurry to get back here," she snickered.

There was so much more he needed to tell her. He needed to come clean about everything. "Mom... Isaiah's not the reason I didn't come home. He's the reason I want to stay. The reason I didn't come back was not only because I didn't want to run the lodge, but..." Gideon's heart was in this throat. "I got sick... But I'm fine now, I swear."

"What happened?"

Gideon heard the panic in her voice. "I got HIV." There was no easy way to say it.

"Oh dear God."

"Mom, I'm fine now." Gideon brushed a tear that was about to fall from his eye. "I'm on medication. I'm not sick. My doctors can't even find it in my body anymore. Really, Mom, I'm okay." Gideon couldn't tell if she was crying. The thought of her crying was too much to bear. He brushed another tear from his eye, but another one ran right behind it. The tears were falling, and he couldn't stop them. He swiped and swiped, and yet they came faster. "I love you, Mom." His voice shook.

"I love you, Gideon. Baby, don't cry. It's okay. I'm glad that you're okay." She sniffed.

"Thank you, Mom." Gideon sniffled, trying to bring an end to his emotional breakdown. "Mom, you'll love Isaiah. He's the sweetest guy I've ever met. I love him so much." All Gideon could think about was going to Isaiah right now and being in his arms again.

"Your father and I have only ever wanted you to be happy. Go be happy."

The dam of tears broke once more. "Thank you, Mom. Thank you." He could barely talk. "I love you."

"I love you, too," his mother said before they disconnected.

Chapter 24

After saying good-bye to Gideon this morning, Isaiah had driven straight to the academy to take his exam. He now sat restlessly in the classroom with Cadets Parks and Thompson, the only three in the classroom whose careers were now dependent on their exam results.

He'd seen a handful of cadets already weeded out through this process, always feeling bad for them but never imagining it happening to him. None of the material had been hard for him. Yeah, some of it he'd had to study, but at least it had made sense. However, Spanish was a beast of its own. Between the irregular verbs and conjugated verbs and changing the order of the words in a sentence, so it was right, it seemed no rule was written in stone.

He looked at his watch. He drew a breath at the reality that, in the next hour, he could be packing up his locker and checking out of here. The thought of it made him sick. He imagined Gideon was thirty thousand feet up in the air, flying along the coastline toward home. What *he* would do to be sitting in that seat next to him right now. There was that small part of him that said failing wouldn't be all bad. He would be on a plane this evening en route to Costa Rica. No question about it. He would be out of here faster than a speeding bullet.

On the other side of the door, he listened as heels clicked on the linoleum down the hall. Every few minutes, his breath had hitched at the sound of heels walking past the door. But, this time, the door opened and Sergeant Perez, their instructor, walked in.

The Sergeant's expression was unreadable. Without a word, the short, but fit instructor, first handed Cadet Thompson his exam, then Cadet Parks his, before walking over and placing Isaiah's exam down on the desk in front of him.

As if the exam was on fire, Isaiah kept his hands at his side as he looked at the upper right-hand corner of the paper. Penned in blue ink was ninety-eight percent. As if he'd fully expected to fail, he couldn't believe it was his test. He stared down at the page. He'd passed!

A large pent-up breath—almost a gasp—poured out of Isaiah as he looked up to celebrate with Cadet's Parks and Thompson. Parks was smiling, and Thompson was flipping through his pages as if reviewing it. His body language was far less enthusiastic than Parks.

"Parks! Williams! You two are excused."

Isaiah wasted no time gathering up his things and hit the door at the same time as Parks.

Once outside the classroom, they high-fived each other as the door closed.

"Shit, I barely passed, but I passed!" Cadet Parks had a big grin on his face. "Williams, what'd you get?"

"Ninety-eight," Isaiah said, trying to hold his exhilaration back so he wouldn't sound like he was rubbing it in. The two made it down to the end of the hall before stopping.

"I need coffee." Parks gestured toward the café.

Isaiah needed a minute to pull himself together before their ten o'clock class started. "No thanks. I got some calls I have to make."

Isaiah hurried toward the parking lot to his car, where he'd left his phone since phones were banned from the classroom.

Inside his car, he checked to see if Gideon had called. No missed calls or new text messages. Although he figured Gideon's phone was on airplane mode, he pounded out a text for him to read as soon as he turned it back on.

I passed! Missing you like crazy already. Xoxoxoxo

All morning he'd been so focused on that damn test that it'd taken his mind off the hollowness of Gideon's absence. But now, off an adrenaline high from passing his test to the reality that Gideon was gone, his spirits plummeted. The churn in his stomach that had been there before he got his test results was back.

Isaiah glanced at his watch. He had about thirty minutes before class. He pulled up his gallery on his phone and slowly scrolled through the photos he'd taken of Gideon over the last six weeks: Gideon holding the giant banana split at the zoo, their hike up to the Hollywood sign, the waterfall. He stopped at a picture of Gideon in his underwear sitting on his kitchen counter. The sweet smile on his face was like a five-year-old on his birthday who was having the best day of his life. He'd cooked him dinner that evening, and they'd had sex right before this picture was taken. The memory of them making love made Isaiah grin.

Their sex was good. As he flipped through the numerous pictures he'd taken of Gideon, he thought of their first night together. It had been anything but romantic; Gideon stumbling drunk, his head in his toilet as he'd puked his guts out, almost naked, except for those red underwear. They were by far Isaiah's favorite pair of Gideon's underwear.

Gideon's poor body curled around the commode that night was etched in his brain. In hindsight, it was likely the moment his heart had opened up to the possibility of having a second chance at love.

More than the number of photos he had of Gideon, what stood out was the number of selfies of the two of them he'd taken when they were in public.

In all the time he and Ronnie had been together, he'd only had a handful of photos of them together, and those had been taken in the house.

He needed to stop looking at the pictures if he didn't want to show up for class with tear-stained cheeks.

He was about to stuff his phone into the glove compartment when his phone rang. Surprised, he looked at the screen, hoping it was his Puppy.

Instead, it was Ronnie.

He debated for a half-second whether to answer it. It seemed that all he'd done at one time was wait by the phone for Ronnie to call.

After leaving Hawaii, he used to wonder what he'd do if Ronnie called. Had Ronnie had any regrets? Isaiah had lost count at how many times he'd checked his phone for a text or message from his ex. Now, the only reason to answer the phone was for answers.

"Hello?" He purposefully sounded like he had no idea who was calling, though Ronnie's name had appeared on the Caller ID.

"What up, Dog." Ronnie's voice was gruff.

Just the sound of Ronnie's voice irritated the shit out of Isaiah. "Hey." *Why the hell did I answer this phone.*

"Why haven't you texted me back? Damn, a brother can't even get a text from your ass these days?"

Yes, I was ignoring you. "What's up?" Isaiah knew he sounded cold, but Ronnie was lucky to get even that.

"Are you busy?" The gruff in Ronnie's voice was replaced with one that now sounded unsure of himself.

"Yeah. Kind of. Heading back to class." Isaiah watched as several cadets exited a building and were walking out into the parking lot.

"Ain't heard from you. I was wondering how the academy was going. Make sure you're good."

"I'm good."

"I guess so since you haven't called."

Isaiah's irritation reached a breaking point. "Ronnie, why would I call you?" Isaiah waited a second for a reaction from Ronnie. "You were quite clear in what you wanted."

"Come on, man. You ain't still pouting over that, are you?"

Pouting? You're an ass. "Matter of fact, I'm not. I've moved on."

"How's that?"

"I'm dating someone."

"Y'all serious?"

"Very." Isaiah would be lying if he wasn't getting a certain amount of satisfaction from this conversation. It took everything Isaiah had not to ask about him if he was seeing someone. He wanted the jealousy to flow only one way. So he said nothing.

Ronnie broke the silence. "Okay, I guess I'll let you go…"

Isaiah was about to say goodbye when Ronnie cut him off.

"Isaiah… I'm sorry."

Ronnie's apology was unexpected. "Sorry for what?" He could hear Ronnie breathing on the other end.

"Sorry I couldn't give you what you deserved. You're a good guy. You deserve to be happy."

Isaiah couldn't immediately accept Ronnie's apology. It was complicated. He knew the apology was sincere—he heard the earnestness in Ronnie's voice—but it also wasn't the first time Ronnie had ever apologized to him either. He needed to marinate on this one.

"Oh." Ronnie's voice climbed a note. "I sent something to your mom's house for you since I ain't got no address for you these days. You can probably just toss it at this point."

Isaiah started to tell him that he was still at his mother's but didn't. "What'd you send?"

"Nothing really. Just toss it."

Isaiah tried to think of what it could have been that Ronnie thought was important enough to send but was now okay with him tossing it. "Okay, man. I gotta go." Isaiah saw several of his classmates in the parking lot walking into the building. "I gotta get to class."

As Isaiah walked back to class, his two-year relationship with Ronnie played from beginning to end. It was now so painfully obvious how toxic that relationship had been and how much of himself he'd given away. In the end, their break-up was like a much-needed surgery where a tumor or growth was cut out, but the doctor guaranteed he'd be much better in the months to come without it. And he was.

By the time he was seated in the classroom, he'd had some time to process Ronnie's apology. He could take it at face value and accept that Ronnie had acknowledged he hadn't been able to make him happy. It was quite the opposite of any of his past apologies where he'd begged Isaiah to take him back, that he would do better. This time, Ronnie had admitted that he couldn't do better.

One of the hardest things Isaiah had had to do was admit to himself that morning when he'd broken up with Ronnie was that he had no longer been willing to be an annex of Ronnie's life. His breakup with Ronnie, leaving the military, had been his way of stepping out of a life that he no longer wanted and examining who he was. He now knew that he wasn't willing to sacrifice who he was by living in the closet.

Gideon loved unconditionally and all-in, the way it should be. The pain in Gideon's eyes last night and this morning validated how much he loved Isaiah. It was also Gideon's love for his family that had driven him home. As much as their separation hurt, how could he be angry with someone who loved like that?

Isaiah wasn't sure how he'd get through this day without Gideon. His heart ached, a pain far worse than he'd ever had with Ronnie during their tumultuous two-year relationship. Not being able to see Gideon for two months seemed like an unbearable amount of time to wait. Maybe he should have just chucked it all and moved to Costa Rica with him.

It was a little after five when Isaiah left class for the day. Back in his car, Isaiah checked his messages. Gideon's flight should have landed about an hour ago. He could picture Gideon and Andrew together. He wanted to feel joyous about the brothers' reunion. He couldn't wait to meet Andrew, as well as their parents, someday.

There was no message from Gideon. However, Daisy had left him a message, telling him there was something at the house for him.

What on earth had Ronnie sent? He couldn't imagine what it could be.

Ronnie had never been right for him because he couldn't commit. As much as Gideon said that he loved him, Gideon, too, had made a choice, and that choice was to go home.

The same as Ronnie.

As much as he tried to say it wasn't the same, the negative bird on his left shoulder refused to let him say otherwise.

After a stop at the gym and a hard hour-long workout, he was now both mentally and physically tapped out. He saw that his mother had sent two more text messages on his phone asking where he was. He shook his head as he tossed his phone onto the passenger seat. He was less than ten minutes from the house; she'd see him when he got there.

With the sun about to set, the sky was lit in hues of pinks, purples, and grays as he rounded the corner to the house. He saw a silhouette of a person sitting on his mother's front step from about five houses away. The closer he got to the house…

Gideon?

He questioned what he was seeing, knowing full well that it couldn't be, but it was. Barefoot and all… *But, how? Why? What happened?*

As Isaiah pulled into the vacant carport, Gideon stood and wiped the seat of his pants as he grinned from ear to ear at Isaiah.

Isaiah's brain wasn't trusting what his eyes were seeing. *What the hell is Gideon doing here?*

Chapter 25

"What are you doing here?" Still not believing he was seeing Gideon, Isaiah jumped out of his car and hurried toward him.

With a grin that ran the width of his face, Gideon's stroll turned into a dash, meeting Isaiah halfway.

Isaiah grabbed him and pulled him up into his arms, and the two tightly hugged. He contemplated never letting go of him. It still didn't feel real. Adrenaline was coursing through his veins; he was deliriously happy. He squeezed tighter, cocooning Gideon's small frame with his arms and chest.

Gideon squirmed. "You're killing me, dude," he groaned.

Isaiah laughed. He'd missed even the sound of Gideon's voice. He didn't want to let go of him, but he did, allowing Gideon's feet to rejoin the ground. "What happened? What are you doing here?" He fought the urge to grab him up again.

"I'm staying." Gideon's blue eyes gleamed. The infinite hues, bright blue and soft, had never been more beautiful.

"What do you mean? What happened?" Isaiah didn't wait for an answer as he kissed him. "Oh my God!" He looked Gideon up and down. *I can't believe you're here.*

Gideon's eyes widened. "It was my eyelash wishes. They came true. I first wished that you would fall in love with me. Then I wished that somehow, I could find a way to stay!" His grin was plastered on his face, his eyes still gleaming with adoration as he stared at Isaiah.

"Your eyelash wishes?" Isaiah laughed, hearing that he'd made several wishes. "Okay, Puppy, do tell. I want to know everything."

"At the airport, I was standing in line at security. It was taking forever. I just kept thinking, what are you doing? Then I realized I couldn't do it. I didn't want to be apart from you. I've always said

229

that I wanted my own life, that I didn't want to run the lodge… and then it hit me, you are my life. What I wanted was you."

After Gideon finished sharing his entire conversation with his mother with Isaiah, they kissed again. Isaiah wanted more than a hug and a kiss. He wanted to make love to this beautiful man standing before him. He'd never loved anyone as much as he was in love with Gideon. "How long have you been here?" Isaiah cast a glance at the house.

Gideon looked back at the house. "About an hour."

"Where have you been all day. Why didn't you call me or text me? I couldn't figure out why you hadn't called yet."

"I wanted to surprise you. After I left the airport, I took a rideshare to go to the beach. I really needed to see the ocean, to process what was happening. I thought a lot about what you said—about taking care of myself. I have some work to do."

Isaiah was proud of him for being able to be so honest with himself. Not only had he told his parents that he wasn't coming back, he told them about them and being sick.

"Now I have to figure out where I'm going to live and sleep tonight."

"Here! With me!" That wasn't even a question. "You're going to stay with us."

Isaiah glanced up at the house. "Is Mom home?"

"She was home when I got here, but her friend Cathy just picked her up."

"Bingo?" That's right, it was her Bingo night.

Gideon snickered.

"Then what are we doing out here?" He hadn't had this much energy all day, and he knew exactly what he wanted to do with his energy. He couldn't have been more grateful for Bingo night.

*****

After a nice hot shower together, which doubled as ten minutes of foreplay, Isaiah was more than worked up when they made it to his bed.

"I love you so much." Isaiah lay Gideon on his back and then lightly kissed him first on his lips, then his Adam's apple, and two kisses down his neck. "There was no way I would have been able to make it until Thanksgiving." He kissed Gideon.

"Me either," Gideon answered through the kiss.

"Loving you is nothing new. But… right now, this… it feels different. It will be the first time that I make love to you without the thought of losing you." With the back of his hand, Isaiah lightly brushed Gideon's cheek. He was used to feeling stubble on a man's face, but Gideon's skin had always been smooth and soft to the touch. In fact, Gideon's entire body, warm from the shower, was still damp as Isaiah brushed the tips of his fingers across Gideon's arm and across his chest. He gently kissed the small, firm nipple that he'd just brushed across.

Gideon meowed as his back lifted. "Oh, God."

You like that, do you? Isaiah kissed the nipple again. This time, followed with a light suck before tracing the areola with his tongue.

Gideon's back arched off the bed as he squirmed. A long low moan streamed from him.

The low, incoherent sounds emanating from Gideon told Isaiah that his man was in ecstasy, and that was a big turn on for Isaiah.

As they kissed, Isaiah moved on top of Gideon and then gently kissed him behind his ear. A slight scent of Vanilla Milk & Papaya from Gideon's hair tickled his nose. He took in another whiff. *How does a man's hair smell soooo good?*

Isaiah sat them both up. With Gideon straddled in his lap, they continued kissing. Their bodies meshed perfectly—like the only two puzzle pieces in a box of a thousand. Isaiah lightly caressed Gideon's ass, and through their kisses, Gideon whimpered.

Their kisses became harder and more urgent, and then Gideon collapsed onto his back and pulled him down on top of him. Gideon gasped when their scorching skin touched.

The tension building between them told Isaiah that this wasn't going to be one of those long lovemaking sessions. The fire was burning way too damn hot.

Isaiah ran his fingers down Gideon's flat stomach until he reached his cock. Warm and hard, Isaiah contemplated going down on him.

"Fuck me," Gideon whimpered.

They locked eyes, just long enough for Isaiah to see that Gideon was every bit as hungry as he was. He reached over and into his nightstand and grabbed a condom and lube.

Within minutes, they were both prepared, and Isaiah drew down into him.

Gideon released a cry followed by a long moan, causing Isaiah to hold still.

When Gideon wrapped his legs around Isaiah's lower back, that was his cue, as he began to make love to Gideon.

It wasn't long before Gideon pushed Isaiah away and then flipped over onto his stomach before raising onto all fours. He pushed back against Isaiah. He'd never been submissive when they made love—and Isaiah loved that side of him.

Gideon lowered his head, causing his hair to fall forward.

Along with the awesome visual, the sensation of Gideon thrusting against him was mind-blowing as heat charged through Isaiah's body. He wouldn't last long this evening.

To maintain some control of his own timing, he grabbed Gideon by the waist, holding his ass in place as he took back control, fucking Gideon until his body collapsed back on the bed. He rolled Gideon onto his back and continued his thrust.

With the penetrating gaze of a jaguar watching his unsuspecting prey, Isaiah never took his eyes off of Gideon as he made love to him.

Gideon gasped and cried out as he tangled locks of his own hair in his hand. "Harder! Harder!"

Isaiah's breathing became heavier as a grunt from the back of his throat came through his chest. His chest and abdomen glistened with perspiration as his body stiffened, and he went over the edge.

Gideon gasped, "Oh my God!" He, too, spilled out onto his stomach.

Not only was it as sexy as hell, it was mind-blowing how Gideon could have an orgasm without even touching himself.

As Gideon spasmodically thrashed and moaned, Isaiah collapsed next to him. They lay in the same position, Isaiah not having an ounce of strength to move. He was sure every neighbor on their street had to have heard them.

"Shit. Can you get me a towel?" Gideon leaned to the side and wiped at the gooey mess on his belly.

Isaiah sprung from the bed and rushed into the bathroom. Within minutes, he returned with a warm washcloth and towel.

"Hey, by the way, congratulations on your Spanish exam." Gideon grabbed the washcloth from him.

"Thanks. I got a ninety-eight." Isaiah watched as Gideon wiped his stomach clean.

Gideon traded Isaiah the washcloth for the towel. "¡Buen trabajo!" He congratulated him in Spanish as he dried his stomach.

When Gideon was all done, Isaiah climbed back into bed and nuzzled his nose into the side of Gideon's arm. His skin was warm, and with one inhale of the faint sweet sweat that coated his skin, Isaiah could easily go another round.

Gideon rolled over onto his side, facing Isaiah. "I love you." He gently kissed Isaiah as he snuggled up under his arms. "I don't know how you do it, but there is something you do to me that is so out-of-this-world gratifying that I lose all control." Gideon's shoulders shivered. "It's so intense. You're lucky I don't pee on myself."

"You're not so bad yourself." Isaiah mentally pictured Gideon on all four thrusting against him. His ass—*wow*! He stared down at Gideon's boney hip bone and the creamy white skin that didn't match the rest of his body. *How had he let this sexy nymphomaniac get out of his car this morning?*

Sex with Gideon was out of this world. But it was also something he'd never taken for granted. It was one of the most intimate acts two people could perform. Sex was something that connected him to the other person like nothing else could. There was a closeness that happened, a bond that he never took lightly.

Gideon left him wanting for nothing… with the exception of wanting to be with him more. Before he met Gideon, he was a different person, afraid to just let it all go and throw caution to the wind. He would rather abstain from something than risk being hurt. His relationships with people, especially his family was a prime example of that. He liked the new him. But with Gideon in his life, could his family really accept the new him?

Chapter 26

Isaiah stood over the hot grill and watched as Josiah tended to the hamburger patties cooking. Behind them, Daisy, Gideon, Tammy, and the baby, sat in the yard at the glass patio table chatting. Although this BBQ was supposed to be a Meet-and-Greet for Mom's boyfriend, Isaiah was nervous about having, for the first time, a boyfriend at a family gathering.

"Mom says he's staying with y'all." Josiah flipped over several of the patties.

Isaiah glanced over at Gideon sitting at the table. He was sure Gideon couldn't hear them. "Yeah, until we find something." He was surprised Josiah was even asking. He and Tammy seemed okay when they arrived and said hi to Gideon. The fact that they'd met before made it a little less awkward.

Josiah flipped the remaining patties. "I remember, back in the day, you had shipped out, and I was dating this chick name Sheryl. Momma caught her sneaking out the house one morning and went ballistic on me. She was screaming and talking about how I had to put a ring on Sheryl's finger before we slept together in her house." Josiah chuckled as he shook his head.

Isaiah forced a laugh. "I remember those skanks you used to date. Mom actually likes Gideon." For the last two nights, Gideon had been sleeping in Isaiah's room, but it couldn't last but a few more days. The walls were paper-thin, and Gideon was a moaner. There was only so much his mother would take, even if it was her own matchmaking skills that made it happen.

Josiah shook his head but didn't take his eyes from the burgers.

Isaiah held his breath, waiting to see if his brother would say any more about him and Gideon. Unlike Elijah, it wasn't like Josiah to actually verbalize his feelings. That was more his nosy wife's style.

With that thought, he glanced over at the table again to check on Gideon. He took a breath seeing that Gideon appeared to look relaxed. It was surreal seeing them all sit there together…. with his boyfriend.

"Who wants cheese on their hamburger?" Josiah yelled to everyone.

Tammy and Gideon raised their hands.

"No cheese, Mom?" Isaiah looked at his mother. She loved cheese.

"No, Honey."

"Hey! Hey! Hey!" a male voice boomed as the side gate slammed closed.

Everyone looked up as Elijah, and an African American woman came around the side of the house. In one hand, Elijah carried a case of beer, and in the other, he held her hand.

Baby Simone stirred and made a noise. Tammy reached into the bassinet and lifted her up out of it.

Elijah and the woman stopped at the table. "What up, momma? Everybody, this is my girl Alicia… Alicia, this is Momma, my brother's wife, Tammy, their baby, Simone and… Gideon." Elijah smiled at Gideon. "Good to see you, man." He reached over the table and shook Gideon's hand.

Isaiah came over to the table. "Hey, bro. I keep forgetting you two have already met." He rested a hand on Gideon's shoulders, making sure he was comfortable with the addition of more family.

"Alicia, this is my brother Isaiah. He and Gideon are doing their thing," Elijah said as he opened the case of beer and pulled a can out.

Alicia gave Gideon a sincere smile and shook his hand first before acknowledging Isaiah.

Isaiah, Elijah, and Alicia all took a seat around the table. "How long have you and Isaiah been going out?" Alicia asked Gideon.

"Almost two months." Gideon reached out to Tammy for the baby.

"Gideon used to live next door," Elijah spoke. "Hey, I saw the For Rent sign is up. Did you move out?"

"Yeah. On Wednesday." Gideon looked down at Simone, who was staring up at him.

"He's staying here at the house until we can find a place." Isaiah watched Gideon as he gently rocked the baby. *He's good with babies.*

"I think that they should rent the place and stay close to me," Daisy joined into the conversation.

Isaiah arched a brow. "Mom, that's actually not a bad idea." He looked at Gideon. "Do you think your parents would go for it?"

Gideon looked up from the baby and shrugged.

Daisy answered as if the question was directed at her. "I don't see why not. Your money's as green as anybody else's."

"Could you buy the place?" Elijah asked Isaiah.

"Don't know." Since returning home, he'd been watching the real estate market and had a general idea of what the house might sell for. With everything he'd saved over the last ten years, on top of a good V.A. loan, he more than qualified for it, if Gideon's parents were willing to sell.

Gideon's eyes widened. "That would be cool."

To rent the house would be nice, but to buy it and be next door to his mother would be perfect. The house was everything Isaiah wanted and move-in ready, thanks to Gideon. He tried to tamp down his excitement over the prospect of it actually happening because the idea seemed almost too good to be true.

Gideon took the baby bottle that Tammy was handing him. "Do you want me to call my mom and ask her?"

"Let me call my bank first." Isaiah tried to tap the brakes a little on the whole idea. He didn't want everyone, including himself getting excited over something that might not even happen. For all they knew, new renters could be moving in tomorrow.

"Who's buying a house?" Josiah walked over to the table and shook hands with Elijah.

"Isaiah," Daisy answered. "The house next door."

"Really?" Josiah looked puzzled.

Isaiah held out his hands. "No, we're only talking about it." He rubbed his temples.

"I love this neighborhood." Alicia snuggled up against Elijah.

"Nobody's buying a house yet. Y'all need to cool it." Isaiah gestured for Elijah to pass him a beer.

Daisy turned to Alicia. "And what do you do for a living?"

Alicia batted her eyes at Elijah. "I'm a Dentist."

"Oh?" Daisy leaned in. "When's your birthday?"

Isaiah shook his head as he watched his mom go to work on the poor, unsuspecting woman. He could only hope Elijah had warned Alicia about their mom's matchmaking.

"April twenty-seventh," Alicia answered.

"Taurus?" Daisy smiled. "Y'all get along well with Virgo's." She cocked her head as she looked at Elijah.

"Ah, Momma, ain't nobody believes in that no more." Elijah looked at Gideon. "Hey, Gideon. Alicia bought this ceiling fan that I've been tryin' to put up for the last three days. I got it up, but when I turn it on, the damn thing wobbles like a son of a bitch and then shuts off. Do you mind looking at it?"

"Sure." Gideon handed the baby back over to Tammy, who was asking for her. "I can take a look at it."

Alicia turned to Gideon. "Are you an electrician?"

"No. But ceiling fans are easy. It sounds like it just needs balancing."

"What do you do for a living?" Alicia took a sip from Elijah's beer.

"I thought somebody told me you were going back to Costa Rica," Elijah asked.

Gideon looked at Isaiah before answering. "Well, yeah. I was planning on it."

"So whatcha gonna do now?" Elijah reached out for his beer.

"Nothing at the moment. I kind of would like to go to college. Maybe take some accounting classes."

Isaiah nodded. "We haven't talked about it yet, but you know I gotcha if that's what you want to do."

Alicia shook her head as she looked at Elijah. "Aww, that's so sweet."

"That was my major," Tammy spoke up.

The side gate banged, drawing everyone's attention.

"That must be Charles." Daisy jumped up and shimmied her dress down over her hips.

A tall, older African American man wearing a bright yellow polo shirt and slacks came around from the side of the house. In tow was a young teenage boy who was dressed in a baseball uniform.

"Hello, everyone!" Charles waved to the group as he approached the table. "I picked up some potato salad from Jimmy's." He put a Styrofoam container on the table.

Isaiah looked at the container. Next to his mother's potato salad, Jimmy's Soul Food made the best potato salad in the world.

Charles kissed her on her cheek before she introduced everyone.

Daisy's boyfriend greeted everyone and then introduced his son. "This here is my boy, Joseph."

Joseph waved to everyone.

"You play ball?" Josiah asked.

"Yes. We had a game this morning," the boy mumbled with a noticeable lisp and a flip of the wrist.

"Seven to three—they might make the championships this year. He's the best shortstop in the league." Charles proudly patted Joseph on the back.

Daisy slid the container of potato salad into the middle of the table. "Hon, can you go inside and grab a spoon for this?"

Tammy was about to get up when Isaiah stood. "I'll get it. I'm going to get the stuff for the burgers."

"Can you bring out the beans too?" Daisy asked.

"Do you need help?" Gideon stood up.

"Sure." Isaiah was ready for some alone time with him—to check in and make sure he was really doing okay.

In the kitchen, Isaiah cornered Gideon by the sink. "Are you holding up okay?"

"Yeah, I'm doing fine. Are you serious about wanting to buy the house?"

Isaiah kissed him. "I am. I think it'd be a good home for us. We know it like the back of our hands. I think it's perfect."

"*Us?*" Gideon stared at him.

Isaiah kissed him again. "Yes, *us.* I know this is fast. We've only known each other for a couple of months." He backed Gideon against the counter and wrapped his arms around him. "I love you and can't imagine waking up in the morning without you."

"Me either. Tell me when you want me to call my mom. If they're not wanting to sell, maybe we could rent it." Gideon held his stare.

"Those eyes of yours…" Isaiah shook his head. *I could make love to you right now… if my family wasn't out back.* "I can't believe how much I love you." He cupped Gideon's chin and kissed him. As they kissed, his hand slid down to Gideon's ass. Isaiah pulled him up against him, wanting to feel Gideon's cock through their clothes.

"Oh! Excuse me…" Josiah back-pedaled a couple of steps.

Isaiah was surprised to see Josiah had walked into the kitchen, and they were caught. Isaiah took a step back from Gideon. "Hey." A little embarrassed they'd been caught, Isaiah wiped moisture from his lips. He was well aware that he had the beginning of an erection in his pants, but he didn't dare call any attention to it by looking or adjusting it into a more comfortable position.

"Sorry about that. Came in to grab a tray for the burgers. They're ready." Josiah slowly walked around them in the kitchen and over to the counter.

Gideon grabbed the slow cooker with the beans off the counter. "I'll take this out." Within seconds, he was out of the kitchen.

Josiah pulled out a platter from the lower cabinet. "So… you two…" He cleared his throat. "Just so you know, I would rather not have the whole gay thing all up in my face."

Isaiah initially held his tongue as he stared at his brother. There was so much about what Josiah said that got his blood boiling. *The whole gay thing? What an ass.*

He looked around the kitchen to look at anything other than Josiah. *How dare you?* Isaiah's gaze drifted to the pair of yellow wooden shoes on the counter that had shown up this morning with the mail—the gift Ronnie had sent, along with a note that said, "Saw these, and they made me think of you. No one can fill your shoes."

No. You're not going to get away with saying shit like that. He needed to put his brother in check. At one time, he would have let it go—for the sake of avoiding an argument and ruining the BBQ or because of his own comfort level. But not anymore. He shouldn't have to, especially with his own family.

"What do you mean the whole gay thing? You mean like you and Tammy pushing your Christianity on me? I was kissing my boyfriend… in my house. Look, Gideon's not going anywhere, so you need to deal with it. I love him. No one in this world has ever made me feel as loved as Gideon, not even you. I absolutely refuse to compromise on any part of this, Josiah. Dude, you're my brother—I shouldn't have to stand in judgment in front of you. Let God do that. He doesn't need your help. All I need from you is for you to love me, but I don't even think you do. The world beats us up every day; it prosecutes us for the color of our skin. I shouldn't be getting it from my family as well. As soon as that boy spoke out there, I saw your face. You probably weren't thinking anything different than the rest of us, but your opinion of who you thought he was sure in the hell showed all over your face. You don't think he can see it? If he's gay, how do you think that made him feel? And if he isn't gay but just happens to be a little feminine, you can bet that he's likely been bullied over it at some point in his life. At sixteen years old, how the hell is he supposed to take being judged over something he has no control over? And by his own people to boot."

Josiah held up his hand. "No! Wait!"

"No. you wait!" Isaiah held up a hand, stopping his brother from speaking. "I pray to God that Simone doesn't grow up with self-esteem issues about the color of her skin or the shape of her body to the point that she's puking her food up right after she eats, or doesn't eat at all, or that her self-worth isn't attached to what some man thinks of her... or, God forbid, she's a lesbian. You're her protector; give someone else's child the same respect you want for Simone."

Isaiah had a lump in this throat. He pushed it back down. "That boy's father couldn't have been prouder of his child. Mom has never held me in judgment because of my sexuality. She supported me when I didn't even know she was supporting me. Josiah, your actions are killing gay people. Do you know that gay kids are almost five times as likely to have attempted suicide compared to straight kids? If you can't dig deep somewhere in you to just love me unconditionally, then do it for your daughter."

Josiah nodded at him. Like a game of chicken, neither broke eye contact. Their stares matching the other's for several long seconds before Josiah blinked and looked away. He scratched the back of his neck as he walked in circles in the tiny kitchen.

Isaiah braced for Josiah's push-back; he'd likely recite some passage from the bible that he interpreted to mean whatever he wanted it to mean.

"I'm sorry." Josiah looked down at the floor.

The two stood in the kitchen, neither saying a word. Isaiah wondered what his brother was thinking.

Eventually, Josiah looked up and took a step towards him. "You're right."

Right about what? Isaiah waited to see if he was going to say anything else. What was he right about?

"Do you really think I don't love you?"

Isaiah shrugged. "I don't know how you can if you can't even see who I am."

The room was so quiet that Isaiah could hear his mother's voice in the backyard.

"I do love you, and I'm sorry if I ever made you feel otherwise." Josiah grabbed him and embraced him in a hug. "This gay thing, it's something I've got to figure out. My pastor's been wrong on some stuff in the past, maybe I need to reexamine this whole thing, but I do love you without a doubt. Momma's been on me and Tammy for years about you gays."

Josiah's words surprised him. He clearly wasn't ready for a Pride Parade with the whole *you gays*, but, shit, he did just give a little. "And when have you ever known Mom to be wrong?" Isaiah attempted to lighten the mood.

Josiah shrugged. "Tammy said that it was Mom who set the two of you up. I ain't never questioned her matchmaking skills before." He shook his head.

Yes, Josiah was absolutely right—their mother had nailed it on this one. To hear his brother say it meant everything. Josiah wasn't a person who said things just to make someone feel better.

He could still feel his adrenaline pumping through his veins. He'd been in fights that took less out of him than what just happened between him and Josiah. But he was proud of himself for standing up to Josiah. Gideon had changed him in ways that he was still uncovering. He liked the new him... No, he loved the new him.

Epilogue
Six months later
Academy Graduation

Gideon fretted in the bathroom mirror, trying to get his hair to lay the right way. *Damn it, I should cut it all off. I hate my hair!*

He thought about rinsing out the gel and just starting over. *You don't have enough time.*

Elijah should have been here five minutes ago to pick him and Daisy up. The last thing Isaiah had said to him before leaving the house this morning was, "Don't be late."

Although Isaiah's academy graduation was at one o'clock, he told them to get there early to ensure the whole family could sit together during the ceremony.

We're going to be late.

There was nothing else he could do with his hair. He'd have to go looking like that man in *Willy Wonka & the Chocolate Factory.* He didn't have time to start over.

Gideon hurried from the hall bathroom back to the spare bedroom that he and Isaiah were sleeping in while Josiah's construction crew worked on the extension of the master bedroom. He grabbed his jacket off the bed and then checked out the window just in case he somehow missed Elijah.

Where the hell is he?

He rushed back out into the living room and stopped at the large mirror in the entryway. He straightened the collar of his jacket. The tie around his neck felt as if it was choking him.

In the mirror, directly behind him, he eyed the new furniture in their living room that Isaiah purchased right after his parents agreed to not only sell them the house but to let them move in while the sale was in escrow.

242

Gideon loosened the tie around his neck enough that it still looked tight but was not choking him. This was only the third time he'd ever worn a tie in his life, and Isaiah had to tie it for him this morning before he'd left. All he had to do was slip the loop over his head and cinch it up. Now, he was trying to loosen it without messing it up entirely.

When Gideon heard the car horn, he rushed to the kitchen and out the door. He and Daisy came outside at the same time. Seeing her lock her door, it jogged his memory to lock his as well.

Before climbing into the back seat, Daisy stopped him to cinch up his tie, and then flattened his collar around it. "I can't have my baby looking all rumpled," she told him.

"Thank you." He caught the scent of her rose perfume and sniffed.

At the Elysian Park Academy campus, the ceremony was being held on the track and field lawn. Gideon squirmed in his seat beside Daisy. On the other side of her sat Elijah and Alicia. Although Daisy had saved two additional seats for Josiah and Tammy next to Gideon, as of now, they were no-shows. He looked around at all the suits and dignitaries under the large white tent in front of them. There were another three rows of empty chairs where he assumed Isaiah and his class would sit.

The ceremony began with a man in a green-and-black kilt playing the bagpipes. The music sent goosebumps up Gideon's arm. As the piper passed between them and the tent, Josiah and Tammy slipped into the two empty seats.

Josiah leaned over into Gideon and whispered, "Did we miss anything?"

"No. It's just starting," Gideon whispered back.

When Isaiah and his thirty-one fellow officers entered the track, they wore their official navy-blue uniforms with black ties and white gloves. Gideon zeroed in on Isaiah, whose back was straight and tall, his head held high. A tear escaped Gideon's eye and fell. Daisy's hand found his hand, and she squeezed it gently.

The class chanted, marching in formation to their seats. A woman standing in the back started cheering, and several others begin clapping. Gideon stared at several of the cadets, wondering which of them was the woman's husband, boyfriend... or son.

The woman made him smile as she reminded him in some way of his own mother, one of his biggest fans. That day, at the airport, when he'd confessed his love for Isaiah, and she'd told him to go for it, to live his dream… and, now, he was doing just that.

With Daisy by his side and the mere presence of the man he was so deeply in love with now seated in front of him, Gideon realized that this was his *new* normal, his new happy place. He'd once hated when the doctors and mental health professionals used to tell him that, one day, life would return to normal. He'd never been able to see how that would be possible, but it had. The closeness he felt with Daisy, the love he had for Isaiah… his new normal far exceeded his old normal. Not in a million years would he had ever dreamed of the life he had now. On some days, Gideon still pinched himself to make sure their relationship was real. Every skin cell tingled, every neuron fired in his body thinking about how much Isaiah loved him.

At the end of the ceremony, all the new sworn officers stood and recited their oath before throwing their hats into the air as everyone cheered and converged on the new officers, celebrating their achievement.

In a crowd of people, Isaiah found Gideon and his family.

"Congratulations, Honey!" Daisy kissed him, tears rolling down her face as she touched the shiny badge on his chest.

As much as Gideon wanted to hug and kiss his man, he held back. The last thing he wanted to do was embarrass Isaiah in front of his peers.

"I love you guys," Isaiah said as he hugged each of them.

"Congratulations!" Tammy stepped up for her hug.

While everyone was hugging, laughing, and congratulating Isaiah, Josiah stepped closer to Gideon. "How's everything going at the house?"

"Great. We finished up texturing the walls on Friday and will probably be done by Wednesday." Gideon and Isaiah had been grateful that Josiah had agreed to provide four guys from his construction company to get the job done. Even as a full-time student at the local junior college, Gideon still found the time to help with the construction every day.

"Cool. I have to come by and check it out." Josiah then turned to Isaiah. "When do you hit the streets now?"

"I report to my precinct on Monday." Isaiah rested his hands on his duty belt above his gun.

Gideon loved seeing his man standing here, especially with all his equipment on his duty belt. He found it sexually exciting seeing Isaiah in full uniform, with his gun and baton on his hip. Since Gideon knew they couldn't use the handcuffs for pleasure, he'd purchased a toy set as a graduation gift, which he would give him when they were alone later this evening.

"Gideon." Isaiah's expression softened, followed by a smile. "I love you."

Isaiah's sudden and so public announcement surprised Gideon. "I love you, too."

"You know, my mom's the greatest matchmaker in the world. The only thing she doesn't have in her resume is a Gay Wedding." Isaiah dropped to one knee. "Gideon Miller, what do you say we give her one?" He held up a gold ring. "Will you marry me?"

Gideon slapped a hand over his mouth in shock. A lump lodged in his throat, so all he could do was smile as tears filled his eyes.

"Puppy? Are you going to answer? Can you say something?" Isaiah remained down on one knee.

Gideon cleared his throat, trying to find his voice. "My wish... It came true!" A thousand butterflies stirred in his stomach.

"*Another* Eyelash wish?" Isaiah laughed.

"Yeah." He could barely talk as the lump in his throat that was holding back a cry threatened to choke him.

"Gideon, how many wishes did you make?" Isaiah repositioned onto his other knee. "You are so freakin' adorable!" He shook his head as he laughed.

Daisy threw her hands on her hips. "Gideon! The boy is on one knee! For the love of God, answer him!"

Through a crying laugh, Gideon barely found his voice. "Of course, Isaiah. Of *course,* I'll marry you!"

Isaiah slipped the ring onto Gideon's finger before standing up. Then, in front of his family and peers, he planted a big, full-mouth kiss on Gideon. He took a step back but still held onto Gideon. "Thank God you said yes. I was beginning to wonder."

Gideon tried to wipe his eyes, but seeing Daisy, Tammy, and Alicia all crying, the tears kept falling. He looked around at the crowd

Bryan T. Clark

that had gathered around them. Several women were brushing away tears from their eyes, and Isaiah's fellow officers began congratulating them.

"Wait!" Gideon tried to stop crying. "I have another wish!"

Isaiah cocked his head. "Another one?"

"A… A… A." He could hardly talk through his cry. "A hummingbird cake for our wedding." Gideon smiled at Daisy.

"Your wish, Puppy, is my command." Isaiah looked at his mother.

"I gotcha, Baby. I gotcha!" Daisy squealed as the entire family came together for one big group hug.

The End

Connect with Bryan

You can connect with me on social media or by signing up for my newsletter, The Reader's Lounge, at https://btclark.com/newsletter. I send newsletters when I have a new release or a sale, and I sometimes include giveaways and access to freebies only for subscribers. You can also find me on

Facebook @ https://www.facebook.com/btclarkauthor,

Twitter @ https://twitter.com/BryanTClarkx2.

And don't forget to visit my website at https://btclark.com.

Love for you to leave a review!

Thank you so much for reading Gideon's Wish, and I hope you enjoyed it. I would love it if you would consider leaving a brief review on wherever you find your books or any author boards or social media groups you belong to. Your review may help other readers discover their possible next read. Thank you again, and wishing you many more Happily Ever After's.

About the Author

Bryan T. Clark started writing mysteries at age thirteen while he and his best friend rode the school bus to school. While he dictated the scene, she wrote it down in her three-ring plastic binder. Those stories were rarely finished before they moved onto the next one. (Those pieces will never see the light of day.) Bryan took a twenty-seven-year break from writing to pursue his desire to enter into law enforcement. He was an investigator for one of the largest law enforcement agencies in California.

Since those days of writing on the school bus, his love for writing has evolved from mysteries and poetry to happily-ever-afters—he does still like a little drama in his stories. Today he is a multi-published award-winning author of gay romance novels: contemporary and historical. Born in Boston, Massachusetts, Bryan and his husband of thirty-six years have made their home and life in the Central Valley of California.

Website http://www.btclark.com/
Facebook https://www.facebook.com/btclarkauthor
Instagram https://www.instagram.com/romanceauthor/
Goodreads https://www.goodreads.com/author/dashboard
Twitter https://twitter.com/BryanTClarkx2

Read more from Bryan T. Clark

Far Away

Eighteen-year-old Noah Rothenberg spent the summer with his first love, the charming and seductive Spiro. He fell head over heels in love from what started as a clumsy crush. But that was twelve years ago. His relationships since have been spectacular failures because of how things ended with Spiro. If he has any hope of moving forward, he needs to find Spiro and get some closure … even if he has to fly halfway around the world to do it. Too bad he instead finds himself falling—again—for the man who ruined him for all other men.

Love isn't an emotion Spiro Papadopoulos entirely trusts anymore. He's far too pragmatic for that. His focus these days has to be on his art and caring for his ailing mother. Being with Noah again is easy and feels so right … but is it love? Spiro isn't sure. Besides, with his entire life being tied to Greece and Noah's to New York, love might just be a luxury neither of them can afford.

Can Spiro and Noah overcome the oceans and years between them—or will their second chance at love end as badly as their first?

PURCHASE NOW

Escaping Camp Roosevelt

"He's a bad boy—cocky and damaged.
So, why can't I stop thinking about him?"

Broken Dreams

Sociable and unselfish, eighteen-year-old Tucker Graves loves two things—his darling little sister and the thrill of playing baseball. He never dreamed that he'd be homeless, but after a series of misfortunes, his life is nothing like he could have possibly imagined. Shocked and shattered, Tucker, his mother, and his baby sister now must brave the dangers of a dilapidated homeless encampment called Camp Roosevelt.

A Wounded Heart

Homeless since the age of fourteen, Dancer has mastered the tricks of living on the streets as a sex worker. The quiet, reclusive, and calculating ways of this twenty-year-old, green-eyed Adonis help him to survive. He hides his emotional scars from the world by interacting only with his clients, whose occasional bizarre requests he reluctantly fulfills. Dancer's past has taught him to trust no one.

A Second Chance

When Tucker and Dancer come face to face on a stormy night, having been thrown together under the same roof, Tucker brings out a feeling in Dancer that he didn't know still existed in him—desire.

Neither man can deny the attraction he feels for the other. But some scars run deep, causing both Tucker and Dancer to question whether falling in love is even possible, especially when survival is on the line.

*** *One hundred percent of the royalties from the first year of Escaping Camp Roosevelt's publication was donated to the Larkin Street Youth Services/Castro Youth Housing Initiative. The CYHI provides transitional housing in the city of San Francisco, California, for LGBTQ youth experiencing homelessness. Fear of being raped, abused, or murdered should not be a part of anyone's youth.*

PURCHASE NOW

Diego's Secret

International Book Awards Finalist for 2019 LGBTQ FICTION

Diego Castillo struggles daily under the weight of his secrets. Not only is he in the US illegally, but he's also forced to hide his desire for other men from his brothers. Lately, the only time he can really be himself is when he's with his landscaping client, Winston—a man as beautiful as he is intimidating. They come from two different worlds, but in Winston, he senses a vulnerable kindred spirit, and even though getting involved could uncover Diego's secrets, putting his entire family at risk, he's powerless to stay away.

Winston Makena is suffering, too. All his millions can't buy a minute's peace from the crushing grief he's felt since his husband's death. The only relief he finds these days is when he's with Diego. Despite their differences, Winston finds himself inexorably drawn to Diego's honesty, kindness, and gentle soul. But he can never truly love again... can he?

It's not long before Diego and Winston's clandestine attraction grows into something much more complicated. As cultures clash, misunderstandings mount, and secrets loom, they're left to wonder if the cost of following their hearts is more than they can ever pay...

PURCHASE NOW

Come to the Oaks

Winner of the 2017 Rainbow Award for BEST GAY HISTORICAL

LAMBDA Literary Award Finalist for 2017 BEST GAY ROMANCE

In 1845, as America is drowning in its own racial conflict, in a time when forbidden love has to remain a secret, can two young men find love when one has everything to lose, and the other has nothing?

For Tobias, a young African man, life has ended before it began. Snatched abruptly from his homeland and enslaved into the Antebellum South, grand homes and majestic oak trees meant little to him. Now he is considered the property of other men, but his spirit would not be broken.

The awkward Benjamin Nathanael Lee lives a privileged life. His father owns the largest tobacco plantation south of the Mason Dixon line. Ben wants little to do with the harsh realities of running a plantation—that is until he meets Tobias, the one person that changes everything for him.

Wealth, greed, and power brought them together. The same now threatens to separate them forever. The two men are on the verge of losing the one thing that matters: their love for one another. Against the odds, they steal off and embark on a journey to find freedom: the freedom to love one another and to live a life without the chains of slavery.

Come to the Oaks is the tale of a forbidden romance—a love forged by two young men as they journey through a land that is tearing itself apart.

PURCHASE NOW

Before Sunrise

USA-Today LGBTQ BOOK OF THE YEAR
Bryan T. Clark has again masterfully crafted a romance where the fine line between right and wrong must be resolved for love to survive-USA-Today

Just Before Sunrise, as the fog lifts from the pool, the light reveals the tapered backs of male swimmers in Speedos concluding their morning workout.

Nicky O'Hare, a promising freshman, recruited to the Tampa Bay University swim team, shows promise both in and out of the pool. The lean Irish kid with the 'boy-next-door' good looks from Brandy, South Dakota, is likely the most talented swimmer on the team. Ready to experience all that college life has to offer, Nicky has even put finding a boyfriend on his wish list.

Coach Phillip Silva, a former Olympic swimmer with a once-impressive swimming career, has recruited Nicky as part of his mission to rebuild the University's failing swim program. Focused on the upcoming season, Phillip's real challenge will be keeping his secrets and demons submerged below the surface.

All seems well until one night when Nicky and Phillip end up at the same Fourth of July celebration. With fireworks in the sky, the hot and humid night reveals the attraction between the two. But can these boundaries be crossed? Suddenly forced to reevaluate his life, Phillip is met with the moral dilemma of discovering true love with the University's rising star.

Before Sunrise presents a story of friendships, love, complicated relationships, and deception woven into a hard-earned happily-ever-after.

PURCHASE NOW

Ancient House of Cards

Sebastian Morales is smart, gorgeous, and has just turned 30. He is also one of the youngest priests to be assigned to the sleepy little town of Morris, Colorado, nestled just below the majestic Rocky Mountains.

Born in a remote village in Spain, Father Morales's life had been perfectly scripted as he obtained his dreams. Now in America, he is tasked with revitalizing an aging congregation. The job seems easy until he meets Ian Stephens. Ian is troubled, good looking, openly gay, and trapped between his own dreams and the responsibility he feels for caring for his aging mother.

Escorting his mother to Sunday mass one morning, Ian's and Father Morales's lives intersect, changing both forever. Ian believes he has seen something in the Father's eyes that morning—a spark, an intuition—or was he just fantasizing about the seductively alluring priest?

Ian is willing to risk it all in order to find the answer, in turn feeding his own sexual desires and causing boundaries to be questioned by everyone.

After an unforeseen yet unforgettable kiss between the two men, will an Ancient House of Cards be toppled when they are faced with the moral dilemma that neither of them can escape?

PURCHASE NOW

www.ingramcontent.com/pod-product-compliance
Lightning Source LLC
Chambersburg PA
CBHW060908250626
47159CB00008B/2919